Kirov Saga:

Armageddon

By

John Schettler

A publication of: *The Writing Shop Press*
Kirov Saga: *Armageddon*, Copyright©2013, John A. Schettler

Discover other titles by John Schettler:

The Kirov Saga:

Kirov - Kirov Series - Volume I
Cauldron Of Fire - Kirov Series - Volume II
Pacific Storm - Kirov Series - Volume III
Men Of War - Kirov Series - Volume IV
Nine Days Falling - Kirov Series - Volume V
Fallen Angels - Kirov Series - Volume VI
Devil's Garden - Kirov Series - Volume VII
Armageddon – Kirov Series – Volume VIII
Altered States– Kirov Series – Volume IX
Darkest Hour– Kirov Series – Volume X
Hinge of Fate– Kirov Series – Volume XI

Award Winning Science Fiction:

Meridian - Meridian Series - Volume I
Nexus Point - Meridian Series - Volume II
Touchstone - Meridian Series - Volume III
Anvil of Fate - Meridian Series - Volume IV
Golem 7 - Meridian Series - Volume V

Classic Science Fiction:

Wild Zone - Dharman Series - Volume I
Mother Heart - Dharman Series - Volume II

Historical Fiction:

Taklamakan - Silk Road Series - Volume I
Khan Tengri - Silk Road Series - Volume II
Dream Reaper – Mythic Horror Mystery

Mailto: john@writingshop.ws
http://www.writingshop.ws ~ http://www.dharma6.com

Kirov Saga:
Armageddon

By

John Schettler

"My friends, tonight we bring you something entirely different. Something special. The poets will rest, the sonnets will be silent, and what words of love there are will not be spoken. Tonight, my friends, and I can hear you out there, sitting alone, like me, in your chairs, your beds, driving down an empty street with no one but me to listen to your weeping; tonight, I'm going to bring you Armageddon."

—Charles Grant

Kirov Saga:

Armageddon

By
John Schettler

Prologue

Curiosity is a powerful urge, and one that has led many men to their doom in ages past. For Mironov, it was a lure he could not ignore, and his mind was always haunted by the strange man he had encountered at the Ilanskiy railway inn, and the odd words he had whispered to him. Was the man working for the Tsar's dread secret police, the Okhrana, he wondered? Was he sent to find and follow me after my release from prison, so that they could find yet another reason to arrest me?

The more he thought about it, the more he began to feel something was very strange about that brief encounter at the inn. The day itself was one he could never forget. A terrible light had flashed in the early morning, there came a loud roar in the distance, an awful tearing sound as if the sky itself had been ripped open and something came burning through, a wild, scintillating light in the heavens, brighter than the sun. A violent wind was blowing outside, sending a hail of debris flying as the dining room windows shattered.

Mironov jumped at the sound, covering his head and face. There were frightened shouts outside, and they heard the sound of thunder or distant artillery firing. Rushing out they looked to see what appeared to be a second sunrise that morning. The entire horizon to the northeast was aglow with red fire, as if the taiga was burning in a massive forest fire. Everyone stared in awe, pointing at the spectacle…and then the stranger came.

Mironov had not seen him in the village before, and assumed he was a recent arrival, a traveler seeking lodging at the inn. The man seemed confused when he had first met him, disoriented, as if he did not know where he was, but Mironov thought it might only be the shock and amazement of the spectacle glowing on the horizon that had the whole town in an uproar. They went back to the dining hall, intent on finishing breakfast in spite of the strange event, and that brief encounter with the stranger had been more than enough to plant that first seed of curiosity.

He seemed oddly dressed, and Mironov remembered the threatening insignia that decorated his jacket and the pistol in the man's side holster. That was enough to add a kernel of suspicion to his curiosity about this man, for the Okhrana were everywhere, and might appear in any guise one could imagine.

"Military?" He had asked, and the man told him he had come from Vladivostok en route to the Caspian. He called himself Fedorov, and claimed he was a soldier traveling to a new post. In time they returned to the hotel dining room and, when the stranger followed them back, Mironov's curiosity and suspicion prompted him to engage the man. He remembered being very blunt with him.

"Tell me you are not a security man working for the Okhrana and I will be happy to share my breakfast table with you," he said. "Then again if you *are* Okhrana, I must tell you I have done nothing inappropriate. I was given a full release, and I mean only to travel to Irkutsk to visit friends. You need have no further worries about me." He looked at the stranger, waiting. "Well? Which is it?"

"Have no fear," the man said. "I have no business with you... "

Yet that had not been enough to quell the suspicion. When the stranger excused himself Mironov watched as he took the back stairway to the upper floor, presumably to his quarters there. He got up and went to the front desk to inquire about the man, but with the village still unsettled by the strange event underway, the innkeeper was gone. So Mironov took a peek at the register, and his suspicion ticked up yet another notch when he could see no recent entry, or any guest listed by the name Fedorov.

Now there was an edge of fear on his suspicion, so he went back through the dining hall to rejoin his comrades, only to find they had gone back outside to look at the fire in the sky. So Mironov decided to see what more he could learn about the stranger, though he knew he was taking a chance at being apprehended again. He crept slowly up the narrow back stairway after the man, his heart pounding and an inner voice berating him for being so foolish. The Okhrana will find you easily enough, he chided himself. Now here you are skulking about and courting their attention! Yet his curiosity seemed all too compelling. He had to know who this man really was.

Sure enough, his worst fears were realized when he reached the top of those stairs. He felt the hard grip of a steely hand on his shoulder, turning to see another soldier had immediately fallen upon him.

"I've done nothing. Let me go!" He protested, but he was soon shoved down the hall and into a room where, sure enough, he saw the man who had called himself Fedorov with yet another soldier, a stocky, rock-like man that looked very threatening.

"So you are with the Okhrana after all," Mironov said sullenly as soon as he saw Fedorov there. "I knew there was something odd about you. What have I done? You have no right to detain me!"

The man gave him a wide eyed look, as if he had suddenly come to some inner conclusion about him, but then he began asking those odd questions.

"Listen to me, Mironov," he began. "What is the date?"

"The date?"

"What is the month and year?"

It was just as he feared. The questions… They always started that way. Who are you? Where have you come from? Where are you going? What business do you have there? But this was an odd one—the date? Mironov spoke, somewhat indignant.

"So you mean to interrogate me, is that it?"

"No, no, please. Simply tell me the date."

It was some kind of test, he thought, to see if his story would hold together. So he humored the man with an answer. "The 30th of June. I arrived late last night. You think I'm a dim witted fool, eh? I knew you were Okhrana the moment I set eyes on you. I have done nothing! I have said nothing, nothing at all!" His eyes were fiery as he spoke, indignant, combative.

The man looked at him as though he had seen a ghost.

"My god," he said in a low voice. "My god, what has happened? Mironov... You came up the back stairs just now?"

"I saw you go that way, and yes, I followed you to see what I could find out about you. It seems I have learned too much, eh? But that is no reason to arrest me again. A man has the right to see to his own safety, particularly after what just happened out there." He turned thinking to point to the awful red glow in the sky outside, and then he, suddenly noticed the darkness, the silence, the quiet night beyond the window lit by a silvery gibbous moon. Now it was Mironov's turn to stare dumfounded at the window.

"What's happening here? Where's the day gone?" He was suddenly as confused as the stranger had seemed when he first encountered him. How could it be night? Was it that explosion? Had the red fire on the horizon blackened the sky with smoke? But no! The *moon*... The moon was up, and all was quiet and still, hushed in the midnight darkness. Then the strangers questioned him yet again, asking his name, and they knew exactly who he was.

Now he was certain they were Okhrana, and he resigned himself to the realization that he would most likely be arrested here again, and taken back to prison. Yet he was suddenly surprised when the man named Fedorov seemed ready to release him.

"You mean I am free to go?"

"Yes, just follow me." Fedorov reassured him.

Mironov looked at the other soldiers, frowning, then followed Fedorov out the door to the upper landing of the back stairway.

"This way, Mironov. Quickly!" The stranger seemed very insistent, an urgency about his movements. There came a rumble of thunder again, and now Mironov concluded that he had been correct, the darkness must be from the smoke of that fire. Perhaps the moon was still up, and only revealed when the smoke obscured the sun, he thought. He went to Fedorov's side, looking him in the eye as though he were staring into the face of fate itself.

"You must go by the way you came," said Fedorov. "Go quickly now, while you see that light." The man gestured to the amber glow from below. "And Mironov—never come up this stairway again. Understand? Get as far away from here as you can."

The stranger had an anguished look on his face, as if he had something more he needed to say, a tormented expression that held Mironov fixated for a time, their eyes and souls locked together in some bizarre twist of time and fate. Yet the man seemed to hesitate, uncertain of himself.

What was this strange look of fear and trepidation in the man's eyes, thought Mironov. Just as I turned to go down the stairs, the stranger reached out, taking hold of my arm to delay me. He leaned forward, close to my ear and whispered something, his eyes vast and serious, his face like that of a man who was seeing a phantom from another world. The words blurted out, an urgent whisper: '*Do not go to St. Petersburg in 1934! Beware Stalin! Beware the month of December! Go with God. Go and live, Mironov. Live!*'

That was how he remembered it. The man finished, then released Mironov's arm. He recalled standing there, uncertain, confused for a moment. Then the urgency of the moment compelled him to move, and he stepped quickly down the narrow stairs.

What was he saying about 1934, a year so far away in the future? Who was this Stalin he spoke of? Why should I be wary in December? What did he mean that I should not go to St. Petersburg? He was speaking as though…as though he saw some distant future in the world that had not yet come to pass, some far off doom, for his tone of voice clearly carried the edge of warning.

Mironov reached the bottom of the steps, bemused to find the morning seemed clear and bright again, and still tinted with the red glow of that strange fiery sky. He sat in the dining hall, thinking about all that had just happened. Then he took the man's advice, deciding he would get himself as far away from this place as possible, heading east to Irkutsk where he had relatives. Yet always the memory of that man's face, and his strange warning, remained with him.

He eventually made up his mind to travel west again, to Baku where the oil workers had been roused to strike against their corporate masters. The incipient fires of the revolution were burning there, the embers stirred by several nefarious organizers rousting about in the region, fomenting trouble and advocating against the wealthy oil barons.

They wanted their damn oil, he thought, and they would do anything to line their pockets with the gold it would bring, and the power. So Mironov decided he would go to Baku as well, and join the revolutionary movement there, but along the way he stopped again at that same railway inn at Ilanskiy, the very place he had met the stranger that day.

Curiosity... that was what drove him that day. His curiosity surrounded that back stairway like a shroud. He was down in the dining room again when he heard the odd rumble, saw the strange glow in the back stairwell, triggering the memory of that strange event he had witnessed. What was happening? Was there a fire upstairs? He remembered getting up, walking quickly to the stairs to climb them again... and his life was never the same after that, for the world he soon found himself in was not the same either!

He emerged on the second floor, but the inn seemed worn down now, a stark and cold place, with none of the inviting warmth it had offered. He looked about, briefly, then went down the main stairway, to look for the innkeeper. The old grey haired man was gone, yet his portrait was hanging behind the main desk and a young serving woman was tending to the inn instead. What was going on here? He would soon find out more than he ever wished to know.

He went to the window and peered outside to a horrific world where he saw hundreds of people being herded into train cars pointed east. The rail yard seemed infested with the security apparatus of the Okhrana, dark coated men with black Ushankas. They spoke to the people in harsh tones, and some used their rifle butts to beat them if they did not move quickly enough. The scene was so shocking that he withdrew quickly, his eyes finding the serving girl by the desk.

"What has happened?" he asked, shaken by what he had seen.

"What do you mean?"

"The Okhrana... Why are they taking everyone? And the soldiers?"

"The war, the work camps, what else?" The woman shook her head. "Comrade Stalin is fighting the Germans with one hand, and his own people with the other. The war will be the end of us. Stalin's dirty war on life itself. This will be the third train heading east to the camps this week. What... don't tell me you have escaped from one of those train cars. You cannot hide here! If they find you I will be punished as well!" She looked around, as if she feared the hard men outside would storm in at any moment and take her away with the others.

"Comrade Stalin?" That was the same name the stranger had whispered to him. *Beware Stalin!*

"What war do you speak of? The revolution? Has it finally happened?"

"What? Don't be daft. You've read the papers. The Germans have reached the Volga! They are after Stalingrad now, and driving on Baku." There was a newspaper on the counter and she shoved it his way. He took it, his eyes scanning the headlines. It was called 'Vpered Za Stalina! Forward for Stalin! And a drawing showed soldiers standing proudly with bayoneted rifles.

"Go! If you have escaped then you must get out of here. Head south and hide in the woods! Quickly, or the guards will find you!"

Mironov moved, on instinct, for he had been a fugitive for years now, the Okhrana always nipping at his heels. He started for the door but, as fate would have it, three dark coated men were walking slowly toward the weathered porch. So he turned and ran up the main stairway, thinking he might get through a window and climb down a gutter pipe to find the woods beyond. Yet no sooner had he made the upper landing when he saw more uniformed men coming out of one of the rooms. This sent him rushing down the hall, turning off quickly to the narrow back stairway, which was his only hope of escape now.

As he started down into the shadows, there came a dark rumble, as if thunder had broken the sky with the threat of rain.

His boots were hard on the steps as he hastened down, and he hoped no one had heard him. Reaching the bottom, he peered furtively around the edge of the wall into the dining room. All was quiet and empty. There was a fire burning softly on the hearth, and the smell of something cooking. He stepped into the room, clearly confused and somewhat disoriented. There he saw the world as he might have expected it. There was no sign of the frenetic activity he had seen outside in the rail yard, no soldiers, no trains waiting, no one being herded into the cars.

He looked down at the weathered newspaper in his hand, astonished by what he now read. Stalingrad... a city named after a man called Stalin, the man of steel. Then another article, on Baku where they showed an image of the city nestled on a wide bay at the edge of the Caspian Sea and surrounded by high hills. Mironov had thought to find the revolution there, but the photo showed the ruin and misery of war. The city looked like an industrial slum, yet the article referenced a name. *"Kirov yet stands his brave watch on the city,"* it read.

There in the photograph he could see the prominent statue of a uniformed man on a high hilltop pedestal of stone. His arm was raised in a proud salutation, as if greeting the masses below while also beckoning to some distant future with the promise of hope. Kirov... Who was that? Something about the name was very appealing to him, and the longer he looked at that image the more he was taken by the odd notion that he was seeing himself there, a distant ghost in a bleak future where every hope had perished but the one he held in his outstretched hand.

Mironov looked over his shoulder, his eyes darkly on the shadowed entrance to the stairway... the stairway the stranger had come down. The stairway Fedorov had insisted he go down again himself after he first followed the man's footsteps that day in late June of 1908. The stairway, and the warning *never* to use it again...

Yet curiosity is a powerful thing. He took two more bold trips up and down those stairs, each one more harrowing than the last. There he learned of the hideous world that was coming, dark and pitiless as the soul of the man who would forge it from the steel of his own hand, Josef Stalin.

There he found another paper, this time a poster extolling the leader of the great Soviet Union—Stalin. In a moment of strange déjà vu he thought he had seen that face a thousand times before—the coldness in Stalin's eyes, the emptiness that yawned open, boundless as the night and darker than perdition. It was as if he was looking into the eyes of death itself, come to make a quiet appointment that would end his days forever. And he also learned why the statue above the city of Baku looked so familiar to him, and the meaning of the warning the stranger had whispered to him that day: '*Do not go to St. Petersburg in 1934! Beware Stalin! Beware the month of December!*'

It was then that he finally knew the meaning of the stranger's warning, and what he had to do.

* * *

The prison was a dark and cheerless place, a place of terror, and isolation and the misery squeezed from one man after another where they huddled in the cold stone cells, behind heartless bars of iron. One man sat there, brooding, yet scheming in his mind. He had been arrested for his persistent criminal acts against the order of the state. The tall, fearsome agents of the Okhrana had tracked him down and dragged him before a court of censure, where he was lucky to have only been sentenced to 18 months in Bayil, the Black Hole of Baku.

He was born 18 December, 1878 in a little town in the Caucasus called Gori. His mother had been a simple housekeeper, his father a cobbler who often drunk himself into a stupor and beat him cruelly in the early years of his life, where the world also branded him with the scars of smallpox, and physical ailments in his feet and left arm that would plague him in later years. Yet he endured the abuse, as if he was nothing more than another piece of stone beat upon by his father, and he grew to a handsome man in his twenties.

His rebellious spirit soon found him in the activist circles and hidden meeting rooms of the incipient revolution in Russia. He read forbidden literature, the writings of men named Lenin and Marx, and soon began to agitate on their behalf. He wrote and circulated papers condemning the wealthy oil barons and bankers who had come to Baku at the edge of the Caspian Sea, and he helped organize workers strikes against them there. He joined the Bolsheviks, helped to print and spread their propaganda, and recruited new cells. He robbed the bankers he saw bleeding the country dry and used their money to foment further revolutionary activity…and he was tracked down by the Tsar's secret police and arrested.

Now he sat in the prison of Bayil, brooding on how he might soon regain his freedom and continue with his revolutionary zeal. It was all arranged. He would feign illness so he could be taken from his cell to the infirmary, and there he would switch places with another patient being discharged, and escape. He had secretly sent messages to his comrades outside, and they would arrange a sleigh and driver to spirit him away into the cold countryside where he would travel north and east, far away from the black hole in which he now found himself. He would then change his name, assuming an alias like so many other comrades in the struggle, and he would find another cell to infect and breed the virus of revolution. The name would be a simple one, easily grasped, and rooted in the Russian word that sounded much like his old family name. He was Iosif Vissarionovich Dzhugashvili, and Dzhuga meant "Steel" in the old Georgian tongue. So he called himself by the Russian name for that word—"Stalin."

It was all set to happen as he planned it, except for one small mishap. Three nights before he would set his plan in motion a man arrived at the gate of the prison, dressed in the dark black garb of the Okhrana. He presented his badge and papers, and was let in through the high metal doors, slowly climbing the stone steps to the warden's office. In his hand he held an order concerning a certain prisoner, and soon the cold clap of his boots were echoing in the long stony hallway that led to the cell where Stalin slept.

The prisoner was awakened in the night, squinting up through bleary, sleepless eyes when a voice spoke from beyond the metal bars, saying his old family name, a question in the inflexion.

"Yes," he breathed, wondering who the shadow was that had come to him in the dark of the night. The shadow was death—his own death—in the hand of a man who held a steel pistol, aiming it right at the center of the heart that would so blacken the world in decades to come. The shadow had a name as well, Sergei Mironovich Kostrikov, though he never spoke it and he wasted not another second as he squeezed the trigger and fired.

That one single act, the flexing of a finger in the night, would change the lives and fates of millions, redraw the borders of nations, and recast the entire political landscape of the world in decades to come. Was it born in Fedorov's plaintive and desperate whisper at Mironov's ear, and given life by his insatiable curiosity that day? Or did it spring from the hollow of Orlov's darkened soul when he leapt from that helicopter and set Fedorov off on the long pursuit that followed. It did not matter. It was done.

Yet Mironov was not the only man to be shaken by their experience on that narrow stairway at Ilanskiy. Captain Ivan Volkov had also taken that journey and he soon learned where he was, the year and day, impossible as it seemed. After the madness passed, the cold logic of his mind perceived the opportunity at hand when his reason finally grasped the fact of his existence in the year 1908. That impossibility soon became possibility, and he knew what *he* would do.

He would become the hidden face in the warning Doctor Zolkin had desperately tried to hand Captain Karpov one day as the two men jousted in the sick bay aboard *Kirov*.

"*Face it, Karpov,*" Zolkin would say. "*Stalin will eventually rise out of the fires of the civil war. What then? You want to face off with Stalin?*"

"Don't you understand, Zolkin? Knowledge is power too. I can know all the history as it is about to unfold. Stalin? I did some reading the other day. You want to know where Stalin is at this very moment? He's in prison at Baku! Why, if I chose to do so I could sail to the Black Sea and send helicopters there and make an end of Stalin before he ever becomes a factor in Russian history."

"My God! Listen to yourself. Sometimes I really wonder if you are serious about all this. Well... I'll give you one thing, Captain. You have power here, that much is obvious. You want to go kill Stalin? I suppose no one can stop you. Do that, however, and another man may rise from the dark corners of history to take his place. Your knowledge of future events will come unraveling the moment he dies. Fedorov will tell you this. Anything you do here will have dramatic repercussions. So this knowledge you think you can use will soon be useless when everything starts to change. Yes, someone will rise in Stalin's place, and you will not know who that man is, or how to reach him. History may be far more resilient than you realize."

Mironov could not see that shadow rising as he stood over the lifeless body of Josef Stalin, watching the man of steel's blood spread out in a dark stain on the cold stone floor of the cell. He slipped the pistol into the holster beneath his dark overcoat, turned on his heel and was gone. Ever thereafter he would go by another name—*Kirov*.

Part I

The Plan

"But that's how it goes; you think you're on top of the world, and suddenly they spring Armageddon on you."

— **Neil Gaiman**, Good Omens

Chapter 1

It was as good a plan as any they might have devised, risky, impossible, yet the only way forward at that moment. Fedorov reached Vladivostok with a heavy heart, the grey skies and late autumn mist still folded about the hills that surrounded the city and the port of the Golden Horn Bay. It seemed a lifetime or more since he had come here on the battered battlecruiser *Kirov*, standing on the weather deck with Karpov as they watched the shoreline grow closer. There they had tried to make sense of the mystery that had taken them to the fire of the past. Was it all a dream, a nightmare?

He had watched, dumbfounded, as the ship dueled with British carriers and battleships in the North Atlantic, and he saw the awful fire of atomic weapons unleashed on an unsuspecting foe. He stood in awe at Admiral Volsky's side as he greeted the famous John Tovey, Commander of the British Home Fleet. He stood astounded and shaken as the battleship *Yamato* burned in the dark of the Coral Sea. Now all these memories and impossible experiences piled one on another in his mind as he contemplated what they had to do next.

"It's the only way, Admiral," he said, a sadness in his eyes. "We started this, and now we must finish it. A submarine is the only way we could get there and still have any authority. It's already clear that Karpov will not listen to reason, at least not from me."

The men were meeting in the deep underground bunker at Naval Headquarters Fokino, and the atmosphere there was now very tense. Fedorov had come in with Chief Dobrynin, and it was a very happy reunion until they realized the enormity of the situation before them.

"Suppose I were to come with you," said Volsky. "Yes, I think I must do this. I could add the weight of my own authority to the situation. A direct order to Karpov to desist and rendezvous with us may be all that is required. What do you think, Director?"

Kamenski raised an eyebrow as he spoke. "Perhaps, Admiral. I was thinking to invite you on a little vacation with me, but now it seems this will not be the wisest course. Yes. I think you should go with this bright young man here, and if you wouldn't mind my company, I should like to come along as well. Perhaps there is something I could contribute to the situation, another mind and voice in the mix."

"Very well, then it's agreed, but this will be a very perilous journey, Kamenski."

"Most likely—are there any other kind when the world is at the edge of Armageddon and it has come down to the four of us here to save it from certain oblivion? Yes, that's a tall order for any chef I know. I must be sure to bring along my very best tea."

Volsky smiled, feeling just a little more hopeful. Something in the manner of this ex-KGB man was most disarming. He had a quiet inner strength that might see him calmly lighting his pipe or brewing up tea as the world came tumbling down in its final, terrible crash. That thought set Volsky's mind on the urgency of their situation, and he reached for the secure line to Moscow, knowing their time could be running out, even as he spoke.

"I think we had better see if Moscow is getting ready to burn down the house. I will put a call through to Suchkov, Chief of the Navy. He will certainly be in on any final decisions to be made on this matter."

It took time, as the persistent electromagnetic effects in the heavily occluded atmosphere due to the Demon Volcano eruption were impeding normal radio communications. In the end he had to switch to a land line.

"That monster in the Kuriles has everything fouled up. Communications are spotty all through the region. The ash cloud is so massive that it is generating its own weather! Imagine lightning in the midst of all that. The only consolation is that the Admirals and Generals may have trouble ordering their sailors and soldiers to kill one another."

Volsky smiled wanly as he continued to wait on the line. Eventually he was able to get through, and they all listened on speaker phone as he and Suchkov spoke of the current situation, discussing the sudden escalation that was now expected after the bold Chinese riposte in detonating a nuclear warhead over the west coast of the United States.

"Listen Suchkov. You and I have had our disagreements in the past, but there is no time for that now. Everything depends on what may happen here in the next twelve hours."

"*Events are taking their course, Admiral.*" The voice of Suchkov was thin and drawn on the speakerphone. "*The Chinese reprisal for those American missile bomber strikes on their satellite facilities was unexpected, and we both know the Americans will not let it go unanswered. We have brought the strategic arm of our forces to a high level of preparedness as a signal to the Americans. Perhaps they will be cautious now, or at least have second thoughts before they lob a missile at Beijing.*"

"Yes, but this could also force the Americans to their DEFCON One! They will prepare all their missiles for launch as well. Then we stand on the razor's edge, and anything could tip the balance into utter chaos. You must do whatever you can to *prevent* a strategic missile launch now, not start one!" Volsky's voice was strident with his effort to persuade the Navy Chief and, as he finished, Kamenski leaned in, whispering something in his ear.

"Hold on, Suchkov," said Volsky. "There is someone else here who wishes to speak to you." He gestured to Kamenski, who sat down slowly, leaning forward heavily on the table.

"Greetings my old friend."

"*Pavel?... Pavel Kamenski?*"

"One and the same, Suchkov. I am here with Admiral Volsky, and I must concur with everything he says. We are going to try something here, and we need time. You must do whatever you can to give us that time. Understood?"

There was silence on the line for a good long while, and they heard other voices murmuring in the background. Then Suchkov's voice returned, more subdued now, yet edged with a tone of fatalism. "*What is it you are planning? What are you going to do?*"

"You must leave that to me, Suchkov, but rest assured, we have a plan. There are others in the room with you that will know something of what I speak of now, but I can say nothing more here, not even on this secure line. I have come to learn in my day that things are seldom as secure as one might believe. You must trust that Admiral Volsky and I will manage the situation. Once the missiles launch they cannot be called back. So do everything in your power to delay that final moment. Call Beijing at once."

"*But what about the Americans? What if they launch first?*"

"Then you will have plenty of time to launch second. What difference will any of that make if this happens, Suchkov? You have already shown the Americans your fist. Now I advise you to stand down the missile bastions for twenty-four hours, and tell the Americans you are doing this. That will send another signal, yes? This too will give them reason for second thoughts about answering the Chinese missile attack. As for Beijing, tell them that unless they desist from any further actions of this nature they will not have our support should the Americans target their homeland. They have seen you readying your missiles, and this only emboldens them. Without us they could never hope to prevail or even deter a strategic strike from the Americans. When they see us stand down to a lower level of alert, that will give *them* reason for second thoughts as well. Then perhaps Admiral Volsky and I will have the time we need to see what we can do here."

Again the murmurs in the background. Then Suchkov returned to the line. "*Very well, Mister Deputy Secretary.*"

"Deputy Secretary? I have not heard that old handle for a good many years, Suchkov."

"*Yet that is how we remember you, Pavel. There are a good many old grey heads in this room. Very well. We will do as you ask, but please keep us informed.*"

"You have my word on it," Kamenski smiled at Volsky now as they concluded the call. "It seems I still have a little bit of pull in Moscow," he said softly. "Now... Let's get on with it. We have no time to waste. What about this submarine?"

Volsky pursed his lips. "There are three diesel electric boats at Pavlovsk Bay. Everything else is at sea."

"That's all?" Fedorov seemed concerned. "We certainly can't use a diesel boat. We'll need something with nuclear propulsion."

"We lost *Omsk* and *Viluchinsk* after that missile attack against the American 7th Fleet, though we made them pay for those kills. We think we may have a confirmed kill on *Key West*."

"*Key West?*" Fedorov was very surprised. "But that was the submarine Karpov spared—the key trigger point for this war we're facing."

"Yes it was, but events have been shuffled like a bad poker hand, Mister Fedorov. *Key West* was snooping for signs of our missing ships and engaged by *Gepard*. That said, we have very little left, a couple *Akula* class boats and the diesel subs. *Kazan* is the only other missile attack boat remaining, and I pulled it off the line for replenishment two days ago. It's in the Sea of Okhotsk with the *Admiral Kuznetsov*. That's the last real fighting ship we have—that, three *Uladoly* class destroyers and a couple old NKVD frigates that should have been retired decades ago. I'm not even sure how they got them running again. I've reformed a battlegroup with those ships, but they will be little more than nice targets for the Americans if we sortie again."

"*Kazan*…That's the new *Yasen* class boat," said Fedorov. "That will do, Admiral. It has a KPM type pressurized water reactor and can make over 35 knots submerged. It's just what we need, fast, quiet, and very deadly."

"This young man knows more about my ships than I do, Kamenski." The two older men smiled. "Very well, I will see what I can do about *Kazan*. Yes, I think this will work out well. We can put the control rods on three helicopters and fly them out to the *Admiral Kuznetsov*."

"Three helicopters? Why so many?"

"So that we can be sure at least one of them gets there! The Japanese are on full alert now, though that damn volcano still has the skies over Hokkaido covered with ashfall. That said, we should not risk losing all three control rods in a single helicopter."

"I agree," said Kamenski. "Yes, this would be very wise."

"Then after we reach the carrier we can transfer to a smaller boat for the rendezvous with *Kazan*. We must do this at night. The Americans have undoubtedly been looking for this submarine as well, and we must not allow them to find it. I would not be surprised if they already have a submarine in the Sea of Okhotsk by now. This war has not gone well for us. If not for the fact that the Chinese are making such a fuss over Taiwan, and drawing off the American carrier battlegroups, we would be out of business as a naval force in the Pacific by now."

"Ironic," said Fedorov. "That is the very thing Karpov thinks he is going to change in 1908."

"Why is it we cannot simply know what has happened by now?" Volsky looked from Kamenski to Fedorov, his two resident guides where the confounding prospect of time travel was concerned.

"I understand what you mean," said Kamenski, "but remember what I explained about that still point in time? We are all there, the four of us, but I think Karpov is there too, and with all the men aboard *Kirov*. He and that ship of his are not where they belong. Their very presence in 1908 is offensive to the flow of fate and time. Yes, they can act and work enormous changes in the past, as we have seen, but I think they exist and sail in the eye of the maelstrom. They are in the sea of time, yet in a protected spot, and things cannot resolve until this whole situation works itself out."

"But everything Karpov does should be concluded by now. He should have been in his grave long ago."

"It would seem that way from our perspective, but I do not think time works that way. She must consider every point of view. Time is not the nice straight line from point A to point B that you think it is. It is all twisted and folded about itself and, in fact, any two points on that squiggly line could meet and be joined. This is why I say we are all together now, in one place, a nexus point where the lines of fate meet and run through one another like a Gordian knot, and we sit here trying to figure out how to untangle it. Karpov is there with us, and we have set events in motion here that have a strong possibility of impacting what he does—deciding whether he does anything at all! Therefore I don't think things have changed yet. The transformation has not yet occurred, though it might happen at any second. Can you not feel the tension in the air now?"

He looked around him as if he could see what he was describing. "It is not merely because of the looming war. I think time itself is waiting to pass judgment and read our sentence for the crimes we have committed against her. But until we resolve this business with Karpov, everything is still in play. All we can do now is work out our plan, and yet I believe our very intention to do so seems to hold time in abeyance. It must wait for us, and see what *we* might do."

"I see… You mean the possibility that we might succeed in stopping Karpov exists now, and so time must wait for us?"

"You have it exactly, Admiral. Wouldn't you agree, Mister Fedorov?"

"That theory coincides with work I have read on the subject by an American physicist, a mister Paul Dorland. He even uses that same terminology—nexus point. He would call this situation a deep nexus, and he believes it has a universal effect on all time meridians passing through this point."

"Then my thinking has good company. In any case, I believe we need only concern ourselves with the outcome of our plan. Let us begin with the submarine. *Kazan* is a very good choice. Then we must decide what to do with it!"

Admiral Volsky looked at Fedorov now. "It is clear that we must try to get the submarine back to 1908. We can do nothing with it here to influence Karpov. Are you certain you can get us there, Chief Dobrynin? This situation is somewhat different, is it not?"

"*Kirov* used KN-3B reactors, and they are pressurized water reactors using enriched uranium-235 fuel. Rod-25 also worked successfully on the *Anatoly Alexandrov*, and it uses a KLT-40S reactor. *Kazan* uses the same basic type. Rod-25 is compatible, and the other two control rods as well."

"Alright. Let us rely on Rod-25," said Volsky. "If it fails us, then we can try the others. And you say you can hear the shift and control it now, Dobrynin?"

"I got us home safely, Admiral. I cannot promise you anything, but I will do my best."

"That is all we have to go on for the moment," said Kamenski. "Alright, gentlemen. Suppose we do get there safely. Then what?" He looked at Fedorov now, wanting to know what the young Captain had in mind.

"As I see things we have two choices," said Fedorov. "The first is to contact Karpov and see if we can all persuade him to relent and rejoin us. This I would prefer, but the Captain may not want to cooperate."

"In that instance, contacting him will give away the enormous advantage of surprise."

"Correct," said Fedorov, though his eyes seemed troubled now. "What you should know, Director, is that Captain Karpov has a kind of phobia where submarines are concerned. Approaching him in any wise with an undersea boat will be dangerous."

"And do not forget Tasarov," said Volsky.

"Tasarov?" Kamenski did not know the man.

"He is the sonar operator aboard *Kirov*, and one of the very best in the fleet. His ear for sonar is every bit as good as Dobrynin's where these reactors are concerned. If we do take the hard road, and that would be to take action without first contacting Karpov, then Tasarov will be the main obstacle to our success."

Volsky folded his arms. "This will not be an easy mission," he said with obvious sadness in his voice. "These are my men—the fighting crew of *Kirov*. That ship has been through hell and back again, and to think of what we may now have to do is most unsettling."

"We need not decide our final course at the moment," said Kamenski, "but I agree, this will be a major fork in the road, and in some respects it influences a choice we must make before we get underway. I assume we have an approximate idea of *Kirov's* general position in 1908, Mister Fedorov?"

"We were able to generalize their signal as coming from the Sea of Japan, and Karpov confirmed that."

"An encouraging start, but ships move, so we must wonder where he might go."

"He will most likely look to dominate the Japanese Imperial Navy," said Fedorov. "This will be necessary if he is to have any real influence there. To do so he will have to engage that fleet in battle, and he will be up against a very wily Admiral Togo, perhaps one of the greatest Admirals in modern naval history. If I had to bet on it, I would guess the action would occur at a key chokepoint waterway—either the Yellow Sea, or the Straits of Tsushima."

"Alright," said Kamenski. "You and the Admiral can plot all this out on your navigation maps, but my question is when do we sail south—in *time*, that is? Do we proceed in the here and now? Or do we shift back to 1908 first and make our approach in that era?"

Volsky nodded his head gravely. "I can see how this choice relates to the other decision we must make. If we sail south now it will be very risky with the Americans and Japanese all stirred up here. That said, we might be very close to *Kirov* when we appear and achieve complete tactical surprise. Then again, if we make our approach south in 1908 the journey will be relatively safe and quiet, except that silence in the sea gives our mister Tasarov the best possible chance to hear us coming. We have a great deal to decide here gentlemen. But I suggest we get to the *Admiral Kuznetsov* first."

Chapter 2

"There's one other matter before we go, said Fedorov. "Orlov has asked if he could come with us,"

"Orlov?" Volsky's face revealed some hesitation over this. "The man has already jumped ship once, Mister Fedorov. This may not be wise."

"That is not how he tells the story now, Admiral. He says there was an electrical fire on the KA-226 and they were unable to communicate with us. The radio was dead."

"I see… And the jamming?"

"I asked him about that, and he claims the emergency systems came on during the fire. Then he saw our missiles and jumped. The pilot could not get out in time."

"You believe him?"

"I would like to, sir."

"Even so, what does he contribute to the mission?"

Kamenski spoke up now, raising a finger to make a point. "This Orlov was the man Mister Fedorov rescued in 1942? That means he has moved in time, Admiral. He is here in the nexus point with us, whether we bring him along or not."

"A lot of others have moved in time as well. I had a full reinforced company of Naval Marines with Mister Fedorov. Are they all in the borscht with us?"

"In some regard, but Orlov is special. This Mister Dorland, the American Physicist, I have read his work as well. I think he would call Orlov a free radical, someone at large in the meridians of time with a great deal of influence. After all, if Fedorov had not gone after him, then we would not now know what Karpov was planning or even where he was. The history might have simply changed, and we would have changed right along with it—in fact, we might not even exist! Orlov led Mister Fedorov to 1942, and from there he fell through to another gopher hole and found Karpov in 1908. That was either very fortunate, or very fated. Time lifted her skirts to show us where

Karpov was hiding, and we have Orlov to thank for that knowledge. You can leave him behind, but somehow his life and fate seems closely associated with the outcome of this saga."

Volsky considered that. "I suppose we could keep a good eye on the man if we do take him. I know Orlov. If we leave him behind he will start talking to anyone who might listen about his little exploits. Very well. He can come, but I will have words with the man before we launch the mission. I want no nonsense."

"As acting mission commander I restored Orlov as a Captain of the second rank," said Fedorov. "He thought we had come to arrest him for court martial. In fact, he thought we were trying to kill him. Those S-300s we fired left him with a bad feeling. I think he attributed it to Karpov, but I was Captain at the time, and the final authorization to fire came from me, though I haven't told him that yet. So I thought restoring his rank would be a good way to start again with this man."

"Perhaps, you are right, Fedorov. Very well. I will let this decision stand and confirm his rank as Captain. Send him along with Engineering Chief Dobrynin."

"There's one other thing, sir." Fedorov looked from the Admiral to Kamenski now, the light of something very important in his eyes. "On the way west to find Orlov I discovered something quite alarming."

"Go on, Mister Fedorov, you have told us nothing of that journey, but I assume it was somewhat dangerous. What happened?"

"We stopped at a small railway in east of Kansk at a place called Ilanskiy."

"Yes, there is a naval arsenal just south of that location," said Volsky.

"Well there is something else there too, Admiral, something very important." He went on to describe the inn, the stairway, and the strange incident that had occurred, along with the meeting with Mironov.

"My God," said Kamenski. "The stairs took you to the year 1908? You are certain it was Kostrikov?"

"I was just as shocked as you seem, Director, but it was him. I looked up photos of his early life, and I never forget a face. I met Sergei Kirov there in the dining hall, but the really significant thing I discovered was on that back stairway. Kirov got curious about me, I suppose. He may have been suspicious of my uniform, and he came up that back stairway. It brought him from his world of 1908, to the one we were in at that moment, 1942."

"Astounding! Then there is some kind of rift or tear in the fabric of time there," Kamenski's face belied that he knew more than he was saying now, and Fedorov could perceive it.

"This is how I came to understand it, Director, and I think it all has something to do with the Tunguska event."

"Yes," said Volsky. "Mister Kamenski and I came to a similar conclusion. These control rods have materials in them that we now believe originate from that event. Whatever it was that exploded over the Stony Tunguska River Valley that day, it has created some very unusual effects."

"It may be that this rift in time was not the only one to result from that event," said Kamenski quietly.

"You know of others?"

The silence after that question was very telling, holding the answer in the affirmative within its emptiness. "Yes, gentlemen, we know of others. This one, however, is something new. This we did *not* know. To think that it may have existed there on that back stairway is most troubling. Who may have traversed those stairs in the past, coming and going from one era to another?"

"The young woman I met there—I think she was the proprietor's daughter—in any case, she told me those stairs were haunted, and she seemed to fear them."

"Perhaps because people may have unknowingly taken that stairway before, and suddenly appeared in her hotel!" Kamenski had a wry smile on his face. "But Sergei Kirov! I have lamented his assassination all my life. Who knows how Russia might have developed had he been elevated to General Secretary of the party instead of Stalin."

Fedorov gave him a furtive glance. "I think I should tell you that I said something to him that I may now have to regret."

"Oh? What was that, young man?"

"I… well I warned him not to go to St. Petersburg in 1934. I told him to beware the 30th of December! I know it was foolish, but I just couldn't help myself. He was always a hero to me. That is one reason I applied for an assignment aboard *Kirov*."

Kamenski smiled. "It was called Leningrad when he was killed there, of course you know that, but it may interest you to know that he was assassinated on December 1st, and not on the 30th. That was the way it happened the first time. Then things changed."

"What do you mean?" said Volsky. "Are you saying there are two versions of the event?"

"Just as there are two dates for the American entry into WWII. Yes, in another meridian of time Sergei Kirov was assassinated on December 1st. Yet Mister Fedorov is also correct. The history he knows will have that date set as the 30th."

"Just a moment, Director," said Fedorov, a troubled look on his face. "It's clear to me that we caused the Americans to enter the war early, yet I would have told anyone that Kirov was assassinated on the 30th *before* we left Severomorsk."

"That is the date I remember as well," said Volsky.

"Yes, and many others will have that date in their heads," said Kamenski. "But this old head remembers it on the 1st of December. A few of the Party elite would celebrate it quietly, behind closed doors. I have drunk many a toast to Sergei Kirov on that day. But the people I can raise a glass with are now are few and far between."

Fedorov was very surprised now. "But that would mean …"

Kamenski looked at him, again with that wry smile. "Go on," he said, waiting.

"Well that would mean something happened to change the history even before *Kirov* left Severomorsk!"

"You are very astute, my young man. Yes. That is exactly what it would mean. There may be only a small handful of people who know what you have just concluded—and know it to be a fact and not mere speculation. I happen to be one of them, and I have lived with that knowledge for a very long time."

Admiral Volsky thought this might have something to do with the strange time shift effects that were discovered after the massive Tsar Bomba detonation. "Tell him about the Kuz'kina Mat," he said, wagging a thick finger. "Tell him about the Tsar Bomba!"

"Yes, that was what Khrushchev called it, Kuz'kina Mat, Kuzka's Mother. The CIA called it 'Joe 111,' and I knew it as Project 7000, but I suppose it was the real 'mother of all bombs.' There has never been a bigger one. Well, you will be surprised to learn, Mister Fedorov, that we first came to understand that time displacement was possible as early as October 30, in the year 1961, on the day that bomb went off. That was sixty years ago, and I was a very young man back then."

He explained how they realized nuclear detonations could cause tears in the fabric of spacetime, and Fedorov listened intently, hearing the details of this now, even though Chief Dobrynin had disclosed some of this to him earlier.

"Then have we done this before? Have we moved things in time?"

"We have tried," said Kamenski. "Sometimes without success, and other times without even knowing or intending it, as in the case of your ship vanishing last July. Yet the real question you wish to ask is something more, Mister Fedorov. You want to know what could have happened to change the course of history—not by much, just a month in this case between the first and thirtieth of December in 1934, but in that brief interval lies a profound mystery. Yes?"

* * *

The last of the three helicopters arrived on *Admiral Kuznetsov*, this one carrying the prize, Admiral Volsky, Kamenski, and Rod-25. Fedorov and Troyak brought one spare rod on another helo, and

Dobrynin and Orlov accompanied the third, with Zykov riding along for security.

The Admiral came dressed in a simple Lieutenant's uniform, and he gave orders that nothing was to be removed from the helicopter for at least an hour, knowing the Americans would be watching the ship closely from space.

"I know very well how good their spy satellites are," said Kamenski. "Ours are good as well. I have read headlines on newspapers using satellites in space! This is a wise precaution. Seeing the Admiral of the Fleet get off a helicopter here would certainly raise a few eyebrows."

"Yes, and this uniform makes me feel young again," said Volsky, smoothing out his jacket sleeve. "We are going to put on a little show for the Americans," he smiled. "Of course they have been watching us very closely since that last engagement. At present we believe they think *Kirov* was destroyed along with the other ships that vanished after that demon of a volcano erupted. Well enough. They have seen us withdraw the *Admiral Kuznetsov* and they are watching that ship very closely. *Kazan* has replenished secretly in the underground submarine tunnels, but they will be looking for her. I have no doubt that they are watching with satellites in spite of the ashfall and cloud cover. The area north of the volcano has not been affected much. Therefore it would be most unwise to attempt to surface that boat to take on our special cargo."

"Then how will we get there?" asked Kamenski.

"We are going to have to use a submersible rescue vehicle, The AS-28 is available and we can move it into the *Admiral Kuznetsov* task force for the show I have planned."

"Where is *Kazan?*" asked Fedorov.

"Right beneath *Admiral Kuznetsov!* The Americans have been looking all over for that submarine, but to no avail. They have been trying to get a peek at my cards, but I have stacked my last two Aces, even though I risk losing both to a single warhead. Yet I reason if that were to happen, then the worst would be upon us and it would be down to the strategic missile forces in the end. So I have hidden *Kazan* below the carrier. Now we must arrange a little theater. The Americans will be watching us, so I am moving one of the diesel subs into the region quietly as well. Our Submarine Rescue Vessel *Sayany* can carry the AS-28 submersible to the scene, and we can quietly load the control rods aboard at night. We board the AS-28 and let it move out a few kilometers on the surface with the *Sayany*. Then we submerge with it and maneuver back to *Kazan*. After we have successfully boarded the sub with our cargo, then we'll send the AS-28 back to *Sayany* and surface the diesel boat right there for the Americans to see."

"Ah, very clever, Admiral," said Kamenski. "You will make it seem like the AS-28 was performing some kind of rescue operation on the diesel submarine, perhaps delivering some needed part or piece of equipment."

"Precisely, and while they are watching the show, *Kazan* can slip quietly out the back door and head for the Sea of Japan."

Chapter 3

Offutt Air Force Base, Nebraska, was a very busy place that morning. Once the center of the US Strategic Air Command (SAC) it was a warren of underground bunkers and command facilities that were now the heartbeat of the U.S. Strategic Command, (USSTRATCOM). Over the years it had seen some memorable events in both war and peace, and had been heralded in film and fiction for its strategic importance in time of national crisis. Henry Fonda was there in the cold war classic "Fail Safe" and Peter Sellers held forth there in Doctor Strangelove as he learned to love the bomb.

On this day it had a very important mission to ready, and one that might fit neatly into the script of either of those two old movies. For among other units stationed there, the base was home to some very special aircraft that would soon rise into the skies in an ominous prelude to what might happen soon after. They were not stealthy, sleek, black-tiled warplanes, or high flying hypersonic reconnaissance planes. In fact, anyone who might have seen them taxi from their secure hangers onto the wide tarmac near the 55th Bomb Wing Headquarters building would recognize their familiar silhouettes at once. One man who saw them that day was in no way surprised when their big engines began to turn over, the sound rolling across the field and reverberating amid the squat concrete buildings housing high level command facilities.

"Hear that?" said Airman First Class Ernie Mason. "I told you they would be flying today. The E-4 hanger doors were open at 04:00 hours this morning."

"You were up at four AM, Mace?" His buddy Airman, James Suder was still working his first cup of coffee that morning, looking tired and needing sleep.

"I had the night shift. Took some down time at the Old Stripes Club, but there was no one there but old stripes. Good name for the place."

"There a lot better clubs in Omaha," said Suder. "Shark Club,

Goodfellas, Whisky Tango."

"Well who can get to Omaha and back on a thirty minute leash, Suder? I had the duty. We had to go over those engines with a fine toothed comb last night. So I knew the spooks were going to be up today."

"Spooks?"

"That's what I call them. They only fly the damn things when all hell is about to break loose. Scares the crap out of you because the only reason they made the damn things is to make certain someone survives to send Emergency Action Messages if we get toasted here on the ground."

"What's on the tarmac this morning?"

"E-4B *Nightwatch* is out there making noise right now. We had to work over the RC-135 Rivet Joints plane and the E-6B Mercury TACAMO plane too."

"Jeeze Louise! That's some serious business, Mace."

The E-6B looked like a white Boeing commercial airliner, and the *Nightwatch* plane actually was a commercial airliner, a big 747 jumbo jet with the telltale porpoise hump and nose and a bright blue stripe down each side of the fuselage. It didn't seem dressed for the part it was to play as the "Doomsday Plane," an airborne command and control plane for the civilian leadership in the event of a major national emergency.

"No shit, Sherlock," said Mason. "You can bet the *Nightwatch* will be heading east to find the President somewhere. And the Air Force brass will be in the E-6 by now. STRATCOM building looks like everyone left for a funeral or something. All the offices are shut down. There's nothing but janitors mopping up over there now."

"They probably all went into their gopher holes," said Suder. "They're all underground by now, which is where we should be. If the President is going airborne with the rest of the stripes, then you and I had better find us a couple cases of bravos and dig a hole ourselves. The proverbial shit is about to hit the fan, my friend."

"Well hell, Suder. Did you think we were going to take that crap the Chinese pulled over the Pacific coast lying down? Hell no! I think we're going to toast something to let them know what's up. Any bets on what they do?"

"Rumors say they might hump Shanghai or some other big city over there. But you know the drill—they throw one, then we throw one, then they throw a few more and on it goes. This business has been wound up tight for the last nine days. Something is about to give, I tell you. Can't you feel it?"

"Yeah, I've had the same feeling. I don't think we're going to back off on this one. It's pedal to the metal from here on in, and that means you and I will either be real busy or very dead in the next 48 hours. Well, I say we make it through."

"How do you figure, Mace?"

"We made it through the alien attack in *Independence Day*. We stopped those wacko alien ships in *Battleship*, and we beat the pants off 'em in *Battle: Los Angeles* and *War of The Worlds*, and even kicked ass in *Signs*—swing away, Merrill… Merrill… Swing away!" He made as if he were holding a baseball bat ready to swing on the first alien that showed its snout.

"Right, we always win against the aliens," said Suder. "But this time we're not up against them. This time it's *us*, the good old primates. We're going to swing away alright, but those planes out there might end up being the only things left around to see what happens. *Nightwatch…* good name for the damn thing."

* * *

High above the Pacific, NROL-52 was up and running, a replacement sent up the previous day for a bird the Chinese had taken down with their surprise ASAT attack. The Americans had seen to it that they would not lose any more of their precious satellites, at least not at the hands of the Chinese. They had sent their B-2s in with a devastating fast new cruise missile and blasted all the key satellite launching facilities the Chinese relied on. To express their displeasure, the Chinese escalated by sending a sub launched missile over the US Pacific coast and, though the resulting EMP burst was not as devastating as originally thought, it had taken down power grids from Seattle to San Diego.

Watching the latest developments very closely from space, 2nd Lieutenant Matt Eden was on the duty roster again that day at the Naval Intelligence Center. He had already lost one bird, and wondered how long this one would fly as he monitored the regrouping of the Russian Red Banner Pacific Fleet. He was told to look for the principle surface combatants, but thus far the only capital ship of note he had been able to identify was the *Admiral Kuznetsov*.

It was time to make his scheduled report to the Deputy Watch Commander, and he punched up line two on his phone set.

"Deep Black Ten, sir. Lieutenant Eden reporting on RB1."

"Anything new, Lieutenant?"

"Yes sir, but communications with the satellite have been difficult. There's a considerable electromagnetic disturbance from that eruption and it's propagated through the atmosphere into space. The high altitude EMP burst didn't help either, but at least our bird was over the horizon at the time and the system wasn't fried. Our optics are still nice and sharp. Lucky for us the ash fall has been blowing south, otherwise we couldn't see a thing."

"I don't need a weather report, Lieutenant. What's up with the damn Russians?"

"Sorry sir. The flotilla was regrouping and replenishing in the Sea of Okhotsk, but that operation appears to be concluded now. They transited the Gulf of Sakhalin and moved into the Tartar Strait off Sovetskaya Gavan and Vanino. There's been some helicopter activity around the carrier but it looks like they were just delivering a few missile canisters. Now they have moved what appears to be a sub tender into the area. I've sent the digital imagery to Section Four for analysis."

"Any sign of that hot submarine PACCOM is still looking for?"

"Nothing has surfaced, sir. But I'll watch this tender and see what it's up to. Where there's smoke, there's fire."

"Good enough, Lieutenant."

Eden hung up the phone and returned to his console, deciding to take a closer look at the new arrival. What would they need a sub tender out here for unless there was a submarine nearby, and possibly one in difficulty? Could this be a blood trail from the submarine Naval Intelligence is all hot and bothered about? Perhaps it was wounded in action on its first sortie, and is licking its wounds in sheltered waters until help can arrive. The Russians sure moved that sub tender there in a hurry. My data points indicate it was making sixteen knots, and that is the top of the scale for that class ship.

He wished he could get a better look on infrared, but that channel was still all screwed up with the heat from that damn volcano making it very difficult to get clear readings in the region. And every so often he would experience a sudden electromagnetic disturbance, even if his satellite was far enough from the eruption to remain largely unaffected.

He thought about the situation…If I was that Russian attack boat Captain I'd be right under that ash cloud. Then again, if I can come up with that, I'm sure our own subs would be searching there as well.

The Russians have pulled most everything in tight—all their diesel boats that were screening that last fleet sortie have turned tail and are mostly on picket duty along the line of the Kuriles and south of Vladivostok. We've already nailed their two *Oscars*, but where is this slippery *Yasen* class boat? Where is *Kazan*?

He would have to rely on his optical feed, and with the ashfall over most of Hokkaido shutting down air operations there, he decided the best place to look was up in the Russian safety zones in the Sea of Okhotsk and Gulf of Sakhalin. Where do you hide a big hungry nuclear attack sub, he wondered?

* * *

Lieutenant Commander William Reed sat uncomfortably in his chair looking at the satellite photography, and he was thinking the same thing.

"I think it's a fair bet we nailed their flagship," he said to the men assembled around the table. "But we lost *Key West* in the undersea duel, though we do have confirmed kills on both their *Oscars*. The only boat we really need to watch out for now is that new *Yasen* class sub."

White House Chief of Staff Leyman was there, along with General Lane of the Air Force and Admiral Stone of the Navy. Called simply the "Stonewall" because of his stalwart opinions on defense readiness, he had come up to the Washington circuit in 2018, and was pressing the palms of Senators and Congressmen to make sure defense allocations kept flowing the Navy's way. Now he was sent in to relay a briefing received from PACCOM on the situation in the Pacific.

"I can't say as that matters a whole lot now," said Lane. "After what the Chinese pulled the other day it's coming down to missiles and bombers soon."

"That decision has not been made yet," said Leyman. "You were in on that meeting with the President. Yes, he's hopping mad, but the general feeling is that if we respond in kind, say with one of these EMP weapons like the Chinese used, it will only escalate the matter further."

"It sure looked grim from what we were seeing in space," said Lane. "The Russians were heating up all their primary missile bastions and dispersing their mobile launchers all over Siberia. Now it seems they've cooled things down." He looked at Leyman, knowing any news on that front would most likely come from him.

"We received a diplomatic message on the red phone from Moscow. They asked us not to retaliate for the Chinese attack, and to sweeten the deal they backed off on their missile bastion alert. It's a strong signal that they don't want this to go any farther than it has thus far."

"I'd do the same after the pounding we gave them in the Pacific," said Admiral Stone.

Lane looked at him askance. "How does Captain Tanner feel about that on the *Washington?*"

"Well at least the ship is still afloat and back in friendly waters. Sure they got through with something, and they hurt us, particularly when *Key West* went down. I can't say as I'm surprised. That was an old *Los Angeles* class boat that should have been retired and replaced years ago. Still, all things considered, we did worse to them. They lost *Kirov*, their hot new destroyer *Orlan* and the frigate *Admiral Golovko*, not to mention that old *Udaloy*. We didn't get the *Admiral Kuznetsov*, but we've got the damn thing bottled up now. Let's face it gentlemen, the Red Banner Pacific Fleet is pretty much out of business. Now that we've got CVBG *Ford* heading east with other Third Fleet assets the Russians won't lift another finger. So if we have to do something about the Chinese, I think the job should go to us—to the United States Navy. Toss this potato to General Lane here and all it does is ratchet this whole thing up another notch because his bombers will be perceived as strategic weapons."

Lane folded his arms. "Hold on just a moment, Admiral, if you please. We've already showed them we can hit their home turf with our B-2s and there's nothing they can do about it. I can put in a limited strike with our new CHAMP missiles and we can take down their local command and control for this planned amphibious operation. That's a well measured response to what they did over the Pacific coast here."

Leyman looked from Lane to Reed, obviously lost in the forest of acronyms. Reed stepped up to enlighten him.

"CHAMP is Mil-speak for Counter-electronics High-powered Advanced Missile Project, Mister Leyman. It's basically a missile that delivers high powered microwaves to the target instead of a warhead. The effect will knock down electronics within a given radius of the strike. Think of it as a precision EMP weapon of sorts, good for a surgical strike if need be, or for wide area deployment if you've got enough of them."

"We have twenty in theater and I can put them on the B-2s in six hours," said Lane. "We can knock out all their key command assets. Hell, they won't even be able to turn over their aircraft engines or use search radars if we hit a few key airfields supporting this operation. Our *Raptors* out of Okinawa stopped that last air strike package they had headed for Taiwan, but that's the conventional way to slow the Chinese down. We can throw in a magic wand or two and go real high-tech on them any time we choose."

"Yes, well we're going to have to establish air superiority over Taiwan if this thing goes any further," said Stone. "That's job one, and it's going to have to come off the decks of *Eisenhower* and *Nimitz*. *Ford* is up north to keep an eye on the Russians, but with those two carriers, and reserve planes from CVBG *Washington,* Admiral Ghortney informs me he believes we can restore order over Taiwan. We do that fast enough and they would be stupid to try and press this attack any further. There's no way they cross the straits in force without air superiority."

"Well, what about these *Vampire* planes of theirs?" Leyman looked at Reed now. "My understanding is that they gave the Taiwanese a pretty good licking. And don't the Chinese have carriers too?"

"They do, sir, and so you can bet that if we do move as Admiral Stone suggests, those assets will come into play on the other side."

" I can take those out of the game real easy," said Lane. "We have enough bombers in theater now to make a real difference here. I can put a hundred cruise missiles on any targets you name, Mister Leyman. Let me get the Bones and Buffs up with the rest, we can plaster their amphibious loading operation in port before it ever gets to sea or anywhere near Taiwan. Air superiority is not necessary. Hell, I can put 24 AGM-158s on a single B-1 bomber! One squadron could lay waste to their entire operation from 600 miles away." The General was referring to the relatively new AGM-158B JASSM-ER, a stealthy, radar evading Long Range Anti-Ship Missile. (LRASM). Six B-1 bombers could send 144 of the sleek cruise missiles at the Chinese amphibious flotilla and wreak havoc.

"So you see we don't need aircraft carriers in the mix to stop this. You all saw what happened to the *Washington.* The right tool for the job here is strategic bomber assets. I hope the President knows that." He folded his arms, well satisfied that he had thumped his chest for the Air Force.

"I'll see that he does," General Lane, said Leyman.

"Then what are we waiting for? I say we take out those Chinese carriers with my standoff bombers, and you can go in and darken the skies over Taiwan with your carriers, Admiral Stone. That's a one two punch that will set the Chinese back on their heels soon enough, and it will still be perceived as a conventional operation. We can stop this planned invasion of Taiwan in 36 hours. Either that or we send our new CHAMP out there, and then maybe they'll think twice about another EMP attack."

"Yes, but what if they *do* respond with another such attack?" Reed cautioned. "The West coast is still a real mess. Yes we can stop their conventional assets, which means the Chinese will then have little more than their ballistic missiles for offensive punch. They can reach Guam with those if they have to, and they can also let slip the dogs of war in Korea. Mister Kim over there would like nothing more than to cross the line after we took out his little missile launch."

"That was an operational necessity, and I will note that they *haven't* crossed the line."

"Only because Beijing has held them on a tight leash. But believe me, gentlemen, the Chinese know the one little nightmare we have had concerning Asia is a ground war. If this thing escalates any further, you can look for one in Korea. It may come down to that. They may tell us they either take Taiwan or we can have the Korean war back again in short order. Is the Navy prepared for that?"

"We can move 3rd Marines over. The planning is already underway, and we have the sealift assets as well."

"Well then let me pose another question here." Reed tacked in a new direction now, playing the devil's advocate well. "Suppose you do hobble the Chinese Navy, just like you did the Red Banner Pacific Fleet. Suppose you stop their planned invasion of Taiwan in the bargain. Then all they have left are the missiles. You saw what they did to Taiwan with those. What if they start lobbing the damn things at Japan? They've got all that area targeted and they could start raining down hell on Tokyo, Osaka, and twenty other cities. The Fukushima complex is still hot as hell over there. What if they dropped a few missiles right into that facility? You all know we don't have enough anti-missile defense batteries to stop them. Look what happened on Taiwan. They had ten patriot batteries over there, and a whole lot more, but they still got smashed."

It was a good point, and Lane shifted uncomfortably in his chair. China's ballistic missiles were their trump card, widely dispersed, difficult to find and kill, and extremely effective on offense.

"The problem with all of this is that when you force the other guy to dig into his haversack for the last weapon he has, he's going to fish around and eventually pull out an ICBM. The Chinese made it perfectly clear with that pot shot they took over Nevada."

"And in my opinion that is the danger of leaving it go unanswered." Lane spoke up now, and with more resolve. "We may want to show them that if they do reach for another missile like that again, we're going to give them the same thing in spades!"

"We have boomers on patrol that can do just that," said Admiral Stone. "It can be a measured response. We can move in a boomer and use a single missile, just like they did."

"Well what about the Russians? You want them heating up all their stuff again?"

"We call the Russians and tell them exactly what we are going to do, and state that it will be a limited, measured response. Oh, they'll try to find that boomer with anything they have, but there isn't much left of the Red Banner Fleet, either above or below the sea now. This is again a job for the Navy. I can give you stealth in a way that even General Lane's B-2s can't deliver. We can creep over with a boomer and turn off all the lights in Shanghai. Then they'll know we mean business."

"Shanghai?" Lane scratched his ear. "Wouldn't that affect Korea and Japan too?"

"I just picked that one out of my hat, but we could go inland with this too. We could hit the heartland cities along the Yellow River, Zhengzhou, Luoyang, Kaifeng. One little missile would turn off the lights there for 15 million people and make a very strong statement. Hell, they took down San Francisco, LA and San Diego! Tit for tat."

"Those cities are starting to recover somewhat," said Reed. "That EMP burst was not as severe as it first appeared. Most of the outage was due to Hoover and Glen Canyon Dams going down, but latest estimates are that they can get back online in a matter of weeks. They found out a lot of the transformers made it through without significant damage. It's still dark there, but the power is coming back in spots. It could take a while, but they'll eventually recover."

"Gentlemen... " Leyman spoke now. "I'll take all these options to the President, but my feeling is that he wants to keep this on a conventional level as long as possible."

"Which leads us right back to this business over Taiwan," said Stone. "Either we stand in defense of that nation or we don't. What's it going to be, Mister Leyman? Admiral Ghortney made a particular point of insisting he was given operational control of the battle space here."

"Within the limits defined by the civilian leadership, Admiral. Now, what we want to know is this: can you do what you claim and recover air superiority over Taiwan in the next 36 hours? If so, you have authorization to proceed. As for you, General Lane, get those bombers armed and ready. If they can do what you say and stop this invasion from 600 miles away, I think the President will want to hear that as soon as possible."

"You have my word on that," said Lane, satisfied.

The meeting rambled on for another ten minutes before Leyman adjourned the session and went to brief the President. As he rose from his chair, Lieutenant Commander Reed handed Admiral Stone the latest satellite photos he had been reviewing.

"Have you seen these, Admiral?"

Stone took a brief look, immediately recognizing what he was seeing. "So that's what's left of the fleet. Still holed up off Sakhalin Island?"

"They've moved."

"Where?"

"Through the Gulf of Sakhalin and into the Tartar Strait, but they don't seem to be in any hurry."

"Lane would love to take a shot at them, if only just to prove his bombers can get the job done. But the feeling is we ought not provoke the Russians any more than necessary here."

"I agree. They took down *Thunder Horse* in the Gulf, and have already lost three subs and the heart of their entire Pacific Fleet."

"Well it will be cat and mouse out there for a while."

"How do you mean?

"The surface combatants have withdrawn and consolidated in to new battlegroups. They pulled their ships up north and we pulled ours south to Guam. That damn volcano is blanketing the sea as much as anything else. It's no place for surface ships in the waters south of the Kuriles. It's down to submarines for them now. So if we move *Eisenhower* and *Nimitz* into strike range off Taiwan, that means we have to worry about their submarines too, both the Chinese and Russian boats."

"That's what all this fuss is with the sub tender? You think they are planning to move their subs out again?"

Stone gave him a long look. "What sub tender?"

"Right there in those satellite images I just handed you."

Stone took a closer look. "That's not a sub tender... looks to be one of their old *Pioner Moskvy* class submersible salvage and support ships. I suppose you could call it a sub tender, but a ship like that usually shows up when there's a rescue operation planned."

"It joined the main fleet group last night, though we have no confirmed report of a sub operating with that task force."

"Are you kidding me?" Stone smiled. "That's the *Admiral Kuznetsov* there, Mister Reed. It's the last surface ship in the Red Banner Pacific Fleet that could pose any threat if it broke out into the Pacific or the Sea of Japan. You can bet your bottom dollar that they have a sub nearby—probably two or three. If I was the Russian Fleet commander I'd have my very best boat right there, on undersea watch for that ship."

Reed raised an eyebrow, then nodded his agreement as Stone handed him back the file. Yes, he thought, that makes good sense… Their very best boat… He looked at the satellite image again, a suspicious light in his eyes.

Part II

Discovery

"No great discovery was ever made without a bold guess."

— Isaac Newton

Chapter 4

"**I must** tell you, Mister Kamenski, even with over forty years in the Russian Navy I have never been all that comfortable sailing in a ship that has to sink first before it can do anything."

"Yes, this is just a little claustrophobic," said Kamenski, "and the thought of having a lot of water over my head soon is just a bit disconcerting, Admiral."

They were aboard the AS-28 submersible, an old boat that was first commissioned in 1986. At 55 tons displacement, it was no more than 45 feet long and just twelve and a half feet wide, with room for twenty passengers. Their party filled half the available seats, the Admiral, Kamenski, Fedorov, Orlov, Troyak, Zykov, Dobrynin and three engineers. Their cargo had been quietly transferred a few hours ago, and now they were making way on the surface, but still towed by the much faster *Sayany* salvage ship. The submersible could do little more than three knots on its own.

"This segment of the mission is all part of the show," said Volsky. "If the Americans do see anything from space, they will know we are at least two kilometers from the *Admiral Kuznetsov*, but now that we are here we will submerge and creep back beneath the carrier to rendezvous with *Kazan*."

"Won't they see us on infrared?"

"Not at the depth we'll be descending to. *Kuznetsov* is sitting atop a deep segment of the strait, close by an area we have used for old explosives dumping. *Kazan* is hiding down there, over 450 meters deep. The only other thing that will notice us there would be the fish, or another submarine."

"Seems secure enough."

"Not to my liking." The Admiral folded his arms. "This vessel had to be rescued itself when it ran afoul of a hydrophone antennae off Kamchatka some years ago. It's not very comforting when you have to rescue the rescue ship!"

Fedorov was seated with them, and he leaned in now, a determined look on his face. "Once we get to *Kazan* things will be more comfortable," he said. "I spent some time on that boat last year. It's one of our very best, highly automated, and with a crew of only ninety, though it can easily accommodate our party here."

It was not long before they had reached their designated diving zone, and the AS-28 was cut loose and began to descend. Volsky and Kamenski watched the water rise above the portholes with some misgivings, but settled in for the thirty minute journey back to *Kazan*.

"It's quiet down here," said Fedorov.

"Too quiet," Volsky tossed out the old cliché knowing that his young ex-navigator wouldn't feel the rising sense of caution that was already turning in his own gut. The man had the bravery to shift back to 1942 from the Primorskiy Engineering Center, not knowing where he might turn up. That took real courage, he thought.

"Mission profile calls for a full scan of the boat's exterior before we latch on," Fedorov noted the information for Kamenski's benefit. They soon heard the submersible pilot, a man named Jakov, speaking quietly with his co-pilot as they made their approach to *Kazan*.

"I'm rolling ten degrees," he said. "We'll look the aft hatch section over first."

"Confirmed." The co-pilot pulled down a view scope and adjusted the rangefinder for close imaging. The green light on the unit drew a thin line over the smooth, bald surface of his head. As he peered through the scope and examined the long sleek lines of the hidden submarine. He adjusted the focus and switched on the record function to log the data.

"Looks clean," he said. "No sign of damage to the propulsion systems or rudder. Hull integrity appears nominal. Some temperature variance on infrared." He was working quickly, and Fedorov, very curious as he watched, could almost see the mental check marks ticking off in his head as he completed one task after another.

They waited until the submersible finished a full exterior scan, but there wasn't much to see. *Kazan* looked to be in good shape, with nothing more than normal discoloration on its missile hatches from the combat salvos the boat had fired in the battle against the Americans. It was a long cylinder with a sleek sail forward that looked like a truncated shark fin. They hovered a few meters off the aft quarter of the ship.

"Light them up," said the pilot, and his partner activated the exterior spotlights. Fingers of light reached out and probed at the cylindrical hull of the other boat, playing over the darkened oval of the access hatch, but revealing nothing unusual.

"I'm taking us over to the emergency hatch on section four," said Jakov, hands on his maneuvering yoke.

"Confirmed for section four."

The submersible danced in response to his commands on the control yoke. In a few moments they were poised over the circular rim marking the location of the emergency access shaft. It was nothing more than a thin lip of metal on the otherwise smooth surface of the submarine. Jakov rolled the submersible on its side, for the only way to dock would be through a six foot access cylinder that deployed from that location. The co-pilot was already checking the docking cylinder controls as he thrust the view scope back into its overhead compartment.

"Ready to dock." Jakov had the ship in a perfect position for the rendezvous.

"Mooring cables clamping on." The co-pilot toggled the switch to enable the computer controlled cables to reach out and fasten themselves to the submarine, a new feature on the boat when it was upgraded in 2018. A small cylinder emerged from the borders of the submersible and extended out to contact the submarine's hatch. "Cylinder operative... Deployed. Permission to pressurize cylinder?"

The kiss would make the marriage, Fedorov thought. After that the two ships would be securely linked.

"Pressurize," said Jakov, and the cylinder hummed to life and rotated a thin rim along the outer lip of the interface until it located a small aperture. The mouth of the cylinder was soon locked in place and the containment within was going to a normal one atmosphere pressure, pumping out the seawater as it did so.

"Engaging processors."

In a few moments a pressurized atmosphere would fill the interior of the cylinder.

"Shall I let them know we are ready, Admiral?"

"Please do," said Volsky, and the word soon came back from *Kazan*.

"Captain Gromyko sends his regards, Admiral."

"May I sir?" Fedorov was eager to be the first one through the cylinder, and Volsky nodded, smiling at the young man's energy.

"He would swim over if he had to," he said quietly to Kamenski.

Fedorov rotated the handle of the interior hatch and a dry hiss greeted him as the air from the docking cylinder mixed with the submersible cabin. The distinctive tang of seawater was in the air. He wasted no time and crawled down into the tube, his service jacket dappled with the drippings of residual seawater. In a few seconds he was poised on the last ladder rung above the submarine deck hatch.

"Open the outer hatch on my hack... Three... Two... One... Engage."

The securing pins rotated and Fedorov heard the muted whir of a small motor as the hatch to the submarine slowly elevated. A faint red light appeared beneath his feet—red emergency lighting from the interior of the boat below him. The oval of the portal beneath him fattened into a circle as the hatch cap opened. Then he slowly climbed down through the opening into the dim airlock of the submarine below.

He waited to assist Admiral Volsky and Kamenski as they climbed down the narrow cylinder. As soon as Volsky's foot touched the deck of *Kazan*, a *Mishman* piped him aboard.

"Admiral on the boat!"

"You can tell that I am an Admiral, even in my Lieutenant's uniform?"

"Sir, I recognized you at once. We all know you."

The three of them exited the airlock hatch first as the other passengers descended into the sub. They found that the main compartment outside the airlock was a diving station where men were standing by in wet suits with reserve oxygen, just in case anything had gone wrong. It was not common for a submarine to receive a visit from the Admiral of the Fleet, particularly under these circumstances, or in this manner. An officer soon appeared, Captain Gromyko himself come to greet them.

"Welcome aboard, Admiral." He offered a firm handshake as the Admiral began to introduce his party.

"This is a special advisor, Pavel Kamenski," he began, agreeing not to dwell on the man's older KGB affiliations. "And here is our former navigation officer and now Captain of the Second Rank, Anton Fedorov."

Volsky looked to see Orlov enter the compartment, eyes averted and quickly stepping aside as the Marines and engineers came in behind him. But the Admiral raised a hand, calling him from the group. "Here we have Captain of the Second Rank, Gennadi Orlov. This man was Chief of Operations aboard *Kirov*, a most capable officer."

Orlov forced a smile, inwardly pleased that the Admiral had singled him out, though he thought the praise was undeserved. He had not expected that to happen, and was not aware that Volsky had confirmed the restoration of his rank. Up until that moment, the two men had not spoken, and the breaking of the long silence between them was a relief.

Gromyko was a clean cut officer, thirtyish with close cropped hair that was close to a buzz cut. He was in a dress white shirt with Captain's insignia on shoulder boards. "Well gentlemen, we have a light meal prepared in the officer's mess, and then I suppose we can hear your briefing."

"Excellent," said Volsky, and the Captain led the way forward.

Twenty minutes later the AS-28 had disengaged and was wallowing slowly back towards the *Sayany* to continue the theater. A small diesel sub taken from fleet reserve was waiting to surface shortly after it reappeared topside. To any watching eyes above, the Russians would seem to have just completed a minor rescue operation for a wounded diesel boat. But there were some very good eyes watching from space, and an eager young analyst thought he saw something that did not seem quite kosher that night as he processed the latest image feeds.

* * *

"**Have** a look at this, sir."

"What is it this time, Mister Keats?" Watch Lieutenant Dickson looked up from his desk, eying the young Ensign in front of him with some impatience."

"It's that sub tender operation up north in the Tartar Strait."

"Sub tender?"

"With the *Admiral Kuznetsov*, sir."

"What in god's name would an aircraft carrier need a sub tender for, Ensign?"

"Well it's really not a tender, sir. This is a *Pioner Moskvy* class submersible salvage and support ship. I was able to see the hull number and I just looked it up—the *Sayany*. We had it in Vladivostok a week ago, but they must have moved it out in the last few days."

"That's not surprising. They pulled most of their diesel boats in tight, and it's probably out on a replenishment run."

"Well they *would* use a tender for an operation like that, sir. This ship carries a deep sea submersible, you can even see it in the image here. These boats are used for undersea salvage and rescue operations."

"That doesn't surprise me either. We took down both their *Oscars* after that engagement with the *Washington*. They got their stuff off and scored hits, but that was like sending *Seawolf* their location via GPS. They were gone three hours later."

"Has that *Yasen* class boat been found yet, sir?"

"You mean *Kazan?* Not yet, but we'll find it. Intel thinks the boat is up in the Sea of Okhotsk to replenish."

"They'd have to put it in the tube to do that, sir." Keats was referring to the deep underground submarine pens built by the Russians for just this purpose. They allowed a stealthy submarine to slip into a secure location and never be seen coming or going.

"That they would…Probably in and back out by now, which is why PACCOM is so hot to find the damn thing."

Keats thought about that. "What would they use a boat like that for LT? Isn't *Kazan* suppose to be one of their sub killers?"

"Carrier killer too. It was a multi-purpose design, built to replace both their *Oscar* SSM missile boats and the *Akula* attack subs. Sucker has a raft of missiles aft of the sail in VLS tubes and also packs ten torpedo tubes that can put a lot of mean fish in the sea."

"Yeah, if they can find anything to shoot at."

"That's always the great game, Keats. Whoever hears the other fellow first gets that first shot. Then it really doesn't matter how much heat these new Russian subs are packing if you put the damn thing on the bottom of the sea before they can fire anything."

"We didn't do that with those two *Oscars*, sir. They hurt *Washington* pretty bad before *Seawolf* got to them."

"Tanner got whacked because he was stupid…but you didn't hear me say that, Ensign. He had no business launching his strike without coordinating with *Nimitz*. The Russians threw everything they had at him—*Backfires*, all their missile subs, and anything that surface action group had that could make the range. With *Nimitz* in support they would have to divide those strike assets between our two carrier groups, and our counterpunch would have been much heavier too. As it was they lost most everything they had out there when that volcano blew its top. Now they've just got the *Kuznetsov*."

"So that's where I'd put *Kazan*, sir."

"Say again, Keats?" The Lieutenant was fixated on creaming his coffee, and lecturing more than listening to the younger officer.

"*Kazan*, sir. If all they have left is that single carrier, I'd pull everything in there to protect it."

"Makes sense, I suppose."

"Well from this image I think they had to mount a rescue operation, sir. Look here, a diesel boat came up about two hours after they sent that salvage vessel out. So it was no replenishment operation, sir. That's B-345, the *Mogocha*."

"How can you know that from that image, Keats? The damn photo was taken from outer space, for god's sake."

"It hit a tug two years ago and they never did repair that ding there on the right side of her nose."

"Ahh…Good eye, Ensign."

"Thank you, sir. But this boat shouldn't be out here now."

"Why do you say that?"

"Well, is was scheduled for refit and they were going to pull all her teeth. Intel says they wanted to make a modification test on this boat to see if they could fit some of the newer torpedoes and maybe extend the life of the remaining *Kilos* a few more years. At least that's what the group concluded when we saw them off-loading the ordnance last month. There's no way they could have it combat ready."

"Is that so…" The Lieutenant was stirring his coffee slower now, his attention finally focused on what the Ensign was telling him."

"Yes sir. That baby should be fast asleep in the old Pavlovskoye underground shelter. They must be scraping the bottom of the barrel."

"Let me see that photo, Keats."

The Lieutenant was very interested now.

Chapter 5

Mississippi was not an old boat ready for retirement, but one of the newer *Virginia* class hunter killer subs on patrol that day—and *Mississippi* was ready. It had moved west as part of the *Nimitz* group undersea screen, but that job was handed over to two *Los Angeles* Class boats out of Apra Harbor, Guam under Task Force 74. This freed up the newer subs to get out and hunt enemy assets that might pose a grave threat. *Seawolf* was now looking for the Russian and Chinese Boomers, particularly the boat that had actually fired a sub launched missile over the continental US. It had good company from units out of San Diego, and the US was slowly scouring the Eastern Pacific throughout 3rd Fleet's area of responsibility.

When *Key West* went down on close in reconnaissance of the Russian surface fleet, it left a big hole in Western Pacific coverage. *Mississippi* was reassigned to fill that hole, and was now on the prowl for anything the Russians might have left behind after their hasty withdrawal to the Sea of Okhotsk. Aside from the state for which she was named, the boat was also proud to bear the name of the old battleship that had been reputedly killed by a sub to begin the Second World War for the United States, BB-41.

But the new *Mississippi* (SSN-782) was nothing like the old battlewagon she was named for. She was commissioned into the navy in June of 2012 with a host of new technology that made her an evolutionary leap in undersea warfare. While not as fast or even well armed as the more powerful *Seawolf*, the *Virginia* class was much less expensive, and went on to become the primary replacement for the *Los Angeles* Class boats and the mainstay of the US undersea attack sub fleet.

It was one of the first submarines to forsake the time honored periscope for a newer "photonic mast," which utilized an array of sensors, including thermographic and laser-based range finders, and high-definition low-light cameras. With no eyepiece, the old classic role of the sub Captain peering through his periscope and 'dancing with the grey lady' was now a thing of the past. Instead the mast was controlled by a joystick to pivot and present visual data relayed directly to several banks of computer monitors displayed in a large control room.

The workhorse of the sub's sensor suite, of course, was her sonar, mounted in a spherical bow array with additional sensors in the sail and keel of the sub. These could be further augmented by both low and high frequency towed sonar arrays, and the equipment was so advanced that good operators claimed they could actually detect the sound of Russian sub crews talking to one another inside their old *Kilo* class boats, once called "the black holes of the sea" because they were so quiet.

The *Kilos* may have been quiet in their day, but that day was now long past. Advances in US sonar technology had now made any boat conceived and built before the 21st Century obsolete. Now the sonar operators would sit before wide panel computer monitors and watch a waterfall of green signal data tumbling down their screens, combining the visual sensory information with anything they might hear, just like old radar operators would monitor signals on their screen. Human eyes now joined ears in the assessment of the undersea environment. The waterfall of data would indicate noise for potential contacts as enhanced white areas within the falling green signal matrix, allowing the operator to watch the contact as much as he might hear it.

Information from all the ship's systems became a data fusion that painted the overall picture of what was happening outside the boat. The net effect of all these listening arrays was to collapse the uncertainty factor, and winnow down the information to answer the same old questions. What was the contact? Where was it? What was it doing? The information was distilled into range, speed, bearing and heading, and the system was so good that operators could even hear sound from a ding on a ship's propulsion blade. A library of sounds was recorded and stored on all contacts made, and various ships or subs could be quickly identified by their sonic "signature."

Situated on the port side of the boat, the sonar operators now shared data with the combat system screens on the starboard side of the control room. Together they combined to give operators an overall "situational awareness" of the undersea environment around them that was unsurpassed.

At the same time, *Mississippi* was one of the quietest subs in the world, with new anechoic coatings, noise canceling technology, isolated deck structures and a novel design for a pump jet propulsor that did not use a rotating propeller and reduced noise from cavitation. It also removed the need for a long rotating drive shaft extending all the way to the boat's reactor. The old hydraulic systems that once controlled rudders and fins were now replaced by a "fly by wire" electronic control system, further reducing noise. Inside the nuclear reactor that drove the ship, water was circulated without the need to rely on noisy pumps, adding additional stealth. All told, it was said by some that the new boats were quieter running at their flank speed than an older *Los Angeles* class boat was sitting idle at a berth in the harbor.

The business end of the boat when it came to war fighting was a set of four torpedo tubes firing the Mark-48 Mod 9 Torpedo. An old warrior from the late 1980s, the Mark 48 held on with many updates and modifications that now saw it capable of delivering a 650 pound warhead to a target well over 20 miles away at a speed of 40 to 55 knots. The boat also had 12 BGM-109 land attack Tomahawk cruise missiles.

So when war came to the Pacific, *Mississippi* was ready for anything the enemy could put in the sea. Her officers and crew were equally ready, and today she was commanded by Captain James Donahue, gliding silently through the waters off the southern coast of Hokkaido. The boat was beneath the big ash plume that had been blowing south from the Demon Volcano, snooping out any potential Russian sub activity there when it received new orders on its secure comm-link channel.

"What's up, skipper." The XO, Chris Chambers, was just getting the word now.

"COMSUBRON 7 wants us to transit the Tsugaru Strait tonight and take up a position here." The Captain pointed at a location on the digital map, just west of the strait, out in the Sea of Japan. "It took them three tries to get us the message too. Communications have been a bear with that eruption still ongoing. In any case, we're supposed to operate in loose cooperation with a Japanese task force coming out of Maizuru... a couple subs and a small surface action group."

"Maizuru? That far south?"

"Chitose and Hachinohe have been forced to shut down operations, just like Misawa. That damn ash fall has practically blanketed all of Hokkaido. Magnetic disturbances have practically shut down most of the comm spectrum as well, so you can forget reliable sensor data from any land based facility there. The base at Maizuru is now top of the list for operations in the Sea of Japan. It's far enough south and the airwaves are clear down there."

"So they're giving us the inside channel this time? I like it much better out in the deep blue."

"They don't think the action there is likely to heat up after that last engagement. Now everything seems to be focused on the Sea of Japan and points south. We'll be playing flank guard on this team. The Japanese want to move up a sea interdiction patrol from Maizuru to monitor the corridor and watch for any new Russian sub deployments out of Vladivostok. Someone at Navy Intel got a hair up his ass and thinks that new Russian boat has slipped away."

"*Kazan?*"

"That's the one. It participated in that missile barrage against Tanner's group on *Washington*. Then it seemed to sail into a black hole. They thought it might be up replenishing, which is a pretty good bet, but the Russians have moved their carrier south through the Tartar Strait off Sakhalin Island, and that raised a few eyebrows at Naval Intel."

"How so, skipper?"

"Who knows. Maybe they think the Russkies will put all their good chips on the *Admiral Kuznetsov* now that *Kirov* has gone down."

"That must have been a hard blow for them."

"Yeah? Well they delivered a few haymakers themselves. Word is *Washington* is going to have to be moved from Guam to Pearl. They're offloading her remaining strike aircraft and ordnance at Guam according to the report I got yesterday."

"What about the Chinese, sir? It seems to me we have more to worry about with them than we do with the Russians now."

"If they have anything in the Sea of Japan it will be ours for breakfast if we run into them. Most everything they've deployed recently is coming out of the Yellow Sea, so it will be in the East China Sea or standing off the Tsushima Straits. That's the real hot zone. This duty here is probably going to be low and slow. I think we'll just sit tight off Oshima Island under a nice thermocline and bide our time."

"Campy says his waterfall looks positively ugly." He was referring to the boat's chief sonar operator, Ensign Eugene Campanella. The visual data waterfall had been very disturbed by the eruption. It wasn't just the constant rumble of migrating magma, but a range of other disturbances as well.

"What's Campanella's problem?"

"Spectrum is all fouled up, sir. We may want to move south away from that Demon Volcano and have the Japanese cover the strait with a couple diesel boats."

"Sounds reasonable," said the Captain. "If we go after this sub we'll need the wax out of our ears, that's for sure. Let the Japanese bird-dog the area and we'll back them up if anything develops."

"I'd be willing to bet the Russians will stand pat where they are now, sir. Without *Kirov* they've lost their real offensive threat on the surface. The atmosphere is just too dirty for air operations off the *Kuznetsov*. In fact, I'd say that ship is just a liability for them now— just a nice fat target for air or sub launched cruise missiles. If that Navy Intel report is accurate, it will tie up all their really good undersea assets."

"Probably so. But if they do have anything left with a mind for blue water, it will be incumbent on us to find and flame the SOB. COMSUBRON 7 wants this new Russian boat located as soon as possible."

"We have a kill order, sir?"

"That remains to be seen. Things have been on a hair trigger the last few days. Right now our mission is to run this patrol and make sure they don't get curious out here."

"Well enough, sir," said Chambers. "I'll brief the department heads."

* * *

Out in the Sea of Japan, Captain Sato was having the same conversation in his own head aboard the destroyer *Onami*. He was leading a small flotilla comprised of his own ship and two smaller and older ASW destroyers, the *Amagiri* and *Abukuma*, which were really frigate sized vessels under 4000 tons full load. *Onami* was a real destroyer at 6300 tons, and had been assigned to duty in the Tsugaru Strait out of Ominato until the Demon Volcano made that watch fairly hazardous. When you can't breathe the air over the sea, you just move elsewhere, so Sato found himself pushed west through the strait to the Sea of Japan to take command of an ASW patrol out of Maizuru.

Submarine watch was his stock in trade, and all the ships in his task group were optimized for ASW warfare, even though they were well past their prime, with every ship dating to the late 1980s except Sato's flagship *Onami*, which had been commissioned in 2003.

Even as Admiral Volsky and his party boarded *Kazan* far to the north, the remainder of the Japanese task force had put out from Maizuru naval base, an installation dating back to the years immediately following the Russo-Japanese war, and a base built with the idea of keeping a watchful eye on the Russians at Vladivostok. They would be steaming north for the next day, intent on mounting a routine anti-submarine watch in the Sea of Japan. A short week ago the Russian surface fleet would have posed a dire threat here, but now they were a beaten force, licking their wounds in the cold northern seas. Sato did not expect to encounter any Russian surface vessels here, but submarines were another matter, which is why he would have his SH-60J *Seahawk* helicopters up on regular patrol. He was carrying a single chopper, as was *Amagiri*. His third ship had no helicopter support, *Abukuma*, a frigate in the range of 2500 tons, but it would weigh in with an octuple ASROC launcher and a pair of triple HOS-301 torpedo tube mounts for some good ASW punch if needed.

Keeping the *Seahawks* up was always a risky proposition given their close proximity to Vladivostok. There was a very real threat of Russian fighter patrols, as the skies over the Sea of Japan were still relatively clear of ash and soot from the Demon Volcano. In this event, Sato was told he could call on a squadron of JF-35 fighters from the mainland, which made him rest just a little easier that morning.

The last two fingers on Sato's mailed fist that day were under the sea, SS-503 *Hakuryu*, the *White Dragon*, and SS-596 *Kuroshio*. As per normal routine, they were already out in front of his small surface group, a pair of diesel electric boats creeping along at a sedate 10 knots for their assigned patrol runs.

They had not seen or heard anything of the Russian Navy for two days now, and did not expect to see anything today either. Yet word came in to be especially vigilant. Apparently the Americans believed the Russians might try to slip a fast new submarine into the Sea of Japan and, as that body of water bore the name of their homeland, the Japanese Maritime Self-Defense Force would stand the watch.

Sato was told to expect American submarine support, but he did not yet know the name or character of the boat that was coming. A *Los Angeles* class boat would be most likely, he thought, as this is a backwater now to the main action further south where the tense standoff against the Chinese was winding up tighter and tighter every day. Soon the American carriers would begin their big counter operation there to retake the airspace over Taiwan. The Chinese were quick to get in those hard first punches, and their new J-20s had soon become masters of the sky, but now they would have to duel with two highly experienced air wings off these carriers backed up by the best squadrons of land based F-22 and F-35 fighters in the Pacific.

The last time we flew land based fighter support off Okinawa the Chinese answered with six ballistic missiles at Naha. Now the island was bristling with new anti-missile defenses, receiving three more *Patriot* batteries in the last few days. We shall see what happens should the Dragon be so bold as to breath its fire our way again.

Yet it would not be the Chinese Sato would have to worry about on this watch. His back was well covered. The navy was watching the strategic Tsushima Straits very closely, and Korea had nothing of consequence to put in the water but a few old *Romeo* or *Whisky* class diesel subs. He doubted if they had anything more than 50 miles from their own coastline, but if found, he had orders to sink any North Korean boat he encountered.

His real nemesis that day was still far to the north, where the chairs were just starting to warm in the briefing room aboard the submarine *Kazan*. There Admiral Volsky was thinking how to outline the desperate mission that would soon add thunder to the quiet of Sato's morning. The Russians were coming south, and they were going to stop at nothing to achieve what they now set out to do.

Ironically, the heart of that mission would mean they were now sending the very best submarine they had to find and possibly engage and sink the former flagship of the Red Banner Pacific Fleet! Sato knew nothing of this that day, but his ships were in the way of that plan now, and he would soon learn the truth behind the rumors of a fast new Russian sub in these waters.

Chapter 6

"**Well,** Admiral," said Captain Gromyko as he finished his tea. The easy route south would be to hug the coast all the way to Vladivostok, and then head south from there into the Sea of Japan."

"Won't the Americans expect us to take this route?" Volsky folded his arms over a well satisfied gut, the meal just concluded, along with the pleasantries, as the briefing began in earnest now. The Admiral was there, with Gromyko and his Executive Officer Belanov, along with Kamenski, Fedorov, Dobrynin and the others.

"I suppose they would, but it is still much safer than trying to go through the Kuriles and then transiting the Tsugaru Strait from the East. That area is very likely being watched by American submarines, and the strait itself could be mined. If we take the route I suggest, we will most likely only have to deal with the Japanese."

"Yes, this is the only route that makes any sense. Captain, what do you think our chances are of getting well south without being detected?"

"*Kazan* is very quiet," said Gromyko, "as long as the crew itself is quiet. We have many new features built into this ship to make it one of the stealthiest submarines in the world. I will give you a tour after we finish, and you will see that our torpedo room is not forward as one might think. The tubes are mounted on the port and starboard side of the ship, on either side of the forward sail. This leaves the nose of the ship acoustically isolated for the new spherical sonar array there. We are the only sub in the world configured this way."

"But can we break through the Japanese patrols undetected?" The Admiral pressed his question again.

"I give us very good odds on that, and if they should discover us by chance, then we can put those torpedo tubes to good use."

Volsky nodded, though his heart was heavy with the thought of more combat, and more lives lost at sea. He had seen more than enough in recent months. Yet now he knew there was another matter at the heart of this mission that needed to be discussed, and he considered how to best broach the matter.

"Well then… Captain Gromyko, every man in this room is aware of something that must now be disclosed to you and your *Starpom* if you are to remain an able Captain of your submarine here. You may have been curious as to what this visit was for, and why you should have the Fleet Admiral and these other gentlemen here asking you about a stealthy trip out into the Sea of Japan."

"That thought has crossed my mind, sir."

"No doubt." Volsky took a long breath. Where to begin? "Captain…as you may have heard I was aboard the battlecruiser *Kirov* last July when we went out for live fire exercises in the Norwegian Sea. What you have *not* heard is what actually happened to that ship, though I am sure there have been rumors."

"We heard there was some kind of accident aboard *Orel*, sir. Those old *Oscars* have served their purpose and should be retired. They are all accidents waiting to happen."

"That may be so," Volsky agreed. "Well there aren't many left. The Americans have recently retired the last two assigned to the Pacific."

Gromyko made a grim nod now, waiting to hear more.

"Captain, that accident involved a nuclear warhead, and the detonation had a very strange effect on the ship—on *Kirov*. Perhaps mister Kamenski here can attest to these effects as they are associated with such detonations."

Kamenski cleared his throat. "That I can, Admiral. But it would take much more time than we have to explain it all in detail. Suffice it to say that in 1961 we discovered that the detonation of a nuclear device caused some rather dramatic effects beyond the obvious physical chaos of the explosion itself. We knew about radiation since the 1940s, but it wasn't until the high altitude tests between 1958 and 1962 that we discovered other effects, like the EMP burst that darkened parts of Hawaii nearly 1500 miles away and knocked out one third of low orbiting satellites with its residual radiation. The Chinese have just recently demonstrated their mastery of this same trick over the Pacific coast of the United States. Well, one other effect was discovered in October of 1961 with the detonation of the Tsar Bomba, and it was very strange indeed. The detonation ruptured the time continuum."

There. He gave it to him plain and to the point, just like his example concerning EMP effects, but it took a while for the information to register on Captain Gromyko's sonar.

"Excuse me, Director... Time continuum?"

"Yes, Captain, the fourth dimension. Time. You know the first three well enough as you move about them in this vast ocean here—length, breadth and height, or depth in the case of your submarine. Well you must also know that you move in the fourth dimension as well—in time. Until Tsar Bomba went off, everything moved in only one direction through time, from this moment to the next in that second by second journey we all take from the cradle to the grave. But Tsar Bomba showed us that journey could also be affected by very powerful detonations—and time itself could be breached. Physical objects could be blown through through that breach, and they would end up in the same spatial location, but in another time."

Gromyko looked at his *Starpom*, raising an eyebrow to see how Belanov was following this, but he sat there with the same serious look on his face all the other men had.

It doesn't sound all that crazy after all, thought Volsky as he listened to Kamenski explain it. Things move in space, and they move in time. In space they go forward and back again, why not in time? As the Director went on, the light of confusion and amazement slowly kindled in Gromyko's eyes.

"And so you see, Captain, we have been experimenting with these effects ever since, and our great problem was how to control them and determine where an object might be displaced in time. We could not solve it, but accidents happen, and they sometimes contain hidden gems of discovery. The incident in the Norwegian Sea last July was enough of an explosion to rupture time, and *Kirov* sailed right through the breach."

"*Kirov?* The entire *ship* moved in... in time?"

"It did." Kamenski let that sit there, knowing what the next question was likely to be as the Captain looked from him to Volsky and back again.

"Where? Where did the ship move?"

"It was displaced approximately eighty years into the past."

"Eighty years? To 1941? And you discovered this to be true, Admiral?"

"I was aboard, as was every other man here except your *Starpom*, and Mister Kamenski here. Yes, it took us some doing but we soon discovered what had happened, and we connected it to that detonation in our minds, but with one more problem. How to get back? I do not believe we have the time to go into all of that just now. But we *did* make it back, as you can plainly see. One strange effect of all this is that the ship itself became far less stable in any given time than it might otherwise have been. Between our Chief Engineer Dobrynin here and young Mister Fedorov, we were able to discover that a replacement control rod we were using in the ship's reactor maintenance seemed to catalyze these effects on every occasion when it was used."

"*Kirov* is quite the slippery fish now," said Kamenski, "and suffice it to say that the detonation of that volcano, and possibly combat actions in the recent naval engagement with the Americans, have caused the ship to displace in time again."

"Again? Where is it now?"

"Much farther back—to the year 1908." Admiral Volsky folded his hands, realizing how difficult this revelation must be for a no nonsense naval officer like Gromyko.

"But… I don't understand. How you can know this?"

"We know it by chance again, another gift of a random moment where something unplanned happens and you fall through to a great discovery. We were going to try and use these control rods in a test reactor to see if we could replicate the effects." Volsky decided to simplify the long twisted tale and try and bring it to some graspable form. He would say nothing of how a missing reactor technician led them to launch Fedorov's mission from the Primorskiy Engineering Center, or why they had first gone in the first place. He would mention nothing of Orlov, quietly shielding the man from any possible recrimination, a tact that the Chief did not fail to notice. The thing to do was to keep everything focused on *Kirov*.

"We wanted to mount a rescue operation, just as we would if your submarine were to get into trouble down here. Yet to do so we did not have to send men in one of those clever deep sea diving submersibles like the one that brought us to you here. No...we had to send men back in *time*. For reasons that remain unclear to us, they ended up in the same year where *Kirov* is now still marooned, and managed to make contact."

"Amazing!" Now Gromyko had transitioned from confusion to awe. Here was a Fleet Admiral telling him a tale the like of which he had never heard in his life. How could he doubt it?

"Yes, very amazing indeed," said Volsky. "Now comes an uncomfortable part of what we must discuss. As you may know, I gave command of the Red Banner Pacific Fleet to Captain Vladimir Karpov."

Gromyko nodded. He had heard of Karpov, though he had never met the man. The things he heard were less than complimentary—that Karpov was aggressive, a climber, somewhat manipulative and not one to trust in any situation where the struggle for power was involved. So it was that he was not entirely surprised to hear what the Admiral told him next.

"We were trying to arrange delivery of one of these control rods to *Kirov*, to see if we might use it to catalyze this time displacement effect again and bring the ship back home. We did this successfully before when we returned from the first displacement. Now we hoped it would work once again, but I'm afraid our Captain Karpov has had second thoughts about it, and other ideas about what he should do."

"Other ideas? What do you mean, Admiral?"

"I mean he has refused to coordinate a rendezvous with that rescue team and now seems intent on remaining exactly where he is."

"What? In 1908? Why would he do such a thing?"

Kamenski leaned in again now. "Power. He is sitting there in the most powerful ship in the world—a very slippery fish indeed—and he has determined that he would prefer to use that power right where he is, in 1908."

Fedorov spoke now. "To put it plainly, Captain, he believes he can cause some very strange effects of his own now—on all the history between that year and this one. His initial objective is to redress the Russian defeat in 1905 at the hands of the Japanese Navy."

"This is unbelievable!" Gromyko looked to Belanov now, but what else could he say or do here? "And yet, you tell me all this with a completely straight face. This is either the best goddamned *Vranyo* I have ever heard or it is an absolutely shocking situation."

"We all went through this same shock and surprise," said Volsky. "Now we are a confederacy of a very few men who know these facts, and you two are the latest new recruits. I must caution you that this cannot be generally revealed to the remainder of the crew on *Kazan,* at least not yet. You must consider it a state secret and a highly sensitive matter, Captain."

"I understand, Admiral."

"I also realize that I may be asking a great deal of you here. The days and mission ahead will be very perilous."

"You may rely on my ship and crew, sir. We won't let you down."

"Thank you, Captain. So…what are we doing here on your submarine with those odd containers? They are, as you may have guessed by now, the very same control rods that we have used to catalyze these time displacement effects aboard *Kirov,* and we intend to use them again—here, on this boat."

"Use them again? You mean…"

"Correct, Captain," said Kamenski. "We are going to mount yet another rescue mission, and your boat has been selected as one that might have just a little more authority in the situation we may soon find ourselves in. You see, our first attempt was able to put men on the scene, but we could only communicate by shortwave radio. This is why we have devised this new plan—to put your boat on the scene and then see what we can do."

"So you wish to try to move *Kazan* in time as well—to 1908?"

"Correct. You must leave off how we can accomplish this for the moment. Our Chief Engineer Dobrynin here has some skill in this business, and he will be placed in charge of your reactor room. But the simple end to this is to understand that we are going to try to get there, with this boat, and then order Karpov to comply with the wishes of this Admiral."

"I see…" The entire insane story suddenly had a dark shadow over it. He had known of several other "incidents" in the past involving Russian Captains that had disobeyed orders and gone off on renegade missions of their own, both in surface ships and submarines. In each instance the Navy had to hunt these men down and enforce the will of the state.

"So," he said in a low voice now. "This will be something more than a rescue mission then, if I am not mistaken here. This Karpov may not wish to comply even if we do this impossible thing and appear in the sea beneath his ship. And what then Admiral Volsky? What then?"

The Admiral tightened his jaw now, obviously troubled. "It is our hope that when I arrive on the scene, with the full authority of the Navy, that this man will listen to reason and comply. If however he does not…Well, I said we selected this ship because it, too, has authority of another kind. I am sure you know of what I speak now."

Gromyko was silent for some time, glancing at Belanov to gauge his reaction to all of this as well. "You are saying we may have to threaten a military solution to force this man's hand?"

"That would be the first escalation, the threat, but we will also have to be prepared to carry out any such threat. We will have to be prepared to engage the most powerful surface action ship in the world with the most powerful undersea boat at our disposal, and we must prevail against a very wily and aggressive sea Captain with a particular hatred of all submarines. This means that our supposed rescue mission may be vigorously opposed, and soon become a red on red engagement. Nothing would be more unsettling to me, considering that these two ships represent the best of the fleet our nation was hoping to rely on in this day and time. Even if we succeed it will be a great sadness, because it will mean that I must engage and destroy the ship and crew I led to sea, and through many ordeals, and I must end the lives of men there that I have come to love. Yet failure is even more difficult to contemplate, because much more than the lives and fate of that single ship and crew are at stake now."

"May I, sir?" Fedorov looked at the Admiral with wide eyes, and Volsky nodded, yielding him the floor.

"Captain Gromyko… the instant we do put this mission in play, and should we actually achieve our goal and displace to the time and place we target, then all the years between 1908 and the present lie on the butcher's block, and our private little war with Captain Karpov and *Kirov* becomes the single most important event in modern human history. The outcome of that battle will decide what happens from that moment on. Should we fail, and allow Captain Karpov to do what he is now planning, then everything could change—*everything*. It could all change so radically that it might occur that your grandfathers were never born! That puts it personally, but there is much more at stake. The world itself, all that we know in this here and now, might never come to be. Should we fail, and survive to return to this year, we could find it all gone, *all* of it, everything that exists suddenly reordered so completely that the world is no longer recognizable. Indeed, we did this before, I think. That slippery fish Mister Kamenski spoke of did move forward again once, and when we leapt out of the dark seas of time all we found was the ash of an entire generation, on every shore and at every city and harbor where we hoped to lie at ease."

Part III

Ultimatum

"In my experience, ultimatums are about control, even when they're presented as a choice. Ultimatums are often couched in anger and/or shame, both of which are very powerful tools for controlling other people. They also have a tendency to be framed as an absolute and a person leveling one isn't likely to be open to hearing explanations, reasons, or other alternatives. And ultimatums are usually given in an either/or, as if those are the only two possibilities in the universe."

— **Charles Glickman, PhD.**

Chapter 7

"Gentlemen, we have before us a most unusual circumstance." Admiral Togo pulled slowly on his white dress naval gloves, one finger at a time, a slow deliberate motion that seemed single minded and thoughtful as he completed the process and carefully laid the gloves on the briefing table. The senior officers of the fleet were all gathered there aboard Togo's flagship, the battleship *Mikasa*, their faces eager for news and the orders that would most certainly follow.

"I have just come from a meeting with Naval Minister Baron Saito. There has been some disturbing news from the north involving the Russians. One of our supply steamers bound for Dailan was intercepted and sunk off the Tsugaru Strait by what was reported as a large Russian warship."

At this there were quiet murmurs and surprised glances as the officers looked from one to another, the junior officers noting the reaction of those senior.

"Captain Kawase of our 9th Torpedo Boat Squadron at Amori confirmed the sighting of a large enemy warship, certainly a battleship, and I ordered our Second Cruiser division led out from Maizuru by Vice Admiral Kamimura to look for this ship. The vessel was subsequently sighted and a brief engagement ensued, but our cruisers were not able to close the range, allowing the ship to slip away to the west. It was last sighted heading southwest."

"And the engagement?" It was Vice Admiral Dewa, a venerable and wizened officer hailing from the province of Fukushima which would one day be rendered practically uninhabitable by a disaster no man in the room could conceive of or ever foresee. Dewa was commander of the 3rd Cruiser Division at the famous battle of Tsushima Straits, and was naturally eager to learn the outcome.

"Inconclusive," said Togo. "It was opened at extreme long range, which is somewhat surprising considering that fast cruisers were involved. Vice Admiral Kamimura's own flagship, *Izumo*, suffered considerable damage and was forced to fall off the line of battle."

"And the enemy?"

"Apparently the ship was able to escape unscathed."

That was not well received, and the lately appointed *danshaku*, Baron Dewa, shook his head. "Kamimura can be a little headstrong at times," he said. "He should have closed the range before engaging this ship."

"From the reports I received it was not a question of Kamimura failing to fire at the appropriate range," said Togo. "The enemy opened fire first, and from well beyond 15,000 meters. Yet the remarkable thing about this engagement was that they did not rely on their main cannon. All the hits on Kamimura's cruiser were obtained by smaller caliber guns, no more than six inch shells."

"This is most unusual. Then it means the Russians have better secondary batteries, at least insofar as range is concerned."

"And I also conclude that this is certainly a new ship," said Togo. "It could not have been any of the cruisers that were still sheltering at Urajio." He was referring to the Port of Vladivostok, called Urajio by the Japanese.

"I see…" Dewa's eyes expressed the concern that was now evident, and the real reason for this meeting. A new ship meant that it must have come from the Baltic or Black Sea, and passed unnoticed through the Straits of Tsushima.

"What do Kondo and Hidake say about this?" The two men commanded small torpedo boat squadrons that had been posted at the Japanese island base at Takeshiki in the middle of the Tsushima Straits. It was their watch that was breached, and Dewa wanted to know why.

"They have seen nothing but commercial shipping," said Admiral Togo. "No warships of any kind have passed through the straits in recent months. This does not mean it is beyond the realm of possibility that this ship slipped by. Bad weather and night can confound even the most vigilant watch, and we have been lax of late."

Dewa nodded his head in agreement, his grey brows frowning as he looked to the other officers with admonishment in his eyes. Vice

Admiral Kataoka nodded his agreement as well.

"We should reinforce those commands," said Kataoka. "Eight torpedo boats is obviously an inadequate force to patrol such an important sector." He was a man of Satsuma prefecture, the naval Spartans of Japan, as Togo was. Small in stature, Kataoka was nonetheless a skillful and aggressive leader. He had commanded an odd assortment of older ships and outmoded gunboats during the last war that the Japanese came to call their "Funny Fleet," but he led them effectively in major engagements in the Yellow Sea and at Tsushima Straits, and also commanded the naval expedition to seize Sakhalin Island after the war ended, giving Japan a strong bargaining chip in the negotiations that followed. He was soon awarded a baronage to acknowledge his successes in battle, and remained a most capable and energetic officer, his eyes bright and lively beneath the dome of his balding head.

"This meeting has obviously been called to redress these shortcomings," said Togo. "Yes, this ship should have been spotted long ago, and yes, it should have been closely shadowed and kept bottled up in Urajio the moment it sailed into the Sea of Japan. But there has been another development that bears upon this matter. During my meeting with Naval Minister Saito a wireless telegraph message was received from the commander of this Russian ship, a man named Karpov. In that message he had the audacity to declare that a naval quarantine has been imposed to prevent any and all shipping from entering the Yellow Sea, and he has threatened to attack and sink any ship flying Japanese colors that attempts to do so."

"This is outrageous!" Dewa was clearly angry now, his cinder brows raising with alarm, and Kataoka's bright eyes glittered with the fire of impending battle.

"Indeed. It is an outrage," Togo continued. "It was reported that the latest incident has involved a Canadian flagged ship en route from Shanghai to Vancouver. It was stopped, boarded and its cargo of mail seized as contraband. We have just received a vigorous protest that came to both our Naval Ministry offices and was undoubtedly sent to the British China Station as well. Needless to say, something must be done about this, and Baron Saito wants the matter settled at once."

"We should immediately reinforce our patrols in the Tsushima Straits," said Kataoka again. "Where there is smoke, there is fire, and more enemy ships could be heading for these waters even as we speak."

"That was Baron Saito's concern," said Togo. "So this is what we will do. I have arranged a convoy of military and food supplies for shipment to Dailan and Port Arthur. This is the obvious aim of the Russian attempt at naval quarantine. They wish to restrict supplies to those important installations."

"The Russians are planning to cross the border into Manchuria?" Dewa raised the most obvious point, as he could not simply see this naval incident as an isolated event. "This must be part of a general plan."

"I would have thought the same," Togo replied, but there has been no sign of any Russian buildup on the frontier, nor any word from our operatives in northern Korea. What we do know is that this new Russian ship pulled into Urajio last week, and with some fanfare. It left soon after, and the sinking of *Tatsu Maru* occurred the following day. The last incident, involving the Canadian ship RMS *Monteagle*, occurred yesterday, so the ship has moved closer to our home waters. That being the case, we will now sortie with the fleet to conclude this matter. The supply fleet will also have dummy ships, and these will make fine bait to lure the enemy in so our warships can deal with it."

"Where will the fleet deploy?" asked Dewa.

"Initially we will do as vice Admiral Kataoka suggests. We leave here this very day and sail for the Straits of Tsushima. Any attempt to enforce such a naval quarantine would be useless in the Sea of Japan. No, it would have to control the vital Tsushima and Korea Straits, or perhaps the entrance to the Yellow Sea itself. Therefore we will strongly occupy the former, and use it as a base of operations until we locate this enemy ship. At that point we can establish flotillas to hunt it down. I have ordered Kamimura to replenish at Maizuru and then sail to the Oki islands. He will linger there, between Dozen and Dogo, and keep watch on that area. This ship has been trying to escalate the situation, and has been obviously keen to approach our home waters. It will be found before it can dishonor us by even sighting Japanese soil on Honshu."

"Agreed," said the bright eyed Kataoka.

"Your Third Cruiser Division will post a flotilla at Mishima Island, Vice Admiral Dewa. You will also command Suzuki's 4th Destroyer Division. As for you, Kataoka, your ships will keep active patrols between Kyushu, Iki Island and the Tsushima Islands." Togo pointed at the map on the briefing table now, indicating these strategic islands controlling the waters off Japan. "I will take the remainder of the fleet to the waters between Tsushima and Korea and close that route. The supply ships, and dummy ships will be dangled like bait in the waters northeast of the straits. The Russian Bear will look for the honey, and then the bees will come with a hard sting."

Dewa smiled, obviously in agreement. "This is a sound plan," he said happily. "Each group should be strong enough to deal with this single ship alone, but all groups remain within reasonable supporting distance. I hope my ships will have the honor of finding these Russians first, and I will end the matter there and then."

"Perhaps Kamimura's Second Division will settle the affair," said Togo. "He has already sortied from Maizuru again, and is probably waving at the lighthouse at Kyogamisaki by now. Yet there is one further consideration we must discuss, gentlemen."

Dewa had been studying the map, eager to get to sea again and assume his post, but now he looked up, his thick hand stroking his short grey beard. Admiral Togo's face was flat and serious.

"We have been informed by operatives in Hawaii that the American Great White Fleet has changed its planned itinerary. It has already left Hawaii and is steaming west towards Japan as we speak."

"Towards Japan?" Dewa was surprised again. "I thought they were going to visit New Zealand, Australia and the Philippines first.

They were not expected here until October."

"That is so, but their course is in a westerly direction and Saito informs me they have just received word that the Americans have requested a visit here instead. There were American citizens aboard that mail ship, and three were killed when the Russians fired to force them to stop."

"Then the Americans wish to make a show of force here? They wish to chasten the Russians as well?"

"That is one interpretation. Saito is not convinced of this, however. He eyes this movement with some suspicion."

"Most likely because he must now have all his invitations and signage re-printed if the Americans visit us early."

At this the other officers laughed, but Togo remained silent. "Saito may have more than his invitations in mind here. I would hope this is, indeed, a matter of no concern, but to flatter the naval Minister, we should be prepared to receive and escort the American fleet when it arrives in our home waters. For this assignment I have selected Vice Admiral Uryu and his 4th Cruiser Division. The 3rd and 5th Destroyer Divisions under Commanders Hirose and Yoshijima will accompany him. Their mission will be to keep a close eye on the Americans and show the flag of the Imperial Japanese Navy when they arrive here."

Vice Admiral Uryu bowed in response, his hair neatly parted down the center and slicked tight on his head. While one of the first cadets to attend the Japanese Naval Academy, he transferred to the United States and so he actually graduated from the US Naval Academy in Annapolis, learning English in the process. Like Dewa and the others he was also made a baron of the realm for his outstanding service during the recent war with Russia, and decorated with the Order of the Rising Sun and Golden Kite. Uryu was a strong proponent of achieving friendship with the United States, and so his posting to this assignment would make him the perfect man to greet and escort the fleet once it reached home waters.

"I am sure this change of itinerary does not bode ill, but I trust

Vice Admiral Uryu will handle the reception of the American fleet with the utmost diplomatic courtesy. Too much has been said about imminent war with the Americans. Let me state categorically that this is not in the interest of Japan."

Vice Admiral Uryu gave a strong nod of approval. "Will the American fleet be arriving at Yokohama, sir?"

"That remains to be determined. Saito is in the process of negotiating the new itinerary. Our concern now will be to find and cow this rogue Russian Captain, and impose calm in the region well before the Americans get here."

"You call this man a rogue Captain?" Dewa spoke up again, a question in his eyes.

"Perhaps," said Togo. "Inquiries have been made to the Russian Legation, but they have denied any knowledge of this man, this Captain Karpov, or even of his ship. Saito is of the belief that this is mere deception, as the ship was received by city officials when it made port at Urajio. The truth is most likely somewhere in that tea, but it is growing cold. No matter who this man is, he must be taught that the Sea of Japan is so named for a very good reason."

"Concerning any encounter with this ship, Admiral, what are your orders?"

"As always, first report the ship's location and heading to me so that it can be relayed to all other divisions. Then, as each division assigned to this mission is of sufficient strength to operate independently, the Russian Captain will be invited to surrender his ship pending investigation of the crime of piracy on the high seas. Should he decline to do so, you are authorized to engage."

"And what if we suffer the fate of Kamimura, Admiral? What if this ship runs and attempts to evade us?"

"At the first sighting of the enemy all other divisions in the vicinity will be ordered to the scene. If the ship runs, then pursue it at your best speed and keep the flag informed of any change in its course."

"This may be all academic," said Dewa. "If this ship is as big as was reported, then it is certainly a battleship, and should not be able to make more than 18 knots. Our cruisers are much faster. We will catch him and bring this Captain to heel."

"I would hope so, Baron Dewa," said Togo. "But I must tell you that the ship is very fast as well, possibly the equal of any of our cruisers. This has been reported many times. It left the *Empress of China* in its wake easily, and that ship can cruise at 18 knots. It also evaded Kamimura's cruisers with uncanny ease, almost as if they could determine his every move and alter course to exactly the correct heading to evade him. All this further reinforces the idea that this is a new ship, something we have never seen before. So I advise you all to be bold and very diligent. Begin live training exercises the moment you arrive at your assigned patrol station. Drill on maneuvers aimed at intercepting a solitary ship, not a set piece battle line engagement. If the enemy flees, drive him towards our other divisions. This ship must not be allowed to transit the Tsushima Straits, for any reason."

"Rest assured, Admiral," said Kataoka, his eyes alight with the excitement of the new assignment. The Navy had done little more than wallow in port with an occasional training exercise in recent years. He was going to sea again, and with the hope of battle. Now all these Vice Admirals made Barons for the glory they brought Japan in the last war could tussle with one another for this final piece of cake. He resolved, then and there, that he would be the one to find and discipline this Russian Captain.

Admiral Togo could see the enthusiasm in his eyes, and had every confidence in all the officers assembled. Then why this shadow rising in the corner of my mind, he asked himself? Why this odd inner warning that there is more waiting for us in the Sea of Japan than any man here might expect?

Chapter 8

Karpov was watching the distant rise of Dogo Island, one of several small outcrops forming the Oki Island group, about 40 miles north of the coast of the main island of Japan. A thin column of smoke was rising from the far shore, and he imagined that some hunter was up in those hills, lighting his mid-day fire for a good meal. Now he walked to the clear Plexiglas map of the Sea of Japan, considering his next move in a brief conference with Rodenko.

He had made a cursory review of the mail obtained from RMS *Monteagle*, and was now satisfied that this could be no other year than 1908. Every letter was postmarked with that date, and he had the mail distributed to the crew for souvenirs, as much as to cement in their minds that they were now sailing the waters of the early 20th Century.

Soon after he had Nikolin transmit his edict on the Naval quarantine over wireless telegraphy. It was sent: *"All ships – all ships – all ships bound for ports on the Yellow Sea and China coast. A naval quarantine is now imposed on the Sea of Japan, Tsushima Strait, Korea Strait, East China Sea and Yellow Sea where all shipping of Japanese origin is concerned. All Japanese registered shipping is prohibited, hereby designated fair prizes of war to be attacked on sight. International shipping will be warned to leave the quarantine zone, and attacked upon non-compliance."*

"That is a fairly ambitious declaration," said Rodenko. "There is no way we can impose it on all these waters. The minute we leave the Sea of Japan, it will fill up with normal shipping again."

"Perhaps, but I have no intention of lingering here now. My real intent is to begin the strangulation of Port Arthur and other Japanese interests in Manchuria as a prelude to persuading Russia to re-enter that region. We don't have to control the Sea of Japan, Rodenko. It's the Yellow Sea that we need to close. To do that I plan to take up a patrol station here."

Karpov pointed at the digital map to the gap between the Shandong Peninsula and North Korea. It was a natural choke point, and all shipping bound for Port Arthur would have to pass through those waters.

"That is the spot we take and hold. From there we become quite a thorn in Japan's side. It's really only the Bay of Korea and Bohai Sea that we have to scour, and nothing can enter those waters unless they move through the Yellow Sea and this gap."

"Agreed, sir, but to get there we will have to transit the Tsushima Straits ourselves, narrow waterways that are easily patrolled and interdicted."

"That is what I expect," said Karpov. "As we move south I want the KA-40 up with an *Oko* panel and returning long range radar data feeds so we can pinpoint the location of every ship in the Sea of Japan. I want this tactical board lit up and notated by color. Designate commercial traffic as green, but any warship identified will be denoted in red."

"You know what they'll do, sir. Sasebo and Kure are their principal naval bases in the south. The bulk of their entire fleet is there, and it will be more than enough to cover the Tsushima and Korea Straits. Granted, those waters span 175 kilometers, but the Japanese also have a base on the central island group. It may not be as easy to slip through as you believe."

Karpov smiled, shaking his head. "You still don't understand, Rodenko. I have no intention of trying to slip through. I'm going to simply sail through, and destroy anything in my path that attempts to impede me."

Rodenko hesitated, then spoke his mind. "That may strain our available ordnance, sir."

"We will use the missiles sparingly, and I have had work crews busy preparing our remaining SAM inventory so it can be re-targeted at surface ships. Many of those systems have an engagement envelope with a fairly low altitude threshold. The *Klinok* system can engage at 10 meters, and be switched to manual guided mode. We used only 28 missiles and have 100 remaining. They are small HE warheads, but I imagine a salvo of six or eight against a capital ship would be most disconcerting. Our remaining P-400s are an even better long range weapon, and I have made it a top priority. They can hit targets as low as 5 meters and those missiles have a 180 kilogram fragmentation warhead which could riddle the superstructure of these old ships with lethal shrapnel. It won't penetrate armor, but the kinetic impact at speeds from Mach 8 to Mach 12 will be considerable. Think of them as shrapnel laden fire arrows."

"I see... You've given this considerable thought, Captain. But are you truly prepared to engage the entire enemy fleet?"

"Why not? There is no undersea threat, no air threat, just ponderous old ships in a line, like sitting ducks. This will be much easier than you may think."

"And what about Fedorov, sir?"

"Fedorov? How he appeared in this same time is a mystery. If he's still here he will be in the Caspian Sea, and after we conclude this business we may find an occasion to sail to the Black Sea and rescue his party if it remains stranded here."

"But what if they use that control rod again and manage to return home?"

Karpov shook his head. "The man isn't even thirty years old. Even if we lead long lives here we'll both be dead well before he is even born."

"If he *is* born, Captain."

Karpov gave his *Starpom* an odd look now. "What do you mean by that?"

"I'm not sure, sir, but I think this is what Fedorov was all steamed up about. From here, in 1908, anything we do to change the history will have a much greater effect on future years."

"Yes, yes, he was always worried about his history. Well, how do the American say it? You can't make an omelet without breaking a few eggs."

"I think he fears something more than that, sir. We could cause a change so radical that it might affect the lives of millions yet to be born. Some that were fated to live may come into the world, others not. Many fated to die may survive and sire descendants that were never supposed to exist."

"Yes, Fedorov tried to explain all that to me once. He used the example of a mirror, and each change we have worked in the history is a crack in that mirror. In places it remains as smooth and unblemished as it always was, in others it is badly cracked."

"And if we look into that mirror our own image may become unrecognizable, sir. This is what I think Fedorov worries about."

"It is all useless speculation, Rodenko." Karpov batted the argument aside, but even as he did so he could hear Zolkin admonishing him: *"Well, here's a thought you can put into your own scheming head. Suppose you do something here; something that changes everything. Suppose the grandparents of men aboard this ship don't survive in the new world you create? What happens to the men then? Do they end up dead, never born, just like the men on that list Volkov was all worked up over, with no record they ever existed? Suppose your own grandfather dies. Then what?"*

He considered that for some time, worried about it at first. The missing men had all died in combat. That was how time accounted for the fact they had never been born. If the warnings from Zolkin and Rodenko proved true, and many others on the ship suffered the same fate, then that would mean they might die in combat as well. That thought shook him for a moment, yet he could not see how he could fail to master the situation here. As long as he kept his wits about him, *Kirov* was invincible. So he decided Zolkin's warning would be an impossible event. How could he do something here to prevent the birth of his grandfather? That man would *have* to be born for him to even be here and do anything at all!

"Look, Rodenko, I don't know how you voted on the question of staying here or trying to get home, and I don't care. All this nonsense about doing something that will alter our own fate is a waste of time. We can't control what may happen in years to come. We may try to shape that world to our liking, but things will happen there that are beyond our power to influence. All we can really do is shape the day before us now, and then stack up one day after another in the shape of our desire. This worry over future generations is useless."

Is it, sir? It was my thought to mention it as a way of personalizing this whole matter. What would we do if the lives of the crew—if our *own* lives depended on the outcome of our decisions?"

"That is so any time you lead men into battle," said Karpov. "The ship and crew are always in the equation, and your own life as well."

"But what about the men on the other side, Captain? They have a yearning for life as well. Alright... I looked in a few of Fedorov's books on my last shift. We'll most likely be up against Admiral Togo, regarded as one of the world's top three fighting Admirals."

"Accolades he won by defeating his peers in this era," Karpov reminded him. "This man can in no wise be compared to me, any more than his flagship can be compared to *Kirov*. What would Admiral Togo have done when faced with a hundred *Super Hornets* off CV *Washington?* Do you think he would have led his fleet out of that engagement intact as I did? It wasn't until that damn volcano blasted us into the past again that our luck turned bad and we lost *Admiral Golovko.* Togo is out of his league here now, Rodenko. I will master him as easily as I master his ships."

"You mean to kill him, sir?"

Karpov seemed annoyed now. "You make it sound like a personal vendetta, but my motives are far broader here. I have no desire to see the man to an early grave, but if he opposes me, and will not submit, then he must be prepared to accept his fate. We all must face the possibility that death will come calling on us one day in the heat of battle. We have faced it many times, but thus far we have cheated death and prevailed."

"Well you saw what happened to *Admiral Golovko,* sir. All it took was a single critical hit."

"True, but that was a fluke, and a massive round fired by a much more powerful ship than anything we face here. Think of this in military terms. *Mikasa* is not the battleship *Iowa.* None of these ships are even truly worthy of the name battleship—not while *Kirov* sails these waters."

"What I meant was that battle often presents the unexpected, sir. I don't think Captain Ryakhin expected his ship would be hit at that range by a random shell, but it was, and we both saw the result. I don't think Captain Yeltsin on the *Orlan* expected to look over his shoulder and find us missing in the heat of that last engagement in 1945, but there he was, alone on a sea of fire, unless he also shifted somewhere else. Who knows? What if he's been blown to another year—1905—1912?"

"We would know it if he arrived earlier than this time period. As for the rest, what you say is true. War is uncertain, battle is inherently risky. But the timid make bad warriors, Rodenko, and you will find the graveyards littered with more of them than the brave men who fell in battle by acting boldly. I intend to fight here and survive. If fate has other plans for us, then let her try me in battle as well."

Rodenko raised an eyebrow at this, but said nothing more.

They steamed almost due south now, slowly approaching the Japanese mainland, and the ship was preparing to send up the KA-40 for a general survey when the Fregat radar system made contact with a small detachment of surface ships near the Oki Islands.

"Con. Radar. Contact bearing One-Five-Zero degrees. Three surface ships. Speed twenty. Range 28,000 meters. Designate Alpha One. Second contact bearing One-Seven-Four degrees south. Two surface ships. Speed twenty. Range 30,000 meters. Designate Alpha Two."

"Feed data to the tactical board," said Karpov. "Twenty-eight thousand meters? How was it they got this close without the Fregat system picking them up earlier?"

"They were probably behind those islands," said Rodenko as the data began to wink on the tactical board. "Yes, the Alpha One contact would have been masked by Dogo Island. They've just come into our line of site now. The Alpha Two contact was probably behind these smaller islands here."

"Give me a Tin Man feed. High resolution please, and

magnification level four."

Nikolin activated the robot-like camera system and fed the data to the wide panel display. The familiar silhouettes of Japanese armored cruisers appeared on the screen, chugging forward and leaving a column of darkening smoke that was now clearly evident in the skies above them."

"Why didn't we see their smoke earlier?" Karpov was not happy.

"Well, sir," said Rodenko, "our men are here with their faces poked into these computer terminals, not out on the weather decks looking for smoke on the horizon."

"I don't like surprises, gentlemen. There's no excuse for us not picking up these ships before they were in our line of sight like this."

"Yes, someone should have seen their smoke long ago. It can only mean that they were lying in wait, sir. Perhaps they came to all-stop and had their boilers fired low. That might control smoke emissions, and the horizon is quite hazy as it stands."

"Are you suggesting they *knew* we were here? How would they know we were approaching? We make no visible steam at all. Get that KA-40 ready, Rodenko. I want better situational awareness. In the meantime... Mister Samsonov!"

"Sir!"

"The ship will come to battle stations. Activate 152mm batteries and prepare to engage Alpha One. Helm, battle speed. Thirty knots and steady as she goes."

"Sir, aye, ahead thirty and steady on."

"Captain," said Rodenko. "If you're going to engage here then perhaps we should launch the KA-40 once the action concludes. We have two batteries aft that will be tossing shell casings all over the place back there."

"Well enough, the Fregat system will do for the moment. We'll let the range close another 10,000 meters, Mister Samsonov, then I'll want all three 152mm turrets to engage Alpha One. I guess these impudent little men did not get enough of a beating last time they stuck their noses into our business. We just blasted their lead ship earlier. Now we'll let them know what they're dealing with."

But Karpov did not entirely know what *he* was dealing with here either. Vice Admiral Kamimura was back on his assigned station at the Oki Island Group, and he was well aware of the approach of the large Russian warship. He had no 21st Century radar systems, but human eyes on the northern coast of Dogo Island had seen the ship darken the horizon long ago, and signal fires were lit that soon spiraled up in thin, dark columns of smoke.

It was happenstance as much as anything else. A sea lion was gliding through the cobalt blue waters off the island, veering toward shore to chase a passing fish and missing his quarry. The rocks near shore beckoned and offered a warm place to sun himself, and that he did, braying with satisfaction as he climbed out of the sea and wallowed up onto the rocks.

The hunter Karpov imagined sitting at his mid-day meal was actually a coastwatcher named Nakai Yozaburo. He had made a lucrative business out of hunting sea lions on those islands, and other small islets further north called Dokdo and Ulleung-do, and the call of a sea lion had interrupted what he hoped would be a nice nap that day. Driven by his greed, he thought instead to get up and have a look from the watchtower and see if he could spot the sea lions. What he saw instead set in motion a series of events that would cascade through the decades ahead, knocking one down after another.

Far out to sea was the threatening silhouette of a large warship! Had it not been for that sea lion's call he would have missed it. Or perhaps it was the greed in his heart, but he ran to light his signal fire as a backup, and then he would transmit the sighting via telegraph as well.

Soon after, the Japanese fed more coal and fire to their furnaces to quickly build up steam for action. The cruisers were indeed lying in wait, just as Rodenko surmised, and now they rushed boldly into the narrow strait between Dogo to the northeast, and Dozen and Nakanoshima Island about ten kilometers southwest. Five cruisers charged forward to engage the Russian foe in a bold surprise attack.

And there was one more thing that Karpov had not seen, nestled in a shallow bay at the heart of the three smaller islands southwest of the channel. Had the KA-40 been up with its *Oko* panel it would have easily detected them, but as it was, the battleships *Tango* and *Mishima* were neatly masked behind the hilly islands around them, and the shovels were quickly feeding coal to the fires on those two ships as crews hastily began to prep the guns for action.

Deception, not discretion, was now the better part of valor, and the Japanese had pulled their first surprise on the seasoned Russian Captain. Now it was time to fight.

Chapter 9

The action opened at 13:20 hours when *Kirov* began firing its 152mm batteries at a range of 18,000 meters. This time there were no pleasantries or warnings on the telegraph. In Karpov's mind he had clearly stated the terms he was operating under, and now battle would decide who's word would prevail. The guns could fire for effect as far as 30,000 meters out, and had a small inventory of 200 rocket assisted rounds that could extend that range over the horizon to 56,000 meters, but none had been used. Karpov was satisfied to close to 18,000 meters, more out of curiosity as to the enemy's capabilities than anything else. He knew he may be navigating restricted waters ahead in the Tsushima Straits and he wanted to test the accuracy and range of the enemy guns.

Kirov's first radar assisted rounds straddled Kamimura's new flagship immediately, and the Japanese Admiral ordered the armored cruiser *Tokiwa* to quickly make a five point turn to port, thinking to avoid the next salvo. There was no way he could conceive of guns being controlled by unseen electromagnetic radar energy that could feed data on his ship's course, speed and exact location relative to the firing weapon. Yet the second salvo quickly repeated the hard experience he had suffered in his first engagement with this Russian dreadnought. The *Izumo* was laid up in port, riddled by the shock of eight direct hits from 6 inch shells.

Two 152mm rounds smashed into his armored bow just at the waterline and sent columns of sea spray up to wash over the forward deck. The distant silhouette of the enemy ship was looming like a storm cloud on the horizon, its flanks lit by gouts of fire that seemed to ripple fore to aft as *Kirov* fired its three turrets in sequence. Each salvo sent 18 rounds, and they came in three sets of six, with the sharp thunder crack of the guns rolling over the sea.

Kamimura felt his ship shudder again, and heard the hard chink and roar of an explosion as the conning tower was struck dead on. The armor was heavy enough to stop the round penetrating, but the concussion threw two junior officers to the deck and prompted him to drop his field glasses and seize a nearby rail to keep his feet.

A sturdy ship, *Tokiwa* was one of six armored cruisers ordered from the British shipbuilder Armstrong Whitworth after the Sino-Japanese war. Just seven feet shorter than the fleet flagship, the battleship *Mikasa*, the cruiser cut a silhouette very close to that ship, with twin turrets housing 203mm 8-inch guns mounted fore and aft and seven 6-inch guns in casements on each side of the ship. She had twin funnels just like *Mikasa* as well, though the beam was much narrower. *Tokiwa's* name meant "Evergreen," and she was destined to be one of the longest serving ships in the Japanese Navy, converted to a minesweeper and sunk in 1945 at the end of WWII by air attack.

"What is the range?" Kamimura shouted over the roar.

"At least 17,000 meters! How can they hit us like this?" His gunnery officer was sitting at the Barr & Stroud naval rangefinder, built by a pair of Scottish professors and now installed on all Japanese warships. It looked like a long telescope, only the lenses were mounted on the sides of each end, and the eyepiece was dead center on the tube. The 'processor' used to align it on the enemy ship was the human eye and cerebral cortex, as the instrument was stereoscopic, and when the operator aligned the images sent from each lens into one picture, the range was reported on a readout by means of triangulation. A telegraph operator sitting beside the equipment would signal the range to the turrets below, and it would also be called out through voice tubes, written on chalk boards, and eventually denoted by moving hands on the face of a clock.

"Just as they hit us before, Lieutenant Hachiro. But we must answer with our forward main gun."

"It can fire no more than 13,000 meters, Admiral."

"Even so, the enemy must see us return fire. I will not be pockmarked with shot and shell again without answering!"

Hachiro sent the signal for maximum elevation via telegraph and then ran to a voice tube and shouted down the order to fire. They heard the hoarse throated shouts of men repeat the order with bull horns below and, down on the forward deck, a young officer ran to the open back hatch on the armored turret housing.

The big guns answered soon after, belching a distinctive yellow fire. The shells were loaded with Lyddite, a derivative of Picric Acid discovered by a Mister Woulffe in Britain when he sought to use the substance as a dye and found it was also very explosive. On impact the shells would emit a haze of yellow gas, the very same dye property Woulffe was trying to harness. The two rounds swooped out, falling all of 5,000 meters short in the sea between the two ships. That distance and the fact that *Kirov* had the speed to maintain it at Karpov's whim, would be the deciding factor of the engagement.

Tokiwa was again being hit, the 152mm rounds possessing much more explosive power and penetrating ability than the same caliber gun of 1908. Before it could fire its third salvo the front twin turret on the cruiser was dealt a severe blow when a round smashed into the 5.9 inches of armor and nearly blasted clean through. The jet of molten steel it sent into the turret space killed three crewmen and badly burned another. Men rushed through the back hatch to drag the bodies out and re-crew the guns, but a second hit jolted them from their feet and now a fire started on the deck just aft of the gun, the raging sheets of flame licking at the open hatch door.

Thick smoke billowed in, and a crewman reached to the hatch handle, screaming as his hands were burned by the heated metal, yet still desperately pulling the hatch shut to keep out the smoke. Men were already choking inside on the fumes, and now the sailor's valiant effort only sealed them in a metal tomb. Another 152mm round struck the turret, and they were knocked senseless by the concussion.

But amazingly, the range was rapidly closing. The enemy ship had turned five points to port, and by 13:30 hours Hachiro yelled out 8,000 meters. "We can now answer with our 6 inch guns!" he shouted, and Vice Admiral Yamimura was quick to order a new heading change.

"Captain Yoshimatsu! Come left thirty degrees to port! All guns fire!" He was turning to present his starboard side where there were seven 6 inch guns in casemates along the upper hull. Now the range was fixed on the clock face, with the shorter hour hand set at number 8 and the longer minute hand set at the number 2 to indicate 8,200 meters. As soon as they fired, however, the Russian ship turned ten points to starboard to prevent the range from closing any further.

Now the difference in accuracy was murderous. *Kirov's* radar controlled guns were riddling the cruisers with armor piercing rounds, gutting funnels, snapping the tall conning masts, blasting into the hull and exploding on the superstructure of the ships to ignite fires fore and aft. Firing at their extreme range, the Japanese guns were still unable to find the enemy ship, most falling short by two or three hundred meters, churning up the sea in a futile reprisal.

Yakumo and *Asama* were soon both on fire, and Yamimura turned to see that *Iwate* and *Adzuma* had rushed up on his port aft, turning to run parallel just ahead of his own line of three cruisers. The Russian dreadnought now turned its attention to them, blasting with those infernal deck guns that could shoot with amazing rapidity and accuracy. The Japanese fought bravely for another ten minutes, but by 13:40 hours all five cruisers were damaged and burning, and the Vice Admiral saw *Iwate* turn sharply to port and run due south for the narrow channel between Dozen and Nakanoshima Islands.

"We cannot prevail," he said grimly.

A ray of sunlight pierced the grey cloud and smoke and gleamed on the water creaming at the sleek bow of the enemy dreadnought. At this range Yamimura could finally see how massive the ship was, easily twice the length of his own cruiser and over three times its displacement. His gunners had scored a few near misses, but had not damaged the enemy ship in any way. To fire with effect, he would want to get in much closer, closing the range to 5,000 meters, but the enemy speed now prevented that. As he watched the big ship maneuver, he realized it had been within their power to open the range any time they chose.

Rounds shuddered against his conning tower again with deafening impact, and only the heavy 14-inch armor had saved the

Admiral and his staff from certain death. They hit us at least ten or twelve times, he thought darkly. Look at my cruiser division! This single enemy ship has shattered it, and now our only hope lies with the battleships.

"Signal *Tango* and *Mishima*. Tell them to move due west now!"

The order was passed by telegraph, and ten kilometers away, Nikolin was listening on his headset, trying to hear the dots and dashes in Kana Code over the sharp report of *Kirov's* guns.

"Captain, they are signaling a course change to two-seven-zero west."

"What's that, Nikolin?" Karpov beamed as he was watching the action through his field glasses, preferring them to the overhead Tin Man display, even if it would not give him as sharp an image. "They are most likely going to run and hide behind that island. Very well. Cease fire, Samsonov. They've taken quite a pounding."

"Sir, securing deck guns, aye."

"What do you think now, Rodenko?" The Captain smiled at his *Starpom*. "Still worried about changing history? Well, it's begun. We put enough damage on those five cruisers to send them all into dry dock for lengthy repairs. I could linger here and sink them, but the damage we've inflicted has already done the job. I doubt any of them will be serviceable in the months ahead."

"Their effective range appears to be well under 8,000 meters, sir."

"Correct. I read this in Fedorov's books, and so I had little fear closing to 8,000 as I did. They got a very good look at us through their field glasses, and that image will now be burned in their memory. A little fear will be a strong ally for us in the days ahead. They will learn to feel it quicken in their chest when they see us appear on the horizon."

"How many rounds did we expend, Samsonov?" Rodenko turned to his CIC officer to determine what they had left.

"Sir, I fired thirty-six salvos with all three batteries, expending a total of 192 rounds. This leaves us with 2,508 standard rounds and 200 rocket assisted rounds for the 152mm batteries."

"Down from a full magazine of 3,000 rounds," said Rodenko, looking Karpov's way.

"A small price to pay for the wrecking of five enemy cruisers," said Karpov. "The range was too short for a test of our re-programmed SAMs, but we'll let that sit for the moment." He watched as the last of the burning enemy cruisers disappeared behind the long peninsula of Dozen Island.

"Congratulations, men," said Karpov. "You have just logged your first victory of the second Russo-Japanese war at sea! It will not be your last."

But the Captain had spoken too soon. The young radar operator had been jubilantly nodding at his mates when he turned and suddenly saw a distinctive blip on his screen.

"Captain. Radar. I have a contact... no sir, *two* contacts bearing one-eight-zero south, speed 16 knots and on a heading of two-seven zero. Range 10,000 meters!"

A distant boom rolled like thunder and they saw the second enemy ship brighten with the glow of its main batteries. The ship was *Mishima*, formerly the obsolete Russian battleship *Admiral Seniavin*, built as a coastal defense ship in 1894, and she was firing 10 inch guns that elevated fifteen degrees to produce a maximum range of just over 13,000 meters. With better elevation they would have ranged much farther but, as it was, the confining space of the turrets would only permit those fifteen degrees, and the same liability would plague the ship following in her wake, the former battleship *Poltava* now renamed *Tango*.

At range she appeared to be just another armored cruiser, actually shorter than Vice Admiral Yamimura's battered flagship *Tokiwa* at only 396 feet, though much wider abeam. Yet that beam of 70 feet gave her the girth to mount two much larger turrets fore and aft of her twin smokestacks and conning tower, and now they lashed out in the second surprise attack the Japanese had staged in this hot, frantic hour. The Krupp 302mm 12-inch forty caliber guns on *Tango* were the mainstay of the Russian pre-dreadnought battleships. Not to be upstaged by *Mishima,* they deafened the scene with their sudden roar, but the ship had fired too soon. The effective range was only 7,200 meters given the maximum thirteen degree elevation of her guns, even more restricted within their turrets due to their larger size.

Both battleships had been lying in the shallow bay formed by three islands. On Yamimura's signal they sailed due west through the narrow mile wide channel and remained masked by the sweeping curve of hilly Nishinoshima, the westernmost of the Oki Island group. So it was that they were not picked up on radar until they were already in line of sight and with good range to open the action.

The opening rounds from *Mishima* actually sailed well over *Kirov* with a long descending whoosh and fell heavily into the ocean behind the ship. Karpov looked at the tall geysers with some alarm, thinking only of the fate of *Admiral Golovko* and Rodenko's warning. Here they had blundered into another surprise hidden away in those damnable islands! Red anger flushed his face as he realized the ship was suddenly in jeopardy. The memory of Rodenko's words now taunted him… *"battle often presents the unexpected, sir. I don't think Captain Ryakhin expected his ship would be hit at that range by a random shell, but it was, and we both saw the result."* A haphazard round could deal them a severe blow.

"Those are heavy rounds. These must be battleships," said Karpov, "and we've stumbled right on them without a whisper on radar!"

"It's those damn islands, Captain," said Rodenko.

"Yes, well we should have scouted them with the KA-40! This is sloppy work, but I will make an end of this nonsense at once. Samsonov, activate *Moskit II* system! Put one missile on each ship. Now!" The second salvo from *Mishima* was already whining in on them and fell much closer as the Japanese began to adjust the range. *Tango* was also firing, but the big 12-inch rounds were still well short."

"Sir, keying *Moskit II* system and targeting now!"

The missile warning claxon sounded the alarm and the forward deck hatches sprung open. Up leapt the sleek daggers their noses quickly inclined towards the enemy ships. Then the engines roared and the Japanese would see what looked to be two demons from hell soaring in like fiery dragons over the sea, impossibly fast as the powerful engines accelerated to devour the distance to the target in just twelve seconds. When they struck they were still accelerating, though already moving at well over Mach 2.

The first heavy 450 kilogram warhead blasted against the side armor of *Tango*, which was almost 12 inches thick, hardened Harvey armor, an older cemented armor method developed in the United States before processes by Krupp made it obsolete. It had a brittle exterior, and more pliant inner segment all melded into one plate, but it was not enough to stop a missile weighing over four tons moving at over 3000 KPH. The side of the ship buckled and was blown completely inward, and the huge store of missile fuel, largely unexpended, exploded in a massive fireball.

Mishima got even worse, when the missile that struck her amidships came in at deck level and smashed into the ship's superstructure, penetrating easily to immolate everything in its path. It blew completely through the ship, destroying every compartment just beneath the conning tower, which now began to collapse as the entire ship heeled to port with the thunderous impact. *Mishima* keeled over, but her conning tower shuddered down into the raging flames amidships, killing her captain and all staff officers on the bridge.

Tango wallowed to one side with the body blow she had taken, and then rolled heavily, flames licking the sea as water careened in through the breach in her hull. Then thick black smoke masked the scene, and Karpov stared with amazement at the awesome power of the missiles.

Aboard *Tango* bulkheads were shattered, water tight doors blasted open, and a torrent of raging seawater was swamping the ship. It rolled to starboard, the crewmen falling on the wet decks and sliding through cinder black smoke into the fire, which had spread to the sea itself, set aflame by the tremendous fuel explosion. Men leapt from the forward gunwales into the ocean, and secondary explosions began to rip through the guts of the ship as the magazines from many of the smaller casement side batteries began to explode with shuddering thunder. Smoke belched from both stricken ships, bludgeoned by a weapon of inconceivable power.

There was no more fire coming from the Japanese battleships, and both would capsize and sink within the next thirty minutes. Japan had taken them from Russia, but now Russia had taken them back, and given them to Davey Jones, who waited with greedy arms to receive them on the sea floor below.

The Oki Island engagement was over.

Part IV

Prelude

"The megalomaniac differs from the narcissist by the fact that he wishes to be powerful rather than charming, and seeks to be feared rather than loved. To this type belong many lunatics and most of the great men of history."

— *Bertrand Russell*

"I think I'll dismember the world and then I'll dance in the wreckage."

— *Neil Gaiman, The Sandman*

Chapter 10

"**We** must decide now," said Admiral Volsky. "I have my mind settled on this question, but I would like to hear opinions."

Kazan was now 40 kilometers south of Nakhodka, having crept down the long coast past Sovetsky Gavan and on south to a point where they would normally round the cape and head northwest to Vladivostok. They were now no more than 75 kilometers from the Fleet Naval Headquarters at Fokino, though the Admiral did not yearn for his desk there, or the damp shadowy darkness of the deep underground command bunker.

A strange lull seemed to have been imposed on the war since the eruption of the Demon Volcano, which was still broiling and belching its sulfuric ash to overshadow the whole region in gloom, the rolling clouds thick and impenetrable to the east, and creeping ever closer on the northwesterly wind. Though no one aboard the submarine could see them now, they could still feel their effects. Lieutenant Andre Chernov at sonar would occasionally report on the deep, dull rumble beneath the sea as the volcano continued its slow eruption, sustained and withering. It was affecting his system performance, with a great deal of sonic disturbance and an odd ebb and flow of general interference.

Dobrynin had taken the time during their journey south to mount Rod-25 in the replacement aperture of the submarine's reactor. It was slow, dangerous work, as the rod was radioactive and had to be handled with utmost caution. It was actually mounted within its radiation safe container by means of a mechanical system designed to allow for this specific maintenance procedure, and the container was not actually withdrawn until it was safely sealed off inside the core area. It was a procedure that should have only been conducted in a secure dock, but the circumstances would not permit that, and Dobrynin's skill was enough to get them through.

Now they had to decide whether to utilize the rod immediately, or to move south into the Sea of Japan and use it when they might appear closer to *Kirov*. The question of the hour was this: where was the ship now, lost in the distant haze of history?

"Mister Fedorov?" The Admiral wanted the opinion of his master strategist, the young officer who had come up with the plan.

"Well, sir. We shifted back here on the nineteenth of July, 1908. If, by luck or Dobrynin's skill, we get back there again with Rod-25, we will most likely appear after that date in time."

"Why do you say this?"

"Because we cannot co-locate, sir. We can't appear the morning of the 19th because many of us, myself included, are already there on the *Anatoly Alexandrov* in the Caspian Sea. My guess is that the earliest we might appear would be July 20th. Karpov said he was in the Sea of Japan, but we are not able to see anything in the history while we remain here in 2021. I suppose once we actually leave, and assuming we get back to our target date and do something decisive, then it will manifest here as history shortly after our disappearance."

Volsky shook his head, somewhat bewildered. "This business is becoming an arcane science, Mister Fedorov."

"In some ways it is, sir. This is theory developed by physicist Paul Dorland, who is presently engaged in a research project involving quantum particle infusion and artificial black holes at Lawrence Berkeley labs in America. His theory draws on the work of others as well, but it posits a Heisenberg Wave that is generated by any decisive intervention in the past, which then migrates forward through the continuum of potential futures from that point in time, like ripples from a stone thrown into a still pool. The wave works a transformation, literally re-arranging every particle of the universe as it propagates forward in time. Paradox eliminates anything that cannot be rationally accounted for in the altered reality. Things literally change, and the world is made entirely new. That's one explanation. Another holds that the intervention actually changes the course of the continuum and it enters an alternate universe. It's all theory, of course, but we have seen it happen more than once already. We have seen it made real, no matter what the process actually is."

"So we can't know exactly where Karpov and his ship is until we get there," said Kamenski.

"That's about the size of it, and so my recommendation would be to shift now. That would give us time to make a search of the Sea of Japan in 1908, sweeping south as we go."

"But won't that also give Tasarov the opportunity to detect us? The undersea world there would be completely empty. His ears are very good."

"They are, sir, but it's a risk that becomes academic if we intend to make contact with Karpov and see if he will comply with a direct order."

"Yes… I suppose the instant we make contact the jig is up."

"Not necessarily…"

They all recognized Orlov's deep voice, and turned to hear him out. The Chief removed his hat, scratching his head. "You called him via shortwave before. Why not do that again? How will he know we are on a submarine?"

"Don't forget Nikolin," said Fedorov. "First off, we would be too close. *Kirov* would be in the shortwave dead zone and we would have to use normal radio bands. The only reason *Kirov* heard us from the Caspian was because the shortwave signal was reflected from the ionosphere. So if we contact him here, Nikolin will immediately know we are very close. He will be able to isolate the signal band in a few seconds."

"But we could tell him we came east on the Mi-26," said Dobrynin. "Might that account for the differing radio signal?"

"Perhaps at first blush," said Fedorov, "but Nikolin will soon determine our location. He's just too good, even as Tasarov is at sonar."

"That's part of what made the ship so deadly in combat," said Volsky. "Each man was a real expert at his post. Rodenko at radar, Tasarov at sonar, Nikolin at communications, Samsonov at CIC, not to mention my ex-navigator here. Now he tries to plot this course through time."

"We don't have to say we are on *Kazan*," said Orlov. "If we broadcast on a line back to Vladivostok, he could assume we are there."

"A good point, Chief. In fact, he might assume we used the test reactor at the Primorskiy Engineering Center and shifted back that way. That uncertainty could be enhanced if we just state that is the case, and then the Admiral can take over and see what he can do."

"That is worth a try," said Volsky. "And the alternative?"

Orlov spoke again. "Sail south now, appear right on Karpov's ass, and put a torpedo into him before he can think twice."

The simple brutality of the suggestion seemed cold and stark in the room, but that was what the surprise option left them with. It meant they might not have to risk battle with *Kirov*, but they would have to appear like an assassin in the dark and stab the ship in the back. They would have to be everything Karpov feared and loathed about submarines, and somehow the notion seemed distasteful to them all.

"Yes, we could appear suddenly like that," said Volsky, "but we would still not know where *Kirov* was when we arrived. Our equipment could be bothered by the effects of the shift as it was on *Kirov*, and they would have the advantage. They might detect us before we could get things in order here. That is one concern with plan B. The second is that I do not like the idea of torpedoing *Kirov* without first trying to persuade the Captain to relent. And from the looks on all your faces I think there is broad agreement on this. What do you think, Gromyko? After all, this is your boat at risk here."

"Not my boat, Admiral. It's just on loan to me at the moment. If you must know, a submarine's stock in trade at war is stealth and surprise. In modern warfare you aim to detect and fire on the enemy before they can do the same to you. A submarine excels at that because of its inherent stealthiness. So while you may all feel uncomfortable sneaking up behind our flagship like this, Chief Orlov is correct. That is how I would fight this boat if asked to take military action against *Kirov*. Speed, stealth, surprise, and a good spread of at least four torpedoes."

"There is one other consideration," said Fedorov. "Karpov's temperament. He has a phobia concerning submarines, and the sudden appearance of an undersea threat has often seen him take extreme measures. In fact, whenever he is truly surprised in battle, either by the skill of the enemy or by the failure of his own tactical approach, he resorts to a sudden, extreme escalation of force. He selects the one weapon which can redress the situation and applies it with absolute, ruthless violence."

"Yes," said Orlov. "That's Karpov alright. I tell you what… Get close and then send me over in a frogman suit. I'll put this fat fist in the Captain's face and another fat torpedo right up his ass."

They all laughed at that, but things settled down quickly to the difficulty of the decision before them now. "Well," said Volsky, "as much as it may be sound submarine tactics, it is against my better judgment to strike as you suggest. Unless the majority here believe otherwise, I think we should do what Mister Fedorov advises. Shift now, while we are here in safe waters. We can drift over towards the Korean coast until we see what happens. Then head south if we reach the targeted time."

"How will we know if we shift successfully?" Dobrynin raised another good point. "How will we know it isn't 1945, or 1942 again? Rod-25 has been very stubborn about that year."

"First we rely on that inner ear of yours, Dobrynin," said Fedorov. "After that we rely on signals intelligence first, and if we still can't ascertain our position in time, we could risk taking a look around by sending a team ashore in Korea, or even Vladivostok. That said, it is my belief that we will reach the target time successfully."

"How can you be so certain," said Dobrynin. "I'm not a miracle worker, you know."

"Because if we failed to do what we now propose… if we failed to stop Karpov, then it *would* be history now, and we should have been able to read about it. No… I think we will get there, because the absence of definite information about what happened to Karpov indicates uncertainty prevails. We are still a primary factor in the outcome."

"Very astute, Mister Fedorov," said Kamenski.

"Then that will be the order," said Volsky, feeling much better about the situation. "Any objections?"

No man had any further argument. They had made the gentleman's agreement. They would contact Karpov and order him to stand down. If he refused it would be pistols at fifty paces, *Kazan* against *Kirov*. Yet like all plans, things can happen that set events off in a most unexpected course... And they did.

* * *

Dobrynin was still very uneasy as he settled into his chair at the reactor monitoring station, in spite of Fedorov's confidence. The equipment here was somewhat different, even if it was still compatible with Rod-25, and he was wondering how this would affect the planned operation. He had spent the last several hours going over detailed charts and data from the two time displacement shifts aboard *Anatoly Alexandrov*. He was noting power levels, output, neutron flux levels, and then topped it all off by simply listening to his tape of the shifts that sent them back to 1908. He was like a conductor being introduced to a new orchestra. The score was in his head, in the delicate weave of sounds he could hear in the internal song of his mind, but the musicians were all new here. Would the sound remain the same?

He would try to repeat that score, yet he knew each player was now subtly different. Each of the control rods on this new reactor had a life span, some old, some young, some ready to be retired. Each would be a player in the music to come, and he wondered if he would be able to still hear the melody required for a successful shift. If he could not, then their whole effort was futile here. They might shift somewhere, but with no guarantee that they would not end up in a year and time that was most undesirable, no matter what Fedorov thought.

He was understandably very nervous about it all, as everything seemed to depend on him now. They could devise their plans, and talk and conjecture, but the real work was his to do, and if he could not get it done, then what?

He closed his eyes, trying to listen to this new reactor to determine its aural characteristics. At one point he had his technicians increase the power output slightly, and then dial it back again. In the same manner he lowered the power slightly, then increased it to normal again, listening to the orchestra play. There was something in the sound that seemed strangely odd, a resonance in the background that he found most disconcerting. He decided to record the sound to see if he could determine what it was, and the longer he sat with it, the more concerned he became. An hour later he went to see Admiral Volsky about it, finding him with Fedorov in the officer's lounge.

"Admiral," he began, "I must report an anomaly."

"Come in, Chief Dobrynin. What is it? I hope there isn't a problem with the control rod installation."

"No sir, that went quite well, but I have been listening to things to get familiar with this new equipment and… well there is something in the background causing interference."

"Interference? What kind of interference?"

"I've tried to isolate the sound, sir. Of course I first believed it was coming from the reactor equipment itself, but this proved not to be the case. So I moved around the boat a bit, and I listened, thinking it might be something on the submarine."

"And what did you discover?"

"Nothing… that's the bad news, Admiral. It's not coming from the boat either. This prompted me to check with Lieutenant Chernov."

"I'm sorry, Chief. Who is Chernov?"

"He's the sonar man here on *Kazan*, sir. I reasoned a man like this will also have good ears, and so I asked him to listen to my recording and see if he could hear what I was experiencing."

"Did he hear anything?" asked Fedorov.

"More than we might wish to know about," said Dobrynin. "It's that damn volcano, sir. It is continuing to spew thousands of tons of electrically-charged ash into the eruption column. This charged ash can cause interference to radio waves and even render radio and telephone systems inoperative. Chernov says he has been having trouble with his sonar beyond the normal sonic effects. There seems to be some persistent electromagnetic disturbance as well, and it is affecting the undersea environment."

"How is that possible," said Fedorov, "an EMP pulse can't even affect us down here."

"True, that's why we must surface an antenna to use normal radio, otherwise we must rely on the Extreme Low Frequency communications module and our ZEVS broadcast from land. That uses a very low frequency, way down at 82 hertz. Chernov says the boat's communications man has heard this disturbance there as well. Whatever it is, it has aural characteristics. He can hear it on sonar!"

"I see," said Volsky. "Yes, we had the same problem with equipment at Fokino, even in the deep underground bunker. We had to use a secondary land line to contact Moscow. That Demon is still grumbling out there, but what does this mean, Dobrynin?"

"It means I have real doubts about this operation now, sir. I can't hear the nuances of the system with this odd throbbing in the background, and I also suspect that this interference might cause trouble if we attempt to shift from this location."

Fedorov produced a pad device and called up a map. "We are almost 1500 kilometers southwest of that volcano. I know it was a very large eruption, but there was no ash fall at Vladivostok when we landed there."

"It is getting closer," said Volsky. "They tell me there is a seasonal wind change that takes place in October here."

Fedorov knew what the Admiral was referring to, being a navigator and familiar with weather effects in the region. "Yes," he said, "I should have considered this. The Aleutian Lows start to form and we get what they call the Winter Monsoon, northwest winds. They must be plowing into that eruption column and driving it in our direction. It has covered all of Hokkaido Island, and also parts of northern Honshu near the Tsugaru Straits. A plume that size can also have dramatic weather effects."

"And you can *hear* this interference, Dobrynin?"

"I hear a kind of general background resonance from the geothermic and electromagnetic disturbances when I am listening to the reactor on headphones. Not here, not now as we speak. I hear it when I listen to the data in the reactor room. I'm worried, sir."

"In what way?"

"Well... to do my job I have to listen to some very subtle sound fields... sound caused by turbines, and steam moving through the system, the coolant water, the servo-mechanical noise, and the sound of the reaction itself. I'm not sure I can hear things well enough under these conditions. I'm not sure I can control the displacement."

Fedorov looked at him with a stubborn expression. "Are you certain, Chief?"

"It was worse earlier, when we were northeast up the coast and closer to the Kuriles. There I could hear the interference on a number of system monitors. It is not as bad here, but I can still perceive it, and it has the effect of someone playing music while you are trying to tune your instrument. You cannot hear the subtle harmonics. I have tried to adjust by accounting for the disturbance in the background, but at times we get a strong emission, a real deep rumble that overshadows everything, and should that happen in the midst of our shift, particularly when I am trying to make an adjustment... well I don't know what to expect."

"What if we got further from the eruption, sir?" Fedorov suggested the obvious. "There isn't much sea room here, but we could still move southwest towards Korea and see what conditions are like there. We could lie off Yonhung-Man Bay near Wonson. That's about as far west as we can get, and it would put us nearly 2000 kilometers from the eruption."

"Very well, I will speak with Captain Gromyko and see what we can do. It would mean entering the Korean Eastern Sea Command region, and the North Koreans are not the most reliable group these days. China thinks they can control that snarling dog, but I have my doubts."

"Those extra 500 kilometers might make the difference, sir," said Fedorov. "It's worth a try." That distance, and the time it would take them to get there, were going to make a considerable difference indeed, but no one knew it just then.

Chapter 11

Admiral Togo received the news with some dismay. He was in the briefing room aboard the fleet flagship, battleship *Mikasa*, and the signals had just been decoded from Kamimura. As he stared at the characters on the scroll he had just been handed, he could hardly believe what he was reading. All five cruisers had been engaged and damaged badly enough that they were forced to break off and seek shelter in the hidden bays of the Oki Island group. All but one, the armored cruiser *Adzuma*, sustained damage sufficient to force retirement to Maizuru and lengthy repairs. Yet this was not the real shock.

Kamimura had laid a skillful trap for the enemy. His cruisers had sat quietly, their boilers suppressed enough to control smoke as the ships lay hidden behind the islands. He had cleverly posted coastwatchers with good telescopes on the highest hills of the islands, and they had seen the approach of the Russian dreadnought and correctly lit their signal fires. Only then did he order the boilers fully fired to get up enough steam to make the attack speed required. Yet the instant they were seen, the enemy opened fire from extreme long range again, 18,000 meters! The cruisers were taking a pounding as they tried to close, and none got much closer than 9,000 meters. They ran broadside to the enemy at about that range for ten minutes, firing every gun they had, but without much success.

By contrast, the Russian guns had found their targets with uncanny accuracy. Almost every round fired was scoring a hit! This was remarkable in that gunners relied on the tall water splashes from their near misses to adjust fire to get those hits in a running gun battle like this. The Russian gunnery was truly astounding! But the real blow had come later, after the cruisers were forced to flee to the safety of a channel protected by Dozen Island.

Kamimura had one last card to play, his two battleships also lying in wait there in the central bay at the heart of the three smaller islands. They, too were able to successfully surprise the Russian ship when they charged boldly into battle, and this time at least their larger guns were able to open fire at a range of about 11,000 meters. But what he read next seemed incomprehensible. The Russian ship had fired a weapon of terrible power and speed, a kind of flying bombshell, a rocket of some type. Such weapons had been used for centuries, since they were first discovered by the Chinese, but they seemed mere toys compared to the much more accurate fire that could be obtained from rifled cannons.

Yet these rockets were as accurate as the Russian guns! Two had been fired, one striking each of his battleships, and the resulting damage was catastrophic. Dragon Fire, that is what the survivors called the weapons. They flew low over the sea, impossibly fast, then struck with thunderous impact, penetrating side armor and gutting the ship with hideous incinerating flame. Both *Tango* and *Mishima*, two ships captured from the Russians, had been completely immolated and sunk. The entire well planned surprise attack had become a naval disaster. The whole Russian Baltic fleet could not inflict that much damage when we fought them at Tsushima, he thought with some amazement. How was it possible that this single ship could so decisively defeat Kamimura's squadron?

Now the ship was heading south and might soon be approaching the island of Mishima where Vice Admiral Dewa was posted with his 3rd Cruiser Division and Commander Suzuki's 4th Destroyer Division. There were not even battleships in this force, and if Kamimura's fate was any guide, it would easily be destroyed, or brushed aside by this powerful new Russian dreadnought. His plan had rested upon the assumption that each division he deployed would have the ability to adequately engage and defeat this ship, but that was now proved to be entirely wrong. With that thought in mind the Admiral quickly called a staff adjutant to the conference room.

"Sir!" The man bowed politely as he entered, then saluted, civility before military protocol.

"Send a signal to Vice Admiral Dewa. He is to immediately bring his force south to lie off the straits west of Shimonoseki. If he requires fuel I will have colliers waiting for him south of Oshima Island, but it is essential he rejoin Vice Admiral Kataoka's 5th Division as soon as possible."

The man bowed again and rushed to the telegraph room to have the order coded and transmitted. Togo turned his gaze to the map now, considering the situation. The Maizuru squadron under Kamimura was one of the strongest in the fleet! It had six armored cruisers and two battleships, and they were all effectively out of the campaign now, with *Tango* and *Mishima* stricken from the fleet register forever.

It was clear to him that he would need to mass the greatest part of all fleet divisions currently available in these waters. But where? The map would tell the tale. Once Dewa moved south to Oshima and re-coaled his ships, he would order both his division, and that of Kataoka, to a position northwest of Iki Island. Yet after reading the results of Kamimura's engagement, he doubted if even these two divisions could successfully engage this new ship.

Dewa had only four armored cruisers and four destroyers under Suzuki. This was meant to be a screening and reconnaissance force, but Togo now believed the course the enemy would choose was inevitable. Kataoka had a much stronger force with the battleship *Chinyen*, five armored cruisers, and four fast destroyers. On paper it seemed more than adequate to seal off the eastern segment of the Tsushima Straits between that island and Iki. This would allow him to patrol the western segment of the straits with his own squadron… but it would also allow the enemy to decide the location and time of the battle by choosing which strait, which side of the Tsushima Island group they would use to break through.

This was most unsatisfactory, and one look at the map provided him with the only solution that seemed promising. The answer lay in speed and surprise. He would have to send his faster torpedo boats and destroyers out as pickets. All the destroyers had mines aboard, and upon sighting the enemy they could deploy those mines and then flee to a pre-designated rendezvous point. If the enemy pursued them, they would lead the unwary Russian Captain toward the main fleet, and perhaps the Russians would even be unfortunate enough to hit one of their mines.

Where to put the main fleet? Where to mass sufficient power capable of smashing the enemy while also preventing him free passage of the straits? The only place was just off the southern nose of Tsushima Island. Strong eyes watching from Mount Ontake to the north of that island would look for the approach of the enemy, just as Kamimura had been warned by his coastwatchers.

They must choose one side or the other, thought Togo. Mount Ontake is seventy kilometers to the north. If they are spotted from there, that distance gives us the time needed to muster forces at the southern end of the island in the proper channel. Then, each group, my fleet and the squadrons under Dewa and Kataoka, will be in position to join and mutually reinforce one another. Black smoke from Ontake will mean the enemy has chosen the Korea Strait, and white smoke will mean they have taken the eastern approach. The whole fleet will be like a pendulum dangling from the tip of Tsushima Island, and it may swing left or right to cover either approach.

This was a good plan, he thought, but it had one flaw. It would be best if the enemy moved down the eastern side of Tsushima. Iki Island forms a strong outpost there, and we would be fighting close to our home ports. Those waters could also be effectively mined to restrict and hamper enemy movement. Yet if the Russians chose to go west of Tsushima, then what? That portion of the straits is 60 kilometers wide, and if they were to skirt northwest near Korean waters they might easily slip through, particularly if the rumors and reports of this ship's speed are true. They could avoid battle altogether, because a fleet massed off the southern tip of Tsushima Island might never be able to get northwest to find or stop them before they were through.

Suppose that happens, he thought? I must have a plan for that contingency as well. Where would they be going if this Russian Captain perceives this weak point and sets his course as I fear? The answer to that is again right before me on the map. They have brazenly stated they would quarantine the Yellow Sea, so they will certainly have to go there to make good on that boast. This would take them on a course between Jeju Island and Korea, yet those waters will not make for a good patrol zone. They are too wide! It is 500 kilometers from Korea to Shanghai, much too wide for a single ship to patrol. Yes, they could stand off Shanghai and interdict all the commercial traffic from that port, but the Chinese are not our friends, and they will not be re-supplying the Japanese garrisons in Manchuria and Port Arthur.

No. The Russians would have to transit the Yellow Sea and go further north, to the waters between Weihaiwei and Korea, which are only 200 kilometers wide. Even that much sea room would be a lot for a single ship to patrol, but from there they could cause a great deal of trouble. If I were this Captain I would just sit off Dailan or Port Arthur itself and challenge any ship to come or go from those ports.

So that is where this Russian Captain is heading, and that is why I must keep the heavy squadron, with all our remaining battleships, on the western segment of the Tsushima Straits. If he chooses the eastern Tsushima Strait, it will mean I am last to the fight, but I believe the pendulum will swing west. I am certain of this. So if I cannot find or stop them there in the straits, then I will pursue them into the Yellow Sea, where they must surely go.

Then another thought occurred to him. The British China Station had a decent cruiser division at Weihaiwei. The British were also their allies at the moment. If Naval Minister Saito could be persuaded to contact the British, those ships could prove to be very useful in this hunt.

Yes... that is what this has now become. It was a hunting expedition. He was gathering all his available ships into two fighting groups, like the two faithful hounds he would always take with him when he was hunting in the hills. Only this time it will not be a pheasant or two, he thought darkly. This time the fate of the nation is again at stake. Our ships are old, and will soon be obsolete. It will take us time, but we will build new ships like this Russian dreadnought. I must see this ship myself! Only then can I take the full measure of my enemy.

Tango and *Mishima* smashed in a single blow... That news continued to harry the Admiral. *Mikasa* was a sturdy ship. She had taken many hits during the battle of Tsushima, and yet fought on bravely to prevail. Togo had her sister ship *Asahi* with him, and also the battleships *Shikishima* and *Fuji*. Two other armored cruisers, nine destroyers and four torpedo boats rounded out his squadron. Yet these few battleships were the heart of the fleet. *Iwami*, another captured Russian Borodino class battleship, was at Yokohama and too far away to participate in the action. The loss of *Tango* and *Mishima* was sour grapes. Those were Russian ships in the first place, but it would be years in the shipyards before his precious capital ships could be replaced if they were lost here.

That is my dilemma, he thought. I must be bold and aggressive here, but also cautious. I cannot allow this fleet to be destroyed. If that happens, the sixteen battleships of the American Great White Fleet will overshadow Japan and relegate us to the status of a third rate power again in the Pacific.

That thought set his mind on his last reserve, Vice Admiral Uyru's Squadron in the Inland Sea. It was merely a screening force of cruisers and destroyers, no bigger than Dewa's, and sent to show the flag to the Americans when they arrived in Japanese waters. Let us hope Saito is very wrong and the Americans do not have any ideas about bold action of their own. It would be most embarrassing if we were unable to catch this renegade Russian ship, and they came along to finish the job.

He did not know exactly where the American fleet was now, only that it was several days at sea after leaving Hawaii on the 16th of July. It would take them a long week to reach Yokohama and one more day to sail to Kure. The earliest they could be a factor here would be the 24th of July. Tonight Dewa comes south and I should have my dispositions complete by mid-day on the 22nd. If this brigand is coming, that should give me more than enough time to sink this Russian ship and then muster the fleet for action in the event... He did not want to think about the prospect of having to face sixteen American battleships at sea, and there was no reason why that should happen. Even so, he had the distinct feeling his navy was already overmatched by the Americans, and it would be a difficult job to catch up to them, particularly with the battleship construction program still relying on foreign ship builders for many of its planned additions to the fleet in the years ahead.

His flagship *Mikasa* was already a wounded warrior. After surviving the last war with Russia, the ship's magazines had exploded while in home port at Sasebo and the battleship wallowed in 33 feet of water, resting on the bottom until it could be re-floated and repaired. Some of the crew on the hard fought ship said that the spirit of the ship itself exploded in protest over how the war ended, with the treaty of Portsmouth such a grace to Russia. This fallen warrior has already risen from the dead, he thought. Let us hope the Gods are not jealous of her now.

The ship was back in fighting trim again by 1908, 15,200 tons, with her hull painted black and a white superstructure. Her bow was crested with a gold chrysanthemum, and her twin black stacks were detailed with three bold white stripes, just like those on the Admiral's cuff. She was a proud ship, and renowned in the empire now for her glorious battle history.

Behind *Mikasa* the battle line of his squadron stretched out in a long sea train, the skies charred by the dark smoke they left in their wake. The Oki Islands were only 400 kilometers to the northeast. If this Russian ship made twenty knots, and it has always been reported as making at least that speed, then it could be on his horizon in as little as ten hours. If Dewa acted quickly, and steamed south at his best speed from Mishima, he might reach Oshima and the colliers in four hours. Three hours to take on coal is all that could be spared if he was to reach Iki Island and be in a position to join the battle that would surely come the following day. It was going to be a very long night.

Togo sent for his adjutant one more time.

"Send a second message to Vice Admiral Dewa. Tell him he must complete his coaling operation at Oshima no later than 05:00 hours, and then sail to the straits west of Iki Island by 08:00 hours tomorrow morning. He is to join with Vice Admiral Kataoka there, and he must not be late."

"Very good, sir. Baron Dewa has acknowledged your first message and is already heading for Oshima. He inquired concerning Vice Admiral Kamimura. Shall I relate news of that action to him, Admiral?"

"You may tell him the outcome was not to our advantage. Nothing more. The details are not important for the moment. The only thing that is important is that he bring his ships south at his best speed, and be here tomorrow morning, ready for battle."

When the man had left him Togo looked to his tea and saw that it was cold. Here we are at the edge of what may hopefully be the final battle in these waters for a good many years. Armageddon... Is that not the name given to a great final battle? We come off a tremendous victory against Russia, and we will have overwhelming odds for success here again. This should be nothing more than a last resounding peal of thunder from that great storm cloud. But why this darkness in my soul?

He reached for the teapot to warm his cup. At least a man should have hot tea on the eve of Armageddon, neh?

Note: For a map of Admiral Togo's dispositions please visit:
http://www.writingshop.ws/html/k-viii-maps.html

Chapter 12

They watched the Japanese ships burning from the citadel bridge, saw the men go into the water, silent shadows on the HD video display. Yet the crew had seen this before, ships struck and burning, keeling over, capsized, broken by the awesome power of *Kirov.*

"Now we know what a single missile will do to these old ships," said Karpov, emotionless, assessing the situation from a pure military standpoint.

"The fuel load at that short range made for most of the damage, said Rodenko. "A missile moving at that speed, with an armor piercing explosive warhead and that much extra fuel behind it is like an air fuel bomb going off—truly awesome destructive power."

"And we still have ten Moskit IIs left," said Karpov. "The MOS-IIIs are even faster, though not as heavy. This is enough missiles to destroy the entire Japanese fleet, all their battleships and armored cruisers, though, as we have seen, it does not take a missile to deal with the cruiser class ships. Mister Samsonov's gunnery was more than sufficient, and unanswerable."

"As long as the rounds hold out in the magazine, sir. We can't manufacture any more, and we may be here for a good long while."

"I am well aware of that, but once we settle accounts with the Japanese Navy things should quiet down. I was reluctant to use the missiles, but against their heavier armored ships they may be the better choice and do in one blow what the deck guns might take half an hour to accomplish. That said, I was not expecting those ships to be in firing range so I had to take quick action."

"The only reason they even got off a shot at us was because they were lying in wait behind those islands, sir."

"Yes, well I will correct that at once with the KA-40. Get it up with an *Oko* panel and do a general survey of the region to the southwest. I want no more surprises."

They ordered the helo up and Karpov slowed to twenty knots, circling in place while they investigated what had happened to the cruisers they engaged near the main island of Dogo. The data feed came in forty minutes later. The shattered cruiser squadron had slipped into a narrow bay behind Dozen Island, and there they sat while the crews fought the fires and tried to keep the vessels seaworthy. They were putting wounded men ashore, and one cruiser was so badly damaged that the Japanese beached it to prevent it from sinking.

The Captain ordered the helo to sweep south along the coast to see what else might be waiting for them. It was well over the horizon for the next two hours, and it soon found a line of eight more ships heading south at 22 knots, a fairly high speed. Karpov believed them to be cruisers or possibly even small destroyer class ships, and gave them no more thought.

"The heading they are on will take them here," said Rodenko. "Oshima Island. The helo picked up several other surface contacts in that region, presumably commercial traffic."

"It's these other groups that we need to focus on now," said Karpov pointing at the digital readout on the Plexiglas screen. There are ten ships here near Iki Island, and eleven more in the Korea Strait west of Tsushima."

"Obviously they intend to try to interdict those passages."

"So we have a choice now as to which passage to take. Opinions, Mister Rodenko?"

Rodenko knew what he really wanted to say here, that they should not engage at all; that they should turn and withdraw north towards Vladivostok and then get out into the Pacific. Yes, that island Volsky had found for shore leave sounded very good now as opposed to yet another sea battle and scenes on the Tin Man display like those they had just watched. Yet he knew that if he voiced these thoughts all he would get for them was Karpov's arguments to the contrary, and most likely his suspicion as well. So he looked at the situation from a purely military point of view and gave his answer.

"I would not take the passage east of Iki Island. It is too restricted and too close to the Japanese homeland. There will be a good deal of commercial traffic there, small fishing boats, steamers, all potential targets if you insist on this quarantine, but also a lot of fish in the net, and not those I think you are after here."

"And the passage between Iki Island and Tsushima?"

"They have thirteen ships on station there now, Captain, and I think this group of eight ships withdrawing south is going to reinforce that flotilla. They must have received news of our recent engagement, so they are consolidating now and this will give them quite enough to close that passage."

"So they may believe. Then you feel that is their main body?"

"In numbers, perhaps, but not their biggest ships. I looked at the return data, and the signal density readings are not equivalent to those we had on the two battleships we just sunk."

"You can determine ship type from this signal strength?"

"Of course, sir, most of the time. I believe the last of their battleships are here." Rodenko pointed to the Korea Strait now, between Korea and the Tsushima Islands.

"Then their Admiral Togo will be there on the flagship *Mikasa*. He is watching the western strait with their best ships, so that is where he fears we will go. The channel is some 60 kilometers wide, and eleven ships isn't much of a force."

"We could probably skirt north near Korea and slip right through at thirty knots, sir."

"Yes, but that would spoil the fun Rodenko. They would have to follow us into the Yellow Sea, and they could only catch us if we allowed it. There isn't much fire for the new history books we're about to write in a maneuver like that. No. I think we will take our time and sail right up to that island. Then we may choose one side or the other, and engage anything that dares to block our path. He has fought here against the Russians before, and like a sly old hunting dog he is going back to familiar ground. Well, we will not disappoint him by trying to sneak through in the dark at high speed. Leave such maneuvers to the Germans in WWII."

Rodenko felt a stab of discontent with that, the same worrisome feeling that this whole adventure was going to cause far more harm than any of them imagined. His conscience nagged that he should speak up and push on this, yet the boundaries of rank and military protocol were hard barriers, and a Captain on his ship was God in his paradise. Yet Zolkin's words returned to him: '*You must do your duty, but yet you are still Starpom, and second in command here now. Your voice counts, so if you have anything further to say about the matter, you must say it to the Captain's face...*'

"You mean to engage their entire fleet tomorrow, sir?"

"Of course, that is the point of this operation, Rodenko. Once I have neutralized the Japanese Navy, all things are possible. Can you imagine the news finally reaching the Tsar in St. Petersburg? When he learns a single Russian ship has defeated the entire Japanese Navy and restored the balance here, that will certainly raise a few eyebrows. Then we can start getting things done."

"What things, Captain? What is it we will do, exactly, after we put another ten or twelve ships out of commission here? What kind of new history will we be writing?" His voice had just enough of an edge to it to indicate his disapproval, but if Karpov heard it, he chose to ignore it.

"Leave that to me. First we patrol the Yellow Sea and I will send messages to that effect regarding the quarantine. When St. Petersburg realizes Port Arthur is cut off and cannot be resupplied easily, it will seem a ripe plum for the taking."

"Are you certain about that, Captain? This Russia was somewhat of a wild beast after they lost the war in 1905. The country was war weary, and trouble rising in Europe overshadowed everything else. That and the revolution slowly building steam might mean the Tsar won't do anything here at all. Instability was the prevailing condition of the day. There was even a rebellion in Vladivostok and they had to declare martial law there in 1905 just after the war. Uprisings continued off and on through 1907."

"We can use that energy to our advantage, Rodenko. Those uprisings were not well led. They arose from grievances within the ranks over poor treatment, repressive rules and restrictions, bad food."

"You plan on sending the ship's chief chef ashore, sir?"

"Don't be ridiculous. All this tells us is that there is good dry kindling there should the authorities, the Mayor and others, not accede to my wishes. It will be necessary to secure two ports in this region, Port Arthur is the first, and once I deliver that, Vladivostok is the real plum that will fall. I must establish authority there to proceed any further."

"That could take a good deal of time, sir, and you will need strong support on the ground there. The ship can sit in the harbor and use its deck guns to make a show of force if need be, but we can't control the city with 200 naval infantry. The garrison there had 60,000 men! There were units of the 10th Siberian Rifle Division, Cossack Cavalry Regiments, Railroad Brigades…"

"I see you have done some reading in Fedorov's books. The obvious thing to do is to recruit those units to our banner. Well, there will be time enough to choose the best course after this naval battle is won. But unless we do win it, none of those options present themselves. To win you must fight, Rodenko. That should be obvious. You fight, you defeat your enemy, and then you dance in the wreckage. I know that sounds cold to you, even heartless, but it is what I call victory. Are you ready for that? It is easily within our grasp here. You saw how quickly we dispatched that squadron today. We will do the same tomorrow. Look… the island splits his available force in two and allows us to defeat them in detail. So that is exactly what we will do. What do we need to steer to come here?" The Captain pointed at the northern tip of Tsushima Island.

Rodenko was not satisfied, but business was business, and war fighting was his job. He had signed on to a battlecruiser, not a luxury liner. Though he had real misgivings about the Captain's state of mind, and his plan in general, he could see no clear way to impede it at the moment. So he spoke by reflex, his eyes scanning the digital map and making quick calculations, but the sound of his voice seemed hollow to him.

"We might best come west a bit first, steering about 260 until we reach a point in the center of the straits. Then turn thirty points to port and steer 230."

"Make it so, Rodenko. You may also recall the KA-40 now. I think we have adequate situational awareness, and the Fregat system should see anything that tries to get close to us from here on in. If we need helo support to monitor enemy movements on one side of the island or another, we'll launch again later. For the moment, we've lingered here about six hours now. Make twenty knots. How long before we would reach the island?"

"A little over seven hours, sir. It looks to be about 275 kilometers."

"Very well, let's get headed southwest on 260 degrees, and I think the two of us can both get a little rest for the next six hours. You can leave instructions with Fedorov... I mean with the navigator."

Rodenko nodded, noting the Captain's obvious slip of the tongue. "I miss him too, sir, we all do."

"Yes, well it can't be helped now, Rodenko."

"I wonder where he is?"

"Probably still in the Caspian trying to figure a way to get the *Anatoly Alexandrov* home in one piece with Orlov. I can't imagine he's very happy with us now either. Believe me, it was not easy to disappoint him. I was privy to plans you were unaware of long before this. I was there when Fedorov first dreamed up his idea to go after Orlov and brought it to the Admiral. I thought it was foolish then, and it certainly seems foolish now. Orlov was never anything to be concerned about."

"No sir, it seems we are the thing he is most concerned about now, but what if they can't get home?"

"He was trying so hard to right the wrongs and preserve his history intact, Rodenko, but it was clear to me that was no longer possible. Yes, we are the issue now. I was responsible for much of what happened before, and I remain responsible for that now as we speak. Don't you see? It's me—not Orlov, not Fedorov or Volsky, and not even that goddamned war we were trying to prevent. It's *me*. All history now turns in the gyre I spin. I am the man that fortune bows to now. But this is the way it has always been in history. A man sees opportunity and he reaches for it. He makes a difference. He changes things. He becomes great. I am one of those men now. Fedorov could never see what I saw."

Yes, thought Rodenko. A man sees opportunity and he reaches for missiles tipped with nuclear warheads. But he could not voice that now.

"And what about the Admiral, sir?"

"Volsky? He was a good and wise man, but too cautious. He was not really willing to take the big risk that I saw necessary to achieve the victory I speak of. Perhaps he would not approve of my choices here. He may even feel I have betrayed his trust. Yet I see things another way. If you go to war a half-hearted warrior then you come back from it in a coffin or body bag. This is war, Rodenko. It isn't nice and it isn't moral either. Yes, Fedorov's history books are all about to be re-written here. Well, if he does get home he can read all about it, though we will never see him again. By the time he gets there we will all be in our graves."

"Strange to think of it that way, sir."

"Indeed," said Karpov. "This is where we live out our lives now, Rodenko. I hope you are prepared for that. Once we achieve our goals here those lives could be quite comfortable. We'll have power—real power—and not just here on the ship. I intend to establish a strong outpost on land and rally the troops in the east to my flag. Believe me, it will give Fedorov something to read if he gets home."

"Suppose he won't leave it at that, sir."

"What do you mean?"

"He's a resourceful man, and very determined. It took a lot of guts to do what he did, going back with two Marines and crossing half the continent to find Orlov. Suppose he decides he can't allow us to proceed here? Suppose he tries to come back after us?"

"On what? *Varyag* is sunk. *Orlan* is gone. *Admiral Kuznetsov* uses diesel powered boilers. There are no more nuclear powered ships left in the fleet here and only a handful of submarines that were all out to sea when that volcano blew us into 1945. They are probably locked in a death struggle with the Americans even now as we speak."

The Captain was heading for the citadel hatch. "Come then, let's get something to eat in the officer's dining room. I'm always hungry after a good fight."

Part V

The Matador

"In bullfighting there is a term called querencia. The querencia is the spot in the ring to which the bull returns and as the bullfight continues, and the animal becomes more threatened, it returns more and more often to his spot.

As he returns to his querencia, he becomes more predictable. And so, in the end, the matador is able to kill the bull because instead of trying something new, the bull returns to what is familiar. His comfort zone."

— Carly Fiorina

Chapter 13

The death struggle Karpov spoke of was about to begin, though he could not know that from where he sat. The outcome of that struggle would determine much, for Anton Fedorov was, indeed, a very resourceful and determined man. *Kazan* moved southwest as Fedorov suggested, until they were about twenty kilometers off the coast of Wonsan harbor. Dobrynin said the interference seemed to diminish somewhat, but kept asking that they continue west.

"Just a little farther," he said. "I think things are starting to clear up and we can begin our operation soon."

"Yes, well we will soon cross into North Korean territorial waters, Chief, so we can't go much farther west. This is a fairly dangerous area. We will have to go south."

They picked up a few North Korean diesel subs on sonar, but there was no indication that they had been detected in turn. Then something quite unexpected happened. The boat's sonar man Chernov had been listening to a small surface flotilla that had deployed from Wonsan as *Kazan* approached. They were very close to it now, and Gromyko even took the risk of sneaking a peek at it from shallow depth.

"Looks to be a couple of trawlers and one large merchantman," he said to his *Starpom*, Belanov.

"What are they doing out here?"

"Who knows? Perhaps they are fishing, eh?"

There was no evidence that they were up to anything that might cause alarm, until Chernov heard something in the water he could not quite recognize.

"Con. Sonar. I have an undersea contact now, very close, very small, on that same heading, bearing 270 true. It's moving, but very slow."

Gromyko scratched his head. "Too slow to be a torpedo?"

"Too small to be one of their diesel boats, sir."

"It doesn't sound like they are fishing either," said Belanov. "Could they have seen our periscope?"

"I doubt that," said Gromyko. "Could it be a submersible? Do you have any transients from the sea floor?" He was thinking there may be some kind of salvage operation underway, as he had noted cranes on the larger commercial vessel in the flotilla"

"No sir, no transients, but I'm on passive systems now."

"You should have heard it well before this, Chernov. Is something wrong with your ears?"

"No sir. I think it was just launched from that flotilla."

"From one of the surface ships?"

Gromyko was running down the possibilities in his mind. Was it possible that the North Koreans had detected them and floated a mine or depth charge? Could it be a torpedo that misfired? Neither seemed likely, but something occurred to him that made more sense.

"This might be one of those damn mini-subs of theirs," he said aloud. "Chernov, look that up in the database."

"Aye, sir. I have it now… *Yono* Class. Twenty-two meter length and just 130 tons. Maximum speed 8 knots. They use those for special forces operations, sir."

"Could be a training mission," Belanov suggested.

"Could be a pain in the ass," said Gromyko, running his hand over his short cropped hair. "Very well, ease us away from this flotilla. Helm, come right five by five degrees. Make your depth 100 meters." He wanted a gradual turn to starboard with a five degree down bubble to slowly descend to the new depth.

"And just in case they get lucky, the boat will come to battle stations. Quietly please."

"Aye sir," said Belanov. "Battle stations. Our red lights are on."

There were no longer loud claxons or alarm bells on the stealthy submarines of 2021. Alert conditions were signaled visually by lights. In the torpedo rooms very near the main operations center the crews now stood ready to load tubes if ordered.

Then it happened.

A maintenance crew had been completing a routine repair operation aft near the turbines. The engineer finished reinforcing a small weld in the turbine room where a piece of equipment threatened to come loose from the deck with a bad bolt. It was very near the turbine itself, which made it careful, dangerous work. He was using a small acetylene torch and when he went to shut it down the valve stubbornly refused to close. As he moved his other hand to assist, the red lights came on indicating battle stations and he glanced away just long enough to cause him to misjudge what he was doing. His elbow struck a shielded pipe in the confined space and the torch slipped from his hands, still on as it fell to the deck with a harsh clatter. The hot blue jet was pointed right at a bearing housing and the lubricant suddenly caught fire.

Seeing what he had done, the man cursed his bumbling stupidity and called out the alarm. "Fire crews! Turbine room! Now, now, *now!*"

The men were already up for battle stations and now they came running quickly into the turbine room in their bright orange suits, one man still pulling on gloves and trying to fasten his rebreather mask. They each carried fire extinguishers, and though the fire was very small, it was in a difficult spot, and the engineer was wedged into a narrow space, the flames blocking his only means of egress. They were forced to deploy a hose, which made for very noisy business the next five minutes as they struggled to knock down the flames and cool the bearings that had been briefly involved.

Back in the main operating room Gromyko saw the fire light, his eyes registering surprise. "What's going on aft?" He looked at Belanov as the information registered, and the *Starpom* was quick to the comm system to find out what had happened.

"We're making a good bit of noise, sir," said Chernov.

Gromyko could hear it now, a dry squeal where the bearings had lost their lubricant, and metal on metal doused by water and fire retardant was causing a real mess.

"Captain," said Belanov. "Fire in the turbine room. The number six bearing housing was involved. They had to deploy a hose!"

"Damn!" Gromyko swore. Just what they needed now, slinking about beneath a flotilla of North Korean boats out for special operations training. Then it got worse.

"Con. Sonar. Torpedo in the water! Range 3,000!"

It was just their bad luck that the special operations deployment in the mini-sub was there to set up sonobuoys on the seafloor to protect the approaches to the harbor. They had already set down three, and this was buoy four, though they had been unable to hear *Kazan* in the water until her turbine bearings started singing. The mini-sub carried two 533mm torpedoes, both armed and ready, and they fired one down the direction of the sound bearing, thinking they may have already caught a Japanese or even an American submarine trying to penetrate their defensive perimeter."

"Countermeasures! Launch decoys, both to starboard side!"

"Sir, launching countermeasures!"

"Left full rudder! Ten degree down bubble!"

"Sir, my rudder is left full and we are diving."

Their luck was not all bad. The North Koreans had been startled by the sudden discovery of a potentially hostile submarine close by. They did not yet have a good fix on the location, in spite of the noise, which was now abating as the engineers quickly got control of the situation aft. Their torpedo was wide of the mark, and when it tried to home in all it would find was noisy sound decoys.

"Load tubes one and two!" Gromyko did not know what the enemy knew. But what he did know is that he wasn't going to give them an opportunity to fire that second torpedo. The North Korean training exercise was now dangerously real, and he was going to take no chances.

He fired, and he would hit the target dead on, ending the spec-ops training mission and setting the entire North Korean Eastern Sea Command into an uproar.

"That was probably not the best choice," said Belanov.

The Captain nodded in agreement. "Unfortunately it was the only choice. Their second torpedo might have been a winner for them. I wasn't about to let that happen."

"Well we've just poked a stick into the beehive. Everything in Wonsan will be out to sea in no time—helicopters, aircraft, and anything they can float. It's going to draw a good deal of attention to this entire sector."

"Sir," said Chernov. "I'm getting active sonar pings!"

"Active sonar? From what?" Gromyko could not believe the trawlers he had seen could be ASW boats.

"It sounds like sonobuoys, Captain, at least three."

"That's what they were doing here," said Gromyko. "They were setting up a goddamned sonobuoy field and we sailed right into the middle of their operation!"

The spider had been slowly spinning out its web and they had been the witless fly. They might have simply moved off undetected, as was Gromyko's intention, but the mishap aft had changed all that, a split second distraction, an elbow that had bumped a shielded pipe, and the dominoes began to fall. One would tip another, then another, until the situation cascaded to a place no one had intended and no one could foresee. That was the way it always happened, a feather light touch that became a push-point to tip some delicate, unseen balance in the universe and change everything.

Gromyko did not know it yet, but they had just sailed across some intangible barrier, past a tipping point that would have grave consequences for all aboard.

"Head southeast," Gromyko said grimly, steering the only place that seemed reasonable given their planned destination. "Right standard rudder. Come to one-four-zero degrees. Make your depth one-fifty."

"Helm answering, right standard rudder and coming to one-four-zero southeast, depth one-fifty, aye."

The Captain looked at his *Starpom* now. "We can go no farther west under these circumstances. So we'll have to skirt south. Maybe the waters will be quiet enough there for that reactor engineer. And speaking of engineers, I'm going aft to see what in God's name happened back there. You have the boat. Get us southeast to safe water."

They really had no other option now and, as soon as the situation in the turbine room was corrected and they could make speed without noise, *Kazan* moved out, as far and as fast as Belanov deemed prudent.

Yet it did not take long for the bee keepers to notice the hive had been stirred up near Wonsan harbor. US satellites soon spotted the engine heat bloom in two North Korean destroyers on infrared, and saw them putting out to sea with three coastal patrol boats and a corvette. They also noticed the frenetic activity at airfields near Wonsan. The North Koreans were reacting to something that had happened off shore, and word soon started to circulate, with speculation as to just what it was that had Kim's mariners all in a tizzy fit. Photos and analysis went from one desk to another, and orders followed soon in their wake.

* * *

Those orders landed right on Captain Sato's bridge aboard the destroyer *Onami* in the Sea of Japan where he was keeping his watch with two smaller and older ASW destroyers, the *Amagiri* and *Abukuma*. They were out from Maizuru, sailing past the Oki Islands when the orders came in. Without knowing it, their wakes had just crossed that of the battlecruiser *Kirov*, where Karpov had ordered a turn southwest, all of a hundred and thirteen years ago.

As Sato looked out on the relative calm of the sea, it was as if he could perceive that passage, the unseen movement of some dark shadow on the sea, a presence… a feeling of unease and disquiet that stirred in his mind. He was not surprised when a signalman came up, saluting as he handed him a decrypt from the secure EAM channel. It was an Emergency Action Message—what else in these waters? He took it with a sullen feeling of foreboding and read it quietly, his brow betraying concern.

"Looks like the North Koreans think they found a hostile submarine," he said to his Executive Officer, Onoshi.

"One of our boats, sir?"

"Not that I know of. We are the only Japanese force in these waters at the moment. Everything else is down south."

"An American boat?"

"Not from the information I've received. The *Mississippi* is supposed to move southwest to cooperate with our patrol, but they could not be that close to North Korea. They came through the Tsugaru Strait last night."

"What would be there, sir?"

"Possibly a Chinese boat that failed to sign in as it approached Wonsan. It could even be a Russian boat." The process of elimination was very simple math.

"Russian? That's our duty call, Captain."

"Yes, and that's what these orders say as well." He handed his XO the recent decrypt. "We're to move northeast and approach Ulleung-do island. They want us to investigate."

"Dangerous waters, sir. That will put us well within range of North Korean shore based aircraft, and we have no carrier support."

"Read the rest. The South Koreans are supposed to put up fighter cover for us."

"Well what do they think this is all about, sir?"

"You want my opinion? I think it's that Russian submarine they were looking for. There's no reason for the Chinese to be up there, but the Russian would hug that coastline heading south if they wanted to slip a boat through the Sea of Japan. That's why we're out here in the first place. That boat was thought to be in the Sea of Okhotsk for replenishment, but no one knows for certain. The Americans want to know where it is, and we are their eyes and ears out here. If it comes south it would very likely hug the Korean coast, neh? And I don't think they would make reservations with the North Koreans any more than the Chinese would."

"Then the North Koreans found this boat, sir? That seems hard to believe."

"Yes… It does. This submarine would be very quiet. The North Koreans would have to be very lucky to stumble upon it, but that would be very *bad* luck. The report indicates a possible sea engagement."

"The Russians and North Koreans? Why would they tangle with one another?"

"Even two old friends might bump heads in the dark while drinking tea, Onoshi. It was probably happenstance."

"Now it falls to us, sir."

"That it does. I'm going to the chart room. Take us northwest at 25 knots, and see that the other two destroyers are notified. Get the *Seahawks* ready. I want them all available for ASW search in thirty minutes. And one other thing, send a coded message to *White Dragon*. They probably received those orders as well, but they are technically under my command. Inform them of our intentions and tell them to coordinate."

"Aye sir. Right away."

Chapter 14

White Dragon was out on point that day, cruising about 50 kilometers north of the Japanese surface flotilla under Captain Nakamura. Loosely translated, his name might mean "middle of the field," and he was soon to find himself right in the middle of the war that had begun just weeks ago when Japan and China had quarreled over the Senkaku Islands to the south.

SS-503 *Hakuryu*, the *White Dragon,* was the lead boat on forward watch. SS-596 *Kuroshio* was cruising some fifteen kilometers to the southwest. Together they were the horns of the bull that was now moving forward with the three destroyers under Captain Sato as its head.

Hakuryu was a *Soryu* class Diesel-Electric boat, laid down in February of 2007 and commissioned into the fleet in March of 2011. The boat was 36 meters shorter and only a third the displacement of the big Russian sub she was hunting that day, her 4200 tons barely a ripple in the sea when submerged, though it was the largest class sub in the Japanese navy at that time. *Kuroshio* was just a little older, a smaller *Oyashio* class boat commissioned in 2004. Both subs were slow movers on the surface at 12 knots, but could make 20 knots submerged where they spent most of their time at sea.

For teeth, the *Hakuryu* had six HU-606 21-inch (533mm) torpedo tubes waiting for her inventory of thirty Type 89 torpedoes, or sub-launched UGM-84 Harpoon SSMs. *Kuroshio* had the same, though it was a little lighter with only twenty weapons in inventory.

With air-independent propulsion that did not need to rely on a snorkel, the subs could stay submerged longer, and were very quiet. They could not match the deep ocean performance of their Russian quarry, as their diving crush test depth was only 900 feet or 275 meters compared to a published test depth of 600 meters on the *Kazan.*

As fate would have it, the two subs were slowly approaching Ulleung-do island, a prominent rocky outcrop isolated in the sea, with the shape of an irregular pentagon. It was actually the top of a large stratovolcano rising 985 meters above sea level, with sheer crags and odd shaped rock columns about its jagged coastline. The volcano had last vented its wrath over 9000 years ago in a major eruption that deposited tephra as far as central Honshu, 800 kilometers to the east. Now it stood in sullen silence, its rocky toes anchored to the seafloor where the water depth fell off beyond 1900 meters and was even deeper to the southeast where the two subs were patrolling above the Ulleung Basin.

A possession of South Korea, the island was a popular tourist destination, famous for squid fisheries, and sometimes called "Squid Island" due to the fact that the locals would hang out squid to dry on clothes lines, and lay them out on their rooftops all over the island. In 2021 it also housed a small radar installation and a single coast guard corvette operating from the main harbor at Dodong, and so the island's only strategic utility was as a watchful outpost, a character it had gained over a century ago during the Russo-Japanese war.

The small island had also been the source of friction and conflict in centuries past, along with the Liancourt Rocks, a series of small rocky islets at the top of a subsea table mount feature about 85 kilometers southeast of Ulleung-do. The Japanese called the rocks the Dokdo Islets, and they coveted the hides of sea lions who often came to roost there, sunbathing on the rocky outcrops.

An enterprising entrepreneur named Nakai Yozaburo wanted exclusive rights to the lucrative hides, and so he sequestered the islands for his sole use during the years Japan fought its wars with China and Russia. He hailed from the Oki Island group and in 1904 he was able to involve the Japanese Naval Ministry, and particularly Admiral Kinistuki Kenko in the acquisition of the islets from Korea. Seeking a way to monitor the movement of ships out of Vladivostok, the Japanese brushed aside all other claims to the islands and erected a series of watch towers on Oki Island, and both Dokdo and Ulleung-do. They connected them with undersea telegraph cables that eventually linked their naval base at Sasebo to outposts in Korea, and they became a kind of early warning line.

As it happened, Nakai Yozaburo was high in the hills of Oki island in 1908, thinking to take his nap. Instead he heard the call of a sea lion, and thinking to spy this lucrative prey, he saw instead what looked to be a very curious ship approaching, and used that same telegraph system along with smoke signals to warn Vice Admiral Kamimura of *Kirov's* approach. It was that warning that led to the battle off Oki Islands, where history now recorded that a large Russian dreadnought led by a renegade sea Captain fought and defeated the Japanese Second Squadron of cruisers and two old battleships out of Maizuru.

Now, 113 years in the future, another Russian vessel cautiously approached the trip wire draped across these isolated island outposts. A deep channel ran along the edge of an undersea escarpment to the north, known as the Usan Trough, and the Russian Submarine *Kazan* had been cruising beneath a thermocline there, moving south at 25 knots and barely making a whisper in the sea, even at that speed. It was slowly approaching the islands, and the horns of the bull that were moving north to look for it in a loose search pattern. The deadly dance at sea was about to begin.

The senior *torero* aboard *Kazan* was Captain Gromyko, still bothered by the odd accident aft that had caused the fire. He was worried that the brief involvement of the turbine bearing housing was going to come back to haunt him, but glad the boat had been able to easily slip away from the Korean coast undetected. As Ulleung-do was South Korean territory, he was taking no chances as they approached, and brought the crew to battle stations again. It so happened that Admiral Volsky and Fedorov were on the bridge in the operations control center when sonar man Chernov reported the first contact.

"Con. Sonar. Undersea contact, possible submarine, confidence high." He gave the bearing and suspected range, though that would only be refined over time on passive systems. Admiral Volsky looked quietly at Gromyko, noting his relative calm on receiving the news.

"Load all tubes and then the boat will rig for silent running," Gromyko said quietly.

"Aye, sir. Load all tubes and run silent," Belanov echoed the order.

"Well," said Volsky to Fedorov. "This is refreshing—a sea Captain who does not lose his composure with the report of an undersea contact."

Gromyko was studying his digital map now, noting the rising terrain ahead that would eventually breach the ocean's surface to become the Ulleung-do island volcano. "I certainly hope this one isn't planning to erupt any time soon," he said with a grin to the Admiral.

He had been musing over all he had learned when the Admiral and Fedorov disclosed what had really happened to *Kirov*, and why they were on this mission. Now they had the first whiff of what was most likely a Japanese or American sub, and the Captain decided to simply run silent for a time to allow Chernov to monitor and record the contact for further analysis.

"That bearing would put that sub on a converging course," said Volsky.

"Yes, that is correct, Admiral."

"Well, shouldn't we turn to avoid them?"

"We could do so, but if they have also managed to detect us that would only tell them we know where they are. No, I think we will hold this course for a while and see what they do."

At this point Belanov leaned in and whispered something to Volsky. "We call him the *matador*," he said. "You have been in the Northern Fleet, Admiral, but out here, Gromyko is a bit of a legend. He has a certain way of fighting the boat in undersea contacts, and the highest scores of any man in the Pacific Fleet."

"Yes," said Volsky in a low voice. "I have read the Captain's file. I suppose that is why he is aboard *Kazan*."

"Yes sir. I have seen him this way many times. We have just entered the bull ring."

Now the *matador* was walking boldly towards his foe. As with any bull fight, undersea warfare was as much a contest to see what the *matador* himself could endure as much as it pitted man against beast, machine against machine. The famous Juan Belmonte took the blood sport to a new level when he began to introduce his luring capework in close proximity to the horns, deftly twisting this way and that to avoid being gored. He stood with disdain, showing the crowd his grace and skill, and seeming to defy the chance of serious injury or death that had claimed hundreds of men before him. Yet many who attempted to imitate his style in later years were mauled by the horns. There was only one Belmonte, and here in the Pacific world beneath the sea, his name was Gromyko.

"Watch and learn, Fedorov," Volsky whispered.

They cruised for the next twenty minutes, the boat silent and tense, and then Gromyko raised his hand, quietly tapping Chernov on the shoulder at his sonar station. "Listen carefully now," he said. Then turning to Belanov he gave orders for a course change.

"Come right fifteen degrees, five degree down bubble."

"Right fifteen, five degrees down."

The order echoed quietly back from the *Starpom* to the helmsman. They waited, while Fedorov studied the digital map of the undersea terrain with some interest. There were two ways around the volcano, the east gap was between Ulleung-do and a submerged seamount called Anyongbok. From what he could see the sonar data was indicating the course of the undersea contact as moving to close this gap. The turn Gromyko ordered now selected the west gap approaching another deep seamount called Igyuwon. Five minutes passed, then ten, and the time seemed agonizingly slow.

"Any course change on the contact?" Gromyko was at Chernov's side now.

"No sir, I have it steady on 280."

"Very well. Keep listening."

They continued on for some minutes until Chernov gave the Captain an odd look. "Sir… I'm hearing noise… I think it's *us*, Captain. It sounds like that bearing is acting up again."

Gromyko was on the comm panel at once. "Engineering," he hissed. "What's going on in the turbine room?"

The report that came back was most unwelcome. The fire near the number six bearing housing had apparently caused more trouble than a quick cleaning an re-lubrication could address. It was squeaking as it turned, and making audible noise. The Engineer promised to suppress it as best he could with additional lubricant, but to Chernov the sound was as if someone was dragging their fingernails across a blackboard.

"Fire control officer. Receive all data from sonar and plot your best solution to the contact. Ready tubes one and three. Type 65 torpedoes."

"Con. Solution plotted and ready on tubes one and three with Type 65."

Gromyko had a choice that day of using the big carrier killer, the 650mm Type 65 torpedo, or the smaller Type 53 which was mainly used for ASW applications. For reasons he did not take time to explain, he chose the bigger weapon, and no one on the bridge thought a second to ask why.

Chernov was very tense. "Sir, I'm hearing more. I think they heard us as well."

"I'm sure they have," Gromyko said calmly. "They are most likely putting fish in the water at this moment, or they soon will. But we will get there first. Fire tubes one and three. Helm, left standard rudder—port five by five."

"Firing now!"

The torpedoes were away, ejecting cold as the submarine executed another turning dive, and then their engines started up and they went streaking away towards the unseen enemy contact.

* * *

Aboard the *White Dragon* things were about to get very interesting, and very dangerous. The bull was advancing in a predetermined search pattern. The two submarines were the horns, well out ahead of Sato's surface ships. Sato's group was the head, and the tail was the SGN *Mississippi*, moving quietly to the scene from the northeast. Captain Nakamura was cruising to his assigned position in the east undersea transit gap, where he thought he might lie in wait for any adversary attempting to skirt the island volcano of Ulleung-do. His sonar man was listening very intently, but he had heard nothing until he suddenly announced a possible submarine contact.

"Undersea noise, Captain. Very audible, and bearing 262 degrees."

The Captain glanced quickly at his chart, noting the bearing and approximate position of the contact and quickly discerning that someone was making for the west gap undersea channel. "Contact Naval Operations and pass this contact data. Battle stations! Load tubes two and four!" Nakamura wasted not a second, but he was already late.

"Sir! I have one, now *two* torpedoes in the water and running true down 260!"

"Firing Control Officer, do you have a solution?"

"Sir, we do not have a lock yet!"

"Then fire down that bearing, minus ten degrees. Now!"

The *White Dragon* fired in return, a bearing only attack that did not have high odds of success, and Nakamura was not going to wait around to see which boat had the better firing solution. Assuming the enemy was heading south, he had subtracted ten degrees from his firing bearing, hoping to get his torpedoes to a place the enemy might be when they arrived to begin their active sonar search for the target.

"Countermeasures! Starboard side noisemakers. Do it now!"

The Firing Officer ejected their decoys which spun out in a wildly cavitating pattern designed to attract any incoming torpedo. Now it was time to be somewhere else, and as inconspicuously as possible. But the noisemakers would linger, moving at a pre-programmed speed to lure in the enemy fish.

"Ten degrees down bubble. Make your depth 200. Speed fifteen."

"Sir, diving planes are ten degrees down and we are passing through 180 meters. Speed fifteen knots."

Both subs had fired, one with a much better solution than the other, as the *White Dragon* had been roused from its undersea slumber by the sudden noise, while *Kazan* had been listening to and tracking the enemy for some time. That difference could be decisive, but now it was up to the four torpedoes in the water, rapidly accelerating and beginning to search for the targets they had been unleashed to find and destroy.

A map of this engagement can be viewed at :
http://www.writingshop.ws/html/k-viii-maps.html

Chapter 15

The Japanese Type 89 torpedo produced by Mitsubishi Heavy Industries was a wire guided, active/passive homing torpedo with a 267 kilogram warhead. It could dive to 900 meters, well below the crush depth of most submarines, and had a range of 50 kilometers at 40 knots, or 74 KPH. It was going to have to go all of twenty kilometers if it was to find the Russian sub, and so it was going to be another fifteen minutes before it reached the hot zone where it might get a definite lock on the target to make its final run.

The wire trailing out behind it allowed two-way communication with the Firing Control Officer on the *White Dragon*, who was still receiving more refined location data on the contact from sonar. The squeaky bearing may have given away *Kazan's* initial location, but engineers were quick to the scene with lubricants as an expedient measure to quash the noise again. Yet now that the Russian sub had fired, the additional sonic information helped the Japanese get a better ear on its general location.

Countermeasures in the water there fired by *Kazan* bloomed like a rose in the sound field, but a well trained human ear could recognize those sounds and feed instructions to the torpedo via the wire to ignore them. The enemy would not be there in the middle of that rose, but elsewhere, lurking off the bearing or speeding away, leaving the noise at its back in an attempt to outrun the torpedo. The contact had been heading south, and so the Fire Control Officer made a course correction, sending his fish to a place he expected the enemy should be in another fifteen minutes.

The Russian javelin was the Big Type 65 torpedo, heavier and faster than its adversary with a 450kg explosive warhead and a speed of 93KPH. It also had a good long range of 50 kilometers, which is why Gromyko had selected it as opposed to his Type 53 weapon, which maxed out at 22 kilometers. At a firing range of 20 klicks, the Type 53 had little margin for error where fuel was concerned, and it was also slower at 83KPH.

The Captain's weapon of choice was also going to make a difference in the engagement. It could fire farther, hit harder, and was quicker to the target zone than the Japanese torpedo. The Type 65 was going to be in the hot zone well before the enemy's weapon became a threat, heating up Nakamura's day at the critical time when his own torpedo was attempting to lock on to the Russian sub. To make matters worse, Gromyko had turned on a bearing that was taking *Kazan* away from the pursuing Type 89s, and he had the speed and power to nearly match the torpedo.

The bottom line in all of this was that the Russian torpedoes had a distinct advantage. Their target was well located and it was approaching them. The Japanese Type 89s were bearing fired, and being nudged to the expected target zone by the best guess of a human operator. As *Kazan* sped away, it was also beginning to put the rising volcanic seamount that became the Ulleung-do island between it and the oncoming torpedo. As the minutes passed it soon became obvious that the Japanese fish were not going to find their quarry that day. The question now was whether the Russian torpedoes could effectively locate the target, for the Japanese sub was also gliding away off its firing axis and attempting to become a hole in the water that would make it disappear.

The big torpedoes came in twelve minutes after firing, and while one elected to go after *White Dragon's* noisemakers, using its passive sensors to home in, the other went active and soon found what it thought was a possible contact. It adjusted its course and ran true, and forced another frantic round of countermeasures aboard the *White Dragon* that barely saved the boat.

The second Type 65 had a choice of a fairly robust sound signature or a quiet echo behind it, and it chose the former, exploding about 50 meters ahead and devouring the noisemakers. The resulting concussion shook up the Japanese boat severely and, in the ensuing wild minute after, they lost their tenuous sonic leash on *Kazan*, which had now put the undersea volcanic mound between itself and the *White Dragon*. The boat keeled to one side, lights flickered, and equipment rattled throughout the sub. Men were thrown from their feet, and anything lose went flying through compartments all over the boat. Fragments of the warhead raked the hull like buckshot, one larger piece of shrapnel lodging in the nose of the boat, but the hull was not breached.

Nakamura was lucky to be alive, and the sweat on his brow was ample testament to the tension. One look at his chart told him what had probably happened. The enemy was still running south, through the west gap on the other side of the island. There was no way his slower boat was ever going to catch up now, and he did not think he would get a second shot. That decided, his only play was to turn south now himself, and take the eastern gap between Ulleung-do and the Anyongbok seamount. If nothing else, he would be moving to a position to better coordinate with *Kuroshio*, which was moving northwest at that very moment from a position well south of the island.

Word was being flashed to Sato's surface action group, and the *Seahawks* were ready to take wing and join the fray. Far to the east, the *Mississippi* was hearing it all as well on their own excellent passive sonar systems, and Captain Donahue decided it might be nice to join the party.

"Looks like we found our bad boy out there," he said to his XO.

Chambers nodded in the affirmative. "They're well west," he said. "Probably running down the other side of Ulleung-do. Any chance the Koreans can bird dog for us?"

"PACCOM says they're a little more than edgy with the way the North Koreans are stacking up on the border. No, I don't think they want a piece of this. To be honest, the Japanese would rather not tangle with the Russians either. They were supposed to flush this bird for us, and that's what they did. I think we'd best get *Mississippi* west before this boat slips away."

"It'll go dark while its behind that undersea massif," Chambers pointed at the map. "There's a lot of shadow there in the sound field."

"Which gives their skipper a number of choices. He can pull an about face and head north again. If he does, we'll lose him, which is fine by me in this situation. As long as we keep them away from our planned operations to the south we've done 90% of our job."

"What if he stays on a heading south?"

"Then game on. In another hour he should be about 10 klicks southwest of the island unless they're running full out. If we push it we just might get close enough for a decent shot. Let's steer about 262 degrees and crank it up. The Japanese will have a diesel boat off our port side and another to our north. We should have *Seahawk* support from their destroyers as well. If this contact insists on pushing south, we'll have one hell of a picket line moving in to nail the bastard."

"Very well sir, 262 it is. Shall I run in Wiki mode or put it on overdrive?"

"Ahead full battle speed," said Donahue. The *Virginia* class had a publically advertised speed that anyone could look up on Wikipedia, but its real numbers were never revealed. It was time to move, and *Mississippi* had the speed to get into the action, which is exactly what she did.

* * *

"**Admiral,** we are going to be in a situation if we stay on this heading much longer." Gromyko decided he had better give Volsky the bare knuckled truth. "I don't think we'll be bothered by that last sub again, but it will have signaled our position, course, and speed to anyone else nearby, and we could be visited again soon. They might have a P-3 up, and that surface action group is obviously heading our way. They'll have helicopters."

Chernov had been listening intently as they slipped behind the imposing undersea flanks of the Ulleung-do volcano. He soon heard the telltale sound of surface ships approaching, and they knew these were most likely Japanese ships on ASW patrol, most likely part of a screen to guard the approaches to the Tsushima Strait.

"What is the situation with your reactor engineer?" Gromyko wanted to know the score.

Fedorov had been in contact with the reactor room at Volsky's request and relayed the news. "Dobrynin says things have cleared up considerably, sir. We're well south now. I think he could run the procedure any time, but that would mean we could use no more than two thirds power."

"Is that acceptable, Captain Gromyko?" Volsky was obviously concerned given the current situation.

"How long does this procedure take?"

"About an hour," said Fedorov. "It took longer aboard *Kirov*, but Dobrynin says he has to alter the tempo of the retraction process to achieve the harmonics he's after."

"Then do it now. Our only other option is to turn about and head north. But if we have to come south again for any reason, I think the other side will be much better prepared. I can give you an hour while we're behind that volcanic massif. After that we'll be in the basin and that is fairly open water. It would be good to have speed if they should find us there again."

"Alright," said Volsky. "I don't think we want to reverse course now only to find out Dobrynin reports this sound he hears again. Go, Mister Fedorov. Tell the Chief to begin, and you may keep us informed." The Admiral turned to Gromyko as Fedorov sped away for the reactor room.

"Captain," said Volsky, "some years ago I took my young nephew with me to Paris and we toured the Disneyland park there."

Gromyko raised an eyebrow, wondering what this was about.

"He wanted to ride the runaway train on Big Thunder Mountain, but when he got a look at the train cars at the end of the ride, and the astonished look on everyone's face, he began to get cold feet. Well, I told him what I must now tell you. We came all this way and you just bought the ticket. Now you're going to take the ride."

Gromyko smiled. "I'll try to keep the train on the tracks for you for a while, Admiral."

"That is good to hear. But what I must also tell you is this..." Volsky lowered his voice. "We aren't really sure this will get us where we hope to go. Rod-25 has had a fondness for the 1940s. Dobrynin believes he can hear the music—that is how he puts it—some kind of nuclear song that will control the displacement if he can achieve the same harmonics during the procedure. But we could end up anywhere."

"I understand, sir."

"I'm glad someone does, because even after bouncing back and forth five or six times I'm still not sure I can believe what happened. Let us hope we have good luck in the next hour." Yet no sooner had he finished saying that when another voice called a warning.

"Con, sonar. Undersea contact, possible submarine. Confidence high. The bearing is 150."

It was the last thing Gromyko wanted to hear just then. Volsky gave him a wide eyed look. "I can countermand that order, Captain. Just say the word."

"No... I think we can proceed," said Gromyko. "What is the heading on that contact Chernov?"

"Listening... Listening... I make it 262 southwest, sir. Moderate speed, perhaps no more than 12 knots, but this is an approximate reading. I will need active sonar to verify that, or a lot more time if we stay passive."

The Captain folded his arms, as if he might be wrapping himself in a cape, lost in his own inner muse for a moment. Something was creeping across his intended path southeast of his present position, most likely another Japanese diesel boat.

"Does this sound like a turtle, Chernov?"

"Yes sir. I think it is."

"Very well, keep listening and feed data to the Fire Control Officer as before."

"A turtle?" Volsky did not understand what he had just heard.

"That's what the Japanese call their older diesel boats, Admiral, *Dongame*, which means languid turtle. Their officers have a self-deprecating way of talking about their work, and they call themselves 'Turtle Boat Captains.' We've got one paddling our way at 12 knots, but if he sticks his neck out too far he just might get a nasty surprise."

For the next ten minutes they drifted silently through the quiet undersea world, each man lost in his own thoughts, listening to something whispering at the edge of infinity, or so it seemed. Chernov was listening to the subtle disturbance of a very quiet submarine moving stealthily through the water somewhere in the darkness ahead. Gromyko was listening to his boat, and hoping he would not soon hear the dry squeal of a bad bearing again anytime soon. Volsky was listening to the voice of his wife in his head, imagining her face as she would sit at the table stirring honey into her tea, and he missed her dearly. Now he was about to vanish again, or so he believed, and leave her just that extra measure away from him, long years, long decades this time if they were successful.

And down in the reactor room Dobrynin raised his hand and signaled his technicians to begin the rod retraction, while Rod-25 waited above in its containment canister, ready to be dipped into the soup. He did not know whether he should choose an odd or even rod this time, but decided in the end to match his exact selection for the shift they made to 1908 aboard *Anatoly Alexandrov*. That was an odd number, always associated with a backward shift. He had just brought them all home by replacing rod number eight on the *Anatoly Alexandrov*, so now he chose rod seven here on *Kazan*, lucky seven. Then he listened, waiting for the sound to become the familiar vibration he had heard so many times before. It would take thirty minutes to withdraw the number seven rod, and all the while Rod-25 would be moving in tandem into the open rod position in the reactor core.

The procedure was a slow game, centimeter by centimeter as one rod lifted while the other descended. As soon as Rod-25 began to move, he heard the song. It was a high chorus of angels singing from above, and their voices deepened, spiraling down and down, ever so slowly. Then there came another voice, as though someone in the audience of the theater had decided to sing along with the choir. He heard the odd harmonic, and decided to try and vary the speed to see if it would be affected. Yes, he could hear the voice change as he sped the process on, and then change in tone when he slowed it down again.

What to do? He had never heard this voice in his choir before. Should he stop the procedure? No, that was impossible now. Once the music began they had to see it through the entire score. So now he closed his eyes, concentrating, trying to shut out all other sounds but the song of this reactor. He had listened to twenty or thirty similar machines in his day and this one was no different, except that it was deep under water, and it was not cooled by pumps to mute the sound a reactor on a ship would naturally make.

Yes! That was it! There was an entire section of his orchestra missing here, that was all. The pumps! He could hear where they were supposed to be playing in his mind, but there was silence in those intervals now. Of course! This was a natural circulation reactor, which is why it was so very quiet. The voice he was hearing had always been there before, but it was overlaid by the sound of water pumps before. If he could just add those sounds back in his mind, and hear what his reactor should sound like with the pumps thrumming like a section of brass behind his strings... Yes! That was what he had to do, and so he closed his eyes again, settling deeper into his chair as he listened.

"Increase to mode three," he said calmly to his technician.

"Mode three, sir."

"Note your flux level and tell me the instant you read anything in the yellow meter spectrum."

"Aye, sir. We are reading green."

Part VI

Gathering Storm

"I have been riding with the storm clouds and have come to earth as lightning and rain. There is no mercy at the edge of my storm, and no shelter from the wrath I now bring."

— *Sitting Bull*

Chapter 16

"**Gentlemen,** the Japanese seem to be somewhat worked up over an incident lately reported in the Sea of Japan," Captain Baker was addressing his bridge crew aboard HMS *King Alfred*. "We have just received word of large fleet movements in the Tsushima and Korea Straits, and Admiral Meux has informed us that this squadron is to sail forthwith to observe the situation. Mister Tovey…"

"Sir." Tovey stood just a little taller, hands folded behind his back and seeming to be at attention in spite of the "at ease" permission given by the Captain. "You will supervise posting of the lookouts, and stand watch on the weather bridge. Lookouts should be especially vigilant once we pass Jeju Island. We have no specific details but the gist of the situation is this, gentlemen. The Russians and Japanese seem to be at it again. Several engagements have been reported describing a large Russian dreadnought."

"A dreadnought, sir?" Tovey was surprised to hear that a ship of that class would be in these waters, particularly after the beating the Japanese gave to the Russian Navy a few years back.

"Yes, a dreadnought, Mister Tovey, reported to be as big and unsavory as our own ship by that name. We've no specific information, but if this is the case, then it must have arrived from the Baltic or Black Sea in recent weeks."

"But wouldn't it have passed through Suez, sir?"

"If it was as big as HMS *Dreadnought*, Mister Tovey, it would be too large for the canal, as you should well know. That said, and given the fact that we had no notice of this ship's arrival in these waters, a transit there seems unlikely. It must have gone round the Cape of Good Hope, and the general notion is that it was sent here as a reinforcement for the Russian cruisers remaining in Vladivostok."

"And this ship is operating alone, sir?"

"My, my, Mister Tovey. Full of questions this morning, are we? Yes, it is operating alone, and it appears to have ruffled quite a few skirts of late. We've been ordered by Admiral Meux to get down there to the straits and have a look around, and you, Mister Tovey will do the looking."

"Very good, sir."

The British China Station, established in 1865, had seen ships come and go, assigned as the situation warranted, year after year. In the volatile years between 1901 and 1905, as many as six battleships might have been anchored there, but now the station consisted of a smaller armored cruiser squadron. They were already a day out of port at Weihaiwei, and HMS *King Alfred* was leading the way south through the Yellow Sea.

Young Lieutenant John Tovey was soon out on the weather bridge, the wind in his face and eyes squinting through binoculars. As the squadron completed a wide turn, he looked back at the graceful line of ships, the skies charred up with smoke from their full coal bunkers. Behind the flagship, the three *Monmouth* Class cruisers assigned to the squadron followed in line, HMS *Kent*, HMS *Bedford* and then HMS *Monmouth* herself. These were 9,800 ton ships with a battery of fourteen 6-inch quick firing guns. In their wake the end of the tail wagging behind was HMS *Astraea* and HMS *Flora*, smaller at a little over 4,300 tons each. The squadron dispatch ship HMS *Alacrity* had been left behind, as it was an older clipper style light cruiser that could make only 17 knots.

The squadron seems in a bit of a hurry, thought Tovey. I hope I wasn't out of place with my questions on the main bridge this morning, but a Russian ship the size of *Dreadnought* coming all this way around the cape without being noticed was most irregular. We have ships posted all along that route, at the East Indies Station, Colombo, Indian Ocean and Australia. Surely someone would have seen and reported on this ship. Well, now that I've been named the lookout watch officer of the deck, we'll amend that oversight. I want to be the first British officer to sight this ship… that is if the Japanese don't put it on the bottom of the sea first.

Tovey did not yet have much experience at sea, but he was already developing a nose for the smell of battle. He could feel something, a strange presentiment of foreboding in the back of his mind and an odd feeling of déjà vu. It almost seemed to him that he had been in the vanguard of other squadrons, hunting at sea for another strange, unaccountable sea raider—that he had done this all before.

Little did he know that many such adventures at sea awaited him. He would stand a watch in the cold icy waters near Iceland when the Germans tried to push *Bismarck* through in 1941, and he would see that ship to a timely end aboard *King George V*. Then, a year later, he would get news of yet another strange raider heading for the Atlantic, and at a most unfortunate time when the Prime Minister, Churchill himself, was putting to sea for a conference with the American President Roosevelt. Tovey knew none of that, however, as it was all long years away in a distant tenuous future, yet somehow, he could feel it all coming, just as he could feel this strange Russian dreadnought coming as well. And through it all he had the odd feeling that he was somehow fated to meet this ship at sea, though he did not know why he should think this.

His muse was interrupted when Captain Baker stepped out onto the weather bridge for some air and was again at Tovey's side.

"Fair weather for sighting, Tovey," said the Captain. "I trust you've posted good eyes on the main mast."

"I have, sir, Jameson and Wilson—a pair of sharp eyed hawks."

"Good then. Word is this Russian ship is a big fellow, so they will have no trouble spotting it. But mind your recognition silhouettes as well. Your first sightings will more than likely be Japanese ships."

"Of course, sir."

"Well then, here's another bit of news for you. The Americans might be sticking their thumb into the pie as well. President Roosevelt has apparently altered the itinerary of the Great White Fleet. This Russian ship fired on an RMS mail ship out of Shanghai bound for Vancouver and three U.S. citizens were killed. That gets Mister Roosevelt a bit worked up, and he's cancelled the fleet's port-of-call in Manila and ordered it to these waters instead."

"Indeed, sir? That is a rather important development."

"Yes it is. With all of sixteen battleships it will be the most powerful naval force in the region. Oh, I suppose the whole of the Japanese fleet would overmatch it, but for sheer, concentrated power in one place, sixteen battleships will outgun anything the Japanese have, and anything we have here as well. We might have made a better show of things some years ago when *Canopus* led the whole of her class out here, but now the squadron in our wake will have to do. We've no quarrel with the Americans, of course, but I tell you this as officer of the watch so that you might be aware of it should a long line of ships suddenly appear on your horizon."

"I see, sir. Any idea where the American fleet is heading?"

"They were scheduled to visit Yokohama, but that would put them on the wrong side of the island for anything developing here. My guess is that they'll steam south of the main island, possibly into the Inland Sea, or even further south. I wouldn't be at all surprised to hear you report them off your starboard bow, Mister Tovey. Do be vigilant."

"I will, sir. And thank you for informing me."

Well, well, well, thought Tovey. This was another interesting development. He didn't think he'd get a look at the Great White Fleet until much later in the year, but now the whole itinerary was turned on its head.

"An interesting stew on the boil, sir," he said.

"Yes, Japanese ships, American ships, British ships, and this Russian raider all in the mix. Very interesting, unless someone tips the kettle."

* * *

The lighthouse of Ko Saki was one of the oldest under Japanese management, and sat at the edge of a sheer cliff of striated black stone on the southern edge of Tsushima Island. It was built to warn ships skirting the edge of the island, or approaching the small fishing hamlet of Izuharamachi Azamo, but now it served as a beacon to rally the gathering squadrons of the Imperial Japanese Navy.

Ten ships under Vice Admiral Kataoka were already there, waiting in the restless waters, their flags and masts stirred by the prevalent rising winds that were common here. They were blowing from the southeast that night, chasing dark clouds across the sharply defined morning crescent moon where it hung low on the sea just an hour after midnight. The sun would rise in about four more hours, and with it would come Vice Admiral Dewa, who had signaled that he now led his squadron of eight cruisers and destroyers here to the rendezvous point as ordered.

Dewa was restless that early morning, awake on the bridge after having taken a long sleep the previous afternoon and evening. He was still troubled by the news that Vice Admiral Kamimura had been unable to deal with the Russian dreadnaught. Knowing Kamimura's squadron was bigger and more powerful than his own whispered the quiet meaning in the orders he received the previous day. He was to be in the straits west of Iki Island by 08:00 hours this morning, and he was early, eschewing the coaling operation at Oshima as he had topped off his holds much earlier, and had ample fuel.

The journey south sighted an unusually large number of fishing boats, and that had proved revealing as well. There were many eyes in the straits now, and some of those boats held more than fishermen. They were joined by six torpedo boats scattered in the wake of his squadron, and more eyes were on the hills and coastlines of every island in the region. All would be searching the gray dawn for any sign of the Russian ship, and Dewa had little doubt that battle would soon follow any sighting.

Now he was to join with Vice Admiral Kataoka south of Tsushima Island and be in a position to move either east or west depending on what that sighting would reveal of the enemy's intentions.

It will be in the Korea Strait this time, he thought. The Russians have bad memories of their last visit to Tsushima. Then again, if this ship is trying to avenge the humiliating defeat they suffered in those waters, it might just return there again just to taunt us. Good. That would mean that my squadron would be the first engaged, with Kataoka behind me and then Admiral Togo swinging down from the Korea Strait. By the time he arrives I will be ready to hand him news of another victory here.

Tonight he was to find Kataoka and meet with him aboard his Squadron Flag. To do so he elected to leave his flagship with his squadron and board one of the faster destroyers he had with him, the *Asagiri.* More talk, he thought. Well, the faster I get there the quicker I will get back. Then we can do the fighting. But when he reached the anchorage near the lighthouse at sunrise, and took the longboat over to the old battleship *Chinyen*, he was discourage to learn that no engagement was to be permitted!

"What do you mean, Kataoka? What are we here for then?"

"We are to spot this ship, report its heading and intended course, and to move away from it, to this location hidden by the headland of Tsushima Island."

"To do what? Go fishing? Enjoy the scenery? Watch that stupid lighthouse spin round and round? It's time we went after this Russian Captain and settled the matter!"

"I know that is what is in your mind, Dewa, but this signal comes directly from Admiral Togo. We are to wait here, and outlying ships should attempt to lead the enemy here as well. Mines are to be placed on the approaches to the headlands, and then, when Admiral Togo arrives with the First Division, we will all engage the enemy as one."

It was very much like Togo, to gather all his hounds together before the hunt. To spin out lines of fast destroyers and torpedo boats as taunting lures, beckoning the enemy to advance across his cleverly laid minefields. But Dewa remembered the sharp crack of the guns, the smell of the battle, the anger in Tsushima Strait those years ago when they had met the whole Russian Baltic fleet and dismembered it, ship by ship.

"This is but one ship," he said, shaking his head. "Why must Togo mass the whole of the Imperial Navy to face it? My squadron alone should be more than enough."

"That is what Vice Admiral Kamimura thought," said Kataoka. "Now *Tango* and *Mishima* are gone and he has one cruiser laid up in port, another beached on Dozen Island and four others black as charcoal from the fires set by enemy guns!"

Dewa was astonished to hear this. "What? *Tango* and *Mishima* gone? Where?"

"They were sunk, Dewa."

"I cannot believe this… It was confirmed?"

"The final report was sent three hours ago to Admiral Togo by wireless telegraphy. Kamimura himself was wounded! So do not be so eager to rush in with your four cruisers and four destroyers. This report has everything to say why Admiral Togo has issued these orders."

Dewa frowned, troubled by the news. "Then the reports are true," he said darkly. "Some of the fishing boats we encountered told us word has spread all down the west coast of Honshu. It is said this ship was a great sea dragon, a monster that could breathe fire and devour an entire ship in one blow."

"This is what we have heard…" Kataoka lowered his voice now, so that none of the younger staff officers would hear him. "*Tango* and *Mishima* were struck by something we do not yet comprehend. They died in minutes, burned within and without in terrible flame. It was said that a flaming lance was thrown at them by this Russian ship, faster than an arrow, and deadly accurate—a *rocket* weapon. We have never faced anything like this. Now do you understand why Togo disposes the fleet as he does? He wishes to mass our fist against this enemy, to make certain the victory that will surely be ours."

"I would see this with my own eyes first," said Dewa stubbornly. "Let them throw their fire arrows. As for me, I will use my cannon and torpedoes."

Kataoka smiled. "You are early, Dewa, but yet your squadron still lingers in the strait. I know you all too well, my friend. You are hoping yours will be the first to spot and engage this Russian ship. Well remember the old saying: be careful what you wish for ..."

Dewa looked at him, with a disapproving frown, but something in Kataoka's eyes disturbed him. If he did not know the man better, having seen him in battle before, he would think it was fear in those eyes, though he could never say as much to Kataoka.

Yes, I want battle, and I will find one soon enough, he thought. That was the way of things. But I will not be frightened by fisherman's tales of sea dragons and fire lances. No. I will see this ship for myself, and watch as my gunners bring it to heel.

Or I will die trying.

Chapter 17

"**Now** we choose," said Karpov as he stood on the bridge examining the situation map. They had reached the northern tip of Tsushima Island and now had to decide their course, either left down the Tsushima Strait or right through the Korea Strait. The Captain seemed in good spirits, the rest he had taken doing him some good, and he was ready for the action ahead.

"From the latest *Oko* panel radar data, it appears that they have pulled back to protect the straits. By assembling at the southern end of this island."

"That is understandable," said Rodenko. "As we come south they will have amble opportunity to spot us from any of these islands. And note all these clutter contacts." He pointed to the Tsushima Strait, indicating many small contacts scattered throughout the sea there. "They are probably trawlers or fishing boats…commercial traffic, but some may be military. It's a thin veil, and nothing that could impede us, but if we take that channel we will be seen in time."

"Then we have the Korea Strait, a much more likely approach," said Karpov. "It avoids all this clutter you speak of and is a much more direct route to the Yellow Sea."

"You believe they are expecting us to take that route, sir?"

"I do," Karpov smiled. "Which is precisely why we will steer for the Tsushima Strait instead."

"You give up the element of surprise. They will spot us much more easily there."

"No, Rodenko, I *create* the element of surprise. You said yourself that they have assigned their heavier ships to the Korea Strait, west of the island. That is where Admiral Togo will be. I would love to sail there directly and engage him, but that would leave all these other ships unfought in the Tsushima Strait. So I will do what Togo does not expect. I will sail boldly into those waters, destroy his squadrons there, one by one, and then, when he comes rushing to the scene from the other side of the island, the surprise will be complete."

"I don't understand, sir. He will be well aware of our movements."

"Yet surprised to see half his fleet burning when he gets there. Then we fire up the *Moskit-IIs* and I will make a quick end of his battleships. The rest is done with mirrors."

Rodenko still seemed troubled, his expression hardened, eyes betraying his concern. "Are you certain we must do this, Captain?"

Karpov gave him an exasperated look. "How many times must we go over this, Rodenko? What is your problem with this? You would rather we take a vacation cruise here?"

"It's just that… Well I was thinking about all this last night, sir. Suppose we do what you plan and smash the Japanese fleet here. Suppose it does have the effect you hope for, and Russia returns to the Pacific as a great power. Japan might eventually be driven from Manchuria and Korea."

"Yes, and led by *Kirov*, our navy becomes the master of these waters."

"Except for the Americans, sir."

"The Americans?"

"Their Great White Fleet is approaching the region. Nikolin said he picked up some telegraphy traffic about an altered itinerary, so I looked it up. They were supposed to be steaming for the Philippines and then on to New Zealand and Australia first, but they have altered course, sir."

"Indeed? Then things have already changed."

"That mail steamer, sir. There were American citizens aboard and several were killed when we fired on the ship. Their Captain was spitting mad and threatened to make a major diplomatic protest."

"To who? The Mayor of Vladivostok? The Tsar won't hear about it for weeks, and would likely give it little notice. Besides that, Nicholas could send me a direct order to cease and desist here and I could tell him to go to hell without a second thought. There's nothing anyone can do about what I now have planned, Rodenko. Nothing."

"Well what about the American Great White Fleet, Captain?"

"If it makes an appearance, which is very unlikely, I can deal with it just as easily as these other ships."

"But they have sixteen battleships, sir! We have only nineteen SSMs left in inventory, and there will never be any more after that. If we use some now against the Japanese that will leave us even less. Can you sink the whole American fleet with the deck guns?"

"I have some surprises planned for the Japanese, but to answer your question, yes. I can sink them all if I wish. Don't forget our torpedo inventory. We have the *Vodopad* system, and a few torpedoes for the KA-40. I have ample ordnance to prevail, against the Japanese or the Americans if they get pushy."

"Alright sir…" Rodenko took another tack now. "Suppose we defeat Admiral Togo here, and the Americans do stay out of things. Then it comes down to a standoff between us and them. Years go by, and they continue to improve their ship designs. We could sink their existing ships, but what if they build more? You saw what they did in WWII. They'll start building aircraft carriers after the First World War."

"Yes, I have thought about all of this too, and perhaps the one thing we *will* do here is change the complexion of WWII in this theater. If I stop Japan now—"

"Then it's the Americans and Russia, sir. You said yourself that you would restore Russia to prominence here, but I don't think the Americans will back down that easily, even if we do destroy their Great White Fleet. They'll be outraged, and simply build another fleet. They know their place on the world stage depends on their navy, just like Great Britain. The enmity we create here could have an effect on the First World War as well. Both Russia and the United States came in to fight against Germany, but with those two countries as enemies who knows what will happen?"

"You worry too much, Rodenko. We cannot control every possible outcome, or even predict what may or may not happen as a result of our intervention here."

"But we can make reasonable assumptions, Captain. And we should. Each second that we pass here widens the rift we tear in history. There may come a point when it can no longer hold together and it all comes rending apart. We have no idea what will happen then, as you just said yourself. We won't be able to control things, sir, not with all the missiles, torpedoes, and shells left to us. This ship is in good trim now, but it is already wounded and will need maintenance. Things will fail in the months and years ahead. The missiles also have a limited life span. We will get weaker and weaker, and the world will get stronger each and every day."

"I don't plan on trying to rule the world, Rodenko, just my little corner of a self-made hell, here. Understand? Yes, we are young men. I am thirty five, so if I live to be eighty-five that gives me fifty years here. I can do a lot with that time… change many things. But that is tomorrow. We start building that future *today*, in the here and now. Nothing happens unless we make a choice to do something about it, and that is what I have done—it's what the crew of this ship chose as well, or have you forgotten that?"

Rodenko was silent, brooding, and still unsatisfied. "Don't you see, Captain? The very existence of this ship arises from a very complex weave of history. *Kirov* was built as a result of the cold war, but we see how fragile that history is now, and you yourself seem to think you can change it all at your whim and no one here will suffer any ill effects. But what if we cut the very strand that we dangle from? What if we do something at affects our very existence?"

"Now you sound like Fedorov."

Karpov looked out to the sea, noting the winds rising and a bank of clouds scudding low over the waves in the distance. It was pristine in its simplicity and emptiness, yet now it was the vast tapestry where he would sew and weave all of that future history. Rodenko's fears were justifiable, but somehow Karpov believed they could do nothing that would affect their own existence here.

"Don't clutter your head with these impossible thoughts, Rodenko. If I could do something to affect the fate of this ship and crew, then how did it ever get here to do that in the first place? It's a paradox! You just go round and round with it in your head and the only result is that you become frozen with fear and uncertainty. Well I cannot live like that. I will do what I choose, and the world can go to hell with me when I leave. So forget tomorrow! Forget fate and time and destiny—all of it. Think of what we must do in the here and now, one thing at a time. This will be an easy engagement. Enough talk and strategy and useless speculation. Let's do something! Let's get moving!"

Karpov turned to the helmsman now. "Come left 10 degrees and steady on two, zero, zero. Speed twenty."

"Aye sir, ahead two thirds and coming round to two, zero, zero."

* * *

It came out of a bank of low clouds, rolling like moving fog on the sea. A shadow darkened the waters there and then took the form and shape of an enormous steel prow. As Onoshi stared at it he realized what he must be seeing. This was the Russian ship he had been told to look for, and his was the only torpedo boat within miles. Boat number 75 was one of four in her class, a Type 67 class TB of 90 tons and relatively slow for the job at only 23 knots. It had three torpedoes available, one in a bow mounted tube, and one to either side on her port and starboard deck.

"Come right and ahead full. Ready all torpedoes!" Onoshi was so excited by the prospect of being the first to find and attack the Russian ship that he almost forgot his primary duty was to signal the location of his sighting. "And signal Lieutenant Commander Fujimoto! Tell him the monster is here, and we are attacking!"

Yet even as he swung round on a new heading, his bow cutting into the sea with the sudden turn, there came a snarling rattle and he saw the sea before the bow of his ship erupt with small white geysers, as though someone had flung a barrel full of stones into the water. The stones were 30mm rounds from *Kirov's* air defense Gatling guns, and they tore into the bow of Number 75, the heavy rounds riddling it to detonate the torpedo there in a violent explosion that sheared off the entire front of the boat. Water flooded in and the boat was soon foundering rapidly in the heavy swell.

Onoshi ran forward, realizing he had been caught completely by surprise and his only hope now was to get off his signal. He had reached the telegraph room back of the bridge where he saw the operator rapidly pecking out his signal. Then a sharp *crack, crack, crack* was heard and three 100mm rounds straddled the boat, one to port, one to starboard, but the third dead amidships, blowing one of his two stacks clean away and knocking everyone around him to the cold metal deck.

Crack, crack, crack—another burst of fire, and his ship was hit again, this time by two rounds. The second smashed the bridge and black smoke and fire poured from the open viewports there. The snarling rattle of the Gatling gun was heard again, and the rounds now came ripping through the telegraph station. Onoshi was not alive to hear the last dying scream of the telegraph operator.

There were now only three other Type 67 Torpedo boats in the Imperial Japanese Navy. Boat Number 75 was down at the bow, slipping into the grip of the sea with a sibilant hiss as the water doused the fires. Minutes later it was gone.

Ten miles east Lieutenant Commander Fujimoto saw his telegraph operator turn, shaking his head.

"That is all, sir. The message was cut off. The signal is gone."

Fujimoto narrowed his eyes. Then the boat is most likely gone, he thought. Only a few words had come to him—*Boat 75 sighting large ship*—but they were enough. He knew where he had posted the Number 75 boat, and now he turned to his wireless telegraph operator and told him to signal Vice Admirals Dewa and Kataoka. The enemy was here, in the Tsushima Strait!

"Say they are heading south from Boat 75's last reported position," he said quickly.

"But sir, there was no heading or course given."

"Where else would they be going? Just do as I say!" He slipped through the hatch and onto the small open bridge, ordering his boat to turn about and head southwest.

"They are here! We have found them! All boats will now execute the plan as ordered. Come to 220 degrees and ahead full!"

The helmsman echoed the order and the boat came smartly around on the new heading. Something had come out of the mist and low clouds to devour Boat number 75, thought Fujimoto. A behemoth—the great sea dragon the fishermen were whispering of so fearfully. Well I will find it and skewer it with my torpedoes if I can. This is no fishing boat.

A voice shouted from the bridge watch, stiff arm pointing ahead where something was streaking through the sky, low over the water. It came at them like a javelin and his eyes widened as it came flashing in to the center of his boat, exploding to send a hail of shrapnel in every direction and cutting down men all over the forward deck. A fire started forward, the thick smoke quickly engulfing the bridge.

Karpov had pulled a surprise out of his hat, using an S-400 SAM modified for low level attack and aiming it by radar at Fujimoto's boat. The Lieutenant Commander staggered off the bridge, seeing men bleeding on the watch deck, one with his face nearly cut clean away by shrapnel where he slumped on the deck. He fought his way to open air, coughing fitfully from the smoke only to see a second javelin roar in from the sea to explode again, careening into his boat.

Fire arrows! He had heard the reports of a fire arrow rocket weapon. This must be what he was seeing! His boat had taken two hits, and many men were down. The bridge was on fire, clotted with smoke. He looked frantically about him, searching every horizon for sign of the enemy, yet there was nothing to be seen. How could it find and attack his ship with all the low cloud obscuring the area? This was impossible!

The fire amidships suddenly exploded, and the small boat heeled over to one side, wallowing in the water, its speed down and fire everywhere. It would be all he could do to get survivors into the sea, and launch a few life boats to see them through. Whatever this enemy ship was, it was truly fearsome if it could find and attack his boat while remaining unseen itself. He would not be hunting the sea dragon today.

The dragon was hunting him!

Chapter 18

Vice Admiral Dewa got the news soon after, fretting on the bridge of the armored cruiser *Kasagi*. He had returned from his conference with Kataoka unsatisfied. The other man's caution and the obvious warning in his tone seemed inappropriate on the eve of battle. Then came the news he had been waiting for. The Russian ship had been sighted to the north about ten kilometers off the coast of Tsushima Island. Yet here he was with orders to withdraw! The news that two of the four torpedo boats from Fujimoto's division had been attacked and sunk was most disheartening, though not unexpected. The boats were there as a trip wire, and now the enemy's location was certain.

Signals filled the wireless channels, leaping from ship to ship, and also coursed along the undersea cable from Tsushima Island that stretched all the way back to Japan. Such means of communication were still relatively new, in the era where men named Morse, Hertz and Tesla still lived, and experiments with the arcane craft of electromagnetism were in their early days. Hertz had proved the existence of radio waves, actually calling them Hertzian waves in his experiments, but he saw no real application for them. "It's of no use whatsoever," he said... "We just have these mysterious electromagnetic waves that we cannot see with the naked eye. But they are there."

By 1895 others soon found new ways to use these waves, though the means of transmitting wirelessly could only reach a mile in range, and two years later it was extended to 34 miles. Soon coastal stations and lighthouses set up Marconi designed instruments and ship to shore wireless communications became a reality. By 1903 Teddy Roosevelt had been able to send a wireless message all the way across the Atlantic to the King in England, and from that day forward the mysterious unseen electromagnetic waves Hertz had talked about began to permeate the air.

Now the wireless telegraphy was chattering out the alert. The enemy was coming. Dewa had little doubt that Togo was already darkening the skies above his squadron with smoke as he hastened south to the planned rendezvous point. Now the 10th and 15th Torpedo Boat Divisions, each with four boats, would hastily form the last skirmish line off the coast of Tsushima. They would have a very special mission, deploying mines in the waters and then withdrawing south to bait the enemy on. Dewa was to take his cruisers and destroyers to effect a conjunction with Kataoka's ships. Though he chafed for battle, he knew that every minute that passed now before the engagement only served to strengthen the Japanese position.

To make matters even more interesting, Vice Admiral Uryu in the Inland Sea had received word that the American Great White Fleet had postponed its planned visit to Yokohama, pausing only for coal, and would now proceed directly to Kure, intending to transit the narrow strait at Shimonoseki. That news seemed alarming to Dewa, and the thought of such a strong foreign fleet boldly navigating the waters of the Inland Sea seemed most disconcerting. The Japanese had intended to meet and escort the American fleet, matching them ship for ship at Yokohama, but that was no longer possible. Vice Admiral Uryu had no more than eight small destroyers and a few cruisers, hardly enough to show the flag of the Imperial Japanese Navy.

Now the rumors and speculation as to what the Americans were really up to began to be whispered on the ship, passing from man to man like wireless telegraphy, and Dewa himself was not immune to the sense of foreboding they carried. What if the Americans and Russians were colluding? What if the attack on that Canadian mail ship had been staged to simply create a pretext for the movement of this massive American fleet into Japanese waters?

Time will tell, he thought. The Americans certainly favored the Russian side in those ill handled negotiations at Portsmouth. If the their fleet were to have any hostile intention, that would soon come to light—the light of battle.

He rubbed his hands together, thinking of the moment his cruisers would first begin to open fire and recalling that glorious day three years ago when they had savaged the Russians with their superior gunnery. We have been lax, he thought, but I have trained my men hard these last few days to see if they can recover their edge. Whatever happens, we must do our utmost now. I am ordered to withdraw northwest to the rendezvous point, but no mention was made of the timing on that movement. If I linger here I will be in a much better position to find this ship…

He smiled, making a stubborn decision that would seal the fate of his entire division.

* * *

Tasarov had been restless of late, with too much time on his hands. There had not been much of anything for him to do at the sonar station in recent days. Undersea threats were all but nonexistent here. Yet his passive system could also detect and track the noisy surface contacts, and at ranges rivaling that of the Fregat system under good listening conditions.

He had been listening to the picket line of torpedo boats ahead of them, slowly fleeing before the oncoming wrath of *Kirov*. The example made of two boats earlier was apparently more than enough to convince them that they had no chance of attacking successfully. Then he heard something he did not expect, particularly given the range.

"Con. Sonar. I have splash transients in the water, sir."

Karpov had not heard Tasarov report for many days now, and seemed surprised. "Splash transients? Are you saying they have fired a torpedo?"

"No sir. I detect no motor noise or any sign of a torpedo in the water. But something big enough to make a fairly distinct noise has been dropped into the sea. I think they are deploying mines, Captain."

Naval mines had been around for centuries, from floating wooden boxes filled with explosives used by the Chinese, to powder keg barrels used in the 17th century. They had always been a cheap, devious and very effective means of interdicting and controlling waterways, and Karpov was not one to underestimate them, even in this day and age. The Japanese had used mines very effectively against the Russians in the last war, killing their best fighting admiral Makarov and sinking the battleship *Petropavlovsk* in the process.

"Well…" said Karpov. "Up to their old tricks again, are they?" He was well aware of Makarov's fate, and determined not to fall into the same trap. "The ship will reduce speed. Ahead one third."

"Aye, sir. Slowing to 10 knots."

"Mister Tasarov, go to active sonar and find me those mines. Rodenko—post lookouts forward to port and starboard and stand ready to engage any floating target with the ship's Gatling guns. We will not blunder into one of these mines on my watch."

"Should we ready the RBU-1000 system?" asked Rodenko. The *Smerch*, as it was called was the very same system they had used to blast the waters around the ship and blow through the Italian minefields in the Bonifacio Strait. *Kirov* was a veritable Swiss Army knife when it came to weapons systems available for any application or defensive purpose.

"No, Mister Rodenko. I do not think it will be necessary. Those boats could not have deployed more than one or two mines. This field will be very porous. I think good eyes and well aimed small arms fire will be sufficient here."

Tasarov's warning proved to be very timely, for he soon began to detect several objects ahead, it was not long until the ship was engaging them with short bursts of the Gatling guns, or from 50 caliber machine guns set up on the weather deck by the Marines. They watched as several exploded, sending tall geysers of seawater up that glittered in the afternoon sun.

"Well done, Mister Tasarov," said Karpov. "I expect that will likely be the last of them, but keep listening on active sonar for the next hour."

They had reached the mid-point of the island, still about ten kilometers off the coast of Tsushima. A little farther south the island broke up into a series of smaller islets and deep bays and Rodenko noted that the Japanese torpedo boat screen had withdrawn into the cover of the bays around Kuroshima Island.

"It's clear they mean to lie in wait there," he said. "They will most likely make a rush at us when we pass that island."

Karpov nodded. "Well, if the example we gave them earlier was not enough of a lesson, then we'll give them more of the same. The instant one of those boats sticks its nose out, I want to engage with the forward deck gun. The 100mm gun should be sufficient."

To the Japanese, the Russian ship seemed to have an almost prescient ability to divine their intentions. Lieutenant Commander Odaki heard and saw the mines exploding as they withdrew south, elated at first to think they had struck a fatal blow and that his small flotilla would have accomplished what the other cruisers and battleships before him could not do. Yet lookouts soon reported that the Russian dreadnought was still steaming stalwartly south, apparently uninjured. Now his small group of four boats, numbers 40 through 43, would take up their pre-assigned position to the north of Kuroshima Island, which sat like a small boot in the waters off Tsushima.

Odaki's 10th Torpedo Division would deploy near the ankle of that boot, and further south, Commander Kondo's 15th Division had four newer boats hidden beneath the long jutting toe. There, watching from a 100 meter hill on the tip of the island, flagmen would signal the moment of the attack. Yet all this was anticipated by the men aboard *Kirov*, so it was no surprise when the Japanese boats suddenly emerged, charging boldly forward at high speed. Odaki's boats could make 23 knots, but Kondo had newer boats that were the fastest in the fleet at 29 knots. It was soon to become a brave and desperate rush to their doom.

"Con, radar reports eight contacts, four to either side of that island off the starboard bow."

"I expected this," said Karpov. "Mister Samsonov, please add the Forward 152mm deck gun to this engagement, and I also want the modified *Kashtan* system to deploy a missile salvo as a test."

The crack of the guns began, their radar eyes quickly finding and targeting the oncoming boats. At 150 tons the torpedo boats looked like tiny destroyers on the high resolution Tin Man cameras, with two stacks puffing dark smoke as they surged forward. On they came, through geysers of seawater with the first near misses. Samsonov concentrated his fire on the northernmost group, and Odaki's boats paid heavily. The penetrating rounds of the modern 152mm guns did severe damage to the lightly armored boats, and within minutes three of the four boats in that division had been hit and were on fire.

Kondo's Division had been given just a little time to get into the action. When he saw the fire and smoke of Odaki's burning boats, he gritted his teeth and stiffly extended his arm, pointing at the distant behemoth that loomed ahead like a dark storm. As the enemy ship approached, it seemed to grow to an enormous size, a huge silhouette that towered above the sea with tall battlements, its long, sharp bow cutting effortlessly through the waves like a sword. In fact, *Kirov* was 20 times the size of his boat and over 200 times his displacement!

Sagi was the first in his division to fall, struck amidships by two 152mm rounds that penetrated to the boat's boilers and exploded with bright fury sending hot tongues of flame jutting from the ship. *Hashitake* fell next, bow hit by a 100mm round, geysers from near misses all around, and then the starboard torpedo mount struck by a 152mm round. The resulting explosion sent men and metal careening into the sky, yet Kondo charged bravely on. He had to get very close to have any chance of hitting the enemy ship, but the range and accuracy of the enemy guns was making his charge suicidal.

"Ready torpedoes!" he shouted boldly, intent on getting through the iron curtain of enemy fire to deliver his sea lances home. Like so many before him, he would never get the chance. There was no mercy at the edge of this storm, just deadly lightning that struck with thunderclap speed and surprise. The dark silhouette of the oncoming enemy ship suddenly erupted with fire and white smoke, and then something came screaming in at his boat, fire rockets that danced wildly up, then angled down to surge in at *Hibari*. His boat was struck by both weapons, shrapnel ripping through the bridge crew, and wounding Kondo himself in the shoulder. He clutched at the wound in pain, then removed his hand, raising his good arm, still pointing out the direction of his attack with a bloodied white glove. Then a 152mm round slammed into the bridge, killing Kondo and every man there.

The navigation wheel was sheered away, and the *Hibari* veered off course, wallowing to port as two more rounds delivered hard body blows. Her sides were ripped open to the sea and the boat capsized to one side, the last of her crew screaming as they leapt into the restless water. Only *Uzura* was left, but it, too, died a quick and painful death, skewered by three hits from the 100mm deck gun on *Kirov's* forward bow. None of the eight torpedo boats got within 4000 meters, still well outside the range of their 14 inch torpedoes. The tricks and surprises that Togo had planned and executed so successfully against the Russian Fleets of 1905 would not avail him now. *Kirov's* ability to see every move the enemy made, and to engage at superior range, was decisive.

The big Russian battlecruiser had expended no more than 72 rounds and a couple of *Kashtan* missiles Karpov wanted to test in their new role as a small anti-ship weapon.

"There you have it," said Karpov, a jaunty rock to his step as he walked to the viewport, lifting his field glasses. "We have blown through their little minefield as if it wasn't even there. Now we put all eight of these torpedo boats to rest. They had no chance to get anywhere within range. What were they thinking?"

"I don't think they knew that, sir," said Rodenko. "But it was a brave charge nonetheless."

"Yes," said Karpov, "and a foolish one as well. You would think they would have broken off and scurried to the safety of those island shoals after we blasted the first couple boats."

"I don't think they realized what we could do, sir. Our radar lock with the deck guns made this a sure kill."

"Well, let's see how the news of this little engagement ripples south. They know where we are, and have undoubtedly withdrawn their heavier assets south to present a stronger threat. This attack was mere harassment."

"That they have, sir," said Rodenko. "I think we can assume we will be facing at least 18 ships in the next engagement." There was an edge of warning in his voice now.

"Eighteen ships, or eighty ships, it doesn't matter, Rodenko. The result will be the same. We will fight that battle just as we have fought this one. Mister Samsonov will engage at 15,000 meters with all our deck guns. I'll fling a few modified P-400s at them as well, just for color. The fragmentation of those exploding warheads is lethal, and there are many open battery gun mounts on those old ships. The SAMs will sweep their decks clean. I'll identify the flagships and make a determination as to whether or not we employ one or two SSMs as well, but I want to preserve that inventory as long as possible. Well," he concluded, "now the real fun begins."

"Vladimir Semenoff thought the same," said Rodenko.

"Semenoff?" The Captain turned to look at him, not placing the name.

"I read his account of the battle of Tsushima in one of Fedorov's books last night. He made that very remark when he witnessed the sudden turn made by Admiral Togo's ships at the outset of the battle."

Karpov gave him a thin lipped smirk. "Well, Semenoff was not aboard the battlecruiser *Kirov*, was he, Mister Rodenko?"

Part VII

Shadow Dance

"A song she heard
Of cold that gathers
Like winter's tongue
Among the shadows…"

— Robery Fanney

"Poetry is an echo, asking a shadow to dance."

— Carl Sanburg

Chapter 19

The *Seahawks* had been up for the last hour, well out in front of Sato's surface action group, scouring the waters south of Ulleung-do. Each helicopter carried two Mark 46 torpedoes, and now they were dipping sonar into the water listening for the enemy hidden beneath the sea.

After the *White Dragon, Hakuryu,* had fired, and was nearly destroyed by enemy counter fire, the Russian sub seemed to vanish behind the intervening undersea massif that made up the island. A long hour passed while Sato considered his options. The enemy could have turned on any new heading after contact was lost, but he stared at the circle indicating their farthest on and knew he was still in the hunt.

They might run due west between those two sea mounts, he thought, fingering two small subsea features west of the main island. Yet they would afford the enemy sub no cover. The water there was too deep, and the Russian sub could not dive deep enough to reach the seamounts, which both had summits at least 870 meters below sea level. The waters south were clear and deep, almost 2200 meters, and that would be a good hunting ground for his helicopters. The Russian sub's best move would be to reverse course and turn north again or even to move slightly east near the steep undersea flanks of the volcanic island. There they could use the scattering effect of the sheer ridges and cliffs to frustrate the searching pings of active sonar.

He had one sub out in front now, the *Kuroshio.* Just after *Hakuryu* engaged, the *Kuroshio* had altered course to 252 degrees southwest, hoping to get a little out in front of the Russian sub if it continued south. Sato's three destroyers were now racing past the Dokdo Islets, also called the Liancourt Rocks. Somewhere off his starboard bow he also knew a sleek new American *Virginia* Class submarine was on the prowl, SGN *Mississippi.* So the table was set for the next meal, and he had several sharp knives at hand.

This Russian boat is very quiet, he thought. He was surprised that *White Dragon* had found it earlier, though that sub was shaken badly by that near miss from a 650mm torpedo. This Russian Captain fired at very long range, and with the only weapon that could do the job, nearly skewering his quarry. Fifty meters made the difference between life and death for the Captain and crew of *Hakuryu*, and that was all too typical of modern warfare, where margins of meters and minutes, sometimes seconds, pronounced the judgment of victor or vanquished.

Flash low frequency message traffic had gone out to all units in the hunt. *Hakuryu* was north in the East Gap of Ulleung. *Mississippi* about twelve kilometers southeast, and *Kuroshio* about 20 kilometers due south of the island. There had been no sign of the enemy on passive sonar from the helos, and he was now ready to order them to undertake a more active sonar search. Where are you? He whispered to himself as he studied the sea charts of the area. Which way did you turn?

He would soon find out.

At 18:20 hours the triangulated sonar scans of his helicopters and submarines thought they finally found something in the deep blue silence of the sea, the barest whisper, a murmur of a shadow passing. It might have been a blue finned whale, or even a large shark, so subtle was its signature on the passive sonar. As per orders from Sato, the first sign of any contact was to be immediately answered by active sonar from the helicopters.

The bright pings radiated out through the hushed undersea oceanscape, rippling against the hull of something dark and solid there. *Kazan's* hull design and skin served to scatter much of the sound, but enough got back to reach the well trained ears of the sonar man aboard *Mississippi*. He had been listening closely to something in the water, an odd repeating scratch that seemed deeply muted, but it was there. Somewhere, he thought, there was a machine out of whack. Some bearing or lever or rod was moving out of balance, leaving a quiet dissonance in the muttering backwash of the sea. He could not tell what it was, exactly, but he had a good idea *where* it was. Then the pings came.

"Con. Sonar. Reporting undersea contact. Possible submarine bearing 265, range approximately 22,000 meters; speed unknown."

The sonic energy from those active pings had radiated out through the deep sound channel in a distinct pattern, the sound waves overlapping until they encountered that shadow in the sea. It had caused the slightest ripple in the pattern, and the barest return of that energy that indicated there was something more there than the empty ocean.

Captain James Donahue turned to his sonar man, Ensign Eugene Campanella. "What's up, Campy? Speed unknown? I can't get a firing solution with that."

"Sorry sir," said Campanella. "Give me a moment."

"That's about all I have to spare. Those pings are radiating our way as well. If the Russians have good ears they just might hear something too."

The Captain did not think that likely yet, but he put a little fire to the feet of his sonar man just the same. "Battle stations. Load tubes one thru four," he said quietly.

"Load tubes one through four," came the echo from his XO Lieutenant Commander Chambers. "The boat will come to battle stations, aye, aye."

"Rig for silent running."

Silence was the order of the day now, and the Captain turned to his communications station and raised a finger, waving it in a tiny circle to indicate the desired action. Orders had been given to use ultra low frequency sound to indicate he had achieved a possible contact and to signal all other units close at hand with the approximate location. It was not something he would have done if not for those orders. *Mississippi* liked to play the game solo, as any submarine would.

Four minutes later a whisper came back.

"Captain..." Donahue went to the signal station, reading the incoming message on screen. It showed the approximate coordinates of the suspected contact as refined by the *Seahawks*, and asked for a concerted attack at 18:30 hours, five minutes away. Every asset in the region was going to put torpedoes in the water to see what they could flush out. If anything got close, the enemy might have to use countermeasures, which would surely give their exact position away and allow a follow on attack to have a high probability of a kill.

The Captain looked at his sonar man. "Give it to me, Campy. You've got some help from those *Seahawks* now."

Campanella bit his lip. "I make it eighteen knots, sir. Twenty at best."

"Run with it and get me a firing solution now."

Computers would take that input, the suspected location and bearing, and calculate the best initial heading for the torpedoes. He was going to put two in the water, to join one from each *Seahawk* and two from each Japanese submarine out there somewhere. They had just heard the music, and now they were going to make the Russians dance. Eight torpedoes in the water, reasonably well aimed, were going to be a real nightmare for Gromyko in about eighteen minutes. That was the time it would take for the Mark 48 ADCAP torpedoes from *Mississippi* to cross the 22 kilometer gulf to the suspected target. Other weapons closer to the target would get there first, but the Mark 48s were the best in the business on the US side of the fence, and they would deliver the coup de grace.

One Japanese boat was closer, firing from a range of about 11,000 meters, and the helos were in that same radius as well. They would fire, listen, and then move to the source of the contact before firing again. If these assets were anywhere close to the mark with their shots, the Russians would have to go defensive with countermeasures, and then the other torpedoes could vector in for the kill. It was a good and well coordinated plan...

* * *

"**Con**, Sonar. I have torpedoes in the water! Two... three... no sir, many more. It looks like eight separate contacts!"

"Eight? My God." Gromyko was quickly at his sonar man's side.

"I have two close contacts, most likely fired by the helicopters that have been searching for us. One bearing 80 degrees, range 12,500 meters approximate; another bearing 138 at about 9,500 meters. Those would be Mark 46 torpedoes, sir, and that first one is firing at maximum range."

"The enemy is very eager today," said Gromyko, seemingly unconcerned. "What is the speed of those torpedoes?"

"I make it 40 knots, sir—that's 74KPH."

"I see they are in no hurry. This is a fishing expedition."

"Then I have two more, medium range at 11,000 meters approximate and bearing 315 degrees. They sound like Type 89s from the profile data match, sir."

"Then we have another Japanese submarine to our south on that heading. Note it as Tokyo-One and place it on the tactical board, Mister Belanov."

"Aye, sir. Designating Tokyo-One."

"Four more contacts at longer range, Captain: two bearing 85 degrees, range 19,000 meters; two more bearing 62 degrees, range 18,000 meters."

Gromyko nodded his head. "Type 89s, Chernov?"

"No sir, not all of them. I think the two fish bearing 85 are Type 48s, sir. The others sound like Type 89s."

"Then we have an American boat on the 85 degree heading, and another Japanese boat on the 62 degree heading. Very interesting. Someone has convened a meeting here today. Designate the second Japanese boat Tokyo-Two, and the contact at 85 as *Orlan.*"

"So designated, sir," came Belanov's deep voice. The *Starpom* was busy setting up the battle on the tactical Plexiglas screen.

"Very well," said Gromyko. "Weapon's officer."

"Sir!"

"Ready on tubes five and six. Set weapons to manual control."

That caused the barest moment of hesitation but the Weapon's Officer, Lieutenant Sergei Leonov, soon echoed the order, his eyes heavily on the Captain now as everyone on the bridge waited.

"Eject ordnance in tubes five and six. Do *not*, engage motors. Understood?"

"Aye sir. Firing now… Weapons free in the water. System on full manual control. Motors not engaged."

Kazan had just ejected two big 650mm torpedoes, with no firing solution plotted, and the weapons had been manually prevented from starting their motors. Leonov was watching the Captain closely, now, waiting on his next order and wondering what he was doing.

Gromyko had but one question on his mind, now: how good was the enemy firing solution? What did they really know? We have been creeping along but they obviously heard something, he thought, possibly that damn bad bearing again, or this infernal maintenance procedure being run in the reactor room. I just gave them another whisper with that weapons ejection. Now here we are with no more than twenty knots available and a whole lot of trouble heading our way. Time to dance.

"Helm, right full rudder. Come to 270 true," he said calmly.

"Helm answering, right full rudder and coming around to 270 degrees west sir, aye."

"Where is the thermocline boundary, Chernov?"

"About 160 meters, sir."

"Helm, make your depth one-five-zero."

Kazan had been at 200 meters, and was now climbing slightly as they turned, aiming to pierce the thermocline and alter the sonic conditions surrounding the boat. The maneuver was also putting more vertical distance between the submarine and the two heavy wire guided torpedoes it had just ejected, which were now slowly sinking deeper into the sea, waiting for orders.

Volsky and Fedorov were still on the bridge, tensely watching the situation, eyes on the Captain. Gromyko folded his arms, leaning Volsky's way as he spoke in a quiet voice.

"I turned to starboard to put as much room between the boat and those last four torpedo contacts as possible. That is their endgame, those Mark 48's off the American boat will have the best sonar for tracking us. Those are their kill weapons, but they will have a very long ride before we have anything to worry about. We're moving west now at 20 knots. They are heading our way, probably at 40 knots. That means their effective speed is only 20 knots, or about 37KPH. It will take them at least thirty minutes to catch up with us, and if I had full power on the reactors they would never catch up with us at all."

"But what about all those other torpedoes?" said Volsky, obviously worried. "They are much closer."

"True, but I don't think they had a good fix on our location. The close in contacts are trying to flush us out of the bush. No doubt they heard those torpedoes eject, and they should now be vectoring on our approximate firing point. In a moment I will keep them running true to that location for a while."

The Matador had swirled his cape and stepped to his right, taunting his adversary, but the bull was charging, and its horns were very sharp.

"Listen to the closer contacts, Chernov," Gromyko said quietly. "Any bearing change?"

"No sir. They seem to be running true on their initial bearings"

"Good. Now let us keep them busy, shall we?"

The Captain was looking at his watch. "Time on target remaining for the closest torpedo?"

"Sir, about six minutes thirty-five seconds."

"Very well." Gromyko waited, inclining his head to the Admiral. "In a minute we start the wild goose chase, Admiral. Any idea how much more time this procedure on the reactors will take?"

Volsky looked to Fedorov to answer that.

"There is no way to tell exactly," said Fedorov. "Sometimes the effects have been almost immediate, but other times it has taken many hours before the displacement happened. Then again... we have never used this control rod in a submarine reactor. The equipment is cooled by self-circulating water, not by pumps. It sounds different, which has me worried somewhat. I hope Chief Dobrynin can control the shift."

"That's an understatement," said Gromyko, still looking at his watch. "Weapon's Control. Activate torpedo motors at lowest speed setting. Guide them on a heading of 80 degrees. No active search—understood?"

"Aye, sir. Activating motors, steering zero-eight-zero with passive sonar."

Gromyko waited briefly before he turned to his sonar man again. "Any heading change on the close in contacts?"

"Yes, sir! The Alpha One torpedo has turned to starboard. It is tracking our torpedoes!"

"Excellent. Let our two big fish swim for a while. They will soon realize what they are tracking and start looking elsewhere, but I think we may have put them off our scent without having to resort to noisemakers."

They waited as the seconds ticked off. The Mark 46 torpedo fired from *Seahawk 2* was now no more than three minutes away. Then Chernov looked the Captain's way, a warning in his eyes.

"The Alpha One contact is starting to circle, Captain. It has switched to active sonar."

"Weapon's Officer, ready on tube number nine please."

"*Shkval* system active on tubes nine and ten, sir."

The Matador was getting ready to swat the enemy lance aside with another flourish of his cape as the bull made its first mad rush. But the bullfight had only just begun.

Chapter 20

Kazan was lavishly armed, with ten torpedo tubes, five on either side of the boat. Two tubes held smaller 533mm torpedoes, six housed the bigger 650mm fish that Gromyko had put in the water, and the last two had been armed with the deadly high speed underwater rocket known as the *Shkval*, the VA-111 *Squall*. It was a supercavitating torpedo that was actually a liquid fueled rocket that generated a gas bubble around it as it moved through the water, allowing it to reach a dizzying speed of over 200 knots. The smaller 210kg warhead was designed to find and kill enemy torpedoes, and the weapon could range out to 15,000 meters.

"Let me know the instant you believe that torpedo has found us, Chernov."

"It's still searching, sir… Active sonar, but I don't think it has found us. They are circling near our firing position."

In the time since *Kazan* turned, the boat had already moved some 3000 meters on its new heading. The nearest enemy torpedo would soon be that close when it reached the point where they turned, but still minutes away as it circled, trying to find its elusive quarry on active sonar.

"Will it acquire us?" asked Volsky, sweat dotting his brow. He was not accustomed to the more confined space of the submarine, or at all well versed in undersea warfare. An enemy weapon that close was cause for alarm, which is why Gromyko had the *Shkval* ready if necessary.

"Their sonar is looking for us, Admiral, but *Kazan* is a very slippery fish too. Even at this speed we make no more sound than typical ocean background noise. It might not acquire us at all. It's those American Mark 48s I'm more worried about. They have good passive sonar, and they are listening to everything happening out there, and sending all that noise back along their control wire to a very good sonar man. If he's smart, he will realize what we have just done, using those two big Type 65s to lure in the weapons fired by their helicopters. They've seen through that ruse already, but seeing is one thing—finding us is quite another. We still have some time, but I wonder what is happening in the reactor room?"

* * *

Dobrynin was listening, listening, listening. It seemed that all human awareness now was focused on sound, and the fate of the boat, their mission, and possibly the world itself was lurking in the subtle whispers, the vibrating quavers at the edge of infinity. The sound of the reaction was not the same as it might be on *Kirov*, or again on the *Anatoly Alexandrov*, but he could still hold the score in his mind and hear the song, just as the music of the great masters like Bach, Beethoven or Mozart had been played by different orchestras through the decades after the composers were long gone.

The trilling vibration had fallen as he expected, and now the deeper basso was asserting itself, tenuously at first, but gathering strength and direction, always descending. The water was very quiet here... until the undersea engagement began, and it was not long before the active pings of the oncoming Mark 46 torpedoes could be heard audibly as they circled like sleek sharks searching for *Kazan*.

Quiet down out there, he thought. I need to make an adjustment.

"Flux readings still green?" he said quietly to his technicians.

"Aye sir, Green and well within expected tolerances."

"Then move to final phase, speed three, please."

He listened again. The bass tones were still descending, but they needed to go lower, another half-octave down to a deeper register. Then something happened that upset everything, a loud boom shuddered in the deep silence of the sea as though a great kettle drum had been struck out of time. Dobrynin jumped at the sound, startled. Quiet down, he thought. A man must think!

* * *

"Detonation, sir! I think it was one of the Type 89s off the Tokyo-One bearing."

Gromyko's expression hardened. That was done deliberately, he thought. That torpedo did not have a lock on his boat. They detonated it manually over the wire to see what we would do, like a destroyer lobbing a few depth charges and then quietly listening.

"There were two torpedoes on that bearing," he said to Chernov. "Is the other one on active search?"

"No sir, it is circling, but still on passive sonar."

Gromyko nodded, knowing his hunch had been correct. The closest enemy submarine to their southwest did not have a good fix on them. They were just shouting at the sea and hoping we would shout back while their second torpedo listens. The tactic was futile. They would have had better results just leaving the fish in the hunt. He knew the second torpedo would not hear him, and have to go active soon in a fruitless attempt to acquire. *Kazan* had moved over 5500 meters since it turned. The other torpedo off Tokyo-One was still over four minutes running time away, easy prey for his *Shkval*, but the Captain knew his best play was to do nothing.

"Active search now, sir. It is circling, along with the Mark 46s off the helicopters. I think we've given them the slip, Captain. Those Mark 46s will be out of fuel soon."

Then it happened, that stubborn bearing in the turbine room decided it needed just a little more lubricant on one side, and the wobble in its housing was just enough to make a small noise, faint and short lived, but audible, even to the Captain where he stood on the bridge. It was as if someone had squealed, though the information was only useful for passive systems that were still listening intently for any sign of their location… And they *were* listening.

* * *

Far to the east, aboard the SGN *Mississippi*, a pair of very good eyes and ears were on the sonar system, and they heard that fleeting squeak after the Type 89 detonation had subsided, just a scratch in the groove of the vinyl, a ripple in the waterfall of data on the screen, but enough to matter to a well trained operator on some of the most sensitive and accurate sonar equipment ever designed. The *Mississippi* could sit off New York harbor and hear shipping in the English Channel. It was that damn good.

"Con, sonar," said Campanella. "I just picked up a transient, and it sounded like that noise I heard earlier. I think our bird just chirped."

"Get me a location," said Captain Donahue.

"Working now, sir... it's farther on from the initial position. I think they turned on 270."

Donahue looked at his XO, and Chambers nodded his agreement. "Makes sense," he said. "You turn away from the long shots to open the range and buy time. Then he pulled that stunt with the torpedoes to lure in the weapons off the *Seahawks*."

"What was it they put in the water, Campy?" the Captain asked.

"Sounded like a pair of Type 65s, sir. But I thought the motors failed."

"One failure I could buy," said Donahue, "but not both. The bastard just dropped a couple turds in the toilet bowl to bait those close in torpedoes like Mister Chambers has it."

"Agreed, sir."

"Why did the Japanese detonate one of their fish? Somebody is getting damn restless out there. You'd think there was a war on here."

That brought a grin to the XOs face, but the Captain was quickly serious again. "Keep listening, Campy. Feed everything you have to the Weapon's Officer. My guess is that they dropped those turds and then ran due west. If that is so we'll keep our two Mark 48's running on that heading, and listen real good. How long before we crap out on the range?"

"Sir, at 74KPH we can run 50,000 meters."

"Can we catch up at that speed?"

"Yes sir, but it will take time. I'm going to assume they may be running at twenty knots, though I have no firm data on that. Anything faster and I probably *would* have a good fix on them by now, but they're damn quiet up to 20 knots. That said, our fish will reach the initial contact point in another three minutes, but if the target has been running west away from that point as we suspect, then we won't catch up with them... for another fifteen minutes, sir. Our Mark 48s will be in the hot zone at 19:00."

"Let's hope we have the legs for this, gentlemen."

"Oh, we'll get there," said Campanella. "After a thirty minute run they will only have traveled about 36,900 meters, with plenty of fuel left in the tank for an active search if we need one. We could even crank 'em up to 55 knots, Captain. That would put them over a hundred KPH and they would be on the target much sooner."

"No, keep them at 40 knots. They have better ears that way and I also want that time in the fuel tanks for active search."

XO Chambers leaned in. "That range has opened up, skipper, and you know they can pour it on if they want to and damn near double their speed over that estimated 20 knots Campy has in his equation. We may not get another shot unless we take it now."

Donahue thought about that. "We're moving fast, XO. They probably don't have a fix on our position yet, as we hit them with a lot of noise at 18:30 when everyone joined the conference call and put weapons in the water at the same time. If we fire solo now, however, they *will* hear us, and you can be damn certain of that. All they might have now is our approximate bearing."

"The Russian sub Captain is a pretty cool customer, sir. That was a nifty trick with those two Type 65s. They spoofed the 46s off the *Seahawks*, if only for a moment."

"A moment is all that matters," said Donahue. "It doesn't sound like they've acquired."

"We might fire another pair of Mark 48s now, sir."

"Yeah? And what if he gets a hair up his ass and puts four Type 65's in the water heading our way at 50 knots? No thanks, Mister

Chambers. It's up to the two fish we have running now. Stay on the trail and get me in the hot zone, Campy, that's all I ask."

"Roger that, Captain."

* * *

Admiral Volsky heard the detonation, and felt the vibration gently shake the ship, his eyes betraying obvious fear.

"Don't worry, Admiral," said Gromyko. "That was a shot in the dark. If I'm not mistaken that was Tokyo-One to our southeast, correct Mister Chernov?"

"Aye, sir. They detonated one of their Type 89s and the other is running passive for a listen."

"They're just beating the bushes, Admiral. They don't know where we are."

"The Mark-48s are still running true, Captain," Chernov warned.

Gromyko thought about that for a moment. "How long before I need to worry about them?"

"I have them at 40 knots, sir. So about another fifteen minutes."

"They don't know where we are either. Otherwise they would be running full out at 55 knots. But they have taken a very good guess that we turned away from their line of fire. Now let's see just how good their sonar man really is. Helm, come left ten degrees."

"Sir, my rudder is left ten degrees and coming to 260."

Gromyko looked at the Admiral, explaining his maneuver. "If they do have us, then they may alter course as well, or fire a second salvo. If so I get my chance at taking down this American submarine."

"What about the Japanese submarines?" said Volsky.

"I think we have a solution on Tokyo-One, do we not Mister Chernov?"

"I can get you red on that one, sir. Close enough to leave it to the torpedoes."

"Not unless they fire at us again, or it appears they have our new bearing. If not, we ignore them. If we engage we just give the enemy more information, and believe it or not, that information is what decides this issue, the weapons just follow suit. Now then... the torpedoes fired from Tokyo–Two... are they still on their initial bearing?"

"They are, sir."

"So they have not altered heading, and they have not gone to active sonar. I believe they will not acquire us either. But listen for those Mark 48s Chernov. What are they doing? That is where the real game is now, a game of shadows, dancing in the sea." He smiled at Volsky, clearly unrattled and in command of his situation.

"Mister Gromyko," said Volsky. "I can see now why you were given command of this vessel. But I hope to God you are correct."

* * *

"Captain..." Campanella looked up at his skipper, a smile in his eyes. "I think the other fellow just blinked. Something just turned off 270. It wasn't a whale, sir. I picked up just the barest trace of that chirp again."

"Where's our bird flying, Campy?"

"I have them bearing 260 now, and diving, sir."

"Running for cold water," said Donahue.

"Shall we stick it to them?" Chambers was still thinking they should put two more torpedoes in the water."

"No..." Donahue waited. "Don't even move our fish running now. I want the bastard to think we still don't see him. Get me a predictive plot on where he would be in ten minutes on that heading, and then get flash traffic to the *Seahawks*. They can get over there a lot faster than we can. In a few minutes we'll shift our Mark 48s into his wake. But for now, I want him thinking all is as it was before."

The dance of shadows continued, with each boat Captain trying to second guess the other, and outsmart him in the murky stillness of the sea. They were like blind men with daggers, groping, listening, one arm taught with the cold edge of steel in its hand as they probed for one another in the dark.

I think I've found you now, Donahue thought. Why did you move? You had a good game going there on 270. I was wondering if you were up there, above the thermocline, but I wasn't sure. Why make a depth change now? You're looking to find the Shadow Zone, aren't you. Crafty fellow… You want me to move my goddamned torpedoes too! Well, no sir. I won't tip my hand just yet. If you've got the balls to show me your backside in exchange for a little information, then I've got the balls to wait you out, as long as I've got the wire.

"Can we still get a command out to our fish?"

"Sir, we've already spun out our first wire and we're using the reserve in the fuel tank now."

The Mark 48 had 9,700 yards of wire in the Torpedo Mounting Dispenser, and an additional 20,000 yards in one of the fuel tanks. That gave them 29,700 yards, or a little over 27,000 meters of wire guided control, but they were rapidly reaching the end of that long, thin tether.

"Another five minutes, sir. We either have to move 'em or cut 'em loose to freelance."

"Then we wait. The boat will run steady on 270 as before. Same for those Mark 48s. Nobody bats an eyelash, understood? We'll let the *Seahawks* take another look and see if they can sniff the bastard out. By the time he realizes what we're doing, it will likely be too late for him to do anything about it. Turn the Mark 48s on the contact's new heading and unleash them in… four minutes."

For the next four minutes *Mississippi* was going to make it seem that the Russian sub had turned unseen in the shadows, safe behind the furled cape of the sea. But the bull was watching from the corner of his eye, and he was about to lower his head and charge.

Chapter 21

The MGK-500 *Shark Gill* low-frequency passive sonar on *Kazan* was working overtime along with Chernov. After processing all the incoming torpedo signatures, and snooping on the bearings they were fired from, Chernov had given Gromyko enough information to paint the probable tactical picture he was facing. Three submarines, at least two helicopters and a surface action group composed of three destroyers was a fairly formidable array. This bull would not be slain easily, if at all. On another day he might try his skill here and fight. He could shower the surface contacts with missiles, but at the grave risk of telling all the subs and helos exactly where he was. Surface engagement was not his mission today. Now it was taking all his guile and experience to avoid the sharp, deadly rushes of those horned torpedoes.

He managed to spoof the short range Mark 46s off the helicopters, and they were now running out of fuel as they continued to circle in a futile search near the point where *Kazan* had made its first evasive turn heading on 270. The two torpedoes fired from the Japanese sub to the southeast designated Tokyo-One, were also confused and had been unable to acquire the stealthy Russian sub. One had committed seppuku to shake up the sonic soundscape and attempt to prompt a response from its quarry while the other listened, but the tactic had proved fruitless.

In spite of these successes, there were still four torpedoes in the water, and they were getting very close to the red zone as Gromyko defined it, that region within 3000 meters where an active sonar search from the weapon just might have a chance to acquire and lock on. Of the four, the two fired by Tokyo-Two to his northeast were less worrisome. Chernov's latest sonar read on them showed them running parallel to his course now, but on a vector that would see them miss by a wide margin.

It was those damn American Mark 48s he was worried about, an advanced capability torpedo with very good passive sonar and a long tether that would allow the even more sophisticated sonar on the firing sub to augment guidance.

"Have the Mark 48s moved?" The Captain had just turned ten degrees to 260 and wanted to know if the torpedoes had adjusted their course to follow.

"No sir, they are still running on 270 true."

"Helm, five degree down bubble."

"Five degrees down, sir, aye."

"Make your depth 170 meters."

"Passing through 160 meters… Now at 170, sir."

"What are you doing?" The Admiral's fear became curiosity now.

"I'm looking for shadows," said Gromyko. "The water is slightly colder down there, just below the thermocline border. Sound propagation is different very near the boundary like this. It tends to split, with some sound waves refracting off the thermocline boundary and bending up towards the surface to form a sound channel at shallower depths. Other waves that do penetrate the boundary are bent downward, but the bottom is very deep here, so there is no bottom bounce for a very long time. If we are lucky we might just slip into the Shadow Zone."

"Shadow Zone?" said Volsky.

"It's that nebulous region right where the sound waves tend to split, a kind of sonic island in the stream. If I can slip into one here, any active sonar waves may not find us easily."

The dance of shadows continued, but the American sub had very good night eyes. They also knew where the thermocline was, and this favored "best depth" for a submarine looking for the Shadow Zone could be calculated and factored into the search equation.

"Range on those Mark 48s?"

"Passing through 4800 meters, Captain."

"Any speed change?"

"No sir, they are still running at 40 knots and gaining on us at half that, considering our speed."

"Time on target if they are tracking us?"

"About 8 minutes, sir.

"He's got to be losing his wire any minute now." Gromyko had a tense expression on his face, eyes scanning the ceiling of the operations center as though he was trying to see through the sub's hull and spot the incoming torpedoes.

"A little under eight minutes out…. So we wait on this heading. If the torpedoes remain steady on 270 in another five minutes, then I think we may just slip away here."

But that was not to be. Four minutes later Chernov heard something and knew the worst. "Speed change!" he said quickly. "I think they are turning their torpedoes to port, sir!"

"Damn!" Gromyko swore under his breath. "They just sent their final course adjustment and kissed them goodbye. They'll go active any second now, and it's about to get very noisy around here, Admiral. I hope your Chief Engineer has a handle on his business."

Volsky had a hand in his pocket, and now he crossed two thick fingers, murmuring a silent prayer. It had been over 90 minutes since Dobrynin initiated his procedure. What was happening? Now we go into battle. Gromyko has been a skillful Matador here, but the last of those eight torpedoes are the best of them, and he looks worried.

"Weapons control," the Captain said quickly. "Do we still have wire on our Type 65s?"

"Yes, sir. They have been circling since we activated motors. We have another 5000 meters."

"That will do. Alright, then we match the Americans, and move as they move. Shift to full speed on those torpedoes and run them east on a heading of zero-nine-five. Go to active sonar."

The Matador still had a few lances in hand, and he meant to use them by sending them hurtling down the presumed line of advance the American sub might be taking. If nothing else the sudden speed change and active sonar was going to be as disturbing to them as the news he had just received. What he really wished for now was the tremendous speed his boat was still capable of, but with the reactors hobbled by the maintenance procedure, he could make only 20 knots. How much longer would it take?

Even as he thought that, he realized what he was saying. If this strange procedure actually works, he might soon be taking the ride of his life! He didn't know which fate would be worse, the battle he had in front of him now, in a world he knew all too well, or the journey into uncertainty at the edge of oblivion. It was madness!

"Active sonar!" Chernov could hear the two American torpedoes starting to sing. He tensed up, trying to keep hold of his sonic leash on the Mark 48s to see if they were making the subtle course corrections that might indicate they had acquired and were vectoring in.

They were.

* * *

Two more voices in the choir, thought Dobrynin as he heard the telltale pinging of the enemy sonar. Here I am stirring my nuclear borscht and now we have uninvited guests for dinner. He had to concentrate! The procedure was nearly complete. Rod-25 had been dipped and was retracting now, and the sonorous timbre of the reaction was quavering ever lower. It had not yet reached that final point when it seemed to fall into a black sonic hole, that great downward *vroom* that would indicate the displacement was actually happening.

He steadied the headphones he had rigged, receiving sounds from the reactors and trying to isolate certain vibrations in his mind's ear. He had already tested all his control options, and he knew what he could do to lower or raise the tone of the reaction. Now he repeated the phrase he wanted to hear over and over in his mind, a conductor raising his hand, seeing it hover over the section of the orchestra he was about to cue, and waiting as the score tumbled toward that moment of fateful timing.

Come on... come on... *sing to me!*

Then he heard the voice he had been waiting for, like a bass soloist suddenly booming out his notes in the midst of the crescendo. It came with cymbal-clap surprise, loud and clear, and he knew they were beginning to move... somewhere. Now all he had to do was control the shift!

* * *

In the tension of the moment Fedorov almost didn't notice it, but some inner sense, a reflex born of so many journeys across that tenuous Shadow Zone of time, told him that a shift had begun. He tilted his head, and then he heard the sound, a deep extended *vrooooom*, as if some behemoth had bellowed from the depths of the sea.

But the Mark 48s heard it too, and the sound was just enough to complete their target vector lock on an unseen enemy ahead. Their mindless brains sent commands to tiny servomechanisms, altering the flow of the propulsion system that drove them on as they accelerated to their top speed of 55 knots.

"Vipers, vipers!" Chernov called. "They have locked on, Captain! Range 2200 meters and closing!"

"The phase change is beginning," said Fedorov. "I think we're beginning to shift!"

Gromyko turned his head sharply. "Well we aren't going anywhere if those torpedoes find us first. Weapon's Officer, ready on tubes nine and ten!"

"Sir, *Shkval* system ready on tubes nine and ten!"

"Fire tube nine!"

"Weapon away!"

They heard the swish and then the sound of the *Shkval's* underwater rocket ignite as it streaked out at high speed, accelerating through 100 knots and beyond in a matter of seconds. This was what it had been designed for. Just as the Russians deployed superb high performance SAMs to protect their surface assets, the *Shkval-2* was the premier underwater anti-torpedo weapon in the world of 2021.

The next minute stretched out to an eternity, and Gromyko clenched his fist, counting under his breath, the sweat now dappling his brow. Then they heard the crack of an explosion as their lethal barb hit home. It had found one of the incoming Mark 48s and bored in mercilessly, destroying it with its 210kg warhead. The second torpedo was close by, and the shuddering sound and concussion radiated out and swamped it, sending it jolting off its intended course. In the chaos of noise it lost its lock on *Kazan*, but its computer brain quickly recovered, like a fighter shaking off a glancing blow to the head, and it began to execute a pre-programmed search maneuver, slowing and then pinging loudly on active sonar.

The Russian submarine was moving, shifting, displacing in time itself, a darkened Shadow Zone of unfathomable depth in the cold waters of infinity. They could all feel it now. Crewmen in the operations center looked around, startled by the strange charge in the atmosphere of the room. They could hear the odd sounds, feel a subtle tingling, and they looked about, clearly startled by the strange effects.

Only four men knew what was really happening that moment, the Admiral, Fedorov, Gromyko and his *Starpom* Belanov. There had been no time to brief the remainder of the crew.

"It appears Chief Dobrynin has pulled us out of the frying pan here," said Admiral Volsky.

"Not yet," Fedorov said with an ominous tone. "That last torpedo—how close was it?" He looked to Chernov now.

"1500 meters, but it has lost its lock on us and will execute a search pattern to see if it can re-acquire."

Fedorov looked at Admiral Volsky, fear in his eyes now. "It could shift with us, Admiral! It was too damn close."

The Mark 48 would not find *Kazan* in the autumn of 2021, where the world still bled at the hard razor's edge of war… but it might find it elsewhere, wherever they were going now as the Russian submarine seemed to sail through a dark hole in the ocean itself, and simply disappear.

* * *

"Detonation, sir!" Campanella shouted out the news when he heard the explosion, and saw the vibrant disturbance in the waterfall of his sonar data.

"Did we get the bastard?"

"Listening now, sir… Listening…" Campy looked up, his eyes betraying surprise. "I've lost them, Captain. All I can hear now are those two Type 65s heading our way like a freight train. There's no sign of the Russian sub at all now… no secondary explosions, nothing sir. I can't even hear our own torpedoes. They put a *Squall* in the water just before that detonation. I heard the rocket ignite plain as day. Maybe they took our boys down."

"But you can hear those big red pain sticks out there?"

"Aye sir, they're running hard and bearing about 275. Range 4250 meters approximate and closing. Pinging like banshees, Captain."

"Then there's nothing wrong with your sonar, or your ears, Campy. Keep listening, that sub is still out there somewhere playing possum. Helm, slow to one third. Left standard rudder and come to 250."

Now it was time for *Mississippi* to dance. The enemy lances were getting too close, and Donahue decided to make his quiet boat even stealthier by reducing speed and executing a soft ten degree turn away from the torpedoes.

"Let me know if those bad boys change bearing," he said to Campanella.

"They're running steady, sir. I don't think they have us."

They waited in the taut silence of the operations center until Campanella confirmed that the Russian torpedoes had continued off on the wrong attack vector.

"They've been in the water a good long time, Captain. They might be able to circle back, but at the moment I think they missed us."

"And what about our Russian friends out there?"

"Gone, sir. Not a whisper or a wobble. My sound field is completely empty on their last heading. It's as if they just vanished. Never heard a sub pull a trick like that before."

"Could they be hovering, Campy?"

"Possibly, sir. But we should still have a Mark 48 out there screaming like a wildcat unless they took them both out with just one shot. I was almost certain I heard one of our torpedoes still running after that explosion. Hell, maybe its motor failed and the damn thing is sinking into the deep, but it's gone too..."

Part VIII

Edge of Perdition

"The man who promises everything is sure to fulfill nothing, and everyone who promises too much is in danger of using evil means in order to carry out his promises, and is already on the road to perdition."

— *Carl Jung*

Chapter 22

They came through the hole in time Rod-25 had opened, but they were far from where they had hoped to go. And something came through with them.

Chernov sat with a look of intense concentration on his face, trying to determine what he had been listening to during the shift. The sounds were amazing, and he could hardly believe his ears. It was as if a chorus of angels were singing to him beneath those headphones, and his face registered a mix of surprise and awe as he listened. Then the static came, more from internal systems reacting badly to the displacement, stunned by the strange effects of the shift, even as those on *Kirov* had been so many times.

"What's wrong, Chernov," said Gromyko. "Your cheeks are on fire. Are you well?"

"It was awesome, Captain. But now I'm having difficulty… No… wait… *Torpedo in the water!*"

"Load large mobile decoy on the number eight tube!" Gromyko did not waste a second, reacting in sheer defensive reflex.

"Tube loading, sir, aye! Ready!"

"Fire decoy!"

"Firing now, sir."

"Hard right rudder. Ten degree down bubble!"

The Matador swirled and danced, flourishing his cape to distract the foe and then spinning about and swooping down onto his haunches as the bull's deadly horn drew near. The large mobile decoy ejected and then went noisily off on its own power as *Kazan* turned and dove away from the scene.

"Any idea how close that thing is, Chernov?"

"Sir, I have bearing only on passive. We would have to ping to get range quickly, but I had a good track on it before and it was inside 5000 meters when that strange interference occurred. Then I lost it temporarily, and there's something else in the water now. Surface contact, bearing one five zero, heavy screw noise. Not sure why I didn't hear it before."

Fedorov was close by the Captain's side now, and he leaned in, speaking in a low, urgent voice. "That was no ordinary interference, Gromyko. We've shifted. The sonar may have been affected and will recover by degrees. That was the work of Rod-25. The torpedo must have been very close if it shifted here with us."

"All stop—rig for absolute quiet running."

"All stop, sir, and silent now."

Kazan's propulsion system stopped, and the boat glided in the water, slowing by degrees, and sinking on the new downward heading. In a few minutes it was drifting, while the large noisemaker was waddling away at twenty five knots, and slowly climbing towards the surface.

Chernov had his eyes closed now, his brow dotted with perspiration in spite of the air conditioned control room. He could hear the spinning whirr of the torpedo, close at first, and then diminishing in sound. The longer he listened, the more he realized what had happened.

"Sir," he said, his voice barely a whisper. "I think the torpedo lost its hold on us. It is circling at low speed now in a programmed re-acquisition search, Captain."

Gromyko nodded, saying nothing; waiting in the silence.

"Torpedo has changed heading. I think it's going after the surface contact!"

"Steady…" Gromyko held up a hand, his eyes on the ceiling of the operations room.

Chernov spun a finger, swirling it about to indicate higher rotations on the torpedo engine. Then they heard a distant boom reverberate through the sea, and seconds later a palpable shock wave shook the boat.

"Steady…" The Captain was standing absolutely still, like a frozen statue, his eyes on Chernov now.

"That was the surface contact, sir. I'm getting secondary explosions. Someone was very unlucky up there today."

* * *

The unlucky ship that day was the Japanese cargo ship *Konzan Maru*, bound for Toyama Wan Bay on the west coast of Honshu, and she was fated that day. Her appointment with death was already logged, for on the 18th of June in 1945 she would run afoul of the USS *Bonefish*, one of three American subs mounting a raid in the Sea of Japan.

The US had been kept out of "the Emperor's bathtub" for most of the war by minefields, but now, in mid 1945, a few subs were fitted with new equipment, high-frequency, short-range sonar that could use frequency modulation to sweep the immediate area around the boat out to about 730 meters and detect mines. A wolfpack was formed at Guam in late May, and "Hydeman's Hellcats," consisting of nine boats, moved north and penetrated the Tsushima Straits undetected to enter the Sea of Japan. Three of the boats split off in a separate pack led by Commander Pierce aboard *Tunney*. "Pierce's Polecats" then consisted of that boat, the *Skate* under Commander Lynch, and the *Bonefish* under Commander Edge.

The three US subs formed a loose patrol that saw *Tunney* come up empty, though *Skate* was able to put a torpedo into the Japanese submarine I-22. *Bonefish* notched her belt by putting down the *Oshikayama Maru* and added almost 7,000 tons to her tally just two days ago. Now she was making a night surface rendezvous with *Tunney* to get further orders. Eager for more, Commander Edge sought permission to head for Toyama Wan Bay before the entire force would withdraw as planned on 24 June.

"Edge is asking if he can ease in towards the coast and scout Toyama Wan Bay," said the lamp signalman as Pierce finished a cigarette on the sail bridge.

"Hell, they've already got one ship on this patrol. If anyone should be eager for more it should be us." Commander Pierce wasn't happy. He wanted to pull his three boats into a tight fist and head for the wolfpack rendezvous point.

"Well, what should I tell them, sir?"

The polecat thought it over, and flicked away his cigarette butt. "Cut 'em loose. But tell them to head for point Zulu no later than zero eight hundred hours tomorrow. Kapish?"

"Right, sir, zero eight hundred."

Pierce went below, not knowing it was the last that he or anyone else would ever see of the USS *Bonefish*. The Boneheads, as they were called, were sailing off to their own little rendezvous with fate that night. Pierce and Tunney would wait for three days at the rendezvous point, but the Boneheads would never come home.

A day later *Bonefish* was sniffing out the wake of that unlucky Japanese cargo ship, and creeping up on *Konzan Maru* as she sought to enter the bay, but the sub would not get anywhere close. Something else had already found the *Konzan Maru*, awakening from a stupor as it circled like a dazed shark in the dim waters of the sea.

The American ADCAP Mark 48 lost its leash on *Kazan*, circled, then heard the noisome thrash of the cargo vessel up on the surface, leaving a nice foamy wake. Low on fuel, it elected to climb to that nearby target instead of trying to locate the elusive submarine it had been tasked to seek out and destroy. That was in the year 2021, some 76 years in the future, but the torpedo would make its kill in 1945.

Bonefish would be denied that day, as would the pack of hyena torpedo patrol boats led by escort ship *Okinawa* that were coming out from the bay to welcome *Konzan Maru* home. It was *Okinawa* and her confederates that swarmed over the American sub to seal her fate, but that history had just changed. Now Commander Edge stared through his periscope in amazement when he saw the Japanese cargo ship blow up, her spine cracked and split in two as she quickly settled into the sea.

"Damn, there goes my ship," he swore. "Who the hell is out here with us? Did Pierce tag along?"

"We don't have anything on sonar, sir," said the XO, Lieutenant Commander Knight."

"Well there's one mean fish in the sea with us somewhere, and it just took one hell of a bite out of that Jap cargo ship. Down periscope! Ten degrees down bubble and make your depth 90 feet. I don't want to be anywhere near the surface until I know what's out there." He shrugged looking around.

"What the hell are you doing there, Vincent?" One of his new recruits was writing with intense concentration on a notepad he always seemed to have at hand. "You making an entry in your personal log?"

"No, sir." Seaman First Class Thomas Vincent Jr. was a fresh faced young man from New York that Commander Edge had picked up to replace a crewman down with an attack of appendicitis before the patrol. That was luck too, for that attack saved the man's life, while taking that of this new recruit in his place.

"I was just figuring out what subs might look like in the future sir. What do you think?" he passed his notepad over so the Commander could take a look.

Edge took the pad, frowning at the sleek lines of the boat, with a bulbous round nose that looked very much like modern submarines. "How they supposed to make way on the surface with a round bow like that, Seaman?"

"They'll spend most of their time under water, sir, and won't need to surface much like we do."

"Is that so… Well what's this other thing here?"

"A rocket, sir. I figure they'll use those to fire at aircraft from under the sea, or even ships too far away for torpedoes, sir."

Commander Edge smiled at that. "You've got quite an imagination, kid," he said. The drawings of the sub and rocket were right next to sketches of Batman and Dick Tracy. "I suppose you figure people will have those Dick Tracy watches in the future too, eh?" Edge shook his head. "We'll get you a medal for that one," he said in jest, "but tend to your station, Seaman, and put that notebook aside."

Seaman First Class Tommy Vincent would get his medal another way, a posthumous Purple Heart awarded to all the crew members of the *Bonefish* after the rest of "Pierce's Polecats" gave up and turned for home three days later.

* * *

"**What** is happening?" Fedorov's face was drawn with concern.

"Explosion," said Chernov. "The American torpedo has struck that surface contact. And I'm picking up another undersea contact now, farther out, and bearing one-two-seven degrees."

"Undersea contact?" Gromyko seemed confused. "What is going on here? Where have all these contacts come from?"

Fedorov knew what was happening. The sonar was slowly gaining strength and resolution to paint a picture of their tactical situation in the immediate area. "Are you certain," he asked. An undersea contact was very bad news. There would be nothing in 1908 that would be skulking about beneath the waves here.

"Getting more surface noise now, Captain. At least five discrete contacts. Screw noise is high and tight. These sound like patrol craft, sir. And that undersea boat is heading our way and leading them right to us here."

"If this shift has happened do I have full reactor power now?"

"I don't see why not," said Fedorov.

"Very well," said Gromyko. "Right standard rudder and ahead two thirds. Make your depth 150."

They waited, with Chernov listening until they heard the sound of active sonar pinging audibly in the sea. It was unlike anything the sonar man had ever heard, and seemed fairly weak to his ear, but minutes later the sound of explosions rippled through the water. *Okinawa* and her group of fast patrol boats had found something, and they were furiously heaving depth charges into the sea in reprisal. One would scud against the side of the American submarine and the Boneheads would all retire to that eternal patrol, joining their brothers aboard USS *Snook*, also sunk by the *Okinawa*, the most successful ship in her class.

Fedorov shrugged, his eyes looking at the ceiling, imagining the scene out there as the American boat died. He knew what they had just heard, and was now certain that *Kazan* had not shifted to 1908.

"We'll have to try again, Admiral," he said hopefully. "Here there will be no further sonic interference from that volcano. Perhaps Chief Dobrynin will have better luck."

"Rod-25 remains very stubborn, does it not? It insists on dropping us into the waters of WWII."

"What is happening, Admiral?" Gromyko wanted to know the score, and Fedorov briefed him quietly, telling them they were going to have to initiate the procedure once again.

"The good news is that there will be no more trouble of the sort we just had. All you need do is cruise very deep and we should be well below any further action here."

"Very well. Where should I point my nose, Mister Fedorov?"

"Here…" Fedorov pointed to a tactical display on the navigation monitor. Put us due west of the Oki Island Group."

"Why there?" asked Volsky.

"If I know Karpov, he will be trying to find and engage the Japanese in a decisive battle. And if I know Admiral Togo, the man will deploy his fleet here." He pointed to a spot south of Tsushima Island, very near the tip. "If you assume a position west of the Oki Islands, that will put us on a general bearing back to Vladivostok. We'll use Orlov's idea and say we came through the Primorskiy Engineering Center."

"Assuming we get there at the correct time," said Gromyko. "Do we have any idea where we are now—I mean the date?" He lowered his voice, glancing askance at a couple crewmen to chase the curiosity from them and set them back to their monitors.

"We really don't know for certain, and we would have to run up an antenna to sample signals intelligence. From past experience we can assume this may be the 1940s, and if I heard what I thought I just heard out there, the Japanese have just sunk an American sub, so I believe it would be very late in the war, 1945."

"How can you know this?" Gromyko folded his arms, unconvinced.

"Because US subs could not penetrate the Sea of Japan until that time in the war. In fact. If I spent some time with my research I think I could probably tell you exactly what happened out there just now, right down to the vessels involved on both sides. All I would have to do is find an instance of a US sub sinking near our present location."

"You assume that history is all undisturbed, Mister Fedorov," said Volsky. "Remember, our nemesis was here earlier—in this very year if this is 1945—and he raised hell up north in the Kuriles."

"Yes…." Fedorov's eyes seemed to sparkle now. "Sir, can we take this discussion to a secure area?"

"Very well," said Gromyko. "Mister Belanov. Make your depth 400 meters and ahead two thirds. Steer 220 degrees and take us west of Oki Island. Then hover. You have the con."

"Aye sir."

Chapter 23

"**Follow** me, gentlemen." Gromyko led the way to the officer's briefing room. Once inside Fedorov removed his hat, eager to speak.

"Admiral, I believe we now find ourselves in the year 1945. That could be verified if we surface for signals intelligence, but I am almost certain if that noise we heard was Japanese coastal defense units attacking a US sub. What else could it be?"

"What is all this noise? Can't an old man get any sleep these days?"

They looked to see that Pavel Kamenski had come shuffling into the briefing room, and the Admiral greeted him with a smile.

"Please sit down and join us, Mister Kamenski. Fedorov here believes we are now in 1945. It appears that our Chief Dobrynin was not able to work his magic after all."

"Oh? Or perhaps your Rod-25 simply has an affinity for the 1940s," said Kamenski. "Remember those gopher holes I talked about. Maybe we must first arrive here before we can discover the hole that leads us deeper into the garden to 1908 where your Mister Karpov is still digging."

"That is one possibility," said Fedorov. "Yet if I am correct, here we find ourselves in 1945, the same year *Kirov* appeared after the eruption of that Demon Volcano. If we could determine the exact day and time here, we could possibly get to the last reported position of the Red Banner Pacific Fleet before that eruption happened. Then, when *Kirov* and the other ships appear here, we will be right there—and with three control rods—enough to get everyone safely home again!"

Kamenski gave him a smile. "Very clever, this young man."

"Amazing," said Volsky, considering this. The Admiral recalled his own internal muse as he struggled with the problem at Fokino headquarters, fretting over Dobrynin and his mission to rescue Fedorov. *If I had it to do over I would have put that control rod we found in Vladivostok on a submarine. Then it would have been right here to find Karpov and surface to deliver the rod. Perhaps it could have hovered beneath the ship and come home when Kirov shifted...* That seemed a better idea to him, but now he did not see how this could work.

"I don't understand one thing," said Volsky. "At this moment Karpov is in 1908. How could we possibly do this? Would not his very presence in that year mean that we *fail* to do what Fedorov suggests?"

"That could very well be the case," said Kamenski.

"But we are here," said Fedorov, and well before *Kirov* arrives. Doesn't that trump anything Karpov chooses to do?"

Kamenski's eyes narrowed. "I believe the Captain was sent here by chance," said Kamenski. "He certainly did not choose anything. It was that volcano, or perhaps fate, that sent *Kirov* and the other ships to this time."

"Then we should be able to intervene here."

Kamenski sighed. "Captain, Gromyko, do you recall any of the history of this period—the end of the Second World War?"

Gromyko thought for a moment. "The Kuriles incident...The Americans claimed that Russian naval units engaged their forces in August of 1945, sinking surface ships, a submarine, and shooting down American planes. That led to Halsey's Kuriles operation, where the Americans made the further preposterous claim that Soviet Russia deployed nuclear weapons against their fleet, sinking the battleship *Iowa*. Yes. Everyone knows that history, Mister Kamenski, and the terrible days that followed."

"Indeed, what followed, if you will indulge us briefly here."

"Why, the American bombing of Vladivostok, sir. It almost started a third world war right after the second one. Zukhov and Patton were eye to eye in Germany and nearly came to blows, but fortunately diplomacy prevailed."

"And to this day Russia still denies it had anything to do with the sinking of the *Iowa*." Kamenski smiled. "Now then, Mister Fedorov, you seem to be very well acquainted with the history of WWII. Do you recall anything about the Americans bombing Vladivostok in late August of 1945?"

"No I do not," said Fedorov. "The war ended after Hiroshima and Nagasaki. Then we altered that and it ended when Admiral Yamamoto managed to persuade the Emperor to capitulate and avoid further destruction and bloodshed. I know nothing of what Captain Gromyko had just said."

"There you have it," said Kamenski. "I suppose if we took a poll most of the men on this boat will agree with Captain Gromyko here. Yet as for myself, the Admiral, Mister Fedorov, and all the other visitors on your submarine today, we all know a very different story of that period in history… In fact I know *several* versions. You get this way with the years, but the point I am making here is that time seems to have closed her books on that chapter of the history. Karpov did what he did, even if Stalin knew nothing about it and denied the whole affair. He was telling the truth, from his perspective, but it was still a lie. You see, gentlemen, time is not a straight line. One thing does not necessarily lead to another, like falling dominoes. Time branches out like a tree, and we are the gardeners."

"Then you do not think we can still prevent what Karpov did in 1945? Why not?" Fedorov still believed they could trump Karpov's hand here. "If we get to him before he arrives here, then we should be able saw off the limb he brought into being."

"I cannot say why, but I have a strong feeling that we may be prevented somehow. Let us think of this from the point of view of Mother Time. We are here because Karpov is in 1908. Now we come up with an idea to prevent him from ever getting there! This is a paradox, yes? So we might go lie in wait as you suggest, and Mother Time might rebuke us by simply sending Karpov back to a different date and time here. In fact, that would be the only way she could avoid the paradox you create with this idea."

"I see…" Fedorov thought deeply about this. "Then we have multiple alternatives. It isn't one single thread of time." The realization shook him somewhat.

Kamenski was correct. Call it a hunch, an inner sense of foreboding, or just a lucky guess. The intercom interrupted them at that very moment, and Chief Dobrynin had something to say.

"Admiral? Captain? Dobrynin here. Something is amiss."

"A problem with the reactors, Chief?"

"Not exactly sir, but I do not think the event has concluded. I am starting to hear those strange harmonics again."

"What do you mean?" said Volsky. "The time displacement has not concluded?"

"Well, sir... It doesn't sound like it has. The song is starting up again. I think our position here is unstable. I will do what I can to control it, but I think we are going to shift again."

"So, gentlemen," said Kamenski. "I think we are about to fall through to another gopher hole."

* * *

It was not long before Dobrynin's song was playing at the heart of the reactor again, and like an aftershock to the main event, *Kazan* slipped again in time. Whether it was his skill in controlling the reactors at that moment, or a strange unexplained magnetism that was calling Rod-25 home to the year its matter first plummeted from the heavens at Tunguska, the submarine fell through to the year 1908. They rose to the surface to listen to signals traffic, and all they could hear was the dot-dash world of Morse code over wireless telegraph systems, a faint scratching of the airwaves that were otherwise clean and silent. So they sat there again in the briefing room, intent on deciding what they must now do.

"This was the answer to your question, Mister Fedorov. Perhaps we might have done something to re-write the history in Captain Gromyko's head, but I think Mother Time had other ideas."

"It appears so, Director," said Fedorov. "Signals traffic gives every indication that we are now in the pre-radio age. The question is when? We do not have a handle on the correct date yet, but I believe that we must be here after Karpov has already arrived aboard *Kirov*."

"Why do you say this?" asked Gromyko. "Why not months before he got here?"

"That is a possibility, though it would be very problematic for time to work out—and for us. You see, many here shifted back to 1908 aboard *Anatoly Alexandrov*. If we have just arrived here *before* that time, then what happens to us at the moment when we first shifted here on the floating power plant? There would be two of us, and something tells me that even in the midst of all these incongruous and astounding events, that would be impossible—two Fedorovs, two Dobrynins, two Sergeant Troyaks, two Orlovs, and so on. We cannot co-locate in any time period where we already exist. Time would not allow that shift, which would upset everything. The backwards shift of the *Anatoly Alexandrov* must happen for us to even be here! Understand?"

"Very wise," said Kamenski. "That would create quite an accounting problem for time when that day rolled around."

"Yes," said Fedorov, "and so I think it is simply not possible for us to shift to an earlier day. We must be here *after* our shift home."

"Alright," said Volsky. "Let us assume that time wishes to impose some order on our shenanigans here. Let us assume we have arrived after that date. What day might this be?"

"The *Anatoly Alexandrov* arrived here August 17, 1908. We went ashore on the Caspian coast to verify that date. We were only there 48 hours, waiting for Karpov to decide what to do. It was August 19th when we shifted all the way back to 2021. So my guess is that we have arrived here from the 20th day of August, or later."

"What if it is months later?" said Gromyko.

"Then we would be too late, and Karpov would have worked his mischief. We would have failed, and so we should have known about that before we left. No, I think we still have a chance to succeed. I think everything is still in the whirlwind. That is why we could not know what Karpov did before we departed 2021. The possibility of our success here existed and forced time to suspend judgment—is that not so, Director Kamenski?"

"This is the way I reason it. I believe the rifts in time are also very limited and specific—the gopher holes, as I call them. Clearly there was a tunnel from 2021 to the 1940s on that back stairway in the inn at Ilanskiy. Karpov may have broken into another borehole in time when his attack on the *Iowa* shifted *Kirov* here."

"Yes," said Volsky. "But I have never understood why *Orlan* did not shift as well, and why it suffered the fate I saw in that old photograph you gave me, swarmed over by a hundred American planes. *Kirov* shifted, but not *Orlan*."

"*Kirov* is the slippery fish," said Kamenski. "It has bounced back and forth in time so often that its position in any given milieu is never certain."

"I agree," said Fedorov, recalling that awful moment on the bridge when the Japanese cruiser *Tone* came barreling out of the mist and appeared to sail right through the ship. "In the early stages the ship seemed to pulse in time, moving in and out before finally stabilizing. That was before we understood the controlling effects of Rod-25."

"So in that light, given a situation where an event causes the fabric of time to break, *Kirov* has an affinity for slipping through the cracks. I suppose that may have happened to *Orlan* as well if it had survived that last battle. But our *Sea Eagle* falls in 1945, never to sortie on the waters of infinity again. Now, gentlemen, we must decide on how we handle *Kirov*—that slippery fish out there somewhere—before it slips away again."

"As I see it we have only those same two choices," said Fedorov. "We either persuade Karpov to come to his senses and rejoin us—we net the fish and then try to get us all home to 2021. The other choice is the hard one—we must kill the white whale—spear the fish and make an end of Karpov that way."

There was silence for some time, then Gromyko spoke. "If I have to spear this fish, will I have tactical command of how I fight this battle?"

Admiral Volsky seemed weary now, his eyes heavy, brow furrowed, and a sense of sadness in his voice. "If we fight, then yes, Gromyko, you will command *Kazan* in battle. I do not know the first thing about how this submarine fights, and I have already witnessed your skills when you dueled with the Japanese and Americans to get us here. As to whether or not you actually engage, however, that will be my decision. I would hope it could be avoided. My first choice will be to try and persuade Karpov to rejoin us."

"So we will surrender the element of surprise?"

"I can see no other way, and I know this presents us all with yet another possibility here, and a rather dark one. What if we fail, even with *Kazan?* What if Karpov is the one who spears this slippery fish?"

Gromyko folded his arms. "I will do everything possible to prevent that," he said, "and I have every confidence we can prevail."

"Mister Fedorov?" Volsky looked at his young Captain now. "What do you think?"

"I cannot say I am well versed in combat, sir. I learned a great deal from Karpov, and from watching Gromyko earlier. It will be a sad thing to watch, but one hell of a fight if it comes to it."

"Well I will say one thing," said Volsky. "I suppose the professors and instructors at the war colleges might also agree. All things being equal, the submarine has the edge if it comes to a duel with a single surface ship like this. How would you attack, Gromyko?"

"Well sir, we have a good array of weapons aboard. Torpedoes are perhaps our most deadly weapon. If I can get within 20 kilometers of that ship I can pose a dire threat with torpedoes. But we can attack with missiles as well. I have 32 VLS tubes armed with an array of P-800s and P-900s. The latter are 3M-54E variants with a range of 220 kilometers and a terminal attack speed of nearly Mach 3 on their final run to the target. A large salvo would be very hard for a single ship to deal with. The only trick is finding the ship before we fire. Our radar seems inoperative."

"That is a residual effect from the time displacement. It will clear up shortly, and then I will contact Karpov and see what I can do to avoid further action. The ship has a formidable SAM defense, and Karpov knows how to use it."

"I have seen Karpov in battle," said Fedorov. "And I also believe I know how he thinks in battle. Perhaps I could assist you if it comes down to combat."

"I would welcome anything you may have to say," said Gromyko. "Were there helicopters aboard?"

"The normal loadout, two KA-40s and a KA-226. But again, I cannot say if they all survived to reach 1908 with the ship."

"I must assume as much," said Gromyko. "Well," he sighed, "we have gamed this many times on maneuvers. I did trials against *Pytor Veliky* before that ship went in for refit. It was the longest serving *Kirov* class ship, and very capable."

"Yes," said Volsky. "Well you will be fighting a piece or two of that ship should you face the new *Kirov*. We used parts of all four vessels in the original class."

"There is one more thing," said Gromyko. "We have special warheads…"

Volsky gave him a sallow look. "What is your inventory?" he said quietly, an uncomfortable edge to his voice.

"We have two RU-100 *Veter* torpedoes with 20 kiloton nuclear warheads. The rest are RU-40 conventional torpedoes, six of those with a range of 120 kilometers." The *Veter* was a rocket assisted weapon that actually entered the atmosphere to cross much of that distance before diving into the sea again to become a torpedo in this new variant. *Veter* meant "wind" in Russian, and these lances carried a dark storm of anger on the wind if they were fired.

"We also have one 15 Kiloton warhead for the P-900s."

"I must remind you that *Kirov* had a loadout of special warheads as well. There is every reason to believe that Karpov has already used one or more of these weapons—in 1945. So you see the Americans were correct after all. The Russians did attack them with atomic weapons, wielded by a madman. God help us all if it comes down to this again here."

"Indeed," said Kamenski. "We have been punching holes in time with our nuclear weapons for decades. Now we have made a veritable Swiss cheese of things. Let us hope this is the end of all that, but it may be necessary if push comes to shove here."

"I fear as much," said Volsky.

Chapter 24

Karpov was standing with Rodenko at the tactical station, reviewing the data that had been fed to the ship on the last long range search by the KA-40. It was clear that the Japanese were now attempting to lead him south. He had brushed aside the screen of light torpedo boats that had challenged him, and now the main event was nigh at hand—Armageddon.

"So there they sit," said Karpov with a smug look on his face. "Four or five old battleships, and perhaps ten to twelve armored cruisers like those we smashed earlier in the Oki Island group. The rest are destroyers and torpedo boats. This will be much easier than you may realize, Rodenko. We will close to about 20,000 meters and begin using the deck guns. That will shock them. We'll just make selected pot shots and shake them up as before. Then I will show them a few of our modified S-400s and shred their decks and superstructures with shrapnel. If a massed flotilla presents itself, the *Vodopad* torpedoes would be an easy reprise. One torpedo should be fairly lethal, and being rocket assisted, they will get to their targets like missiles. As soon as Togo has the temerity to present himself on his flagship, I will put a *Moskit-II* into his belly and see how he likes the fire. Even if we have to use five missiles here, that should wreak havoc on those old ships and still leave us a considerable inventory for post-operations maneuvers."

Rodenko raised an eyebrow at that. "What is it you have in mind, Captain?"

"Once I smash the enemy fleet here, we will push on through the strait and into the Yellow Sea. I'll sink anything that bears a Japanese flag, and then we stand off Port Arthur and impose our quarantine."

"Captain, sir." It was Nikolin in communication with the KA-40. "The helicopter is on return approach and they say they have one final data block to upload to the CIC here."

"Ah, so our tactical board is not complete. Have them send it now, Nikolin. We need all the information here before I open the action."

"It's a video feed associated with their last radar sweep."

"Put it on the overhead HD panel."

The two men stepped from behind the glowing Plexiglas Tactical Board and stood waiting for the feed to display. Then Karpov squinted, his head inclined to stare at the image on the screen. It was clearly a line of warships, laboring through the rising seas.

"Well, well, well," said Karpov, hand on his chin. "Freeze that shot Nikolin…. Good. Now zoom in please…. There. What do you make of that, Rodenko? Note the standard that lead ship is flying."

"British, sir."

"Indeed. It seems we may have missed something in our research. What would British ships be doing out here?"

"I believe they had ships at Hong Kong, Captain."

"No," said Karpov, holding up a finger. "These can't be from Hong Kong. Now I remember! They had to come from the China Station at Weihaiwei on the Yellow Sea. Well this is getting very interesting—six more ships joining the party."

"The radar returns are showing up on my tactical board now," said Rodenko. "Course and speed indicate they are moving towards the battle zone. This will bring the total force deployed to 35 ships, sir, assuming the British side with the Japanese."

The Captain folded his arms, somewhat annoyed. "This complicates things," he said. "If the British get involved that forces my hand into a conflict with the Royal Navy. That doesn't matter militarily. I'll deal with those ships as easily as I handle the Japanese, but it does bode ill for Russia's prospects in the future if we go to war with Britain."

It was the first surprise Karpov would have that day, but it would not be the last. Nikolin was sitting at his station, quietly monitoring telegraph traffic. The Japanese had been very silent and the signals he was listening to were in plain Morse. It appeared to be routine commercial traffic. Ships were checking weather information, sea conditions, requesting berthing, and traffic was very light. Then his HF secure coded military band suddenly indicated an incoming transmission, and he nearly jumped out of his seat. He stared at the light, quickly adjusting his headphones as he reached for the switch to activate that channel.

"...*Vladivostok. Over. Repeat. This is Captain Anton Fedorov on station K-11 Vladivostok. Calling Kirov, come in. Over.*"

Fedorov! What was he doing on this channel? Nikolin quickly checked the signal vector on his automatic Radio Magnetic Indicator and noted the bearing as almost true north. A quick look at a chart told him the signal was right on axis for Vladivostok. How did he get there? Just days ago he was in the Caspian on shortwave. His heart leapt and he looked to see where Karpov was, standing near the Plexiglas situation map with Rodenko. The glow of the illuminated digital map traced lines over the features of the two men, drawing the map of the region on their uniforms and faces. Then some inner instinct whispered a warning to him. Whatever this message was, it was coming at a critical time. It was important, and so he reached over and toggled a switch to record the transmission, and also placed a backup on a memory key.

"Captain," he said. "I have HF traffic on the coded military signal band!"

He saw Karpov's head turn, his eyes narrowing, a cloud of suspicion on his face. "A coded signal? On our standard HF channel?"

"Yes, sir. It's Mister Fedorov calling again. He's in Vladivostok!"

"What?" Karpov was moving now, stepping quickly from behind the Plexiglas screen. "Vladivostok?"

"Shall I put it on speaker, Captain?"

"No, Mister Nikolin. I'll take this call personally. Busy yourself with the weather data for the moment. This is command level business." Karpov waved him from his chair, and Nikolin retreated to the weather monitor, looking furtively over his shoulder as the

Captain settled in and quickly put the headphones on. His hand was unsteady as he reached for the handset, thumbing the send button.

"Fedorov! What are you doing on this channel?" Karpov's voice was low, a raspy whisper as he spoke, his eyes looking up to chase any curious glance from bridge crew members away with an angry stare.

"*Captain Karpov! Fedorov here. I report that we were able to return successfully to our home year, and I have flown to Vladivostok with the control rods. Over.*"

"But what are you doing *here*, Fedorov. How did you get back to 1908 again?"

"*Just as I left before, Captain. We used the reactor test bed at the Primorskiy Engineering Center, and Dobrynin was able to calibrate it to reach this year. I am now in an old cottage in Vladivostok, with a military radio set. There is someone with me who wishes to speak to you. Please hold...* "

Karpov waited, a thousand thoughts swirling in the hiss of the background noise. Then a familiar, low voice came through his headset, and he knew exactly who it was.

"*Captain Karpov. This is Admiral Leonid Volsky. I have accompanied Mister Fedorov on a most remarkable journey here, and I hope I do not have to tell you why. Your decision to intervene here is most unwise, and as Admiral of the Fleet I am now giving you a direct order to cease and desist. The consequences of anything you may do here are simply too severe. Bring the ship here, Mister Karpov, to Vladivostok. We have control rods with us that can get you safely home. This is a direct order from me to you. Beyond that, Moscow has also been informed and this order comes directly from the entire naval board. Over.*"

Karpov's pulse pounded at his temples, his eyes casting about in sharp, nervous movements. He had to think quickly. What could he say to buy more time? "That is not possible," he said in a low whisper. "We are at the edge of a major engagement!"

"*Then use your speed and break off that engagement, Captain. This is an order! What in God's name are you doing here, Karpov? I have heard of mission creep but this is outrageous! We know what you did in 1945. You and your ship must return home at once! You were gifted with command of the fleet flagship, with my trust in you, and the fate of that ship and crew is now in your hands. In exchange for that honor you gave me something I thought you considered of great value at that time—your word and promise. And do not tell me the men have decided this course. You as Captain are responsible. You must return Kirov and the men home safely. This is imperative!"*

Karpov hesitated, a tormented look on his face. "That is my intention, sir," he lied. "But to do that I must assure there is a safe home to return to. We could not do that before—not in 2021 or in the 1940s. But here I can accomplish everything we hoped to achieve. I am within an hour of changing the entire course of history in the Pacific! Japan will never rise as an imperial power. The Second World War will never be fought here. Don't you understand?"

"Com. Radar." Came the report from Kochenko. "Range is now18000 meters and closing."

"Karpov. Listen to me. We have seen the history. The change will be more than you realize. It will be catastrophic! You must desist at once and obey this order. We can explain everything to you at Vladivostok." Volsky could here Karpov trying to argue with him and so he lied as well, hoping to convince him his attempt to re-write history would end in failure.

The Captain squeezed the handset, hunching over Nikolin's desk to mask his voice. "We are in battle!" he rasped. "I do not have *time* for this, Admiral. The ship is in jeopardy! I will contact you after we conclude this action and the ship is safe."

"No, Karpov! Break off now! Do not engage! I repeat. You are ordered to disengage and withdraw at once. This is critical! If you fail to obey, this order falls on your Starpom, and should he fail to heed this command, then it falls to the next senior watch officer on the bridge, Mister Samsonov, through Tasarov, and then to Nikolin. If no man among them stands up and obeys, then I hereby appoint Dr. Zolkin as the ship's commander, whether he knows a thing about operations or

not. At least his judgment will be sound. Do you hear me, Karpov? It is vital that you comply at once!"

Then, just as the Admiral was finishing his urgent order, Karpov heard something quite unexpected in the background, another voice, another name, and his face registered alarm, even as his heart pounded out a warning and the rapid pulse of imminent danger.

* * *

Aboard *Kazan* the Admiral had been huddling with Fedorov, both men with headsets on at the communications station, their faces drawn and serious. Captain Gromyko was standing by, hands on his hips as he listened to the transmission being played over the comm speaker. Even as Volsky repeated his urgent order, a *Mishman* stepped through a nearby open hatch with a clipboard.

"Captain Gromyko, sir. I have the maintenance log for—"

Gromyko whirled about, his eyes wide, arm extended as if to stop the man. Fedorov twisted in his seat holding a finger to his lips to indicate silence as the Admiral finished. There was a brief interval of quiet. Then they heard Karpov's voice come back, quick and urgent. *"Very well, Admiral... Karpov out..."*

"Captain Karpov?" The Admiral thumbed his send button. "Are you there, Karpov? Respond. Over." There was nothing on the channel but the dry hiss of background static.

* * *

Aboard *Kirov* the Captain set the handset heavily on the comm panel, his other hand reaching up to slowly remove the headset. He stood up, and the torment in his eyes fled like storm clouds before the wind. Now they were dark and empty, a cold, lifeless expression on his face, cheeks drawn beneath his sallow gaze as he stared out the forward viewport. He seemed to be standing in the midst of a great void, an emptiness of the soul, his shoulders hunched and stooped.

Then he straightened, taking a long, deep breath as if to draw in energy from the tension of the moment.

"Mister Nikolin. There will be no further signals traffic over the HF Military band until this action is concluded. Understood?"

"Yes, sir." Nikolin looked like a schoolboy being dressed down, and returned to his post.

The Captain walked deliberately to the flag briefing room, quietly closing the door behind him. The eyes of the bridge crew followed him, particularly Rodenko where he still stood by the digital situation map, the lines of distant ships now glowing softly red on the screen.

Inside the briefing room alone, the Captain now moved with urgent swiftness. He activated a system monitor and quickly typed in a password to log on to the fleet manifest. His hands were unsteady as he typed, backspacing to correct two errors. The words on the screen finally scrolled up, *GROMYKO, IVAN, CAPTAIN of the 1st RANK,* Karpov's finger ran across to the column indicating current fleet assignment. There it was…. SSGN *KAZAN*…

Karpov tapped the name of the ship with a taut finger, and the display quickly called up the profile:

Yasen Class, *Boat No. 2* - SSGN *Kazan*.

Commission Date. June 15, 2015. *(Modified Severodvinsk)*

Displacement: *12,800 Submerged, Length: 120m, Beam: 15m, Draught: 8.4m*

Propulsion: *One modified KPM Pressurized Water Reactor*

Speed: *20 Knots Surface; Submerged: 35+ Knots. Test Depth: 600m*

Compliment: *32 Officers, 58 Enlisted*

Current Loadout:

16 x 3M-54E Klub P-900(VLS)

16x Onyx P-800 (VLS)

8x650mm Torpedo Tubes (83R): Load of 24

2x533mm Torpedo Tubes (82R): Load of 16

2 x Veter Rocket Assisted Torpedoes (RU-100 Nuclear Capable)

6x Veter Conventional Long Range Rocket Assisted Torpedoes

Additional Munitions: *VA-111 Shkval (6)*

Special Warheads: *Classified*

The longer Karpov looked at the data the more the blood seemed to drain from his face. They were *lying...* They were *not* in Vladivostok as Fedorov claimed. They did *not* use the test bed reactors at the Primorskiy Engineering Center. They were here, now, aboard one of the most lethal attack submarines in the navy. Now the full measure of what was happening here suddenly rose in his awareness like red heat.

They were out there in the silent darkness of the sea, hidden like a venomous adder that had crept quietly into his bunk, and there might be nothing more than the faint, sibilant hiss of the torpedoes as they fired to warn him of imminent destruction. They are trying to *kill me*, he thought, his mind at the edge of a barely restrained panic. *They are trying to kill us all!*

He leaned heavily on the counter, and then he remembered it, the service revolver he had secreted away there a week ago after they had first displaced to this time period. It was as if he anticipated trouble here, possibly a restive crew or opposition from one or more officers. Certainly Zolkin would oppose what he planned to do, though he felt he could handle that challenge. Rodenko, however, was another matter. He was *Starpom*, and in that position had a great deal of authority, and he had been somewhat squeamish of late, raising objections and questioning decisions at almost every turn.

So Karpov quietly placed a service revolver behind the chart box in the plot room, and now he stooped to retrieve it, slipping the belt around his waist and concealing the weapon beneath his service coat. He sighed, feeling better, but noticed a discernible nervous jitter in his hand.

A goddamned submarine!

Part IX

Trials

"The time to take counsel of your fears is before you make an important battle decision. That's the time to listen to every fear you can imagine!"

— **General George Patton**

Chapter 25

Nikolin returned to his station, a nervous look on his face. He sat down, eyeing the Captain with a furtive glance, and when Karpov withdrew to the flag briefing room he fixed his headphones in place and reached for the message recording bank. His hand hesitated briefly as he wondered whether he should play the recording back, but curiosity overwhelmed him and defeated his caution. Who would know? It would seem as though he were just monitoring signal traffic. So he toggled the switch to replay the message, listening with surprise and then growing alarm as he realized what was happening. Fedorov was in Vladivostok with Admiral Volsky! The Admiral was ordering the ship to disengage and return to that port at once!

His gaze strayed to Rodenko, who seemed to be fidgeting uneasily at the Plexiglas situation map, his eye drawn upward to the Tin Man HD screen as he looked at real-time images of the symbols being tracked on the digital display. He was putting the two systems into synchronization mode, so that he could simply tap the Plexiglas screen and the Tin Man would zoom on that precise location to display the hi-res optical feed. At intervals Rodenko looked aft to the flag briefing room where Karpov had sealed himself away, and Nikolin could see the same curiosity in the *Starpom's* eyes. What was the Captain doing? More to the point, Nikolin wondered what he was doing himself? Should he tell Rodenko what he heard? What if the Captain suddenly emerged from the flag bridge in the middle of that?

The urgency of the Admiral's voice alarmed him now… *"If you fail to obey, this order falls on your Starpom, and should he fail to heed this command, then it falls to the next senior watch officer on the bridge, Mister Samsonov, through Tasarov, and then to Nikolin…"* My God, what was happening? What if no one else obeys the order? What should I do? His heart beat faster as the message concluded. Then the hatch to the flag briefing room opened and the Captain stepped onto the battle bridge, his face set and grim.

"Mister Tasarov, come here."

Tasarov looked up sheepishly, not knowing why the Captain would want him. There had been very little to do at his station in recent days. This era presented no undersea threats, but he had busied himself listening to the sea around them, noting the special quality of its emptiness and silence when the ship was alone, and then honing in on the sonic characteristics of the Japanese ships when they were present. They seemed to slosh through the water with a ponderous noise, and he could easily hear their approach on passive sonar from many miles away, well over the horizon.

Now the Captain was waving at him impatiently, and so he removed his headset and slowly stood up. The look on the Captain's face made him feel he was about to be disciplined for something. He knew he had been told not to listen to music at his post, but he had pocketed his music player and never used it now when Karpov was on the bridge. He had been sending text messages back and forth to Nikolin as the two men played an old favorite Russian game of riddles. Did Karpov discover the surreptitious messages?

"Com. Radar." Kochenko was reporting again to note the current range interval. "Range is now 16,000 meters and closing."

Rodenko gave the Captain a look, as though he expected an order, but Karpov simply shooed Tasarov into the flag briefing room and then closed the hatch. This was enough of an irregularity to prompt him to move from behind the Plexiglas screen and onto the main bridge area, his eyes fixed on the closed hatch, and then straying upward again to the HD feed where the image of a long battle line of warships was clearly evident, under the long billowing charcoal smoke from their stacks as they labored into the rising wind.

Inside the flag briefing room Karpov now fixed Tasarov with a hard stare. "Mister Tasarov, there has not been much work at your station for some days, but that is about to change."

Tasarov thought the Captain was angry with him and going to assign him to some new duty, but it seemed very odd to him that he would take such a disciplinary action at the edge of battle like this.

Then the Captain asked him a question that set the conversation off on a most unexpected direction.

"You have sonic signatures of undersea boats stored in our computers?"

"Sir? Well, yes sir. Of course."

"How extensive are they? Do you have profiles on our ships and boats as well as those of the enemy?"

"Yes sir. Our ships are in the secondary memory, but I can call them to the live profile track when we exercise with fleet units."

"Excellent. Then you have sonic profiles on all our submarines?"

"Those we have maneuvered with are current, sir. Other boats would be in the data library, but they would be general recordings, and all the data would not be considering our current sound field. They are more like templates."

"Could you identify one of our own submarines if it were anywhere nearby?"

"That depends on many things, sir, yes, I suppose I could, yet I don't understand—"

"Alright. Then we will liven up your duty here a bit. I want you to assume undersea alert one when you return to your station. How would you look for one of our very best submarines—just as an example."

"Sir?" Obviously the Captain had some kind of drill in mind to keep him busy. "Well if it was a very quiet boat I would use the KA-40 and the towed Horse Tail sonar to augment my normal shipborne systems."

"Excellent. Do this. Assume you must find the best submarine we have. I will be sending up the KA-40 as soon as it replenishes, and you may issue direct orders to that asset as well. Deploy the towed sonar array if you wish, or even use active sonar if you would deem it necessary to hone in on a contact. I want you to do anything you might normally do to provide the ship with the best possible awareness of any undersea threat. Understood?"

Tasarov raised his eyebrows beneath the dark crop of brown hair protruding from the edge of his service cap. "Is this an exercise, sir?"

"Of course. I cannot simply let you sit there musing on the ocean floor and listening to whales. You must be as sharp at your post as any of the others."

"Very well, Captain. I will assume undersea alert level one."

"And to make your exercise a little more demanding, assume we are actually in a war situation with one of our very best submarines. What boat would you select?"

Something in the Captain's eyes made Nikolin very nervous now, a darkness that held fear as well as the cold logic and calculation of war. "In this theater, sir? Why I suppose I would chose *Kazan*. That's a *Yasen* class boat, sir, very quiet, very stealthy." He noted what he thought was a flash of trepidation on the Captain's face when he said that, as if he had hit some deep nerve of fear.

"Good... Assume it is out there somewhere, that very boat. Listen for it. Report anything you hear."

Tasarov nodded, but the order made little sense to him. "But I won't hear anything, Captain. *Kazan* is not out there."

"Listen as if it *was* here. That is the only way to drill, Tasarov. Yes? Now, we are about to go into battle. Your job may be difficult here, but I want to know immediately, *immediately*, if you hear anything at all that might indicate the presence of a hostile undersea contact—of *any* undersea contact. Understood?"

"But sir, there won't be... Yes sir."

"And at undersea alert one you realize you will also have the RBU rocket defense system as well as the *Shkval* torpedo system and the RPK-2 *Viyugas* primed and operational at all times, correct? I want full readiness."

"Yes sir." Squalls and blizzards... That's what *Shkval* and *Viyuga* meant. The undersea weather was going to be very bad, it seemed. He wondered if the Captain would ask him to fire any of the weapons.

"Do not look so confused, Mister Tasarov. You may not fully understand why I order this, but it has come to my attention that there are, indeed, fledgling submarines in this era." A little *vranyo*, a simple garnish on the salad. That would do the job here, Karpov thought. "So if you are listening for our very best, and searching for it out there, then you will certainly find anything they might have deployed from this era, correct?"

"Of course, sir."

"Alright then." The Captain turned and punched the wall comm-link panel, taking the handset. "Flight deck," he said tersely. "Prepare the KA-40 for operations as soon as it is recovered—full ASW loadout."

There was a brief silence on the line before a voice came back. *"Anti-submarine loadout, sir?"*

"That is what I just ordered. Now be quick about it! Mister Tasarov will be authorized to conduct this launch at his discretion. You will coordinate with him."

"Aye, sir. The helo is landing in five minutes. We'll be ready soon after. Flight deck out."

"There you are, Tasarov. I'm counting on those sharp ears of yours now, and I may join your exercise during this action. Understood? Be sharp. I will be watching. Now back to your post."

* * *

Nikolin sat paralyzed for a moment, not knowing what he should do. The Captain had taken Tasarov into the Flag Plot briefing room and closed the door, and he wondered why. Curious, he toggled inter-ship communications and listened to any routine traffic underway. It was not long before he knew that there was activity aft on the helo deck, and that an ASW loadout mission was being prepared. That surprised him, but given the sudden conference with Tasarov, he now knew that the Captain was getting ready to defend the ship from a submarine. But why?

He played back the conversation again, hearing the urgency in Admiral Volsky's voice as he ordered Karpov to cease his current operation and return to Vladivostok. Then, near the end, he heard another voice he hadn't noticed before, and the name of another officer—Gromyko. He paused the recording, and played it back again. There is was: *"Captain Gromyko, sir. I have the maintenance log for—"*

Captain Gromyko? Who was that? Curious, he decided to solve the riddle by simply keying the name in the naval register. That data was always on file at his terminal, as he was responsible for maintaining all ships compliment and updating them in the general register to note promotions and service details. Seconds later he had the answer, and when he saw the notation for Gromyko's present command the adrenalin rose like magma in his chest.

Now he found himself at a real precipice. What should he do? His instinct was to try and warn Rodenko, or at least get him the information he had uncovered so he could decide what to do, but they were at the edge of combat and Rodenko was across the room near the Tactical Situation screen plotting the position of all enemy contacts with radar feeds. I can't just blurt this out, he thought. Nor can I leave my station and go over there. What can I do?

Then another idea came to him. The game! The game he had been playing with Tasarov! With little to do in this environment, he and Tasarov had been sending riddles back and forth secretly. He was opening a quiet channel to Tasarov's station, and the other man had a toggle switch that allowed him to receive Nikolin's secret little messages using the ship's closed short range cellular system. He could text Tasarov and send him his riddle, and then they would count the time it took to solve the word puzzle. The man who solved it first was declared winner that day, and they had been exchanging things in payment for the prize.

Nikolin's last riddle had been simple and yet devious: *It neither barks nor bites but guards the house well.* Tasarov had not been in doubt for long. Two minutes later he sent back a text message with his answer—a lock! Then three minutes later he fired off his own riddle for Nikolin to solve: *I have four legs and feathers, but I am neither beast nor bird.* Nikolin knew that one easily enough, and sent back the answer in under a minute—*a bed!*

Tasarov was now busy loading in his sonic profile data and getting ready to set up his comm-links and data point feeds to the KA-40 when it launched. Then he saw the red light indicating a text message was coming from Nikolin and he looked over at Nikolin as if to shake off the incoming message. He had no time for games now—not with the Captain all hot like this and detailing him with this new duty. But something in the look on Nikolin's face wasn't right. He looked frightened, nervous, and there was an urgency in his eyes, in the nod of his head as he seemed to plead for Tasarov to answer.

With a shrug the sonar man reached for the toggle switch and enabled station to station text, casting a furtive glance at the Captain as he did so. He just thought to signal back NO TIME, but then he saw the message. It was not a riddle…

* * *

Karpov walked slowly to the view ports, his hand reaching for his field glasses as was his habit in a surface engagement. He stared out at the sea, then raised the binoculars to his eyes, his hand unsteady. For a long minute he searched the grey wave tops, as if he might spy out the tiny white wake of a periscope or sensor mast from a hidden submarine. He could see the distant silhouette of Iki Island off the port bow and now he knew what he had to do. He meant to use his deck guns here to open the action, and pepper the enemy with those S-400s to rake their decks with lethal shrapnel and start fires. Yet now the dire threat posed by *Kazan* forced him to open, or at least maintain the range and seek a better tactical position until he could get the KA-40 up and out to try and hunt down that infernal submarine. He looked down at his watch, considering.

I have to know where they are, he thought. I cannot get too engaged here until we have located the *Kazan*. We would be in the midst of battle for the next two hours if I attack now as planned, and what if Tasarov suddenly hears incoming torpedoes off that damn submarine. No! I've got to find defensive cover and eliminate attack bearings for torpedoes. That island there is perfect, but what if they hit us with a missile barrage? I've been reprogramming all the remaining SAMs to be used as anti-ship missiles! How far has that progressed?

"Mister Samsonov."

"Sir!" Samsonov sat up stiffly, expecting battle orders, as he could see the range was inside 16,000 meters.

"How many S-400s remain?"

"We have thirty-one missiles, sir."

"And how many have been converted for ship to ship usage?"

"Twenty-two, sir." The big man's hand hovered over the S-400 bank, expecting Karpov to order them into action.

My God, thought Karpov. He had given orders to restrict the missiles to low altitude flight paths with reduced speed. That leaves us only nine long range SAMs that could hit anything at altitude like an incoming cruise missile before it dives to its sea skimming approach. "Halt all conversions. Send down a message to the weapons bays and tell the crews to begin restoring the S-400s to normal operating parameters until further notice."

"Restore to air-to-air configuration, sir?"

"That is what I said! Why is it I must repeat an order twice?"

"Sorry, Captain. I will send down the order at once."

That got Rodenko's attention, and he walked slowly to the Captain's side, folding his arms as he leaned into the interaction with Samsonov.

"Air-to-air defense, Captain? I don't understand. I thought you wanted to use the S-400s in SSM mode. If I am not mistaken the Japanese have no aircraft here."

Karpov turned his head, eyes dark, lifeless, like those of a shark, but he spoke only to his CIC officer. "How long will this take, Mister Samsonov?"

"Sir? Well the men have been working for the last eight hours and doing about four missiles per hour."

"Tell them to work faster. I want another dozen S-400s returned to original configuration within the hour. Activate *Kashtan* system and establish air alert two."

"Captain," said Rodenko again. "As *Starpom* I must understand what you are doing here."

"What I am doing here, Mister Rodenko, is giving orders. Your task is to second them and see that they are accomplished in a timely manner. Now... Thirty degrees right rudder. The ship will come to one-five-zero. Battle speed! Ready on all 152mm batteries."

Rodenko was ready to ask another question, but he turned his head and seconded the order. "Helm, come right thirty degrees and steady on 150. Battle speed. Ready on all deck guns."

"Helm answering, and ahead at thirty knots, sir."

"All batteries report ready," said Samsonov.

"Captain?" Rodenko was even more insistent now. "What was that radio message about, if I may inquire, sir?"

"The main enemy column will be northwest of us on this heading, Mister Rodenko. I want to open the range." Karpov deftly ignored the question, focusing on giving Rodenko information as to his battle strategy. "That surprise we had when we stumbled upon those other two battleships is also in mind." He strode over to the tactical display and Rodenko followed to see the Captain increase magnification, centering the map on Iki Island. "Look there," he said. "See those bays and islets at the southern end of that island? Who knows what they may be hiding there, eh?"

"We had no radar returns from that sector, sir. All their capital ships are massing to the northwest off our aft quarter after this turn. It looks like they are trying to get into a position to prevent us turning on a heading to the Yellow Sea."

"I can hit them any time I choose," said Karpov. "But the helicopter is now replenishing, and they may slip something behind that island—perhaps a flotilla of those pesky torpedo boats. I intend to go over and have a look. This maneuver south may also compel them to move in this direction. I want to see what this Admiral Togo does. If they follow me they will be strung out like a string of pearls."

Nikolin had been watching the scene, knowing exactly what was happening and why, but unable to say or do anything about it. Rodenko was slowly beginning to perceive that something was amiss, he thought. The incoming radio message, the Captain's speedy retreat to the briefing room, the conference there with Tasarov had all been noticed, and started some suspicion smoldering. Now the odd order to Samsonov to refit the S-400s and an air alert order must have him thinking something is wrong. I can add fuel to that fire if I just speak up now.

The adrenaline pounded in his chest as he considered what to do. "Sir," he said, trying to sound like he was making a routine report. "KA-40 reports ready for operations in ten minutes. Full ASW loadout." He looked at Rodenko briefly as he said that, hoping it would be the last match required to light the fire. It worked.

"A word, sir," said Rodenko firmly. "I still don't understand what we are doing. Why the order to reconfigure those S-400s? There is no air threat here. Why is the ship on air alert two? And what is the KA-40 doing with an ASW loadout?"

Karpov's jaw tightened, the emotion there intense. Rodenko thought the Captain might yell at him for a moment, but he saw how he mastered himself. Then he spoke in a hushed tone. "The ship will steer one-five-zero. Mister Samsonov, engage the nearest enemy ships with the two forward deck guns. Walk with me, Mister Rodenko, if you please."

Chapter 26

Tasarov suddenly knew what was happening. He read the text message again, eyes widening with surprise and disbelief. It read: "*Admiral and Fedorov are at Vlad – Have ordered us to break off and return there! Direct order from Moscow! If not obeyed command falls on Rodenko!*"

Tasarov began to text back: *Does he know?* He looked over at Nikolin after he sent it, waiting until the communications officer slowly shook his head in the negative. Now Nikolin was furiously typing another message and when he saw it cross his screen everything suddenly made sense to him.

"*I think the Admiral is aboard a submarine!*"

This was no drill, Tasarov suddenly realized. The unusual nature of Karpov's conference with him and the questions about the submarine were most telling, and it was a riddle he now easily solved. They must have come back on a nuclear submarine! It was the only thing that united all the pieces of this puzzle together and made any sense. Yes! They came back on a submarine, and there were only a very few they might have chosen. The Captain had mentioned the most likely candidate by name—*Kazan*—and he told me to load that profile and listen for it. If they were on a submarine then the order to reprogram the S-400s and the Air Alert made perfect sense as a defensive measure against *Kazan's* missiles, as did the order to launch the KA-40 and this undersea alert drill. This is why he ordered me to make the *Shkval* and RBU rocket systems ready for action. He's afraid they are going to attack us, and if I report any contacts he might strike at *Kazan* too!

He suddenly realized that the instant he opened his mouth the dominoes would fall.

* * *

Karpov and Rodenko were heading for the flag briefing room, and when the hatch was sealed the Captain turned to his *Starpom*, a grim expression on his face, his eyes animated with urgency and an edge of fear. "The message was from Fedorov," he said quickly. "They have come back."

Rodenko was very surprised. "What did he want, sir?"

"He is up to his old tricks again," said Karpov, very edgy, arms folded, eyes shifting this way and that. "He could not persuade us to sail to the Bay of Bengal to make that ridiculous rendezvous, but they managed to shift home. Now he is back again insisting we return to Vladivostok."

"Vladivostok?"

"That is where he claimed to be."

"Well what does he want us to do, sir?"

"Use that damn control rod again! They say they have a spare and they brought it with them. Doesn't he realize what's happening here? We are right at the edge of battle and now I'm supposed to rendezvous with him at Vladivostok? This is nonsense! We don't even have Chief Dobrynin here any longer. There is no way the men we have could mount that control rod under these conditions. Even if we did this there is no way we can control where we shift without Dobrynin. What is he thinking?"

Rodenko considered a moment. "If we sail for Vladivostok conditions may be better, sir."

"No! We cannot go north. We have come all this way, and too far to just turn tail and withdraw now after issuing an ultimatum as we did. I will not run in the face of the enemy fleet."

Rodenko could understand why Karpov said that, but there was something more that did not make sense here. "And the orders to Tasarov and Samsonov? Why are we on air alert here? And what is the KA-40 doing with an ASW loadout? It should have an *Oko* panel instead, just as before."

"Look, Rodenko. We have whole sections of the crew specializing in those areas and when they stand to battle stations they have nothing to do. That is a bad situation, so I have given these orders to keep the men sharp and involved." Again, the well measured lie, told with a straightforward look that Karpov had honed to perfection over many years of hard trials.

"Beyond that, you saw what happened up north. We had to use the close in defense guns to engage those mines as well. Last evening I did some additional research. The Imperial Japanese Navy purchased its first submarines during the Russo-Japanese War as early as 1904. They had five Holland class boats from the Americans, and also purchased several more from the British. They will only be able to operate in littoral waters, but in battle you must be ready for any contingency. I may be maneuvering near that island to the southeast. Tasarov has just been sitting there, so I gave him something to drill on. Besides, the KA-40 can still give us eyes in the sky that could be valuable. We haven't scouted east of the Shimonoseki Strait."

"I see…" Rodenko nodded.

"Satisfied now? What more?" Karpov's anger was evident as he saw his *Starpom* stiffen with the hard edge in his tone, the line of his jaw tightening.

"Why have we turned southeast like this? We are entering littoral waters if we stay on this course. The area ahead could be mined, and you just said yourself that we have not yet scouted the Inland Sea. If anything emerges from the strait it will block our way north should we need to maneuver in that direction."

"Don't be a fool. Nothing will prevent me from maneuvering in any direction I please."

"Captain… we are now facing thirty-five enemy contacts. Things are about to get very hot out there. At least let me understand your thinking on this. Surely it's not because you suspect something is hidden behind that island."

"I have my reasons. We will draw the enemy out in a long line of battle with this maneuver."

That was not why the Captain turned southeast, of course, but it would cover the real reason. What he really wanted to do was get into the shadow of Iki Island to put it between *Kirov* and the open waters to the north. He reasoned that *Kazan* was out there somewhere, and the island would serve as a shield against torpedoes coming from the north. There was a small bay at the southern end of the island where he thought *Kirov* might hover, safe from incoming torpedoes on all but one axis, and that is where he would post his KA-40. The island would also prevent *Kazan's* Klub P-900s from coming in at low elevation on a high speed terminal run. In effect, Karpov was maneuvering to fight *Kazan* more than Togo's fleet, and the turn southeast also gave him the added benefit of buying time with the Japanese. He explained that much to Rodenko, hoping it would quell his irritating resistance.

"We'll buy ourselves a little time on this course and extend their line of battle before we turn west again."

Rodenko was ready to say something more, but he stopped himself. "Very well, sir."

"Good. Now just *listen* for a change before you open your mouth and don't give me that stupid look every time I issue an order. Must I explain all my tactics? You are *Starpom*. Act like it!"

There was sting in Karpov's words, but Rodenko kept his cool. "I'm sorry, Captain. I just wanted to be informed as to your intentions."

"My intentions? I've explained that many times. I intend to smash the rest of the Japanese fleet and change everything here. Understood?"

Rodenko hesitated, his features taut, eyes hard. It wasn't the sting of the Captain's words, but the long held reservations that had been building like a storm front within him, and now the thunder rolled.

"Captain," he said sharply, "on that I disagree."

"What's that? You disagree? Yes, you have held doubts about this course of action all along, haven't you. Well, you can disagree with me in private—in the officer's mess or briefing room—but not here, not on the bridge, and *not* in front of the men! So now you are informed as to my intentions. You've stuck your opinion in the borscht and expressed your vote of no confidence, but I have vetoed it. That's the *end* of it! If you have any further reservations then look at my cuff and note the thickness of the stripe there. How many stars do you see on my shoulder?" He stared at Rodenko, angry and perturbed. "Now enough of this. Let's get back out there. We have a battle to fight."

* * *

Togo stared at the flag plot, noting the positions of the ships assigned to their long battle lines. Dewa was to the south with four cruisers and four destroyers. He should have come further north by this time. What was he doing? Just north of him was Kataoka with five cruisers, four destroyers and the ponderous old Chinese battleship *Chinyen*. It was his intention that those two groups unite as one, but Dewa was still too far south. The Admiral' squadron was still close by the southern tip of Tsushima Island with four battleships, two cruisers and five destroyers.

Now he had yet another squadron to note. An officer of the watch reported a column of smoke in the skies to the west, and he knew without asking what this must be. Naval Minister Saito's call for support from the British must have been well heeded. These can only be the ships from the China Station out of Weihaiwei. Good. We are reinforced with another six cruisers if they have brought their best ships. This balances our loss of Kamimura's strong division up north. But will the British fight here, or simply observe? And what about the Americans?

He had received a coded message sent by Admiral Uryu via the new undersea cable to their base on Tsushima Island. It was relayed to his ship by wireless and read simply: *Thunder on Mount Adachi.* That was a high mountain just south of the Shimonoseki Strait that connected the Inland Sea to the Sea of Japan. It meant that from that promontory, looking east, the smoke of the American Great White Fleet could now be seen darkening the sky in the Inland Sea. They had hastened here from Hawaii in just eight days, a remarkable pace. Even now he knew that Admiral Uyru was steaming in the van of that fleet, waving the flag of Imperial Japan.

Uryu was ordered to delay the Americans. His English was very good, and he was to invite them to drop anchor there in the Inland Sea and take tea with the local ministers of Nagasaki Prefecture. But the offer was politely declined. It seemed the American Admiral Sperry had other orders that compelled him to sail to the Sea of Japan at once. So be it…

"Admiral, sir! The enemy has been sighted!"

Togo turned to regard his watch officer, his face stolid and unrevealing of any emotion. He stepped deliberately to the weather bridge, an open area outside the armored conning tower and looked in the direction the watchman pointed. Now he slowly raised his odd looking binoculars, the Marine-Glasmit Revolver, a German made field glass by Carl Zeiss Jena. It had four eyepieces instead of two, with two mounted on each ocular section that could be rotated to select one of the two eyepieces. Depending on how they were paired, the Admiral could get different magnification settings.

He stared through the glasses for some time, noting the dark silhouette of the enemy ship and seeing it turn to his starboard as if to present its broadside. It was true, he thought. There is no smoke! How does it make way without charring the sky as we do? Could it be using some new means of heating its boilers that does not produce smoke? And yes, it looks to be a massive ship, even at this range.

Now his gaze turned to the ships ahead of him in two long battle lines. Dewa was in the lead, and undoubtedly getting a much better view of the enemy ship, and chafing at the bit to attack. But we are much too far away to engage. The range looks to be over 18,000 meters, even in the van. If I point the fleet at this beast to close that range, the enemy will be able to fire all their guns at each ship in the line, smashing them one by one as they present themselves. They would be crossing the T. This I cannot allow, but it does not look like we will have the speed to gain the advantage of position here. Look at that bow creaming the sea. It is completely different from any ship I have seen!

He turned, seeking Captain Hikojiro. "The fleet will turn all lines to a heading of 140," he said firmly. He intended to run on a converging parallel course to the enemy that would allow his ships to also fire from broadside. He could then slowly close the range by making five point turns to port. This maneuver would see his ships trail out from Dewa's leading cruiser and stretch back like a net to the tail of his own formation near Tsushima Island. Should the enemy turn to starboard, they would be aiming to pierce that net and break through his battle line. So *he* must close the range with us now, or else he must turn away to the north, or east toward our home islands where many torpedo boats wait in the shallow waters. There lies Iki Island, and the minefields we have moored in the dark between that place and Kabe Island to the southeast. If he goes there, he must either turn and fight, or else wallow among my iron puffer fish.

Seconds later the flag men were signaling, and he saw the tail ship in Vice Admiral Kataoka's battle line passing the message forward. It would ripple ahead, stiffening in the breeze flag to flag, until it was spotted by Admiral Dewa's watchmen aboard *Kasagi*, the flagship of the leading 3rd Cruiser Division.

* * *

"**At** last," said Vice Admiral Dewa. "Look! The enemy has turned south towards Iki Island. This means they will be heading in our direction, and the course Admiral Togo now orders will put us in the vanguard instead of the tail of the action. Make ready all guns and torpedoes. This will be a glorious day!"

Officers scrambled to obey his directive as Dewa held up a long telescope, studying the dark shape on the far horizon. So this is the ship that defeated Kamimura, he thought, and he had at least two battleships. I still do not believe it. We will soon see what my cruisers can do. I will form them into a tight fist to concentrate all their guns along the same axis. Then I will send my destroyers forward to harass and distract the enemy to weaken their counter fire against us. We will not need Kataoka and Togo here. I will settle things easily enough, and they will be watching behind me as I have the honor of engaging first!

He smiled, snapping the glass shut and stepping back into the conning tower to check with his fire control officers. At that moment there came a distinct *crack, crack, crack* as naval guns punctuated the noise with their fire. He stopped, his head jerked around again to see the enemy ship in the distance, and then, to his amazement geysers of sea spray dolloped up just ahead of his cruiser, wetting the bow there. The enemy had fired at tremendous range!

"Quickly!" he ordered. "What is the range?"

"At least 16,000 meters, Admiral!"

So it was true. The enemy had a long arm, but from the looks of that shell fall these were small caliber guns, just as he had been told. "Signal the destroyers! They will break formation and turn towards the enemy in a torpedo attack!"

Crack, crack, crack... Again the sound of enemy fire, and this time he saw the wink of red and yellow fire from the bow of the distant shadow, and spied the smoke rising from their guns. Seconds later the shock and explosion of impact shook his cruiser. *Kasagi*, guardian of the holy mountain it was named for, had been struck amidships by at least two of the three shells. His instinct was to immediately fire back, but he needed to wait just a little longer.

"Raise main guns to maximum elevation!" The cruiser had two 8 inch Type 41 naval guns, one each mounted fore and aft on two large turrets. They could elevate 18 degrees, and achieve a range of just over 13,000 meters at that angle, though they would rarely engage until inside 10,000 meters, with 7,000 being the norm. But something told Dewa that he was going to have to fire with everything he had, and as soon as possible. The accuracy of the enemy guns was disturbing. Crews were already fighting a small fire near his number two stack, and now he could see geysers of sea spray straddling the cruiser *Chitose* behind him, sister ship to his own.

If I turn slightly to port I will angle in toward this enemy ship as we approach Iki Island. This will allow me to keep my ships broadside to him if he turns in our direction, but it appears that the Russians have other ideas. They look to be steering 150, right for the island. In due course I can fire with our secondary guns as well. They are smaller but can elevate 25 degrees to reach over 9,000 meters. I will have to wait just a little longer while the enemy continues to rake his glove across my face! So this is what Kamimura endured.

The ship shuddered again, this time well aft where Dewa turned to see a fire near the main 8 inch turret there. "Five degrees to port!" he ordered, thinking to throw the enemy's aim off. It was uncanny how they had found his ship so far off, but have they nothing bigger to sting me with?

He was about to learn yet another hard lesson.

Chapter 27

Volsky slowly placed the handset in the holding cradle, his eyes sad and deeply troubled. All the men were huddled near the communications station now. *Kazan* had sprinted south at high speed after they shifted, streaking silently through the dark seas at depth. Then, as their systems recovered one by one, they slowed and crept up to the surface to use the radio and make the call to *Kirov*.

What was Karpov thinking, thought Volsky? The man had relapsed into his delusions of making a decisive change to the history, and though the Captain's final response was vague, Volsky did not think he was going to comply with his order to cease and desist in this operation.

"I'm afraid he is just buying time," he said to Fedorov.

"Then what do we do sir?" The young ex-navigator had a pleading expression on his face. "I know it will be hard to raise our hand against *Kirov*, but we must act before the Captain does something irreparable."

"Mister Kamenski?" Volsky looked to the Deputy Director where he stood nearby the console.

"I do not know the man, but he certainly made his intentions clear enough. We chose to come here aboard *Kazan* for a reason. I know we have put off the decision before us now, but the time has come. Yes, Armageddon is at hand, but what do we do here? Has it occurred to any of you that if we engage *Kirov* now the outcome of this event will be far from certain? You have missiles and torpedoes aboard this ship. Suppose we use them and the ship is damaged to an extent that it can no longer pose a threat here, yet here it remains, with weapons, computer systems, technology, and men who know all about them. And if we damage its reactors in any way, all these control rods are useless. This does little to solve our problem."

"You are saying *Kirov* must be sunk?"

"At the very least, though that would still leave a remarkable shipwreck on the seafloor here, which is quite shallow in the straits, is it not?"

"The average depth is only 140 meters," said Fedorov. "If he gets near any of the islands that will shrink to 50 meters or less."

"Well, as time passes, a recovery of that shipwreck is a real possibility, if not a certainty. Then what?"

"I see…" Volsky shrugged with resignation now, knowing this question would eventually arise.

"Beyond that," said Kamenski. "What about the question of survivors? Suppose your Mister Karpov goes into the sea and winds up washed ashore on a nearby island?"

"We could try to rescue them," Fedorov suggested. "Assuming we prevail in this battle. If I'm not mistaken we have an emergency VSK pod in the sail that can hold up to 110 people."

"That is correct," said Gromyko.

"Well that is encouraging, but *Kirov* has quite a few more than that, if I am not mistaken."

"About 700 men and officers," said Volsky. "No, I do not think we can rescue them."

"Which means we are facing a situation much like the one that sent your Mister Fedorov off to hunt for Chief Orlov." Kamenski was playing the Devil's advocate now, though they had all mused on these dark questions in silence before they were voiced here. "You would have to hunt down any man who might survive a conventional engagement. And there is still the other darker possibility that *we* may not survive, and *Kirov* sails on."

"What you say is all too true," said the Admiral. "It leaves us with only one option. If we engage *Kirov*, then we must prevail, and decisively. The ship and every man aboard it must be destroyed."

"Completely destroyed," said Kamenski.

"But Admiral," said Fedorov. "We would have to use a nuclear weapon to insure this."

Volsky lowered his head, eyes closed as he pinched the bridge of his nose. "Captain Gromyko. Can you use your sensory antenna or sonar to acquire the ship at this time?"

"Our radar has cleared up but we will have better luck with the sonar. It will hear *Kirov* long before we might acquire it with the Snoop Pair surface search radar. With your permission sir, I would like to move into the sound channel and see about that."

"Do so. And you may also prepare your missile inventory for action."

"Then you have decided to engage, sir?"

"I intend to fire a single missile as a last warning shot to Karpov. Would this compromise your defense of this submarine, Captain?"

"That depends on the range, sir. If I am not mistaken *Kirov* has *Vodopad* torpedoes that can fire out to 120 kilometers. Our P-900s can beat that by a hundred kilometers."

"Yes, but that would mean we would have to open the range considerably. My feeling is that *Kirov* is no more than a hundred kilometers to the south at this time."

"They must be in the straits preparing to engage the Japanese," said Fedorov.

"If it comes to combat I would risk a missile launch even inside the *Vodopad's* effective range. We are very stealthy, and the sonar on that system is not very sharp."

"Agreed," said Volsky. "I have seen all the live fire exercise data. We have never had good results with the *Vodopad* against our quieter submarines. So this is what we will do… We will fire one warning shot, a single missile. We will tell Karpov that he either alters course to Vladivostok or we must engage with a full barrage." Volsky took a deep breath, as though he had just set down a heavy burden that he had been carrying for some time.

"With conventional warheads?"

"No, Mister Kamenski, you have ably demonstrated the folly of that. *Kirov* has a very robust SAM defense. If all our missiles struck home I would rest easier and believe we might have a chance to rescue the few survivors that remain. Then we could also assure the wreckage is completely destroyed. But I am afraid that *Kirov* will get many of the missiles we fire. We upgraded the SAM inventory to P-400s before Karpov sallied with the fleet. They also have the *Klinok* system, then the *Kashtan* system, and the 30mm Gatling guns. Something may get through if we fire a full barrage, perhaps we might even get several hits, but not enough to assure the destruction we have spoken of."

"Then we will use the nuclear warheads?" Gromyko waited.

"I'm afraid we have no other choice. We will have to hit the ship with everything we have. If the P-900s do not get through, then one of those torpedo rockets must do the job."

There was a long silence as each man considered this, and then Fedorov offered a grim smile. "Now we are the madmen flinging nuclear weapons around. But something tells me that if we do not do this, and Karpov remains free to do what he wishes here, it is only a question of time before he uses another nuclear warhead himself."

"Yes, and there is also the possibility that he will be so possessed by the threat we pose now that he will do so at once to assure our destruction. He may think we are at Vladivostok, as Fedorov told him, but the instant *Kirov's* Fregat system picks up our warning shot he will know otherwise. I know Karpov. That hot minute will be one of intense peril for us all. He has undoubtedly done an aerial survey of the region and knows no other surface ships are behind him, so he will quickly deduce we are in a submarine. The list of those available with nuclear reactors is very short."

"And he will know our bearing and approximate range the instant we fire," said Fedorov.

"So the question is this—what will he do? Will he perceive the action for what it was intended, a warning shot, or will his fear of undersea boats blind him and compel him to make an immediate reprisal? If he does counterattack, how will he come after us? This is the crucial question. If he uses the *Vodopad* system, Captain Gromyko and I both feel our chances of surviving to make a second launch are fairly good. But what if he uses a MOS-III with a special warhead, just as he did in the North Atlantic? That missile could be over us in a matter of seconds, and we would have to be very deep to avoid serious damage."

"The water here is not that deep," said Gromyko.

"Any action we take will have risks," said Fedorov. "If he uses a MOS-III, we will see it coming, and then we could still fire everything we have with the hope one of our own warheads gets through."

"Unfortunately, in this event we may not survive to find out what happened." Kamenski folded his arms, still kibitzing.

"Then I will contact the ship just as we fire and give fair warning. That is only just. It means we will have to drop the pretense of our being at Vladivostok, and all element of surprise, but that vanishes the instant we fire anyway."

"Unless you make the first blow the final one," said Kamenski.

Volsky looked at him, very troubled. "You suggest we make a pre-emptive nuclear strike?"

"We have always based our naval strategy around the struggle for the first salvo, Admiral. You know this as well as I do. Here you have pointed out the dangers inherent in a limited response. The warning shot could set Karpov off like a time bomb, and he could lash out with every intention of destroying us completely. The conventional barrage will not assure what we need to achieve here. So it is a process of elimination."

"I understand what you are saying, Director, but I feel we must at least make one last chance at resolving the matter before the missiles fly. Find your target, Gromyko. In the meantime, we are going to send one last message before we do anything else."

"Very well, Admiral. I'll see what our sonar man has for us and report the moment I have any news, but this raises one last question." Gromyko scratched his head, continuing. "Only Belanov and I know what has happened. The rest of the crew still believes we are out here facing the Japanese and Americans, but Chernov is very good. He will find *Kirov*, and he will recognize its sonic profile as well. How do I explain the situation when it comes time to fire on our comrades?"

"I had not considered this… Well I will be right there by your side, Captain. Leave that to me."

Gromyko saluted and went forward to the main operations center to check with Chernov on sonar.

When he had gone Volsky shook his head, a discouraged look on his face. "What can they be doing out there? What about Rodenko, and Samsonov and the others? Did they not hear my order?"

"They may not know, Admiral. Karpov would have certainly been startled by the radio call. He may have taken it on a closed channel. You saw how devious he can be when he tried to take the ship before. It took Sergeant Troyak's Marines to regain control last time."

"Yes, well I cannot send Troyak over on a cruise missile, can I?"

"No sir."

"This is very hard… I can still see Nikolin sitting at his post with those headphones on, Tasarov lost in the sea beneath his headset, Samsonov stiff backed and ready at the Combat Center. They were good men, and it is a good crew—a good ship. To see it end this way…"

"There may still be hope, sir," said Fedorov.

"I do not see it. And I have had my fill of weapons and missiles and war. It has also occurred to me that Karpov might be correct."

"Sir?"

"What if he can prevent Japan from becoming the Imperial power it was in the Pacific? What if he can stop Japanese aggression and keep that nation out of the Second World War? Do you realize how many died during the war in the Pacific?"

"It is estimated that 22 million died in China alone, sir, and another 10 million died in other theaters."

"So if Karpov succeeds in preventing that, all those lives are spared. It sounds noble enough, does it not?"

"Who can say?" said Kamenski. "Who knows what they would do in the years ahead, and all their ancestors?"

"You seemed to be convinced that this would cause some great catastrophe, Kamenski."

"Perhaps…" The Deputy Director had a distant look in his eye now. "Then again, we were hard at work on catastrophe as we left it."

"Well as we cook in the oven, I cannot help but wonder whether Karpov is doing the right thing here. I know we saw Karpov's acts as those of a madman when he used that tactical warhead on the Americans in the North Atlantic. But look what happened! There was no Japanese attack on Pearl Harbor, and no bombing of Hiroshima and Nagasaki with atomic weapons."

"No," said Kamenski, "that sad fate was reserved for Vladivostok, or so Gromyko would tell us."

The Admiral gave him a quiet look, still thinking. "Indeed it was, though I know nothing of that. Events are all jumbled up like a puzzle now, and I have no idea how things will look when we finally get it back together again. The history is so broken by what we have done that it seems impossible to heal, Fedorov. I know this is what you want, and what you hope for—a chance to set it all right again as it was, but that may not be possible now. Too much has happened."

"We can try, sir." Fedorov did not know what else to say.

"Yes, we can try by becoming madmen ourselves and smashing *Kirov* to dust with our own little cataclysm here in 1908. The catastrophe that was upon us in 2021 was the result of the history playing out just as you might wish to restore it! We could not stop it, even knowing it was coming. So here I am haunted by the notion that Karpov was correct after all. He thinks he can shape the years ahead with the power of *Kirov*. Imagine that power redoubled with *Kazan*. We could truly impose our will on the world, here and now, just as Karpov envisages it."

The admiral looked for a chair, wanting to get off his tired feet, and slowly sat down.

"Don't mind me," he said. "I'm just a worried old man, like Kamenski here. We will try to set things right. I have no intention of conquering this world, and only hope we can get safely back to our own. But you must brace yourself against the possibility that we may not succeed. I doubt Karpov will relent. He will fight. That said, we will certainly have to destroy *Kirov* to be sure the ship and its weapons and technology do not further pollute this era of history, and then we must take the blood on our hands home, if we can get there. I wonder what we will find this time, even if we do prevail here?"

They were all silent, the depth of the irony and the sadness of it all weighing on them. Then Volsky spoke again, his voice dark with misgiving. "I dread the moment Gromyko calls us to the bridge with news of *Kirov*, Fedorov. I dread the order I must give to unleash the missiles in this submarine, and send them on their way. I dread this whole dirty business of war…"

"So do we all," said Kamenski, "but it seems we cannot avoid our fate here, Admiral. There was even war in Heaven."

"Indeed," said Volsky. "Well here we have war in Hell, one demon facing another in the abyss, and I shudder to think that the world waits on the outcome."

The Admiral's worst fears were soon realized, though Gromyko's voice sounded hollow when he returned to say that Chernov believed he had a contact nearly matching the profile stored for *Kirov*.

"As you might expect," said Gromyko, "this was some news for the bridge crew. We all believed *Kirov* was lost. And Admiral," he added with an edge of caution, "Chernov believes the ship is engaged in battle at this very moment. There's a lot of noise off to the south now, and we've detailed a long line of surface contacts emerging from the Shimonoseki Strait—a very large formation of ships, sir. It has caused a bit of a situation, Chernov can't understand why he has no profiles on any of these contacts. Beyond that, the mood of the crew is hot to get to *Kirov's* side and join the battle. Chernov says the ship is making a hell of a lot of noise on sonar."

"Yes, the thunder and clamor of war. Well it is time I went forward to speak with the men. Now we come to what may be the final log entry—for *Kirov*, for *Kazan*, or for time itself insofar as all this history is concerned. Now we come to the final battle, here on the edge of perdition. What is the word for it, Mister Fedorov?"

"Armageddon, sir. Armageddon."

Part X

Armageddon

"And starward drifts the stricken world,
Lone in unalterable gloom
Dead, with a universe for tomb,
Dark, and to vaster darkness whirled."

— George Sterling: The Thirst of Satan

Chapter 28

Vice Admiral Dewa sat stolidly in the life boat, shame burning the back of his neck as he watched his flagship burn. For the last hour his line of four cruisers had run southwest, slowly angling toward their adversary, but taking a fearful pounding. He perceived that the Russian ship was trying to steer for the southern tip of Iki Island, which gave him heart at the outset.

They will run afoul of our minefields there, he thought, but the damage his ships were taking from the lethal accuracy of the enemy guns was mounting rapidly. At one point he was thrown to the hard metal deck by a direct hit on the conning tower of *Kasagi*. The armor there saved his life, and those of his bridge crew, but the smoke and fire of battle obscured all and he found himself senseless for a time.

"Admiral!" a voice came as he was roused from his stupor. "*Chitose* has sunk, and we are burning badly. Our aft stack has been blown clean away and we have fallen off the line. You must transfer your flag, sir."

"What? *Chitose* has sunk?"

"And we will follow her in a matter of minutes. Come sir, we have a boat rigged on the port side of the ship. The fires are not as bad there."

And now Dewa stared in horror at the scene before him, watching *Kasagi*, keel over to starboard, her hull riddled by enemy fire. *Chitose* was gone, but cruisers *Otawa* and *Nitaka* were still bravely firing at the enemy, though he could see their effort was futile. The range had barely closed to 12,000 meters, and the enemy had targeted and destroyed the 8 inch guns on his cruisers, picking his ships apart with those deadly small caliber rounds that seemed to have tremendous penetrating power. None of his four destroyers could get anywhere near the Russian ship without being riddled with fire, and one endured a barrage of what looked to be very small rockets dancing over the sea with wispy white tails. They smashed into the destroyer, killing men all over the exposed weather decks and igniting the torpedo tubes there. *Asagiri* died a miserable death. *Murasame* and *Shirakumo* were both burning fiercely.

The Russians had once called his brave division the "Greyhounds," as they would dog the old Russian ships, appearing suddenly out of the mist and then racing off, sometimes to lead the unwary enemy into a trap or a hidden minefield. His cruisers would dance about the Russian battleships, but not this time, not against this new monster. How could it move so fast? His entire division had been shattered in a single hour, and the enemy was unscathed! The Greyhounds were gone.

"It seems there will be no place to transfer my flag," Dewa said sullenly.

"*Nitaka* has seen our signal, Admiral. She has broken off and is heading our way."

"So I will climb aboard her burning decks?"

"At least she is seaworthy, sir."

"Yes, and my shame will be that I must order her to withdraw the instant we arrive there. We are no match for this Russian dreadnaught. Now I know what Kamimura suffered."

"Sir, we can try and rendezvous with Vice Admiral Kataoka's battle line there to the northwest. They are very close, and Admiral Togo's ships are right behind them."

Dewa followed the man's arm where he pointed. There was Kataoka, steaming in the ponderous hulk of the old battleship *Chinyen*, a line of five armored cruisers and four destroyers in his wake.

* * *

When Admiral Togo got the news of Dewa's fate he showed not the slightest flicker of emotion. Circumstances had conspired to place Dewa's force in the vanguard. His most impetuous leader was therefore too eager to prove himself and avenge the shortcomings of

Kamimura in the north. Unfortunately, the lesson learned was a hard one, and now Dewa was dragging himself up from his lifeboat onto one of Kataoka's armored cruisers after transferring from the damaged *Nitaka*. He had nothing left to command. It was karma.

Now the remainder of fleet had finally been united when Togo brought his division up at the best speed he could muster. Out on the weather bridge he could see the smoke and fire of battle ahead, Dewa's last cruiser, *Otowa* burning and dead in the water, one of her stacks sheared off at the top, and another broken and collapsed on itself like a crumpled stove pipe hat. Farther ahead he could see the silhouette of the enemy ship, a sinister threat at the edge of the sea.

By all Gods and Kami, he thought, where have you come from? The long raked bow of the ship seemed completely empty. He could see no big gun turrets, and only noted the last wink of what looked to be secondary batteries firing from the mounting shadow of the dreadnaught's superstructure. He saw the white splashes as the rounds struck very near *Otawa's* listing hull, and then there was a lull in the action.

The Admiral knew without asking that the range was still far beyond the capability of his own main guns. The Japanese had purchased 44 Armstrong Whitworth 12-inch naval guns from Great Britain, and *Mikasa's* forward turret held two of them, with two more aft. They were now designated as "Type 41" in honor of the 41st year of the reign of Emperor Meiji. An early version of this weapon had served well against the Russians here in 1905, but *Mikasa* had been re-gunned in 1908 with an improved, better rifled version that could elevate 18 degrees to fire at a maximum range of just under 15,000 meters.

"Sir," said the Lieutenant of Arms. "We can finally fire!"

Togo looked at the man, his face a mask of calm. Patience, he thought.

"Sir, shall I give the order?"

"We will wait," said Togo, seeing the obvious frustration on his Lieutenant's face. The officers had all seen the punishment Dewa's division had taken, he thought, and they were now eager to join the fray. Yet firing now would only waste ammunition, even if it might bolster the spirits of my ship and crew.

He raised his field glasses, studying the ship more closely. The Russians did not have this ship in 1905. This is something entirely new. It is bigger than anything I have ever seen afloat, faster than the wind, and fierce as the biting sting of a typhoon. The enemy was now at his maximum range, and running for Iki Island. Why this ship runs to the shallows near Iki is a mystery to me. If he keeps on that way perhaps I can catch this spider is my own web there. The minefields at the southern end of the island will soon force him to slow his pace, and then we will close to a better range.

Kataoka leads with the ponderous *Chinyen*, and those two armored cruisers just behind her, *Matsushima* and *Hashidate*. They have that heavy gun forward, and so to fire they must turn and present their bow to the enemy. The turret is so heavy that if it attempts to rotate and fire from broadside they will surely capsize in these rising seas. It should never have been mounted on a ship of that size.

He looked at the gathering clouds, the warning of a storm clearly evident as the winds began to whip the seas higher. The Gods themselves bellow with anger in the sea and sky. So be it. We will stay on this heading and when the enemy reaches Iki Island they will soon find my barnacled friends in the sea and be forced to reduce speed. Then we will close and I will give the order to turn.

His gaze shifted farther east where he saw smoke on the wind. That must be Admiral Uyru escorting in the American Great White Fleet. He has signaled that Admiral Sperry will support us. If this is true they come to our aid at a most opportune time. Hopefully we will all share tea in the Imperial Gardens when this is over, but that is for another day.

Togo smiled inwardly. While this enemy ship threads its way through my minefield I will close the range protected by those islets southwest of Iki Island. Then, when he blunders into the thicket of my floating thorns, I will be there with over twenty ships, and we will charge boldly in from the west like a mighty lance of steel and skewer this monster! His only recourse would be to turn on a heading of 130 and run for deeper water, yet if he does that the British will engage, and the American Great White Fleet soon after. Hopefully that will not be necessary and I will end the battle long before he escapes my trap.

No, he thought. This is not about hope any longer. This Russian Captain has maneuvered foolishly to place himself within my grasp, and now my mailed fist will close and crush him. I could not have planned it better!

* * *

Oronshima Island was a tiny speck in a region of the Sea of Japan known as the Genkai Sea. The island was endowed with many shrines and offerings to the Shinto kami, the spirits of the Gods who would take shape in natural forms. As a stepping stone in the sea between Japan and the Asian mainland, the island was also a way station for that sea faring nation, and prayers were offered there for the safety of all sea going souls.

The stories about the place dated back centuries. It was said that Amaterasu, the Shinto Goddess of the sun, was suspicious that another deity was envious of her land there, and so she suggested a trial by ordeal to test the intention and honesty of the god. She took his sword, broke it into three pieces and swallowed them, exhaling a thick fog that then spawned three Kami spirits now inhabiting the islands. So it was that a test of loyalty came to be associated with the ancestral rituals of the region, and now another sword would be unsheathed to test the loyalty and intentions of Captain Vladimir Karpov and his ship of fallen angels.

Kazan had obtained a bearing on *Kirov* and was now approaching the lee of that island, ready to fire the last warning shot across Karpov's bow, a single P-900 cruise missile. Admiral Volsky insisted that it be programmed to self destruct once it came within visual range of the target, if it managed to survive to even get that close, and he would announce it in warning. But first he needed to explain what was happening to the bridge crew of *Kazan*.

"Gentlemen," he began heavily, "we have a difficult situation here. As you know, we believed *Kirov* was lost, but that turns out not to be the case. Our mission was to find her and bring her safely home. Your Mister Chernov here has sharp ears, and we have now located the ship. Fortunately for all of us, Moscow has been trying to negotiate an armistice to end this conflict before it gets out of hand. Though I have ordered *Kirov* to break off and return to Vladivostok, the Captain there refuses to comply with that direct order. That is why we are here, and now we must take stronger measures to convince this Captain. I could simply threaten to fire, but the sight of a missile will speak volumes," he said. "We are going to fire a warning shot and see if it will put some sense into this man and give us the hope we can end this war before the *real* missiles fly. I do not have to tell you what that will mean…"

He let that sink in, waiting as he looked from one man to another. "So you may receive some difficult orders here, but I expect every man to do his job. Captain Gromyko has been fully briefed and knows what we must do. Follow his orders faithfully, and without fear or hesitation."

"It would be good if we could fire now, sir," said Gromyko. "He is running southeast toward Iki Island and will soon place that land mass between our position and his. I would fire now and then move quickly off this bearing at high speed. We'll round that little island ahead, then swing southwest toward that long line of surface contacts. Their noise will mask our position well. In fact, we could get right beneath them and I doubt *Kirov* could hear us, or find us there, no matter how good their sonar man is."

The range to target was only 45 kilometers, so they knew they were taking a risk that *Kirov* could return fire now with her long range *Vodopad* missile torpedo system. Yet Gromyko was told to stand ready to launch a full missile barrage should that happen, another fifteen P-900s that would mass on the target in reprisal. One of those missiles would carry a nuclear warhead, and both *Veter* system 20 kiloton warheads would also be fired. They would take no chances that *Kirov* would survive. The question on everyone's mind was hinging on Karpov's response. What would he do?

"Spin up missiles one through sixteen on the P-900 system," said Gromyko.

"Sir," said the weapon's officer, "the number sixteen missile is mounted with a special warhead. Do I include it in this order?" Protocol required that he point this out.

"Confirmed. Missiles one through sixteen," Gromyko repeated flatly, and Belanov seconded his order immediately.

"P-900 system. Missiles one thru sixteen, aye, sir."

"*Veter* system," said Gromyko. "Load tubes one and two. RU-100 torpedoes, *with* special warheads." He reached for the missile key that dangled from his neck, making his way to the console with Belanov quickly at his side.

"Sir, load RU-100s on tubes one and two; special warheads enabled, aye, aye."

There was a long moment of tension in the control room, then Gromyko nodded to the communications station. "The floor is yours, Admiral."

* * *

Kirov ran southeast, well ahead of Togo's converging column. Samsonov had been given the order to open fire with the forward deck guns. As the Captain had not been specific, he was using the 100mm bow gun to range in on the leading ships of Kataoka's division in the long line of contacts that now presented themselves on his tactical display. The gun fired in three round salvos, with a brief pause between each one while Samsonov refined his radar lock and fed the data to the bigger 152mm deck guns fore and aft. Soon they were making short work of the enemy ships, punishing them severely with their precision radar controlled fire. Kataoka's leading battleship and flag, *Chinyen*, was hit three times and already fighting fires, and *Kirov* was so fast that the enemy could not close the range to answer.

"What is the range?" The Captain was pleased with his results so far as he watched Samsonov target the unwieldy Japanese battleship in the vanguard of the enemy formation.

"About 15,000 meters, sir."

"Good. Give them a good pounding, Samsonov. Light that one up and let the rest see what's in store for them. Helm, ten degrees to port. Come to one-four-zero and reduce to twenty knots."

"Sir, coming around to one-four-zero, aye."

Chinyen was among the oldest ships in the Japanese fleet, built by Germany in 1882 and sold to China where it deployed as a "turret ship" in the Sino-Japanese war of 1894-1895. Called *Zhenyuan* at the time, she was damaged at the battle of the Yalu River and transferred to Weihaiwei after repairs where she struck an unseen rock, forcing her Captain to beach the ship to avoid sinking. There she was taken as a prize of war by the Japanese at the battle of Weihaiwei, and after refurbishing, she became the only battleship in the Japanese fleet for a brief time.

Like so many other ships, once the pride of the fleet, she was soon relegated to the status of an obsolete troop escort ship. Togo had reservations about letting her sail at all, but Kataoka had insisted that her four Krupp 12 inch guns would provide much needed firepower for his division. Yet those guns could only elevate thirteen degrees, restricting their range to an anemic 7,200 meters, so *Chinyen* remained silent as she labored forward at 15 knots, her best speed in the rising swell. The only thing she would end up providing Kataoka would be a harried trip to the salt of the sea.

"Give me a single *Moskit-II*," said Karpov. "Blast that lead ship out of the water. That will be the flagship of this squadron."

Samsonov wasted no time, keying the target and assigning his weapon. The roar of the missile launch followed soon after, devouring the short 15 kilometer range in just 25 seconds from launch to impact.

To Kataoka, it seemed like a demon from the deepest hell, howling in at his flagship and smashing the vessel amidships with a terrible explosion and raging fire. As with *Tango* and *Mishima*, the missile had barely touched its fuel reserve, yet was hurtling at near Mach 2 speed when it thundered home. *Chinyen* had a thick shell of 14 inch armor, but at only 7,600 tons she rode very low in the water and the missile struck well above her armor, ravaging the superstructure and burning completely through the ship.

Kataoka was well forward of the impact on the weather deck of the bridge, but the concussion was so severe that he was hurtled off the deck and right into the sea along with several junior officers. When he finally managed to break the surface, clinging to a shattered spit of the ship's forward mast, he gaped in horror as *Chinyen* buckled and broke in half, the ship completely gutted by the terrible fire dragon that had devoured it. He would be a long time in the water before being rescued by the destroyer *Oboro*. In that time his division plowed forward gallantly, the five remaining armored cruisers sailing past the ravaged ship, their crews gasping at the carnage inflicted on their flagship, yet determined to seek vengeance.

Chapter 29

Aboard *Kirov* Karpov raised his fist in jubilation. "You see, Rodenko? When the others see what we have done to their flagship I wonder how eager they will be to close with us?"

"Captain," said Tasarov.

Karpov's ebullient mood was suddenly iced over as he turned to his sonar man, but the report was of another surface contact and he calmed himself. Tasarov had been listening to the wallowing slosh of the old Japanese navy ships off to the west of their position, but now he heard a strong surface contact to the east, some 60 kilometers away. The Fregat system soon confirmed it as yet another line of enemy warships emerging from the Shimonoseki Strait and heading south at 18 knots.

"We should have scouted the Inland Sea," said Rodenko. "I have another twenty-eight surface contacts on that heading now."

"They could have twice that number there and it will not matter," said Karpov. "They are just more grist for the mill."

"It appears the Japanese fleet is larger than we expected, sir. We've just dealt with this group of eight ships but there are still two large formations closing on us like pincers, and sinking that old gunboat has not dampened their enthusiasm. Look sir, they are still coming. Then we also have this group of six ships here southwest of us. Those are flying the British flag."

"Six, eight, twelve, a dozen—what does it matter? You saw what we just did to the first of this group. The rest will get the same."

"Mister Samsonov," said Rodenko. "How many rounds have we expended in this engagement?"

"Sir, we have fired 240 rounds from the 152mm guns, and another 36 from the 100mm bow gun. We still have 2432 rounds remaining on the 152mm guns, and 914 on the bow gun."

"And missiles?"

"Nine each for the *Moskit-II* and *Mos-III* systems, sir."

"I know what you are trying to prove, Rodenko," said Karpov. "That is more than sufficient. I will use our remaining SSMs sparingly."

"Well sir, this new group to the east is returning much stronger signals. Those are battleships. I read at least sixteen, and they will take far more punishment to sink than these cruisers and destroyers."

"That's not possible. I researched the Japanese order of battle and they do not have that many ships in that class."

"The Fregat system does not lie, sir, and you know I can read it like a book. I am certain there are sixteen larger ships. The remainder will be smaller cruiser and destroyer class vessels."

Rodenko was correct. Karpov ordered the KA-40 to swing over Iki Island and have a look east where they soon received HD video from their long range camera system. They were staring up at the screen to see a line of chalk white warships steaming at a good speed, the skies dark with the soot of their coal fired boilers. In their van were squadrons of smaller ships, but they flew Japanese naval ensigns.

"Look at those flags on the battleships, sir. Those are American ships!"

Karpov stared at the screen for some time. "What in the world? This can only be their Great White Fleet, but it was not supposed to be anywhere near here at this time. They should be sailing to the Philippines."

"Well things have clearly changed, Captain. Are you prepared to engage the American Navy here as well?"

My God, thought Karpov. What a gift! Now I can destroy both the Imperial Japanese Navy and the American Navy in one great battle here! That will make *Kirov*, and Russia, the undisputed master of the Pacific for decades to come. After this I can sink any ship they build and send here to challenge me. This is perfect! But Rodenko's warning about the munitions is now more important. I cannot waste my remaining deck gun ammunition on those battleships. They will have to be crushed swiftly, and I have only eighteen SSMs available.

Then there is still the matter of *Kazan*. That is my main fear at the moment....

Rodenko was watching the Captain closely, seeing the mix of emotions cross his face as he studied the screen. He was hoping the Captain would see that the odds were stacking up here, and creating a situation that could prove very difficult to manage without resort to more force than their conventional arms could wield. That was *his* great fear. Karpov had a reflex to suddenly escalate in the face of such odds, and he was worried.

"Sir?" He pressed the Captain. "We now have both American and British ships in the mix here, and they seem to be intent on joining this battle. Engaging the Americans will set a powerful enemy on Russia's trail in the history ahead. Are you certain you wish to do this?"

Karpov turned, his eyes smoldering. "We will have to face them one day or another, Rodenko. If not now, then they will grow beyond our means. I admit that I bit off more than I could chew by confronting Halsey and Nimitz in 1945. But these ships can be mastered easily enough."

"Yet at great expense of our conventional munitions, sir. These are old pre-dreadnaught battleships. Their dreadnaughts are now in the shipyards being built in the shadow of the First World War. After that will come the pre-WWII battleships, and then their better designs. You saw what it took to sink the *Iowa*. So how many irreplaceable rounds of ammunition do we use here on these old ships?"

Karpov gave him an irritated look. "Leave that to me. I will show you what can be done. Navigation! How long before we reach that island?"

"A little over 20 minutes, Captain."

They were now just 20 kilometers northwest of Iki Island, the place that Karpov had chosen as his shield against possible missile or torpedo attack from the north. He was worried that he had to opened the engagement too soon, for *Kazan* would surely have a good idea of his location after that initial gun duel. Now his intention was to swing around a cluster of small islets south of the main island and find the sheltering bay beyond. Once there he would be in a well protected area, the island a strong shield against any torpedo attacks, and he had the ranged firepower to pound anything that dared to approach him. I must find that submarine before I leave those waters, he thought. But what if they strike with their missile battery first? With all this noise from the surface contacts Tasarov will have a hell of a time trying to locate that submarine. Yes, they will certainly get the first salvo, but we can defend ourselves well with our SAMs, and then we strike back.

"Navigator," he said. "I want to move the ship into this bay. How deep is the water there?"

"29 meters, sir, and a little deeper further south at 38 meters. We'll have to avoid the channel to the north, it is much too shallow for us to transit." Kirov's draft was only 9 meters, but Karpov did not want to run aground on a hidden sand bar or shoal.

"Then take us south of those islands and approach from that direction. Alter speed if necessary. I will be too busy to instruct you, so I rely on your skill to pilot the ship while we finish this combat."

"Aye, sir. Programming in the course now."

Then Karpov eased over to Tasarov, his voice muted as he spoke.

"Anything, Tasarov?"

"Sir?"

"You know what I mean. Are you listening carefully?"

"Yes sir. But the sound field is very cluttered."

"As we approach that island ahead, you will go to active sonar. These waters could be mined."

"Very well, sir."

"The KA-40 is over Iki Island now. Move it south to watch the channel east and south of the island." The Captain was pointing at the location he had in mind on the map. He tapped the screen with a thin finger, and Tasarov nodded.

"Very well, sir."

"Don't forget those submarines I warned you about."

Then the Captain drifted back to the tactical screen near Rodenko where the two men continued their discussion concerning the Americans.

"Sixteen battleships, Captain. Yes we could put a missile on each and every one, but then we would have only two left. It will be deck guns and modified SAMs for all the years ahead of us, long decades, sir. Think about it."

"I tell you I have no intention of squandering my missiles as you suggest, Mister Rodenko. We have ample means to carry the fight to that enemy at a time of my choosing."

"What means sir? Surely not another special warhead."

"Those weapons are in inventory for a reason, yes? I have not hesitated to use the full power of this ship. Why are you so squeamish?"

Rodenko had finally realized that his opposition to Karpov had to be framed in ways the Captain would accept. He knew there were no moral considerations in Karpov's mind now. That was evident in the way he so casually ordered the destruction of that last ship, watching it break and burn without the slightest twinge. It was just as he had ordered the annihilation of the American TF-16 in 1941, and again in 1945 with the *Iowa*. Where the Americans were concerned he would have no qualms, the verdict of future history claimed as ample reason for his murderous rage.

There was no way their remaining conventional munitions would suffice to destroy all these ships, and he was certain Karpov would soon opt for stronger measures. Yet if he could couch his objection in strategic terms, he might convince the Captain that using nuclear weapons here could jeopardize everything he was aiming for.

"Well, sir... A special warhead would certainly do the job, but look what happened the last time we did this. We were blown another thirty-seven years into the past! The ship's position in time has never been stable. Consider what happened when that volcano went off. Rod-25 was long removed, and yet it appears that any major explosive event like that can still cause us to shift in time. What if that happens again? You'll lose your entire strategic position here, and everything you have been planning."

Karpov gave Rodenko a narrow eyed look. "So you are starting to think rationally now," he said. "You are finally seeing the big picture. Well don't worry, Rodenko. There are always other options. I am not concerned with this Great White Fleet for the moment. First we deal with the Japanese."

"On this heading? Those look to be very restricted waters ahead, Sir. I'd feel more comfortable steering 240 if you must engage the Japanese."

"I have good reason to hold this course. Watch and learn."

Tasarov gave Nikolin a wide eyed look. Nikolin had been agonizing at his post, considering a number of ways he might get the news he held to Rodenko without provoking a major scene on the bridge with the Captain. One scenario he ran through his head was that he could feign illness, even pretend to collapse with dizziness so that he would be relieved and sent to sick bay. There he could tell everything he knew to Zolkin, and the Doctor would certainly know what to do. Could he get away with that? At least he would not be here when the shouting started.

Another option presented itself. I have recorded the entire message, he thought. All I would have to do it play it back over the ship's intercom system! Then the entire crew would hear Admiral Volsky ordering the Captain to break off this engagement and return to Vladivostok. Yet there will be a firestorm if I do that. I would have to face the Captain's wrath right here on the bridge, and I do not want to imagine what he might do.

What about Tasarov? If I go to the sick bay he's still stuck in the borscht here. He knows about the Admiral too. Is he sitting there wondering what to do just as I am? He glanced at Tasarov's sonar station, seeing him stooped over his headset, deep in concentration. Nikolin toggled the station to station link again and keyed a text message. WHAT SHOULD WE DO?

At last he could bear it no longer, and he was working himself up to call Rodenko to his station to certify his ship's log entry. He thought he might then rasp out the truth he was holding when Rodenko was close, but he would not get the chance. Events took another course.

Tasarov heard it on sonar, a distinct sound that he had come to associate with an undersea missile launch. Yet it was oddly diffused in all the noise and he was not certain about it. Instinctively, he began to calculate bearing, making ready to report the contact, his heart beating fast as he did so. That single contact finally pushed the tentative house of cards on the bridge of *Kirov* to collapse.

"Con. Sonar. I believe I have—"

"Con Radar! Airborne contact inbound bearing five-zero degrees and sixty kilometers out." A junior radar operator had seen it much more clearly on the Fregat system as the missile climbed over the peak of Oronshima Island roaring like a kami. "Captain, I believe it's a missile!"

"Confirmed," said Tasarov. " I picked its launch up on sonar as well, same bearing."

Rodenko was standing sullenly by the tactical display, an uncomfortable look on his face that soon became real surprise. His eyes expressed both alarm and suspicion.

"Missile fire?"

Karpov spun about, his features ashen, eyes seeming to bulge a bit in his sallow face, and he reacted on sheer instinct. "Ready on S-400 system! Prepare to fire on my command!"

"Captain," Rodenko pressed. "A missile? How is this possible?"

"Mister Samsonov…"

"One moment, sir. I have a red light on the system board for the S-400s. The crews had to pull several missiles from the silos to reprogram as you ordered. They have equipment all over the deck!"

"Damn!"

Rodenko rushed to the radar station, unable to believe what he was hearing. Yet there it was, a clear signal lancing in at the ship at subsonic speed. He knew the signature well, and could even read the IFF data on his secondary screen It was very close.

"My God! It's a P-900, and no more than 45 kilometers out!" He looked directly at Karpov now, who stood frozen near Samsonov.

"Switch to *Klinok* system!" said Karpov, ignoring his *Starpom*. "Key all 30mm Gatling guns and begin tracking."

They had only seconds to decide what to do. Even at subsonic speed the missile was going to reach them in less than three minutes and then begin a high speed terminal run with dizzying evasive maneuvers.

"Switching to *Klinok* missile system and tracking on all starboard side 30mm guns." Samsonov moved, robot like, his big arms engaging switch toggles and sounding air alert one. The claxon blared through the ship's corridors and compartments, and they heard the scramble of unseen crewmen below.

"Captain!" Rodenko's voice cut through the tension.

"Not now, Rodenko, we have a missile inbound!" Karpov held up an arm as if to ward his *Starpom* off. "Fire when ready Samsonov! It will begin its terminal run any second. We must get it in cruise mode!"

At that moment Nikolin saw the amber light on his HF radio panel. It was another command channel message, and he had no doubt as to its origin. His heart pounded, pulse racing as he flipped the switch, realizing that it was now or never.

"Captain," he called, his voice unsteady. "I have another emergency HF command level message from Admiral Volsky!" There, he spoke the name, removing all doubt, and Rodenko heard it as clear as the message now playing on the overhead intercom speaker.

"*...This is your final warning. I repeat. This is Admiral Volsky ordering you to immediately break off your engagement and turn north to Vladivostok. If you do not comply we will have no choice but to fire in earnest. This is your final warning. Respond at once!*"

Everything seemed to be happening at once in a wild cacophony of sound and motion on the bridge. Karpov wheeled on Nikolin's position, shouting his name in anger. Samsonov fired, and two medium range missiles snapped up into the air above the aft section of the ship and ignited one after another, streaking away to find the incoming threat. The roar of their ignition drowned out the Captain's strident voice. Then Karpov stiffened to look outside for the incoming missile. They could already see the white contrail of the P-900 beginning its descent to sea level, and the two SAMs danced in the air to vector in on the target. Then something happened that no one expected. The P-900 exploded.

Chapter 30

"**Turn** that damn thing off, Nikolin!" Karpov was enraged. "At Once! Who gave you an order to relay command channel traffic to the intercom? Get off the bridge, you stupid fool. Move!"

Shocked by the twisted expression on the Captain's face, Nikolin quickly dropped his headset and slid out of his chair, a look of real fear on his face as he headed for the aft hatch of the citadel.

"Send up Chekov," Karpov said sharply after him. "And be quick about it. You are confined to quarters until further notice."

Nikolin shrugged and slipped through the hatch, his cheeks red and a downcast expression on his face. Yet he had done what he hoped. Everyone on the bridge now knew that Admiral Volsky was out there somewhere and heard his order for the ship to turn for Vladivostok. Rodenko knew, and was soon standing stiffly at the radar station, his eyes darkly on Karpov as he spoke.

"Captain, that was a warning shot. What is happening?"

"That man is insane," said Karpov. "What is he trying to do here? Thank God I got that missile with the Klinok's."

"Those SAMs had nothing to do with it, sir. Look, they are still in the air! The missile was detonated deliberately. We must open a command channel to the Admiral at once."

Rodenko wasn't stupid. His initial confusion and surprise evaporated quickly. He had been musing over the incongruities on the bridge the last hour and feeling something was very wrong here. He knew that Fedorov was back, supposedly at Vladivostok, but now the P-900 set that assumption to rest. They had to be on a ship if they fired that missile, and a ship with nuclear propulsion. He knew the fleet as well as any man, and could see no surface contacts on the radar screen at the point of origin for this missile. They were on a submarine, and the list of possible boats was a short one. Why hadn't he seen this earlier? It was right before his nose, the ASW loadout on the KA-40, the order to re-configure those S-400s...

"Captain, it is now obvious they have managed to return aboard a submarine. It's not an *Akula*; they have no SSMs, and it's certainly not an *Oscar*. They have to be aboard *Kazan*. That is the only boat in the Pacific armed with the P-900."

"Very clever, Rodenko. I deduced this long ago. What of it?"

"Sir, why didn't you inform me? Now we have orders from the Admiral and I would like clarification."

"Since when do you have anything to do with orders from the Admiral? You take orders from only one man on this ship—the Captain."

"But we all heard what the Admiral said, sir. We *must* comply."

"We will do nothing of the sort."

"Captain, I must insist."

"You insist? Don't get bigger than your britches, Rodenko. You insist nothing here, is that understood?"

The tension on the bridge was razor sharp. The two men were standing some ten feet apart, Rodenko by the radar, Karpov next to Nikolin's communications station, still eying the switches and controls there with offended suspicion. Tasarov was listening beneath his headset, eyes closed tight as if he were trying to shut the scene out and lose himself in the depths of the sea. Samsonov was waiting at his CIC post, but there was a light of uncertainty in his eyes as they moved from the Captain to Rodenko. All the other junior officers and watch standers seemed frozen in shock.

Rodenko stood taller, hands on his hips, squaring off as he faced the Captain now. "Sir, with all due respect. I am *Starpom* of this ship. It is within my right to question any order you issue, and to demand clarification should any order be unclear, particularly if a senior officer is at hand. Now the Admiral is out there somewhere, and I have heard his direct order—"

"I am countermanding that order as Captain of this ship!" Karpov's anger was barely controlled now, like a team of stallions straining at the reins. "Volsky knows *nothing* of the immediate tactical situation, and therefore cannot understand what needs to be done here."

"Which is why we need to contact him, sir. If nothing more you can explain our present situation and prevent an incident that we may all soon regret. You saw that P-900. That was a warning shot! *Kazan* has considerably more to throw our way and our primary SAM system is not ready for action. We must open communications at once."

Rodenko was playing it by the book. He knew his rights and obligations as *Starpom*, and if he had heard the whole of Admiral Volsky's first message he would have taken a much stronger line here. As it stood, only Nikolin and Tasarov knew that Volsky had ordered Karpov relieved upon non-compliance, but the Captain knew that as well, and he was not about to allow any further 'clarification' of that little matter.

"The man is insane if he would fire on us like that, and if he tries it again, we'll be ready for him, right Samsonov?"

"Sir?"

"I want all S-400 batteries active and enabled at once. Put the deck guns on automatic and have them engage contacts at 15,000 meters or less. Then key up the *Vodopad* torpedo system, four tubes. We have been given no choice and we must defend ourselves. Tasarov! Find me that goddamned submarine!" The Captain was staring at his sonar man now, a sinister look in his eye.

Rodenko realized that Karpov would not listen to reason, and that the subtleties of protocol would not avail him here either. Karpov was going to ignore the Admiral's order, and more, he was making ready to do battle with him! The Captain's blind insistence on this course, his overweening desire to strike a decisive blow to smash the history that had brought so much strife and sorrow to Russia, were his only concern. He knew that Karpov would not hesitate to fire *Kirov's* ASW torpedoes, and that *Kazan* would hear that and immediately retaliate. They were seconds from a situation that no man alive could forestall or control once those weapons were fired, and now

Samsonov was the key synapse in the chain of command. Instinctively, reflexively, he was reaching to enable the weapon systems on his command board, and Rodenko knew he had to act.

"Belay that order! You will stand down, Samsonov."

"Stay out of this, Rodenko! Mind your place! This is your last warning. You are so concerned over orders here, but can't seem to hear one when it's given to you. Now either second my orders or stand aside and keep your mouth shut. Understood?"

"No, sir. I cannot second this order and I will *not* stand aside."

"Then you are relieved! Go below at once and commiserate with Nikolin. The two of you have been nothing but trouble for days."

"No, Captain, I will not. I have heard a direct order from a senior officer, and you have failed to comply. As *Starpom* of this ship that order now falls on me. I must relieve *you* sir, if you do not comply."

* * *

What are they doing out there," said Volsky, his voice edged with impatience. "Anything?" He looked to the communications station now, hoping to hear that *Kirov* was signaling them.

"There has to be some confusion on the bridge," said Fedorov. "That warning shot will have certainly surprised Karpov, and he must now know we are not at Vladivostok. The question is whether or not he can master his demons. I believe he will be preparing defensive measures now."

"Yes, and the *Vodopad* system is all he has that could bother us this far away. But I do not think he has located us yet, even with our missile launch."

"Probably not, given all the surface noise from those ships to the south. But he will at least have bearing and general range."

"This does not bode well. If he fires I cannot take any further risk that one of those rocket torpedoes will find us, even if they have proved unreliable in the past. So here we have it, that cold reflex of war. A push on the shoulder becomes a shove, and that becomes

Orlov's punch in the face. The next thing we know we will feel the shock wave of another nuclear detonation. We fled to this distant past because that was precisely the situation we were facing in 2021, only it was not just this single submarine at stake, and not just *Kirov*, but the whole world waiting for the missiles to fire. This is but a microcosm of everything we set in motion. All that darkness is sitting right here. Yes, we are the demons from hell that we all shirk from in fear. Words fail us, then out come the clubs, knives and guns. This time it will be missiles."

Fedorov's eyes were sad and troubled. Then they seemed to kindle with newfound fire, the light of another idea there, and he leaned forward.

"Admiral…There may be another way we can handle this."

"Oh? I would certainly like to hear it, Mister Fedorov, but I think you must be quick about it. The longer we go without a message back from *Kirov*, the darker the swells in this turbulent sea."

"We have Rod-25 aboard, and we discovered that the radius of its effects is far greater than first believed. When the *Anatoly Alexandrov* shifted forward from 1942 we took a Soviet fishing trawler with us over a kilometer away! That was how we managed to find Orlov. Those British commandos I told you about had him on that trawler."

"Yes, yes, and what does that have to do with this situation now, Fedorov?"

"Sir… *Kazan* is a very stealthy sub. If we could get close enough, we could initiate the procedure again and possibly take *Kirov* with us, willing or not!"

The Admiral looked at him now, raising his heavy eyebrow. "You mean our shift would pull in *Kirov* as well? Are you certain this would work?"

"Nothing in all this business is certain, sir. But it is one last possibility short of a missile barrage laced with nuclear warheads."

Volsky folded his arms, inclining his head to Captain Gromyko now. "Just how quiet can this boat be, Captain?"

The hot potato was now in Gromyko's hands, and it was very uncomfortable. "Well, Admiral...I turned on a heading of 215 and began a high speed sprint just after we fired. As Fedorov says, there is a great deal of surface noise, and that island is now masking our position. Even at high speed we are very quiet, as long as that bearing aft doesn't give us away."

"What if *Kirov* used the *Vodopads*?"

"I believe I could evade them, sir. They would likely fall well behind us near our missile firing point, and if any were lucky enough to lock on I could probably outrun the damn torpedo at the pace we're going now."

"How close could we conceivably get to the ship without being detected. Don't forget, *Kirov* has the *Shkval* system as well, and it is much more lethal than the *Vodopads*. They can range out fifteen kilometers at 200 kph. That means he could hit us with one in under five seconds at that range and you certainly cannot approach at high speed."

"No, sir. I will slow to 10 knots on final approach."

"Well we must not forget the man sitting at sonar out there. Tasarov is very good. If he hears us..."

Fedorov spoke now, knowing that this was their last chance to avoid a cataclysm here. "We have his heading, sir. He is steering right for the southern tip of Iki Island. He knows from our first radio communication, and from our warning shot, that we are to his north."

"And so he seeks to put the island between us and the ship. I have seen him use this tactic before."

"Yes, sir. He did the same thing just after that accident on *Orel* that first displaced us in time. He wanted to get the ship north of Jan Mayan and use the island as a shield against those contacts we had to the south."

"Do not forget the KA-40s," Volsky warned. "They could be up there dropping sonobuoys as we speak."

"There must be a good deal of confusion and doubt aboard *Kirov* now, sir," said Fedorov. "They had to hear your orders. Karpov said the crew voted to stay here, but that was before your direct order to the contrary. I would bet there is some tension over all of this, perhaps even conflict aboard."

"Unfortunately Sergeant Troyak is here, and I do not think Karpov will make the same mistake twice and allow the ship's Marines to settle the issue."

"Just the same, sir, if we have any chance to attempt this and succeed, now is the time to act. Otherwise it is your hand on our missile key, and Karpov with his."

"If it comes to that choice," said Gromyko, "I can fire at any point as we head southwest, but realize if we have to use a special warhead the blast effects could be up to five kilometers wide. I'll need some room. It is very shallow in the Iki Channel and Genkai Sea. If I had to fire I would prefer to do so soon."

Volsky passed an agonizing moment in the silence of his mind. He remembered that night in Vladivostok just after the meal he had shared with Fedorov and Karpov. The Captain was another man then, rehabilitated, a phoenix risen from the ashes of everything he had done in the North Atlantic. Now he counted on them both to find a way to save the world and prevent the war they knew was coming.

He had rushed to a waiting taxi for the ride out to Naval Headquarters Fokino when the alert was sounded and the fleet was called to arms. The memory was still as fresh and cold in his mind as the cool night air when he rolled down the window, beckoning Karpov near.

"*We both know what is happening now,*" he had said to the Captain. "*We may have plugged one hole in the dike by sparing that American sub, but now the water seems to be coming up over the top. Remember, you are acting Captain of the battlecruiser Kirov. Don't let Kapustin and Volkov push you around. And one more thing... Fedorov... Listen to him, Captain. Listen to him.... Do what you must, but we both know that there is something much greater than the fate of the ship at stake now, something much bigger than our own lives. We are the only ones who know what is coming, Karpov, and fate will never forgive us if we fail her this time."*

"Fedorov will stand right beside me, Admiral, and we will do everything in our power to prevent that future we saw together. I promise you."

"I'll have faith in you both...There's one more thing..." The Admiral recalled how drew out his missile key, removing it and slowly handing it to Karpov. Their eyes met, a thousand words unspoken, and then he nodded at his Captain, raising his heavy hand in a salute, which Karpov returned briskly with a farewell smile. He could still see the Captain turn and rush away to the nearby quay where the dark threatening profile of the world's most powerful surface action ship rode quietly at anchor. He was animated with energy, and there seemed to be hope in every stride he took as he approached the gangway.

What had happened? Where had that hope gone? Was it the stress of combat with the Americans in 2021, the jolting shock of that Demon Volcano and the realization that the ship was again lost in time, marooned, with no way home? And then how was it *Kirov* was sent hurtling further into the past, to 1908? Was Kamenski correct in thinking that Rod-25 had been trying to work its way home to this year all along—the year of Tunguska?

In an instant he knew what had happened. Karpov had spoken the same cold logic to him long ago, aboard *Kirov* when he first asked him why he had tried to take the ship. The Captain had been surly, disrespectful, but he finally spoke his mind.

"What future are you talking about, old man?"

Volsky remembered bringing his fist down hard on the thin wood of the table, and the sullen Captain started with the unexpected blow. "Address me by name and rank, Captain! You are talking to the Admiral of the Northern Fleet!"

"Admiral of the fleet? What fleet is this you presume to command now, comrade? We are one ship, lost at sea, and lost in eternity. God only knows where we are now, but I can assure you, the fleet is long *gone, and there is no one back home in Severomorsk waiting for us to return either. It's all gone, Volsky. Gone! Understand that and you have your fat fist around the heart of it. If you want to understand what I did you need only open your hand and look at it. All we had left was this ship, and no one else seemed to have backbone enough to defend it. If I had not taken command it is very likely that we would all be at the bottom of the sea now—have you considered that? So do what you will. Choke me. Shoot me! ... I had my hand on the throat of time itself and I let it slip from my grasp. Don't you understand what we could have done with this ship?"*

The man found himself in 1945, and he fought. Now he is blown into 1908 and here he fights again, only now he believes he can finally win. Here the siren song of temptation is simply too great for him to resist. Then we return, with the one thing he has always feared most, a submarine. Now I think he will fight again. I have never seen him run, or quail in the face of combat. So I must either raise my sword now while we have the advantage and every prospect for success, or take the grave risk that Fedorov suggests.

Could we get there undetected? Even if we could get close enough, would Rod-25 have the power to sweep us both away into the chasm of time again? Can Dobrynin control the reaction under these circumstances? Even if he can, where will we end up? Will we get home? Will there be any world left there at all when we arrive? Will it all be charred and burned as it was before? ... *It's all gone, Volsky. Gone!... I had my hand on the throat of time itself and I let it slip from my grasp. Don't you understand what we could have done with this ship?*

He glanced at the ship's chronometer, seeing the second hand of the clock moving swiftly on. He had to decide.

Part XI

The Devil's Horn

"We are each our own Devil, and we make this world our hell."

— Oscar Wilde

Chapter 31

On the bridge of HMS *King Alfred* Captain Baker was studying the silhouette of the distant ship through his glass, astounded by what he saw. It was a monster, easily twice the size of his own ship, even bigger than the fleet's newest battleships. How could the Russians have built a ship like this?

"My God," he whispered. "What would old Jackie Fisher say if he could get a look at this." He was referring to 1st Baron John "Jackie" Fisher, the First Sea Lord and Admiral of the Fleet, the man who single-mindedly spearheaded the effort to design and create the first new battleship with all big guns as its primary battery, HMS *Dreadnaught*. That ship had spawned a new arms race at sea when it launched in December of 1906 with 11 inch belt armor and ten 12 inch Mark X naval guns in five turrets. It had more than twice the firepower of most any other ship then afloat, rendering entire navies, even proud battle lines like the American Great White Fleet, obsolete overnight.

Yet as he studied the Russian ship his amazement gave way to a confused expression. "Have a look at that, Mister Tovey," he said to his First Lieutenant of the watch. "Do you see any main armament forward?"

Young John Tovey raised the Captain's glass to his eye and squinted at the dark ship ahead for some time. "Can't see a thing, sir. Nothing more than those secondary batteries winking at the Japanese, but they can't be anything more than six inchers, sir."

"Indeed… Well then what is all the brouhaha concerning this ship? It looks to be no more than three twin turrets from the fire I've observed. We have sixteen Mark VIIs at hand and a pair of 9.2 inchers to throw in with them. Size is one thing, but firepower quite another. I don't see that this ship has much to fight with, unless it's hiding a row of casemate guns beneath its gunwales."

"Look, sir. That old battleship in the lead is already burning very badly." He was pointing at Vice Admiral Kataoka's *Chinyen*, now wallowing as a burning wreck in the sea while the armored cruisers behind her maneuvered to her port side, charging bravely on toward the Russian ship. They had not seen the missile that struck her down, and attributed the damage to the Russian naval gunnery.

"They may be few in number, sir, but those Russian guns appear to be deadly accurate. Now that lead cruiser has just taken two hits amidships!"

They watched as the armored cruiser *Matsushima* was hit and set afire, soon to be masked by thick black smoke licked by tongues of orange and yellow flame. *Kirov's* deck guns were firing on automatic, selecting targets at will within the engagement range Karpov had ordered as he tussled with Rodenko on the bridge. Before the *Starpom* intervened, Samsonov has carried out that order, and the result was a methodical, computer controlled gun duel that saw *Kirov* selecting targets and riddling them with 152mm rounds in precise radar guided salvos. The Japanese cruisers were still too far off to reply, and the lead ship, *Hashidate* pressed forward into the van, still waiting for a chance to fire their main gun on the foredeck.

"Those small islands will force them to slow down, sir," said Tovey, handing the glass back to the Captain.

"That will give us a little time to get our ships up." Baker studied the situation. "Yes…If we keep on this heading we'll cross their bow when they get past that island. At maximum elevation we might announce ourselves shortly." The two Mark X 9.2 inch guns on the cruiser could elevate 15 degrees and achieve a range of just over 15,000 yards with a full charge.

"We would do little more than that, sir," said Tovey, hoping he was not out of line with the remark. Captain Baker gave him a brief glance, his attention riveted on the enemy ship. "What in blazes is that whirling about on her main mast?" He had spotted *Kirov's* spinning Fregat radar panels, seeing them catch the light of the fading sun as they turned.

Then they saw a wink of light from the shadow of the Russian ship and Baker was experienced enough to know that his ships had been fired upon. The first rounds fell just ahead of the cruiser, their white geysers splashing up from the sea and soon awash in the ship's bow wave as the water was plowed up ahead of *King Alfred.*

"That was close. Damn good shooting for an opening salvo. Go to the helmsman, Mister Tovey, and have him come five points to port. I want to have a look at this ship for another moment and I'll be there shortly."

"Aye, sir. Port five." Tovey ran off into the armored conning tower leaving the Captain and his XO there on the weather bridge, the two men pointing at the Russian ship and discussing it further.

Then *King Alfred* shuddered and they heard an explosion well behind them. Captain Baker turned to have a look aft, seeing that his number two funnel had been all but decapitated by a direct hit, jutting like a broken tooth in the row of four stacks, and bleeding heavy black smoke. His executive officer was pointing a stiff arm at the scene. The next round changed the whole character of the engagement and plunged Lieutenant Tovey into the crucible of war in a way he never imagined.

There was a bright flash and a deafening explosion. *King Alfred* had been struck again and the entire bridge trembled with the vibration of the shock. Tovey was knocked from his feet, but unhurt. Yet, as he reached for a guide rail and pulled himself up, he saw that most of the outer weather bridge had been blown clean away, and with it both the Captain and his Executive Officer!

In an instant Tovey realized he was now First Officer of the watch and in de-facto command of the ship! He saw men crawling on the deck, the signalman struggling to his feet, a flagman hanging on a rail to the starboard side. Then he ran to the nearest voice pipe and did what should have been done long ago.

"Action stations!" he shouted. "Helm, port twenty!"

"Port twenty, sir." The ensign's hands were white on the wheel as the ship turned.

"Signal all ships to follow!" Tovey had turned to point his bow at the enemy ship, waiting until he saw the bow of *King Alfred* line up on the shadow ahead. "Midships," he shouted, "Steady as she goes and ahead full!"

"Steady on and ahead full!"

The bridge crew had recovered and leapt to their jobs with remarkable pluck and efficiency. Some were not even aware that Captain Baker was gone, but Tovey's strident voice was enough to lash them into action. They heard an order and they carried it out.

"Forward turret make ready to fire!" Tovey shouted that order down the voice pipe now, even as he saw two more shells hiss into the sea and bring the forward deck awash with their spray as the cruiser was straddled yet again. Now he knew why Kataoka's ships were burning off his port side. It wasn't the volume of fire that was doing the damage, but the infernal accuracy of the guns. He knew his rangefinders were desperately peering through their eye pieces, and could hear their voices calling out the numbers.

"Sixty cables!" called the Warrant Officer. That was just under 12,500 yards, a long shot for the single Mark X gun up front, but within its range.

"Elevation twelve degrees!" came a voice. "Ready sir!"

"Fire!" Tovey wasted no time. *King Alfred* would announce herself, as Captain Baker had put it. He looked for a pair of field glasses, finding one scudding across the swaying deck and scooping it up to sight on the enemy ship. There he saw the tall white spray of an explosion in the sea right on the Russian ship's bow as it emerged from the lee of a small island and near the sheltered bay just south of the main island. It looked as though the ship had drastically reduced speed, and it now seemed a massive, ponderous target in the restricted waters.

We'll rush in at high speed and get inside 10,000 yards, he thought. Then I'll remember what Captain Baker told me and we'll turn hard to port, presenting the concentrated firepower of the whole formation. But first this mad dash, and hell in the teeth of those enemy guns. He could see that the Russians had rippled their fire down his line, putting rounds on three more ships behind him. *Kent* and *Bedford* seemed bothered but were faring well, but *Monmouth* had a severe fire on her forward deck, obviously taking direct hits there that put her main gun out of action.

Just a little longer, thought Tovey. Soon we turn and hit them with everything we have. Then, to his amazement, he saw the sea erupt with explosions near the Russian ship, the booming report of the detonations rolling like thunder, and huge white gouts of sea spray in the waters on every side. It was as if an entire division had put fire down on the ship, but he could not see where the fire had come from. Yet every round missed! They were all arrayed in a neat arc about the ship! Amazed, he steadied himself and counted off the seconds, ready to give the order. It was now or never.

* * *

By the time Tasarov heard it there was nothing they could do. They had slowed to ten knots to navigate the narrow channel between the main Iki Island and a group of three small islets. The hidden bay Karpov was seeking as a sanctuary from *Kazan's* wrath had once been the hiding place and operations base of the famous Wokou pirates. It was said that a great demon had set foot on the island once, using it as a stepping stone at a place now called the Devil's Footprint. Yet now the demon that cast its darkness over the island was in the shape and form of a man on the bridge of *Kirov*, and the great ship that loomed as his shadow.

There was something in the waters ahead, as *Kirov* rounded a small islet and entered the sheltered bay beyond. It was adrift on the rising seas, a hulking, unseen devil of another kind, an oval of metal packed with an explosive charge. Five "Hertz Horns" jutted from the upper portion of the sphere. Each contained a canister of acid, and when crushed by the hull of an oncoming ship the container of acid would shatter and cause a battery to energize and detonate the mine.

Inside the metal sphere of the mine was a densely packed charge of nitrocellulose, called "guncotton" at the time. Mixing nitric acid with cotton was discovered by chance by a Swiss chemist, who spilled the acid and then hastily swabbed it up with a cotton apron, only to find the apron spontaneously exploded after it had dried! Its explosive power would later serve as a solid fuel for the famous Russian Katyusha rocket. This time it was in a Japanese mine, and the bulbous end of *Kirov's* Polinom "Horse Jaw" sonar beneath the bow of the ship struck it just as Tasarov detected the mine field and realized what was happening.

The devil's horn was broken, the acid burned, and the guncotton exploded, all 56 kilograms, or a little over 120 pounds. It was a small mine compared to modern standards where some might pack 3000 pounds of explosives, but it was enough to wreck the sonar there, and cause a minor hull breach that soon saw *Kirov* shipping water at the bow. The mightiest ship in the world had just been struck on the jaw by a lowly sea mine.

Yet a far more significant result was the shock to Tasarov's sensitive ears when the mine detonated. The noise cancelling suppressor on his headphones kicked in to stop serious damage, but he had been given a severe jolt, and his ears were ringing when he threw his headset on the console table. The explosion was felt on the bridge, where Karpov and Rodenko were still locked in their intense standoff, and it forced the Captain to take immediate action.

"Mine!" Tasarov had the presence of mind to call out the warning, putting a name to the noise and vibration they experienced. His voice seemed weak and lost between the sharp crack of *Kirov's* deck guns, still engaging targets with computer controlled fire. Now he stood with his hands cupped over his ears, as if to hear no evil in the sharp interaction that was transpiring just a few feet from his station.

"All stop!" Karpov barked out an order. "Watchmen to the weather decks with anti-mine details!" He was shouting the orders on instinct, but no one repeated them or sent them down to the decks below. The helmsman responded by stopping engines, but otherwise, the bridge crew seemed paralyzed with the conflict unresolved between the Captain and his *Starpom.*

"Hold on those torpedoes, Samsonov. We need the RBU systems now, full array on minimum range, forward and to both port and starboard quarters, fire *now!*"

It was *Kirov's* modern version of the old 'Hedgehog' system developed by the British, a kind of seaborne mortar that could fire a pattern of twenty-four explosives out in front of an advancing ship. Russia's modern day equivalent could range out to three kilometers with salvos of rockets bearing 300mm warheads. In this the big CIC officer quickly complied, and soon the sea ahead erupted with explosions and geysers of white frothing seawater as the first salvos landed, the detonation of the cure sometimes more jolting than the explosive power of the mines it was seeking to destroy.

It was this massed fire that Tovey had seen around the ship, and a typical reaction from the Captain, particularly when he was heavily stressed. He applied maximum force, thought Rodenko, the precise weapon required to do the job, an instinct to bludgeon the face of any unseen enemy. He knew what was coming next.

"Captain you *must* comply with the Admiral's order or I am forced to take command!"

Rodenko took three steps forward as he spoke and then stopped short, amazed at what he now saw. Karpov was holding a service revolver!

"You stupid bastard!" said Karpov. "You? Relieve me? Don't be a fool. You would not last ten minutes at the helm in this situation."

"Captain!" Rodenko persisted in spite of the obvious threat. "Listen to reason! You cannot do this!"

"I can and I will. Now get below or I will put a bullet into you for insubordination. Radar! Feed bearing and range on that missile fire to the CIC at once." Karpov's eyes were fixed on Rodenko's, watching every move he made. "Samsonov! Ready on the *Vodopad* system and prepare to fire."

Now I am the enemy, thought Rodenko, and Karpov has a pistol pointed right at my gut. Would he hesitate to use it if I press him further? He had his answer in short order.

"Get off the bridge, Rodenko! I can't *think* with you standing there staring at me like the stupid fool that you are. Get below or I swear I will kill you where you stand." The Captain extended the pistol with an unsteady hand and Rodenko held up his palm, warding off the weapon.

"As you wish, sir. Stand easy." He started for the citadel hatch.

"And don't get any stupid ideas about returning with Marines! I'm going to lock this bridge down tight as a fortress until this is over, and then I will come see about you and anyone else involved in this goddamned mutinous behavior. You are relieved!"

Rodenko thought how ironic that remark was, for it was in this very place that Karpov tried to seize control of the ship after locking the Admiral away in the Sick Bay. There were a hundred things he could have said at that moment, but he did not get the chance. Another voice spoke from the shadow of the open citadel hatch.

"No Captain, *you* are relieved."

Every head turned, including Rodenko, for they all knew the voice that had spoken those words. It was Doctor Zolkin.

"Not now, Doctor. The last thing I need is your nonsense or another lecture. The ship is in danger! We have just struck a mine and there may be more out there."

"Yes, it certainly is in danger, and from a Captain who has lost every vestige of self-control and all power of reason! I saw that missile coming at us off the port bow and knew it could only have been fired by one of our own ships. Then Mister Nikolin was kind enough to inform me as to what was happening up here."

"Nikolin? That little shit was confined to quarters!"

"Yes? Well he came to see me first, and with a recording of everything Admiral Volsky said to you when he contacted the ship earlier." The Doctor held up Nikolin's memory key, and Karpov's pallor reddened with anger.

"You have been given a direct order to break off this engagement and return to Vladivostok," Zolkin said quickly. "That order cascades from you to Rodenko, to Samsonov, to Tasarov, and then to Nikolin himself if not obeyed. Yes, don't look so surprised, Mister Samsonov, and don't sit there like a wind-up toy or a puppet dangling from the Captain's strings. You are next in line if the Captain sends Rodenko off in Nikolin's footsteps. The Admiral's order falls on you."

Karpov gave him an evil grin. "Don't listen to a word of this, Samsonov. He's making it all up! Mind your station. We have a battle to fight here."

"Of course, don't listen," said Zolkin. "Don't think, just react, and the next thing you know the Captain here will be ordering up another nuclear tipped missile to get himself out of the stew. Well, don't worry gentlemen. If Samsonov is not man enough to stand up here then I think I will spare the rest of you the trouble. The Admiral clearly stated that command of the ship would fall to *me* should his order be disobeyed. I have observed you for some time, Captain, and here you are holding a service pistol on Mister Rodenko, obviously quite disturbed. I hereby deem you unfit for duty and relieve you of command on medical grounds and for your obstinate failure to comply with the Admiral's direct order. Now, put that weapon down and stand aside. I did not come alone. Those Marines you were worried about are right behind me."

Karpov's eyes widened when he heard the echo of heavy footfalls on the ladder leading up to the landing in the hatchway behind Rodenko. He did not think. There was no plan, no carefully thought out strategy. It was nothing more than the mindless reflex of fight or flight, a broken horn, burning acid, and a spark of hideous ignition. There was just one more enemy before him, and he had a weapon to deal with him in hand. In a moment of sheer rage he cursed at the Doctor and fired.

Chapter 32

Kazan crept forward after its breakneck high speed run to the south, converging on the heading being taken by a noisome line of contacts arriving on the scene from the northeast. They did not know it at the time, but these were the venerable battleships of Teddy Roosevelt's fleet, sent hurriedly west in a massive show of force. Their commanders had been monitoring the telegraph wireless traffic and they knew there was a battle ahead. So as the Great White Fleet hastened forward, the crews were rigging out the guns and prepping for action, thinking there might be a major battle underway between the Russians and Japanese.

Kazan was moving like a grey shadow in the sea, silent and swift at a depth of just under 50 meters in these shallow waters. Gromyko was counting on the noise coming from that surface fleet to drown out any whisper of sound his stealthy boat might be making at this high speed, but soon he outpaced the ships above and was well out in front. He had surged south at over 40 knots, a speed *Kazan* was capable of, yet one never published on any spec sheet. In thirty minutes he had closed rapidly on the southern tip of Iki Island.

Now the depth was very shallow, and he had to slow to 10 knots and alter depth to navigate around shoals in the Kanasiro Channel. There were numerous rocky outcrops and shallows but the channel soon deepened out to 50 meters again once he had slipped through, elated to think he had made the run south undetected.

Yet that was not the case. While the situation on the bridge of *Kirov* and the sudden collision with that horned mine had made it all but impossible for Tasarov to hear the sub, the KA-40 was still up on the ASW watch where he had posted it, and Karpov had instinctively fingered the exact spot where *Kazan* was approaching, tasking the helo to watch that channel when he had last visited Tasarov's station. Just after they reduced speed to a gliding 10 knots, sonar man Chernov thought he heard some odd transients in the sound field.

The rumbling approach of the surface fleet was behind them now, and he had been able to filter out much of that noise, concentrating on the forward arc and the subtle sounds he was hearing there.

"Con. Sonar," he reported. "I think I'm hearing sonobuoy drops off our port bow, and something more in the water."

"Torpedo?" Gromyko fingered the worst possible option.

"No sir, it sounds like…mines! I think there's a minefield ahead." He could hear the heavy sea kettles sloshing about on the surface, lightly moored to the shallower waters ahead by thin tethers tied to anchors. They jostled in the rising swell, their reins rattling against the underside of the sphere of the mine.

"All stop," said Gromyko.

"All stop, sir aye."

"Make your depth forty meters." Gromyko was leaning heavily over the horizontal navigation screen, noting the depth indicators for the waters ahead. He did not have much sea room here for depth or maneuvering.

Admiral Volsky gave him a worried look. "What now, Gromyko?"

"Your Mister Karpov is more clever than I thought," said Gromyko. "It seems he's deployed a defensive minefield ahead of us, and we've come upon it like a spider's web. If these are moored mines we could easily snag a cable. *Kirov* is out their waiting for us and those helicopters you mentioned are going to beat the sea with sonar pings any moment and flush us out."

"Do you think they have located us yet?"

"Perhaps not, but this was a perfect place to post a KA-40. I was afraid this might happen."

"I doubt that Karpov deployed those mines," said Fedorov. "They are probably Japanese mines, meant to restrict this channel south of Iki Island and protect the bay." He was pointing to the digital map on the screen now. That's what Karpov is really up to. He wants to get the ship into that little bay where he'll be covered on three sides by land.

He'll sit there like a Moray Eel in his rock cave and devour anything that approaches him. Meanwhile he'll use the helicopters to find us."

"How deep is it in there?"

"29 meters average depth."

"That a fairly shallow tub. We'll barely have water over the sail if we try to enter. Our sensor masts will start to break water at 18 meters."

"It's deeper here," Fedorov pointed to the navigation chart. "There is 49 to 51 meter depth off this cape on our approach vector. It could possibly put us within the shift radius as he makes his approach here."

"And what if they get up into that bay?" Gromyko scratched his head. "You can time this shift perfectly?"

"They'll have to come from this direction," said Fedorov. "They'll swing around those islets and then approach from the south. If we can get here and hover, they'll come right to us. Dobrynin is already working on the reactors. The procedure is already underway."

"Yes? Well this is a very big risk we're taking here. We could be discovered at any time, and your shift may not happen in a timely manner. If we suddenly vanish into the ether what then? On top of that, now we have mines to worry about." He folded his arms, clearly unhappy.

"The mines will be riding the surface. Unless we snag a tether we should be fine."

"This is a big boat, Mister Fedorov. We could snag two or three if they are closely spaced, and we cannot detect their positions accurately without going to active sonar. One ping, however, and *Kirov* will know exactly where we are and spear us with a *Shkval*."

They heard a distant roll of thunder, clearly large explosions, and Gromyko raised his eyes to the ceiling. "That's some battle underway up there."

"Sir," said Chernov, "Those were RBU-1000 rockets! I recognize that sound anywhere. It has a very distinctive signature on my screen."

"So he's after us already? He may have a possible read on us."

"No," said Fedorov. "They must have detected the mines! Karpov used that same tactic to clear minefields when we were in narrow channels in the Med. If they heard us they would have fired much closer to our present position."

Gromyko nodded, realizing that was probably true. "Then perhaps he will be doing us a favor…unless he turns those 300mm rockets on *us* any time soon. Admiral…" Gromyko looked over his shoulder for Volsky. "I can put four torpedoes in the water in a heartbeat. At this range we would be certain to sink that ship. They would have no chance. We could then ease off and send in a *Veter* torpedo with a 20 kiloton warhead to finish the job." He waited, the seconds drawn out as Volsky considered all that had been said between the two men.

Gromyko was correct. Their situation was precarious here, and unless the shift was timed before *Kirov* slipped into that bay they would disappear and lose any chance of further intervention here. It was a desperate plan, a crazy plan, but he realized his alternatives were even worse. He would have to fire now, sink the ship, and put every man aboard in the water. Then he would have to slink away and send in a nuclear tipped missile before the ships and men of this era got too close, and what a sight that would be for all of them as they watched an atomic explosion erupt from the sea before them. It was insane. It was all utter madness.

He leaned in, his face grave. "Yes, we could sink *Kirov* here and now, but it won't go far, will it? Twenty nine meters? The Fregat radar would still be poking out of the water! We would have to drop a nice fat nuclear warhead here as you say to obliterate the wreckage, and there is probably quite an audience out there. I think we have no option but to hope we can pull Fedorov's plan off."

"Very well, Admiral. We're gliding now, about as quiet as a passing fish. I'm going to hover in about five minutes and let them come to us. I think we will end up somewhere here…" He pointed at the map to a position just south of the bay, the very same waters

Karpov hoped to occupy to hide from the submarine. *Kazan* had beaten the battlecruiser to the scene, but was still in grave peril. "We're already inside *Shkval* range," he added quietly, "and just seconds away from destruction if they detect us."

* * *

"**Look** there, Vasily! A Submarine!" Airman Lev Leonov pointed out the forward pane of the KA-40.

They saw it as the water depth faded to only 30 meters and *Kazan* was forced to move very near the surface on her run south. The speed and shallow depth made the submarine very visible from the air, and what human ears could not hear in all the noisome sea, human eyes from above could easily see.

"That looks like one of ours!" The pilot, Vasily Kovalenko had seen every class of Russian sub from above, and he knew the sleek lines of a *Yasen* Class boat. My God! That has to be *Kazan!* What are they doing here?"

"Maybe they have come to join us! Now there is no force on earth that could bother us."

"Yes, but weren't we ordered to look for submarines? We have a full ASW loadout for good reason, Lev. Get busy."

"What? You want me to drop sonobuoys here?"

"What else?"

"And report on our own submarine? That's ridiculous. Just call the ship and tell them we've spotted *Kazan* approaching from the northeast. That will certainly bolster morale."

"Alright, but drop your buoy just the same. We're supposed to be on ASW exercise. You want to get in trouble with the Captain after we land?"

"Very well, Vasily. You report, I'll deploy."

The pilot nodded and touched his helmet microphone to call the ship but when the signal came winking in on Nikolin's station he had already been chased below by Karpov, and there was no one there to see it! Chekov had not yet arrived and the light winked on and off plaintively, with no response. Kovalenko droned on with his call litany, waiting, but soon realized that no one was listening. Frustrated, he looked over his shoulder and saw *Kirov* approaching Iki Island from the west after navigating around the cluster of small islands. He, too, saw the ring of explosions around the ship, and realized they had fired the RBU-1000 system.

"Lev! They have fired the 300mm rockets! Things are getting serious down there." The rockets primary use was as ASW defense against close in submarine contacts, torpedoes or mines.

"Still exercising in the middle of a surface engagement? Look at all these old ships approaching from every heading! Why is the Captain making us run this stupid drill?"

"*Kazan* will deal with anything on this side of the island, and *Kirov* can handle the rest. But we may be ordered to fire a torpedo at one of those ships as well. Stay sharp."

It had never occurred to them that the submarine they had found was Karpov's mortal enemy and the real target of their mission.

* * *

Zolkin fell back against the bulkhead near the aft hatch, clutching his shoulder where the bullet had struck him. Whether it was Karpov's unsteady hand, or some inner instinct that saw the Captain aim his shot to a non-vital area, the Doctor was not mortally wounded. The shock of the gunfire was stunning, however, and Karpov moved like a dark shadow, bounding toward the open hatch and violently slamming it shut just as the first of three Marines had reached the landing above the ladder.

He sealed and locked the hatch, immediately toggling the intercom there, one eye on Rodenko. "You men! Return to the helo deck. The situation here is under control. This is the Captain."

Now he wheeled towards Rodenko, seeing he was kneeling over Zolkin where the Doctor had slumped to the deck, bleeding from the gunshot wound.

"Well it seems you'll be staying here after all, Rodenko," said Karpov, breathing heavily. "I can't risk opening this hatch until I've dealt with those enemy ships out there."

"Samsonov!" He looked for his CIC chief, the fire of battle smoldering in his eyes. "No more fooling around with the deck guns. Now the gloves come off. Key up the Moskit-IIs, two full silos. Prepare to target on my command."

Samsonov turned his thick neck and saw Zolkin and Rodenko, the wild light in Karpov's eyes, the revolver in his hand, and then the Doctor's words burned in his mind.

"Don't think, just react, and the next thing you know the Captain here will be ordering up another nuclear tipped missile to get himself out of the stew. Well, don't worry gentlemen. If Samsonov is not man enough to stand up here then I think I will spare the rest of you the trouble."

He looked at Zolkin now where he clutched his wounded arm. Then Samsonov stood up, man enough, his jaw set, towering like a chiseled statue over his post, his face resolute and grim. He had been just that for one engagement after another, a man of steel and stone, a mindless automaton, a fighting machine, as if he had been part of the ship itself, a mere dial or switch the Captain might throw to vent his rage on the unsuspecting foe. His work had been precise, clock-like, emotionless, like any other machine on the ship. Yet now he stood there looking at Rodenko where he knelt by the Doctor, seeing the blood staining Zolkin's shoulder and arm, and he found the mind and soul within him and spoke.

"No Captain. I will not comply. You heard the Doctor. The Admiral's order has fallen on me now."

Karpov gave him a look of complete shock. "Samsonov! What are you doing? Those ships will have us in range within minutes!"

"I'm sorry, sir…" He stood there, a look of anguish on his face, the fate of the world on his broad shoulders, though he did not know that, could not know it. But what he did know was that the fate of at least one man he loved was at stake. Zolkin could bleed to death right there on the deck of the citadel. He also knew if he fired those missiles the last would bear a nuclear warhead, and thousands more would die here today. The Captain knew but one way forward in the heat of battle, a certain escalation that could only lead to fire and doom.

Who would judge him this day? Perhaps it would be a bullet from the Captain's pistol and he would fall as Zolkin did. Yet now he finally stood before the unforgiving court of his own conscience, even as he stood adamantly before Karpov on the bridge. Now he stood as a man and not a machine, and he could do no more. Karpov once stayed my hand as I made ready to kill that American sub. Now it will be my hand that stays his, thought Samsonov. He found inside himself this single budding moment of morality, the bane of all warriors who kill by trade, yet it was enough. It was enough.

"Tasarov!" The Captain turned, his face frantic now. "Ready on the *Vodopad* system. Target those oncoming ships!"

Tasarov was still standing, eyes wet, and now he walked to Samsonov's side and stood at attention, unable to speak. Then, one by one, the Junior Officers at every station set down their headsets and light pens and came to their feet, standing like terracotta warriors, in serried rows at their stations, motionless, their eyes on the Captain as a black hole of silence seemed to open beneath their feet. Their silence and stillness was an awful reproach, and the look in their eyes was the final unspoken verdict.

Karpov looked at them as though they were ghosts, the spirits of the damned, the fallen angels he had led to perdition now arrayed against their lord and master in an act of supreme defiance. He saw the fear there, the doubt, and behind it all the awful spike of recrimination, a dagger to his soul.

"*Get back to your posts!* What are you doing? You'll get us all killed!" The Captain's words lashed at the men, but they would not be moved. He craned his neck to see outside, but cinder black smoke obscured the seascape. Then he ran to the weather bridge side hatch, opening it with a vicious wrench of the handle and stepping outside to see what was happening. A battle line of oncoming enemy cruisers was knifing through the waters in the distance, the ensign of the Royal Navy snapping stiffly in the breeze above the main mast of the leading ship.

Chapter 33

On that ship stood another man, leaning on a hand rail with one hand, the other holding a pair of field glasses. Lieutenant John Tovey had closed the range. His ships had taken a fearful pounding, but they had closed, and now he meant to make his turn at 9,000 yards and give return on every shot and shell the enemy had flung upon them.

"Port thirty, and signal all ships to follow!"

"Port Thirty, aye sir!"

"Come round to two-seven-zero and set your range!"

"Sir, coming to two-seven-zero," the helmsman echoed back.

"Range 9,000 yards, aye sir, and all guns ready."

"Steady… Steady… *Commence firing!* All ships to fire in turn!"

The guns roared in anger, retribution, vengeance; the justice of Lyddite and shrapnel. Tovey watched to see the first shells from the Mark VII 6-inch guns falling near the enemy ship. They had the range, and he hoped some would find their way to the heart of that monstrous shadow.

His own ship trembled again with the impact of yet another enemy shell, this time at the base of the armored conning tower where it rattled the heavy armor there. He had a fire amidships, one funnel sheared off and bleeding smoke, one of his stacked casement guns on the starboard side was blasted away, the weather deck was gone and the Captain with it, but the ship was fighting back now, and behind it came *Kent*, and *Bedford, Monmouth,* and then the light cruisers *Astraea* and *Flora*. They were turning smartly, following the arc of his frothing wake, and one by one their guns opened fire, adding their thunder to the raging skies above.

Well off his port quarter he saw the last brave cruisers of Kataoka's battle line still firing as they, too, came into good range for their well trained gunners. The main body of the Japanese fleet was coming up behind them, and farther off his starboard side he could see yet another long line of tall battleships laboring forward, the ships of the American Great White Fleet. They would surely join the action in half an hour, with more ships under Japanese flags due east of his position.

The crash of the guns was reassuring now, his two big turrets joining in with their loud booming 9.2-inch guns. He looked to see the first shell hit home, high up on the dark battlements of the distant ship where a 6-incher flashed in explosive anger.

"Pound them, gentlemen," he said coolly. "Give them the shot and shell."

It was the grandest battle he had ever seen at sea, with all of forty ships or more dashing forward in a wild surge of steel and violence. It was Armageddon and he was right in the middle of it all, thrust into battle with a nemesis that would haunt him the remainder of his long life. One day he would see this ship again, and the strange, unsettling feeling would settle in his gut as he reached for the faded memory of this hour. He would wait, through long decades, unknowing and unaware that this demon before him would return again and again, a dire threat that he would guard against to his dying day.

* * *

When Togo finally saw the enemy ship at a closer range his face hardened, taking on a stony quality, as if the weight of that inner warning that had possessed his mind had now frozen him to a rock like thing. There was something otherworldly about the ship, the way it moved, shark-like, its guns turning, barrels jerking to elevate on a target in sharp precise movements, then recoiling in three crisp salvos that were so rapid it seemed beyond the realm of possibility that human hands could have achieved that rate of fire and reloading.

It was a monster from the deepest sea, twice the size of any ship he had ever seen, intent on devouring all that came before it. By comparison his own fleet seemed a hapless school of tuna, lumbering forward in formation only to see one ship after another struck by the lethal fire and accuracy of those guns. He could see only three of them, turrets mounting what looked like two medium caliber guns each. Yet their rate of fire and accuracy was awesome!

And what happened to *Chinyen*, he thought? He arrived on the scene to see the burning flotsam of wreckage where it once led in Kataoka's Fifth Division. What was that blur of fire that had struck it? Where was the Vice Admiral now? Was he suffering the fate of those men flailing about the sea, or did he manage to escape and safely transfer his flag to another ship?

He looked over his shoulder, seeing the battle line behind him, his proud warriors, the victors of Tsushima. The battleship *Shikishima* followed his own, and then came *Fuji* and *Asahi* followed by the armored cruisers and then the destroyers. The ragged line of Kataoka's division was still well ahead of him, and half those cruisers were now on fire. He spied the brave 2nd Destroyer Division of Captain Yajima sweeping up in a wide turn, their wakes white behind them as they began to charge the enemy ship. The aft turret of the Russian ship rotated and fired, its shells immediately finding the formation—two, four, six—white fire and smoke as the lead destroyer was hit. He knew none of those ships would ever get close enough to fire their torpedoes under the murderous fire of those guns.

A desperate feeling came over him, as if he could sense the fate of the Empire hanging by the barest thread here, the line of ships remaining behind him. If I lose this fleet today, then Japan has nothing, he thought darkly. It will be years before we can build more ships, and there to the east is the smoke of the American Great White Fleet, a force I know we must one day face as an enemy. All history will turn on this battle, yet if I do not prevail, if I turn now and leave these waters to the enemy, the dishonor would surely break our nation as well, even as it crushes me with shame. That was something he could not bear.

So we will charge next, he thought grimly. I still have ten ships behind me, but if Russia has ships like this demon before me now, how will Japan ever survive?

* * *

Kirov was still firing its guns, a mindless thing in the sea, a steel Leviathan, flagship of the Red Banner Fleet. The ship had written a legacy of death and destruction on the decades from this moment to the distant future of 2021. It had fought, and prevailed over every foe, but now it was a headless horseman, wallowing at the edge of a minefield in a merciless sea, moving only by its own ponderous momentum, and a reflex guided by the cold logic of its computers. It was hemmed in on every side by lines of enemy ships, and now their guns began to fire, led by the brave charge of a young Lieutenant aboard the armored cruiser *King Alfred.*

The sea around it was awash with the white vengeful geysers of seawater where the hostile rounds fell. Most were short or wide, yet others struck home. The tall parapets of *Kirov's* superstructure endured the impact of the first shells, like a gladiator shrugging off the sharp edge of cold iron when an enemy's sword drew blood. Crewmen bled and died where those shells hit home, lives to be extinguished in the cracked mirror of the history yet to come. Like the men found missing, faceless, unborn on the list Inspector Kapustin and Captain Volkov ferreted out during their inspection tour, they would never exist in the years ahead, so they died here and now as Time mercilessly balanced her books.

Yet ships bleed only smoke and fire when they die, and now the mighty *Kirov* began to burn with two fires amidships. There men still fated to live rushed to fight the flames in their orange life preservers and yellow helmets. And high above them, at the edge of the weather deck stood their Captain, watching the scene in utter shock and disbelief. A 9.2-inch shell from *King Alfred* straddled the ship with a great eruption of seawater. Karpov looked aft to see smoke rolling from the fires amidships like black blood, thick and impenetrable.

The Captain had a haggard, haunted look on his face, gaunt with fatigue, his cheeks sallow and drawn, eyes shadowed with pain and remorse, and now the barest glimmer of fear. There he stood,

Vladimir Karpov, Captain of the battlecruiser *Kirov*, acting commander of the Red Banner Pacific Fleet, Viceroy of the Far East, yet with no one and nothing to command but his own forsaken soul. In his hand he held a pistol, and now in one last act of frustrated defiance he raised it at the far-off silhouette of HMS *King Alfred* and fired three shots… And the last he saved for himself….

* * *

Hidden beneath the turbulent sea Dobrynin sat huddled in the belly of another behemoth, and he was listening… listening… The rumble of battle sounded faint and far away, a muted background to the song that was playing in his head. *Sing, choirs of angels*, he thought, *sing in exultation…*

Rod-25 was home now, in the year it had reached for all along. Yet it was tasked again to rend the fabric of time and open the yawning, endless night of infinity. Dobrynin heard the rising chorus and knew it was happening. How far they would go, to what distant year, he could not say. Would time find a place for them, for *Kirov* and *Kazan* where they sailed at the edge of the maelstrom of Armageddon? Would time have a life waiting there for them, the Admiral, Fedorov, Orlov and all the rest?

He did not know any of this, but he could feel them moving now, slipping over the event horizon of the maelstrom and being sucked away into the void. *Kazan* was close enough to the turmoil and strife above, close enough to *Kirov*, and when the submarine fell into the empty hole in time it reached out and dragged the embattled ship along with it.

To those that saw it, rising on the heavy seas as they aimed and fired their guns, or puckered their eyes behind field glasses, telescopes and range finders, it seemed that a vast mist enfolded the ship, a shadow deepening at its center. Iridescent light played in the mist, like the strange glowing ripple of luminescent sea fire. Others thought they saw the discharge of Saint Elmo's Fire from the tall spinning mast atop the ship, coronal jets of plasma that crowned the shadowy sea fortress in a halo of gossamer green light. It had always been regarded as an omen of bad luck when it afflicted a ship at sea, or the ominous portent of stormy weather to come.

The ship glimmered in the wreath of mist and shadow, there and gone again, seen and unseen. It quavered at the edge of eternity…

And then it was gone.

The smoke and fire was gone with it, and it was over.

Part XII

Tomorrow is Yesterday

"You cannot escape the responsibility of tomorrow by evading it today."

— *Abraham Lincoln*

Chapter 34

The wan light of a grey day gleamed on the wet surface of the boat when it broke the surface of the sea. *Kazan* rose from the shallow hiding place where it had crept so close to the imminent possibility of annihilation. Yet no one on the bridge of the burning ship in the distance was listening for it, or seeking its death in the sharp explosive tip of a rocket torpedo or missile.

There sat *Kirov*, the smoke and fire of war charring her hull and superstructure, but yet sound and seaworthy, and still a dangerous shadow on the sea. All about the two vessels the sea was calm, rippling gently away from an unseen center point of stillness. *Kirov's* guns were silent as well, the computers that aimed and fired them bludgeoned into a stupor by the effects of the displacement. There were no other ships anywhere to be seen, not the dogged battle line of the British squadron, not the remnant of Vice Admiral Kataoka's embattled division, not Admiral Togo on *Mikasa* charging boldly forward to join in battle, nor the Great White Fleet that had sailed so far and fast to reach this place, only to find the enemy it sought had vanished.

They were all gone, far away and lost in another time. Only one man alive on any of those ships would ever live to see that dark shadow again, John Tovey, and he would shiver with the memory of that first sighting, and strange disappearance, the remainder of his life. It was said the Russian ship was sunk, yet no vestige of the vessel was ever found in the shallow waters off Iki Island. Rumors of the ghostly encounter would be passed from sailor to boatswain and back again over the long years ahead, but the incident was never explained. It remained one of the great mysteries of the sea, a place where so many other ships had vanished at the edge of a storm, never to be seen again.

The ship was there, they said. It was real, and the holed hulls, sheered funnels, burning weather decks, and ravaged superstructures of many who fought against it that day stood as undeniable testimony to that fact. The list of ships sent to the bottom in the brief time the rogue vessel blighted the seas off the Imperial homeland of Japan was a long one. Kamimura's entire division was all but destroyed in the Oki Island engagement, and the battleships *Tango* and *Mishima* obliterated. Dewa's cruisers paid a high price for his impetuous desire for battle, with *Kasagi* and *Chitose* sunk, *Otawa* and *Nitaka* set afire, and the destroyer *Asagiri* broken in two. Kataoka's flagship *Chinyen* and the cruiser *Matsushima* were also sunk that day, with *Hashidate* burning and falling off the line of battle, never to fight again.

Karpov and *Kirov* exacted a very high price for the privilege of closing the range, until one man finally stood up, refusing to fire any longer, and said no to the horror the ship had visited upon that unsuspecting world. The blow against the Japanese fleet was a hard one, but not fatal. The recent commissioning of HMS *Dreadnought* had rendered most ships afloat that day obsolete, and they would all soon be scrapped for new construction. Without the ceaseless patrol of *Kirov* in the Sea of Japan, that nation's imperial ambitions, and the navy that would one day conquer half the Pacific, were still on track.

Russia was severely censured politically for a time, but was too possessed with its own internal strife and rebellion to notice or care. Great Britain was now living beneath the looming shadow of the First World War, and the Tsar was soon courted again as an ally against Germany. And so Karpov's dream of a Russian Pacific power would never come to pass. It was not on the restless swells of the sea that history would turn in the maelstrom, but in the tempestuous storm of revolution on land.

There, the iron will of another man rose like a demon from the ashes of the Romanov dynasty and slowly took hold of the growing revolution in his cold hand—Ivan Volkov. With an uncanny insight for things to come, his close confederates soon came to call him "The Prophet," and he soon found himself at the center of the Bolshevik party, its new master, and a shadow that would fall over Europe and the world in days ahead.

Only one man stood in his way, resolute, unyielding, and with enough of a power base to contest him—Sergei Kirov. He had seen the world that Stalin would build, and learned of the fate that awaited him. Now he saw that same iron and evil in Volkov, and he stalwartly opposed him. It would be Sergei Kirov who stood like Rodenko, and Zolkin, and Samsonov and the others and said no to Volkov's meteoric rise to power, and the fate of Russia would hinge on the outcome of that struggle.

* * *

Rodenko stood up now, looking at the empty seas around the ship, and he knew it was over, the terrible ordeal finally ended. We have moved again, he thought. There sits that island, there is the bay the Captain was steering for, yet we are somewhere else now, in some other time. But when?

He could not answer that while Doctor Zolkin lay bleeding beside him, and so he ordered the men to open the citadel hatch and called for a medical team to get the Doctor below. One by one the men sat back down at their posts, still silent, as if unable to speak in the face of the heavy stillness around the ship. Then Rodenko walked over to Samsonov and placed his hand on his broad shoulder, nodding with a half smile to Tasarov where he stood in the big man's shadow.

"Well done, Samsonov, and you Tasarov. You have done the right thing, and you will never regret it."

"Sir," said Tasarov. "Where is the Captain?"

Now Rodenko looked over his shoulder at the still open hatch to the weather bridge, his eyes darkening with misgiving. He walked slowly to the hatch, stepping out and expecting to see Karpov huddled against the outer bulkhead of the bridge, but there was no one there, only a stain of blood on cold grey metal, where a bloodied hand may have gripped the gunwale. The Captain was missing in action.

He heard the thumping of a helicopter emerge from the silence, and looked to see the KA-40 coming in slowly off the port bow. It had been unable to raise the ship, and so it circled back towards *Kirov* as the action began to heat up and became another fly caught on the web woven by Rod-25. The bulbous round nose of *Kazan* broke the sea as the big submarine leapt up from its silent patrol. He ran back into the citadel, and was quickly at the communications station, eying the dials to open a channel. A shadow fell on the console and he turned to see both Chekov and Nikolin had come back to the bridge, so he stood up, arm extended to the chairs as he invited them to take their posts.

"Mister Nikolin, please signal *Kazan* that all is well aboard *Kirov*, and that I have assumed command as per the Admiral's orders."

The voice of Admiral Volsky was soon on the overhead intercom speakers. *"Well done, Rodenko. And to all of you there I express my deepest regrets for what you have just endured. You have all done your duty. Mister Fedorov and I will be coming over in a few minutes."*

He did as he promised, dragging himself up the ladder from a boat tethered near *Kirov's* aft hull and returning the stiff salutes of the men there as he was piped aboard. Then he walked up to the nearest man and extended his arm for a warm handshake. Fedorov, Orlov and Troyak followed after him, coming aboard to cheers and warm salutations, though a few men shirked when Orlov appeared at the gunwale gateway.

Volsky turned to Fedorov and gave him a quiet order. "Go forward to the bridge and see about Karpov. I will be there shortly."

Several Marines were there for security, and when they saw Sergeant Troyak return they saluted crisply, then came forward to clasp him heartily on the back and shoulder. "Welcome back, Sergeant! I see you brought Corporal Zykov too."

"Lieutenant Zykov," the former Corporal exclaimed. "Mister Fedorov gave me a nice promotion, and Orlov here is a Captain again."

"Don't let it go to your head, Zykov," said Troyak. "That was a temporary assignment, you are as much a Corporal as they come these days, so don't think we'll be shining your boots tomorrow."

They all had a good laugh, even Orlov, who looked around, feeling strangely out of place now as he stood on the aft deck. He had thought he would leave this ship and crew behind forever, and make his way in the world of 1942 with little more than Svetlana whispering in his earbuds to remind him of his old life, the life that lay somewhere far ahead of him, concealed in the obscuring and uncertain mists of time.

Yet he, like Karpov, once thought he could shape that life into an image of his own making by using the foreknowledge of all the days yet to come to good advantage. Unlike the grand scale of Karpov's plans, it was only his own personal fate that he had been concerned with. Now, however, when he felt the hard metal deck beneath his feet again, and the subtle roll of the ship, he was as much at home as any place he had ever known. He was glad to be back again, if the men would have him.

Volsky took some time, working his way through every section and compartment of the ship to greet the men, offer his praise and reassurance, telling them that all would be well.

"I see you have been in quite scrap or two," he said looking at the thin column of smoke still rising amidships. "Chief Byko has some work to do again."

"Don't worry, Admiral, sir. We have already put those fires out, and the damage is not serious."

"That is good to hear."

"Where are we now, sir?" one *Mishman* asked plaintively.

"Where are we? We are aboard the finest fighting ship in the world," he said with a smile. "Do not worry. I have business to attend to on the bridge now. All will be made clear in time."

Papa Volsky was back, and the mood of the crew elevated perceptively with each step he took on those embattled decks. He made a point to go by the sick bay, thinking he would find Doctor Zolkin there tending to any man wounded in the action lately fought. To his great surprise he saw Zolkin lying on his own medical examination table, his arm and shoulder being wrapped and attended by two medics.

"So you have joined the fighting too," he said with a smile.

"I did what I could," said Zolkin, and when the medics left to look after other wounded men, Volsky closed the door and sat down heavily on the chair by the bed.

"I am so sorry, my old friend. When the ship left the harbor at Vladivostok and sailed by the bay south of Fokino, I saw you all go, and wished I was there with you. But they strapped me into Abramov's chair and there I sat, learning one thing after another from the pages of the history books, and wondering if I would ever see any man aboard this ship again, particularly you Dmitry. I had no idea any of this would happen."

"None of us did, Leonid."

"And how were you wounded?"

"Karpov." He told the Admiral how Nikolin had come running breathlessly into the sick bay, holding a memory key with that recorded message traffic.

"He recorded it? God bless Nikolin. I was very worried when Karpov did not comply with my order. How sorry I am to have put you in front of his broken soul. You were very brave to go to the bridge as you did, Dmitry."

"It was either that or we would have seen another mushroom cloud. There is a lot you have yet to learn about what happened."

"I'm sure there is, but rest now, my friend. I will go forward and see about the Captain. It's time I was on the bridge."

When he got there he learned the news from Fedorov first, who had been talking with Rodenko when the Admiral stepped through the hatch. The eyes of the entire bridge crew were on him at once, the men smiling and obviously very happy and relieved to see him again. After a time he took Rodenko and Fedorov into the flag briefing room, and learned all that had happened.

"Karpov drew a gun, yes, I have seen Zolkin, and I am pleased to tell you the good Doctor will do just fine. The man who skewered a score of enemy ships with his missiles apparently could not shoot strait, and for that I am very grateful."

Rodenko had the same question that many crewmen had asked. "Any idea where we are now, sir?"

"We do not know yet," said Volsky. "I imagine Gromyko is over on *Kazan* wondering the same thing. I have told him to submerge for reasons of security. For all we know we could be back in 2021 and right in the middle of that war again, or even in the 1940s in the middle of *that* war. Fedorov may have told you we made a brief stop there on our way back to 1908. Any way we look at it, we must assume these are unfriendly waters here."

"We have ship-to-ship, sir," said Fedorov, "but Nikolin says longer range communications are still down. The ship's systems will most likely recover slowly in the hours ahead."

"Well, as soon as possible I think we should at least have a SAM battery operational, just as a precaution."

"I'll see to it, sir," said Rodenko.

"As for Nikolin, I'm going to give that young man a Papa Volsky bear hug. If he hadn't recorded that message I sent, who knows what may have happened? Now then... Mister Fedorov, if you would set that enterprising mind of yours to finding out how we should reset our watches and calendars, I would like to address the crew. But first I must ask where the Captain was last seen alive?"

"He was out on the weather deck off the side hatch of the bridge, sir," said Rodenko. "I was out there to see about him just after we shifted, but he was gone. I did hear gunshots, Admiral, just as we began to shift."

"I see... Well I think I will go and have a look. See to those matters for me, will you both?"

"Aye, aye, sir." Rodenko saluted.

Volsky stepped out, first congratulating Nikolin and expressing his gratitude to all the junior officers as well. Then he turned to Victor Samsonov, and leaned in, saying something quietly to the man. The light of appreciation was evident in the CIC Chief's eyes, and when he sat down he seemed just a little bigger, if that were possible. Then Volsky walked slowly to the side hatch and stepped through, closing it behind him.

He stood in silence, his eyes playing over the deck, as if looking for any sign or remnant of the Captain. Then he spied the blood on the gunwale railing, and saw more blood spatter on the deck just below it. He thought of Karpov and all he had done, their many arguments and discussions, his intransigence and unyielding ardor for battle, and his obvious skill when it came to the fire of war. He remembered how he had shared a drink with him, asking him why he had tried to take the ship so long ago. He recalled the Captain's pledge and promise, broken now, yet another victim to the man's ravenous ambition.

You thought we all had the wax in our ears, Karpov, he said silently to the missing man, and only you could hear the siren's song. I gave you this ship and crew, and it was only by the grace of God that they are still alive and well—the grace of God and a few good men who were willing to stand against you in that final hour. There are thousands dead now, scattered all through the decades, and thousands more unborn because of all we have done. How can we ever measure it? And how can we ever be forgiven? The worst of it all is this haunting fear that you were right, and there is nothing more we can do now to set things as they were.

He lowered his head, at the edge of tears, and sighed heavily. Then he turned, straightened his hat and uniform jacket, and stepped through the hatch.

"Lieutenant Volsky on the bridge!" Fedorov was grinning now.

"Ah, I see I am still wearing a Lieutenant's uniform. Well let no one think that a simple Lieutenant cannot be the most important man alive one day." He winked at Nikolin now, and smiled.

Fedorov stared at him with admiration and hope, yet his attention was ever drawn to that open hatch where Karpov had gone missing. What had happened to him? Did he take his own life? Why was there no body found? These things and so many others settled like heavy anchors on the silted bottom of his mind. Kamenski had posed more than one challenge to him with his subtle hints and innuendo. The differing stories of how the war ended, the revelation that he had long been aware that time travel was possible, the strange fissure in time at Ilanskiy, and the unsettling notion that others had walked there were most troubling to him.

Like Volsky, he sighed with resignation. Nothing was certain. The history he once thought of as secure and safe in the past, stony and solid, unchangeable, had been proven to be a mutable and ephemeral thing. In fact, he thought, if what I now suspect is true, then other men from the future have returned to the past and worked their will upon it... Just as I have.

The loss of innocence in the face of that hard reality shook him to his very soul. *Nothing is written,* he thought, remembering the novel by Vladimir Bartol, *Alamut.* In that ancient stronghold of the Assassins the credo was stark and unyielding: "Nothing is an absolute reality; all is permitted." If that were so then Karpov may not have been the madman he seemed. Perhaps I am the one deceived by my own delusions of grandeur, he thought. The idea that I could make everything whole again was foolish, even selfish.

Yes, he knew now that other men from had walked in the Devil's Garden of history, and trampled the flowers there. He knew that he would never look at the world the same way, and his own life was now forever changed. His heart was heavy as he turned to the Admiral again, seeing him reach slowly into his jacket pocket to draw out a small book, opening it, his thick fingers turning the pages slowly.

"Gather round for a moment, men... I thought I would say something to you all, perhaps something profound. I know we have all done many things we came to regret, and taken many lives with the power beneath our feet, mighty *Kirov*. We have blood on our hands, and many tears to shed. Yet we did not hate those we engaged in battle, and for most of us it was not for gain or glory that we ever fought. We fought for each other, though now we may feel at times the need to hide from the gaze of sane men in this world who do not ever wish to find themselves in the service of war.

"One man among us fought his battles, within and without, as we all must do. He thought we could shape the image of our future by changing the past, and so for him tomorrow was yesterday. While his actions may have seemed incomprehensible and cruel, we must also remember those times when he stood with us, a comrade in battle, and fought to save this ship and crew. He was our brother once, though wayward, lost, and consumed by emotions that many of us will never feel or understand.

"I am told that was a British cruiser that led the final charge against this ship in battle. While we have seen the British as foes many times on this journey, I have always held a certain admiration for them, in many ways—except when they are chasing me with battleships!"

At this the men laughed, one moment of levity at a time when their hearts were heavy, weighted with remorse and sorrow. The Admiral sat down in the Captain's chair, swiveling to face the men as they waited.

"So this is written by a British poet, Lord Byron," he began, his eyes soft on the well worn page. "And it speaks well to how we sailed together these many long months, and through uncounted days, across decades and even centuries to reach this place. We do not know where it is just yet. We may still be lost in time, but we will find that out soon enough. Then again, it may be that we have no place in this world any longer and that we have murdered all our tomorrows in the yesterdays where we fought and extinguished so many souls...

"We fought, says this man...

'Midst a contentious world, striving,
Where none are strong.
There, in a moment, we may plunge our years
In fatal penitence, and in the blight
Of our own soul turn all our blood to tears,
And color things to come with hues of Night;

The race of life becomes a hopeless flight
To those that walk in darkness: on the sea,
The boldest steer but where their ports invite—
But there are wanderers o'er Eternity
Whose bark drives on and on, and anchor'd ne'er shall be."

Epilogue 1

Captain Gordon MacRae was down in what appeared to be a long, shadowy tunnel, constructed entirely of the same heavy reinforced titanium and tungsten carbide steel alloy as the hidden door that had led to this place. He stared up at the ladder, but strangely could see no one else above him, only a pale, wan light filtering down from above, a wavering fog that seemed strangely luminescent.

It was not long before a pair of feet and legs appeared, Elena Fairchild in the typical pants suit styles she wore so often. There was only room enough for about four people below, a room the size of a small elevator or closet. Elena brought down a flashlight and the Captain could see the walls of the chamber seemed perfectly smooth, but he could see no other doorway or passage.

"Looks like a dead end, Elena," he said.

"Dead end?" She ran the light over the pristine metallic walls, searching. "Stand aside, Gordon. I think there's something behind you."

The Captain side stepped, seeing the small recessed area in the wall behind him for the first time. There was a rectangular outline, as if a steel drawer was mounted inside of the wall, and dead center was another keyhole.

"What have we here?" said MacRae, running his hand over the cold smooth metal.

"That's odd," said Elena, appearing somewhat confused. "I thought there would be another door or passage here, but that certainly doesn't look big enough to get anything more than a cat through this wall."

"Perhaps it's just a control lock for another mechanism," MacRae suggested. "Maybe one of these walls moves… or even the floor." He looked down at his feet as if to spy out another obvious hatch or trap door, but there was nothing but the unblemished steel alloy beneath his feet. Elena pulled out the key, still on a sturdy chain about her neck, eying the keyhole with a puzzled expression.

"Well," said MacRae, "I was going to ask you where the hell we are, but from that look on your face I don't think you have the slightest clue either!"

"I didn't expect this," she said, her brow betraying concern. "But I suppose I'm meant to use my key again here, so that is exactly what I will do."

"Just a moment," the Captain said quickly, his head craned up towards the shaft above them. "Where's Mack? Suppose the damn floor gives way beneath our feet here when you turn that key? What if this is an elevator down? I think we should get some rope and secure ourselves to the ladder."

"That will take forever, Gordon. Here… Why don't you step up onto the lower rung of the ladder, and then I can take hold of your arm with a free hand."

MacRae shrugged, but stepped up and the two joined right arms in a firm hold. "I hope to God you don't find yourself dangling above a hundred foot shaft in another thirty seconds.

She smiled, and then reached with her left arm to insert the key, stretching as she leaned over to get close enough to the lock while still keeping hold of MacRae. With a quick click, there was an audible beep and the key seemed to activate a receptacle in the wall. A metal box, completely sealed on all sides, slid out from the wall like a bank safety deposit box.

"Hello?" said Elena, not expecting any of this. Yet she could see a third keyhole on the top of the box, and what looked to be a recessed handle that folded out so it could be carried.

MacRae let go of her hand, thinking the floor looked secure enough under the circumstances. "You seemed in such a God awful hurry to get here, Elena. So what's going on?"

"I don't really know…" Her mind was working furiously now. These were the correct coordinates. This was the place, and there was no mistaking the singularly iconic landmark above them. They had found the way in. Her key opened the door and the upper hatch and ladder down all made sense to her. She had been told to expect as much, and to follow the passage to its end. Then what? There had been no further instructions in the secure briefing file she received nine days ago. Only a single word—Godspeed.

Another key hole. Very well, one more time. She inserted the key, but this time there was no click, no beep, and it would not turn in either direction. She struggled with it for a moment, but realized, with a sinking feeling, that the key would simply not turn. They had, indeed, reached a dead end!

Frustrated, she stood up, illuminating the whole area in a careful search while MacRae stood there, hands on his hips, watching with a look on his face like a school master who had happened upon a student trying to cheat on an exam.

"What are we missing?" said Elena, somewhat exasperated.

"The key won't work?"

"It won't turn or engage in any way. It's as if I've got the wrong key, but it got me this far, so I can't imagine why this should happen."

"Suppose I have a go at it." MacRae stepped into her light. "Here… the thing has a handle. Let's set it down on the floor." He stooped down on his haunches, looking up at Elena with his dark eyes brightened by her light.

"Very well…" She handed him the box, thinking to check inside the recessed area where it came from first, feeling about to see if there was anything she might have missed. It was smooth and empty. Then she got down next to him, and their close proximity in the darkened, confined space seemed magnetic. MacRae put a reassuring arm around her, and then reached for the key with his other hand, inserting it and testing its operation in all directions.

Nothing happened.

"Well now," he breathed. "An emergency trip to nowhere—that's what we have here. Something tells me the answer to all this is inside that box, but why won't the damn thing open? Are you sure you have the right key?"

"It's the only one I have."

"Might it be timed to operate only at a certain hour?"

She hadn't considered that, but even so, what could the box possibly hold? How would it help them in any way, given what she knew was about to happen in the world above?

"This is maddening," she said, clearly bothered. Are you certain there was no other opening or hatch?"

"I can't see anything here. Give me your light and I'll have a look along the upper shaft. I can go up and get some better light down here." He took the light and began searching all the walls, yet they seemed solid and presented no apparent seam or opening of any kind, so he climbed higher.

As the shadows folder about her, Elena stood up. What was going on here? She had expected to find a passage, one that would take them along the nebulous edge of a fissure in time. That was how it had been explained to her. Upon receipt of the go signal she was to get to Delphi as quickly as possible with a security team and excavate the site above. The rest should be obvious. Godspeed. She looked up at MacRae, suddenly realizing he was no longer there.

"Gordon?" She stood there in the pale light, noticing the odd sheen above her in the ladder well for the first time. "Gordon? Are you still there?" Surely he could hear her. Why couldn't she see his light?

"Now where has that man gone? We don't need more light. The flashlight was working fine."

Frustrated and somewhat angry, she started to grope for the metal ladder, then looked down at the box on the floor, barely visible in the dim light. On an impulse she reached down and took hold of the box by its handle, then started climbing up. There was a strange sensation, and she felt suddenly light headed half way up the ladder. A voice was heard, strangely distended, a hollow echo that seemed to reverberate back on itself with a cellophane timbre. The sound solidified as she climbed, and became more distinct, the familiar Scottish brogue of Gordon MacRae.

"Well it's about time. I was calling for you. Dinna ya hear me?"

Elena felt very odd now, and claustrophobic in the narrow shaft. "Climb up," she breathed. "I think I need some air."

He was up the ladder and extending a welcoming arm to help her up, taking the box with his other hand when she handed it to him. Mack Morgan and several Argonauts were standing there, curious and eager to see what was happening.

"I looked the whole passage over," said MacRae. "If there's another hatch or opening anywhere else, then I'm a jackass. Did you look into the recessed area where the box was mounted?"

"Nothing there," said Elena. "I checked every one of the interior surfaces."

"We can get better light and send the engineers down. They might see something we missed."

She thought about that, looking at her watch. Something had gone wrong. Something was wrong, wrong, *wrong!* It was getting late, but they still had time. Her mind was a whirlwind as she considered what to do. Why didn't the key work? Unless… perhaps it *did* work. Why didn't she hear Gordon calling to her? His voice should have resounded through that well loud and clear. Perhaps that was the passage, that brief descent on the ladder. Where were they at the bottom? The past?

Then something else occurred to her, and it gave her the shivers. Who could have built this well in the past—those titanium alloy doors? She had been told there were fissures, passageways through time, and assumed they would always lead *backwards*, to the past, but that might not be the case. They could have also descended into the future!

Maybe she was meant to find something with here and not to go anywhere as she had anticipated. But why the key hole on the box, and why wouldn't it turn or open? Could other members of the Watch help her solve the riddle? Protocol now required her to report the incident. That was mandatory, but there was so little time and only one place she could do that—back on *Argos Fire*.

"Get the men to the helicopters," she said firmly. She was obviously meant to find what she now had in hand. The box may not open with her key, but it might be opened with another. She had to report this! She had to get back to the ship, re-enable her secure command line and report. They had precious little time, but enough to get there and back again if need be on the fast X-3s.

"We just leave that hole there in the middle of the shrine?"

"Secure the hatch. It should lock upon closure. Cover it with a few feet of earth and leave the rest as is. It won't matter anyway in a few hours time. But we've got to get back to the ship."

Her own words echoed in her mind as the Sergeants whistled, calling back the Argonauts from their security perimeter and shouting to fire up the helicopters.... It won't matter anyway in a few hours time. It won't matter...

But it did matter. It was going to make all the difference in the world, at least to them and the lives they would lead in the world they returned to. The helos landed on the after deck of *Argos Fire*, and the Argonauts dismounted, laden with arms and equipment and feeling like passengers at an airport whose flight had been cancelled. Yet they were glad to be back aboard the ship and soon settled in below decks, thinking nothing more of the strange mission.

The Captain went forward with Elena Fairchild, carrying that small box they had retrieved from the dig site at Delphi. They reached the executive suite, tired, and somewhat confused. Morgan came in last after having stopped on the bridge to confer briefly with Commander Dean.

"What's happening out there, Mack?" said Elena as she cast a worried glance at the clock on the wall.

Morgan scratched his dark beard, a puzzled expression on his face. "Well, Mum, there's been nothing on the black line while we were gone, so I've no hard intelligence over that channel. Funny thing now is that Mister Dean says we've got some strange interference on all the normal communications channels."

"Interference? Anything wrong with the equipment?"

"No, Mum, they've checked it top to bottom. It's very odd. We can't even pick up anything on either AM or FM bands, not a word, not a whisper. It's as if there's just no one out there."

At this Elena's eyes clouded over with a squall of fear. MacRae was watching her closely as she stood up, slowly walking to her desk to depress a hidden button that would open the rear bulkhead to secret room harboring the red phone.

"Come with me, gentlemen. There's one more line we can try."

Morgan looked at MacRae, and the two men passed a knowing glance with one another. This was the hidden inner sanctum of *Argos Fire*, and messages coming across that line had been the seed of many missions in the past. Neither man had ever been permitted to enter the room before this, and so it was with some surprise and an equal measure of curiosity that they both stood now, quietly following Elena into the small room.

There was a single chair sitting before a small pedestal crowned by a Plexiglas dome over the red phone. It had a keypad for code entry and Elena quickly used it to re-enable her phone. MacRae set the box heavily down on the pedestal desk, waiting while Elena seat herself on the chair.

"Well," she said, "protocol has it that I should report any red mission irregularity at once. I never thought I would find myself sitting here in front of this damn phone again. This is all quite unexpected."

"What was the failure?" MacRae folded his arms.

"You saw yourself. The key would not operate, and there was no other passage or door."

"But there was that box," he pointed.

"Yes, and now I've got to report that and see if I can find out why my key won't open it."

"Try it again," MacRae suggested. "No sense making your call unless you're sure it won't work."

That sounded reasonable, and so she nodded, drawing out the key again on its chain and slowly inserting it into the hole. It turned!

There was an audible click and a quiet tone from some mechanism inside the box, and now the front side tilted open, revealing a small drawer that held a rolled scroll. She glanced at MacRae, perplexed, and then slowly reached for the scroll to open it.

There was a brief message, addressed to her, and she read it aloud. "Should you read this your mission will have concluded as planned. Keep this device within a secure room aboard *Argos Fire* at all times and it will serve to hold you in a safe nexus. As of this moment, you are now Watchstander G1. Godspeed."

"Watchstander G1?" MacRae did not understand.

"There were nine of us left," said Elena. "It seems I've been promoted."

"What does it mean, Mum?" said Morgan. "A safe nexus?"

She turned, looking at him with a new light in her eyes, and then smiled. "It means I know why you can't raise anything on the radio now, Mack. It's begun. It's happening right now, and we're right in the eye of the maelstrom..."

Epilogue 2

It had taken some time to debark at the port of Ostend, as it was quite busy that morning. Sir Roger had his footman Thomas retrieve their luggage while he thanked the Captain of the *Anne* roundly for taking his small party on a minute's notice The Captain was all to gracious and willing to do more. The glitter of the diamond the Duke had left in his palm was more than ample inducement.

"May I look for your ship in these waters again, sir?" Ames had inquired as he made ready to leave the ship.

"Most certainly, Mister Ames. I make this run from Edinburgh to Ostend once every fortnight, and then sail on to London before returning north again."

"That will work out well, Captain, as I shall have business in London soon," said Ames.

"Excellent. Well I do hope the French don't complicate matters for you. I would advise you to stay well away from the border."

"I take that as good advice, Captain Cameron. Very good, sir. Farewell."

The Duke quickly found a pawn shop and brokerage near the wharf that agreed to buy a few of his diamonds for a considerable sum in coinage, which he thought would make for much easier commerce in the days ahead. He soon had a nice leather pouch full of pounds, shillings, and pence, though the old 240 pence pound was still being used, with a pound equal to twenty shillings, and a shilling equal to twelve pence at the time.

The first order of business was then to secure a good coach for the journey to Brussels, some 80 miles inland which was accomplished in an hour's time. Thomas and the coachman loaded the luggage on a sturdy post-chaise, a common four wheeled carriage of the day, and the two men climbed aboard. Sir Roger leaned out to speak with the coachman, intent on giving him firm direction.

"Now then," he said. "We will not be going to the principle residence of the Duke of Richmond on the Rue des Cendres. There is a coach house back of the property with an address on Rue de la Blanchisserie. Make for that location, my good man, and an extra shilling if you get us there before sunset." The exact location of the ball being given by the Duchess of Richmond was in some doubt for many years, but the Duke had discovered it was held in that very coach house, and not the main residence. He recalled attending mock events of the famous ball, the last given on the 200th anniversary of the battle in 2015. Yet none will be so grand as the original, he thought with some satisfaction.

He eased back in his seat now, exhaling and pleased that they were finally on their way, though the Duke's companion and would be footman sat in sullen silence. Ames regarded him sympathetically, knowing the shock of his present circumstances must be very hard to take, even in the comfort of the plush riding coach. He reached up, sliding the window shut to make certain the driver would hear nothing, then regarded his hired hand Thomas with a steady gaze as he fished in his pocket for a pipe.

"I managed to get my hands on a bit of Bull Durham tobacco while we were at the wharf. I don't suppose you'd care for a smoke?"

Thomas shook his head, saying nothing.

"Well," said the Duke, "I don't partake often, but I rather feel like getting into the swing of things here. You know the saying… When in Rome, do as the Romans do. My meerschaum pipe is an old favorite." He held up an ornately carved pipe in a pale cream meerschaum, a Black Sea mineral that was perfect for the application and used for pipemaking since the early 1700s. "Much better than a clay pipe," said Ames. "The stone is soft and porous, and it cools the smoke wonderfully. I'd favor a pipe like this over briar wood any day. Manzanita is another fine wood for a pipe, but meerschaum stone is top drawer."

He could see that his attempt at simple civil conversation was having little effect on Thomas, so he inclined his head and got round to the trouble at the bottom of his footman's depressed mood. "Well,

Mister Thomas. I suppose you think you have been hoodwinked here, eh?"

"Sir?"

"Come now, I can read that glum expression. Yes, I know this has all been quite a shock, and perhaps more than you bargained for when I first proposed this journey."

"It's just too much to believe, sir. I can't imagine how any of this could be happening!"

"Of course not. You have taken it all bravely, my man. I suppose you thought it was all sport and theater to tickle my fancy at first, though I tried to put you off that mindset several times."

"Well who could believe it, sir? Who could believe *this* without seeing it all first hand?" He gestured to the world outside, passing the windows of the coach as it started off down a narrow road.

"Indeed. Seeing is believing, however, and we have only just begun. You will see a good deal more before we're through here."

"How, Sir Roger? How did we get here?"

I'm afraid that is a very long tale, my man. But I do suppose I owe you a bit more of an explanation. That business at Lindisfarne was no mere sightseeing tour. The place has a long history, and hides more secrets than many know. You have just seen one of them—that passage at the back of the closet on the upper bedroom. It was that stairway, and the tunnel after it, that led us here. We walked only that very short distance, but traversed long years with every step we took."

"What… through *time*, sir? How is that possible?"

The Duke regarded him with narrowed eyes, considering. "I suppose you have both feet in it now, Thomas, and you did not know the full measure of what I was asking of you when you signed on to this little adventure. I tried to convey the indefinite duration of the assignment, and its potential hazards. Yet I apologize for not revealing everything. If I had told you this beforehand you would simply not believe it. There was no other way. Sometimes you cannot go by rope or ladder when you come to a precipice in life, my man. You must simply throw yourself over. Very well then, in all fairness I will be candid with you now. Few men or women will know what I will now tell you. To put it simply, the world we have just come from is in real jeopardy, not just with that war brewing up like a storm on our near horizon, but because it seems time itself has simply run itself down there. Things are starting to come apart and it's about to get very strange, which is why it was necessary that we go somewhere else."

"I don't understand, sir. How could we move in time?"

"Of course you don't. Let me see if I can explain it. You are given to thinking of time as something you always have, and always spend, like these shillings in my leather pouch here." He cupped the pouch under his waistcoat and went on. "You think of your life as beginning at birth, when you are handed a nice big bag of coinage in time and you spend two pence a day until you run out. You move through time every day. Yes? But you always move in the same direction, forward. The thought that you might ever take a step back, to unsay an ill made remark, or correct some other misjudgment often crosses every man's mind, but it's not something he can ever do—or so he believes. You've heard the poetry by Omar Khayyam: The moving finger writes; and, having writ, moves on: nor all thy piety nor wit shall lure it back to cancel half a line, nor all thy tears wash out a word of it. So it has seemed to be true for most of our lives. Yet I have found it to be in error, Mister Thomas. Other men have too—though they are very few in number."

"Others have done this—they have traveled back here?"

"Not here. This is my keyhold, and I paid handsomely for it, believe me. But there are other places like Lindisfarne in the world, and they open hidden doors like the one you and I just went through. I only know of a very few, but they are there."

"You're telling me these doorways and passages exist elsewhere?"

"They do. There's one in the Great Pyramid, and others in Greece and China. There may be more that I do not know of, and each one leads to a different place—or rather I should say, a different *time*. This one led us here to the eve of a great moment in history, and it was much coveted. I had to pay a great deal for the key, and there it is." He touched the chain that held the key where it hung about his neck.

"But… how? Who built these passages?"

"The short answer is that we do not really know. There is no doubt that the portals exist, though they are really more like fissures in time. The one we traversed was discovered in the early 19th century when the restoration of the castle was underway. How they managed to determine its unique nature remains a mystery. There were signs that they tried to open the doors, without success. Those works were beyond the means of anyone in the 19th century. They could not be breached by force. The doorways were six inches of tungsten-carbide steel and titanium alloy! That is technology we may master in 2021, but not in the 1900s."

"Then they were built in our day?"

"I could find no evidence of that, which means that they were built in the past."

"But how could they achieve that? You just said the technology was beyond them."

"So one would think. Well, we don't know who built them, do we? They may have been built in the past, but that does not mean they were built by anyone native to the time of their construction. I could undertake a project here, for example, using knowledge and methods known only in our time."

"You are suggesting they were built by… by someone from a *future* time?"

"Very good, Mister Thomas. I knew you would come round to it one way or another. It's really just a process of elimination, isn't it? If past generations could not master the technology required to build those doors, and they were definitely not built in any of the modern history we know, then they had to be built by men who *could* complete the project, and also built *before* they were discovered by architect Sir Edwin Lutyens in 1902. In fact. He may have been privy to their existence."

"How would that be possible?"

"Easy enough, Thomas. He may have been from the future! I've given all this a good deal of thought, you see. Suppose Lutyens deliberately engineered his restoration to deftly conceal those doors, stairs and passages? He would have to have rather specific knowledge of the subterranean layout and all."

"Did he have that key, sir? The one you used to open those doors?"

"Perhaps he did. Perhaps he was a warden of sorts—a gatekeeper. In any case, those who did know of the passage kept it under their hats and quite secret."

"Then how did you come by the key, sir?"

The Duke folded his arms, considering. "I'm afraid that would be a very long story, Mister Thomas. Let me put it to you this way. Men of privilege, wealth, and power have a handle on things that go on in this world that few would realize or ever know about. This is a perfect example. Suffice it to say that I had the means and the will to find out about this passage, and to obtain the key."

"Amazing, sir. Though I still can't get my mind around this. How does it work?"

"It's not a machine, Thomas. It's a physical rift in time. Think of it this way. You may now believe time is fluid, that it flows or moves like water in a river, and you are on a raft simply being carried along. Well these little passages are like whirlpools in the stream. Happen across one and your little raft might be swept under and pop up somewhere else entirely. That's one way of grasping it."

"I think I follow you, sir."

"If you want to know the truth, however, time is more like a solid thing, but it has cracks, fissures, little tears that can take a man from one moment to another. You live your life in one, day by day, like the grooves scratched into an old vinyl record. The music as you go along is your life, and you never think the song can be stopped in mid stream, reversed, or ever played again, just like Omar Khayyam's poem, even if you do know it will come to an end one day. But it *can* be played again. Scratch that record and the needle skips! Sometimes it may get stuck and simply repeat a segment over and over, like a time loop. You've had brief skips like that in your own life, coming upon a person or place and knowing you have been there before."

"You mean like déjà vu, sir?"

"Yes, exactly. Now, we believe we are stuck here in our song— track number five on the album if you will, and it never occurs to us that we might skip back to track number three. But that needle can run across a scratch in the record and skip a whole segment of the tune, or even skip backwards again to play a part over, or go to an entirely different song! That's what these passages are like. They are physical scratches in time. They were discovered by chance, I suppose. Someone stumbled through one and then found a way to stumble back. When one is found, it is well hidden, and well secured, as you have seen. And it is my belief that men from a future time are behind all this. Only a very few are known to exist. Scratches, tears, grooves, fissures, whirlpools. I mix all these metaphors to make it understandable, but the simple fact of the matter is that if you find one, you can move the needle of your life somewhere else—and that can be quite thrilling."

"And quite daunting, sir. Yes, I did think this was all theater, until we finally made port and the sheer magnitude of it all finally struck me."

"I thought it might work better that way," said Sir Roger. "Wade in gently before you take the plunge, eh? Well, now here we are, on the eve of great events. We'll have a long carriage ride to Brussels today, and then rest up at a hotel near the ball room at that address I gave the driver. A room may be difficult to come by, with the British army garrisoning the town, but I've enough coin to loosen things, and more diamonds if coinage fails. Then we get down to business. I will explain it all to you in good time. Lord knows we have enough of that now that we're here."

"That passage we took," said Thomas, his mind still wrapped about the mystery the Duke had related. "We can go back?"

Ames raised his eyebrows. "I suppose we could try, though I have no intention of doing so any time soon. This is a very exciting world here, Mister Thomas. Men were real men in this day and age. They fought with swords, pistols, and rifled muskets with a good bayonet, and not missiles and machine guns. They still rode horses into battle, and this one here is going to be rather grand."

"Waterloo?"

"What else?"

"And this... business. This business you speak of, Sir Roger. You said we were going to kill—"

Ames held up a hand, stilling him. "No need to discuss that here," the Duke said quickly. "But yes, we have some urgent tasks at hand, and then I've a mind to get back to England after the battle."

"To Lindisfarne, sir?"

"To London—Piccadilly in fact. I need to see the 7th Earl of Elgin there."

"The 7th Earl?"

"It's a special matter. We'll discuss it all later. For now, my man, get your mind and thoughts around the business at hand! We're here, just a few days before the battle, and we get to see sights and breathe air that no man of our day could ever imagine. Smell that air, Thomas. Not a hint of pollution on the breeze. There's nothing in the sky but the clouds and wind by day, and the stars by night. This is a world still unspoiled by modernity—no radio waves, cell phone traffic, or microwaves flitting about carrying a blather of nonsense and text messages, eh? I think we'll have the time of our lives here, and then, after we've done what I came here to do, we'll see about a matter that I have recently stumbled across myself—a very interesting matter indeed."

"Yet you do plan to return when this is concluded?"

The Duke sighed heavily. "Well I suppose I should be forthright about this as well, Mister Thomas. We could reverse our footsteps, even rejoin Captain Cameron again on his ship if we choose. He would be more than happy to deposit us on Lindisfarne Island again.

And we could make our way back through that passage, though I shudder to think of what we might find if we do so."

"What do you mean, sir?"

"What I mean is that the world we have come from is going to hell, my man, and it's not going to be a place where you and I might wish to be at all. We were warned of this some time ago, and those in the know have made arrangements, if they could. There are some that will simply try to go underground—you've heard all the stories and rumors about the deep underground shelters and bases... the Denver Airport and such. In fact, they even modeled some of it by way of disinformation in those Hollywood movies about the end of the world. Well it was all true. Anyone in their right mind back home is going underground by now, but only the key holders have any real chance for a life in another time."

"The key holders?"

Sir Roger held up the odd key he had used to open the hidden passageways at Lindisfarne, smiling. "Yes, the key holders. This little adventure is the arrangement I have made. It is my chance, and by extension *your* chance at life as well. I have no intention of returning to discover what might be left of the world in 2021. I mean to stay here, Mister Thomas. There's real adventure here, and that passageway at Lindisfarne is not the only fissure in time I am privy to. There are others, and we can do a good deal of exploring if you have the stomach for it. For us, tomorrow is yesterday. The only way to traverse the years between this date and the world we came from will be the old fashioned way now—one day at a time—but we will make a grand adventure of that."

He looked at Thomas now, a smile on his lips and a challenge in his eye. "Come along with me, Mister Thomas, and I'll show you worlds you could only dream of. Are you with me?"

Afterword

Dear Readers,

"We started this, and now we must finish it," said Fedorov at the outset of this story....*But not quite yet!* If your eyes now scan these lines then you have been with me since that first moment on the bridge of *Kirov* as Admiral Leonid Volsky shifted uncomfortably in his chair, staring out at the slate grey sea. It has been a long journey and I thank you for coming along. In truth, I meant to move on to some other tale after I first wrote *Kirov*, but your enthusiasm for the story, and your loyalty as members of a very elite crew, kept the ship sailing.

Many of you have written to me expressing your enthusiasm and enjoyment of this long saga. Some have even told me that their escape into the world of Volsky, Fedorov, Karpov and Orlov was a balm that comforted them when faced with the pain and challenge of their normal life, be it illness, work, or other issues. I was delighted to hear that, and to know that you were out there literally entering my stream of consciousness as it was when I wrote the lines of these stories.

Writing always was, and remains, my first love in life. (If only my typing skill equaled my knack for spinning out prose, I would be a contented man indeed!) As many of you have told me, I have also grown very attached to this story, the characters and their fate. They have become brothers in my mind as I labor to give them life on these pages, and ending the story here would leave a strange emptiness in me for some time after these two long years writing the series.

Thankfully, many of you felt the same way, writing to me and also voting in the reader poll on the web site to choose a new direction for my restless pen. The book most asked for was that this saga should continue, and so it will, as I now evolve the series further in *Altered States.*

Hemmingway once wrote: "All good books are alike in that they are truer than if they had really happened, and after you are finished reading one you will feel that all that happened to you, and afterwards it all belongs to you: the good and the bad, the ecstasy, the remorse and sorrow, the people and the places and how the weather was. If you can get so that you can give that to people, then you are a writer."

I hope I have given you something here that rings true as I continue that never ending journey, and also hope one day to call myself a writer. I would like to thank you all again for coming aboard and steadfastly manning your post with your support of the *Kirov Saga*. It was a tale that grew in the telling, and it was all for you. And so, with my deepest thanks and gratitude to have you as a reader…

The Saga Continues…

Kirov Saga: Altered States

Kirov and *Kazan* move forward yet find themselves stuck in the midst of WWII once again, only the world is not the same! The consequences of all their interventions in history have now calcified to a new reality. The political borders of nations have been re-drawn, Colonial powers vie for control of the undeveloped world, and Russia itself is a divided nation. Discovering they still possess a decisive edge in weapons technology they must now decide which side to take to end a long and terrible war that threatens millions more lives.

Altered States ~ Volume II: Darkest Hour

The first rounds have fallen, heavy shells smashing against the armored conning tower of HMS *Hood*, stunning the ship and its stolid Admiral Holland. Yet *Hood* fights on, her guns raging in reprisal as the pride of two navies meet in the largest naval engagement since Jutland. Even as Admiral Tovey reaches the action, the shadow of Hoffmann's battlegroup looms over his shoulder and the odds stack ever higher against the embattled ships of Home Fleet. Off to the north the *Stukas* rush to re-arm aboard carrier *Graf Zeppelin*, while far to the south another ship hastens north to the scene, from a time and place incomprehensible to the men now locked in a desperate struggle raging on a blood red sea that may decide the fate of England in 1940. Can they engage without shattering the fragile mirror of history yet again?

Learn the outcome and follow *Kirov* north as it heads to home waters, determined to meet the man that may have changed the course of all history, Sergei Kirov. Meanwhile the action moves to the Med where the young Christopher Wells is dispatched to Force H. The British must first prevent the powerful French Fleet from falling into enemy hands. The fighting has only just begun as *Altered States* continues the retelling of the naval war in an exciting second volume.

The Series will continue in Altered States ~ Volume III: *Hinge of Fate*

OTHER BOOKS BY JOHN SCHETTLER

Kirov ~ *Book 1 in the Kirov Series*

The battlecruiser *Kirov* is the most power surface combatant that ever put to sea. Built from the bones of all four prior *Kirov* Class battlecruisers, she is updated with Russia's most lethal weapons, given back her old name, and commissioned in the year 2020. A year later, with tensions rising to the breaking point between Russia and the West, *Kirov* is completing her final missile trials in the Arctic Sea when a strange accident transports her to another time. With power no ship in the world can match, much less comprehend, she must decide the fate of nations in the most titanic conflict the world has ever seen—WWII.

Kirov II – *Cauldron of Fire*

Kirov crosses the Atlantic to the Mediterranean Sea when she suddenly slips in time again and re-appears a year later, in August of 1942. Beset with enemies on every side and embroiled in one of the largest sea battles of the war, the ship races for Gibraltar and the relatively safe waters of the Atlantic. Meanwhile, the brilliant Alan Turing has begun to unravel the mystery of what this ship could be, but can he convince the Admiralty? Naval action abounds in this fast paced second volume of the *Kirov* series trilogy.

Kirov III - *Pacific Storm*

Admiral Tovey's visit to Bletchley Park soon reaches an astounding conclusion when the battlecruiser *Kirov* vanishes once again to a desolate future. Reaching the Pacific the ship's officers and crew soon learn that *Kirov* has once again moved in time. Now First Officer Anton Fedorov is shocked to learn the true source of the great variation in time that has led to the devastated future they have come from and the demise of civilization itself. They are soon discovered by a Japanese fleet and the ship now faces its most dangerous and determined challenge ever when they are stalked by the Japanese 5th Carrier Division and eventually confronted by a powerful enemy task force led by the battleship Yamato, and an admiral determined to sink this phantom ship, or die trying. In this amazing continuation to the popular *Kirov* series, the most powerful ships ever conceived by two different eras clash in a titanic final battle that could decide the fate of nations and the world itself.

Kirov Saga: *Men Of War ~ Book IV*

Kirov returns home to a changed world in the year 2021, and as the Russian Naval Inspectorate probes the mystery of the ship's disappearance, Anton Fedorov begins to unravel yet another dilemma—the secret of Rod 25. The world again steering a dangerous course toward the great war that blackened the shores of a distant future glimpsed by the officers and crew. Fedorov has come to believe that time is waiting on the resolution of one crucial unresolved element from their journey to the past—the fate of Gennadi Orlov.

Join Admiral Leonid Volsky, Captain Vladimir Karpov, and Anton Fedorov as they sleuth the mystery of Orlov's fate and launch a mission to the past to find him before the world explodes in the terror and fury of a great air and naval conflict in the Pacific. It is a war that will span the globe from the Gulf of Mexico to the Middle East and through the oil rich heart of Central Asia to the wide Pacific, but somehow one man's life holds the key to its prevention. Yet other men are aware of Orlov's identity as a crewman from the dread raider they came to call *Geronimo*, and they too set their minds on finding him first... in 1942! Men of war from the future and past now join in the hunt while the military forces of Russia, China, and the West maneuver to the great chessboard of impending conflict.

Kirov Saga: *Nine Days Falling ~ Book V*

As Fedorov launches his daring mission to the past to rescue Orlov, Volsky does not know where or how to find the team, or even if they have safely made the dangerous transition to the 1940s....But other men know, from the dark corners of Whitehall to the KGB. And other men also continue to stalk Orlov in that distant era, led by Captain John Haselden and the men of 30 Commando. The long journey west is fraught with danger for Fedorov's team when they encounter something bewildering and truly astounding, an incident that leads them deeper into the mystery of Rod-25.

Meanwhile, *Kirov* has put to sea and now forms the heart of a powerful battlegroup commanded by Captain Vladimir Karpov. He is soon confronted by the swift deployment of the American Carrier Strike Group Five out of Yokosuka Japan in a tense standoff at sea that threatens to explode into violence at any moment. The fuse of conflict is lit across the globe, for the dread war has finally begun when the Chinese make good on their threat to secure their long wayward son—Taiwan. From the pulsing bitstream of the Internet, the deep void of outer space, the oil soaked waters of the Persian Gulf and Black Sea, to the riveting naval combat in the Pacific, the world descends in nine grueling days, swept up in the maelstrom and chaos of war.

This is the story of that deadly war to end all wars, and the desperate missions from the future and past to find the one man who can prevent it from ever happening, Gennadi Orlov. Can the mystery of Rod-25 and Orlov be solved before the ICBMs are finally launched?

Kirov Saga: *Fallen Angels ~ Book VI*

The war continues on both land and sea as China invades Taiwan and North Korea joins to launch a devastating attack. Yet *Kirov* and the heart of the Red Banner Pacific Fleet has vanished, blown into the past by the massive wrath of the Demon Volcano. There Captain Karpov finds himself at the dying edge of the last great war, yet his own inner demons now wage war with his conscience as he contemplates another decisive intervention.

After secretly assisting the Soviet invasion of the Kuriles and engaging a small US scouting force in the region, Karpov has drawn the attention of Admiral Halsey's powerful 3rd Fleet. Now Halsey sends one of the toughest fighting Admirals of the war north to investigate, the hero of the Battle off Samar, Ziggy Sprague, and fast and furious sea battles are the order of the day.

Meanwhile tensions rise in the Black Sea as the Russian mission to rescue Fedorov and Orlov has now been expanded to include a way to try and deliver new control rods to *Kirov* from the same batch and lot as the mysterious Rod-25. Will they work? Yet Admiral Volsky learns that the Russian Black Sea Fleet has engaged well escorted units of a British oil conveyor, Fairchild Inc., and the fires of war soon endanger his mission.

All efforts are now focused on a narrow stretch of coastline on the Caspian Sea, where men of war from the future and past are locked in a desperate struggle to decide the outcome of history itself. Naval combat, both future and past, combine with action and intrigue as Volsky's mission is launched and the mystery of Rod-25 and Fedorov's strange experience on the Trans-Siberian Rail is finally revealed. Can they stop the nuclear holocaust of the Third World War in 2021 or will it begin off the coast of Japan in 1945?

Kirov Saga: *Devil's Garden ~ Book VII*

The stunning continuation to the *Kirov* saga extends the action, both past and present, as the prelude to the Great War moves into its final days. The last remnant of the Red Banner Pacific Fleet has fought its duel with Halsey in the Pacific, resorting to nuclear weapons in the last extreme—but what has happened to *Kirov* and *Orlan?*

Now the many story threads involving Fairchild Inc. and the desperate missions to find Orlov launched by both Haselden and Fedorov all converge in the vortex of time and fate on the shores of the Caspian Sea. Fedorov and Troyak lead an amphibious assault at Makhachkala, right into the teeth of the German advance. Meanwhile, Admiral Volsky and Kamenski read the chronology of events to peek at the outcome and discover the verdict of history. Can it still be changed?

Turn the page with Admiral Volsky and learn the fate of Orlov, Fedorov, Karpov and the world itself. Follow the strange and enigmatic figure of Sir Roger Ames, Duke of Elvington as he reveals a plot, and a plan, older than history itself on the windswept shores of Lindisfarne Castle.

Kirov Saga: Armageddon ~ Book VIII

The lines of fate have brought the most powerful ship in the world to a decisive place in history. Driven by his own inner demons, Captain Karpov now believes that with *Kirov* in 1908 he is truly invincible, and his aim is to impose his will on that unsuspecting world and reverse the cold fate of Russian history from 1908 to the 21st century. But it is not just the fate of a single nation at stake now, but that of all the world.

Shocked by Karpov's betrayal, Anton Fedorov plans a mission to stop the Captain before he can do irreversible damage to the cracked mirror of time. Now Admiral Volsky must do everything possible to launch this final mission aboard the nuclear attack submarine *Kazan*. The journey to the Sea of Japan becomes a perilous one when the

Americans and Japanese begin to hunt *Kazan* in the dangerous waters of 2021.

Join Anton Fedorov, Admiral Volsky, Chief Dobrynin, and Gennadi Orlov aboard *Kazan* as they launch this last desperate mission to confront the man, and the ship, that now threatens to change all history and unravel the fabric of fate and time itself.

The *Kirov Series* continues with Book IX: *Altered States, Book X: Darkest Hour,* and *Book XI: Hinge of Fate....with more to come!*

The Meridian Series (Time Travel / Alternate History)

Book I: *Meridian – A Novel In Time*
ForeWord Magazine's "Book of the Year"
2002 Silver Medal Winner for Science Fiction
The adventure begins on the eve of the greatest experiment ever attempted—Time travel. As the project team meets for their final mission briefing, the last member, arriving late, brings startling news. Catastrophe threatens and the fate of the Western World hangs in the balance. But a visitor from another time arrives bearing clues that will carry the hope of countless generations yet to be born, and a desperate plea for help. The team is led to the Jordanian desert during WWI and the exploits of the fabled Lawrence of Arabia.

Book II: *Nexus Point*
The project team members slowly come to the realization that a "Time War" is being waged by unseen adversaries in the future. The quest for an ancient fossil leads to an amazing discovery hidden in the Jordanian desert. A mysterious group of assassins plot to decide the future course of history, just one battle in a devious campaign that will span the Meridians of time, both future and past. Exciting Time travel adventure in the realm of the Crusades!

Book III: *Touchstone*

When Nordhausen follows a hunch and launches a secret time jump mission on his own, he uncovers an operation being run by unknown adversaries from the future. The incident has dramatic repercussions for Kelly Ramer, his place in the time line again threatened by paradox. Kelly's fate is somehow linked to an ancient Egyptian artifact, once famous the world over, and now a forgotten slab of stone. The result is a harrowing mission to Egypt during the time frame of Napoleon's 1799 invasion.

Book IV: *Anvil of Fate*

The cryptic ending of Touchstone dovetails perfectly into this next volume as Paul insists that Kelly has survived, and is determined to bring him safely home. Only now is the true meaning of the stela unearthed at Rosetta made apparent—a grand scheme to work a catastrophic transformation of the Meridians, so dramatic and profound in its effect that the disaster at Palma was only a precursor. The history leads them to the famous Battle of Tours where Charles Martel strove to stem the tide of the Moorish invaders and save the west from annihilation. Yet more was at stake on the Anvil of Fate than the project team first realized, and they now pursue the mystery of two strange murders that will decide the fate of Western Civilization itself!

Book V: *Golem 7*

Nordhausen is back with new research and his hand on the neck of the new terrorist behind the much feared "Palma Event." Now the project team struggles to discover how and where the Assassins have intervened to restore the chaos of Palma, and their search leads them on one of the greatest naval sagas of modern history—the hunt for the battleship *Bismarck*. For some unaccountable reason the fearsome German battleship was not sunk on its maiden voyage, and now the project team struggles to put the ship back in its watery grave. Meet Admiral John Tovey and Chief of Staff "Daddy" Brind as the Royal Navy begins to receive mysterious intelligence from an agent known only as "Lonesome Dove." Exciting naval action and top notch research characterize this fast paced alternate history of the sinking of the *Bismarck*.

Historical Fiction

Taklamakan ~ *The Land Of No Return*

It was one of those moments on the cusp of time, when Tando Ghazi Khan, a simple trader of tea and spice, leads a caravan to the edge of the great desert, and becomes embroiled in the struggle that will decide the fate of an empire and shake all under heaven and earth. A novel of the Silk Road, the empire of Tibet clashes with T'ang China on the desolate roads that fringe the Taklamakan desert, and one man holds the key to victory in a curious map that guards an ancient secret hidden for centuries.

Khan Tengri ~ *Volume II of Taklamakan*

Learn the fate of Tando, Drekk, and the others in this revised and extended version of Part II of Taklamakan, with a 30,000 word, 7 chapter addition. Tando and his able scouts lead the Tibetan army west to Khotan, but they are soon confronted by a powerful T'ang army, and threatened by treachery and dissention within their own ranks. Their paths join at a mysterious shrine hidden in the heart of the most formidable desert on earth where each one finds more than they imagined, an event that changes their lives forever.

The Dharman Series: Science Fiction

Wild Zone ~ Classic Science Fiction – Volume I

A shadow has fallen over earth's latest and most promising colony prospect in the Dharma system. When a convulsive solar flux event disables communications with the Safe Zone, special agent Timothy Scott Ryan is rushed to the system on a navy frigate to investigate. He soon becomes embroiled in a battle with a virulent new organism that has infected the planet to produce a world of dangerous mutant life forms. Aided by three robotic aids left in the colony facilities, Ryan stands alone to mount a desperate defense against a ravaging horde of vicious creatures as he struggles to solve the mystery of Dharma VI, and find the source of the strange mutations that now threaten to make humanity their next target! Book I in a series of riveting classic military sci-fi novels featuring robots, incredible alien life forms, duels in space, and a mystery that threatens to unravel the very fabric of evolution itself.

Mother Heart ~ Sequel to Wild Zone – Volume II

Ensign Lydia Gates is the most important human being alive, for her blood holds the key to synthesizing a vaccine against the awful mutations spawned by the Colony Virus. Ryan and Caruso return to the Wild Zone to find her, discovering more than they bargained for when microbiologist Dr. Elena Chandros is found alive, revealing a mystery deeper than time itself at the heart of the planet, an ancient entity she has come to call "Mother Heart."

Dream Reaper ~ A Mythic Mystery/Horror Novel

There was something under the ice at Steamboat Slough, something lost, buried in the frozen wreckage where the children feared to play. For Daniel Byrne, returning to the old mission site near the Yukon where he taught school a decade past, the wreck of an old steamboat becomes more than a tale told by the village elders. In a mystery weaving the shifting imagery of a dream with modern psychology and ancient myth, Daniel struggles to solve the riddle of the old wreck and free himself from the haunting embrace of a nightmare older than history itself. It has been reported through every culture, in every era of human history, a malevolent entity that comes in the night... and now it has come for him!

For more information visit:
http://www.writingshop.ws or http://www.dharma6.com

Made in the USA
Lexington, KY
15 October 2014